I0764497

RISEN

By
Krystal Lawrence

TELEMACHUS
PRESS

RISEN

Cover Art Design: Telemachus Press, LLC
Cover Art Illustrations:
Copyright © istockphoto.com/Sophia Tsibikaki (Trapped Man)
Copyright © istockphoto.com/Andrew Parfenov (Gravestone)
Copyright © istockphoto.com/eszawa (MoonBats)
Copyright © Douglas Vitkauskas (VTS Estilosa Font)

Edited by: Allen Klavons

Published by: Telemachus Press, LLC
http://www.telemachuspress.com

Visit the author website:
http://www.darksidestories.com

ISBN: 978-1-935670-05-6 (Paperback)
ISBN: 978-1-935670-06-3 (Hardback)
ISBN: 978-0-9841083-6-7 (Ebook)

Printed in United States

10 9 8 7 6 5 4 3 2 1

For Uncle Allen

Reading Sherlock Holmes and smoking his pipe in Heaven

RISEN

CHAPTER 1

Late Summer 2004

The boy was unremarkable. Nothing about him would have made you think he was anything other than a somewhat unkempt young man pushing twenty, walking aimlessly up Lombard Street. His shoulders were too slender to fill out the green army fatigue jacket he wore. His long black hair obscured most of one side of his face, and looked like it needed to become better acquainted with a comb. He ambled down the road with his shoulders slumped and his scuffed tennis shoes kicking up dust as he walked. No different than thousands of other guys stepping out of their teens and entering their early twenties all across the country. No reason anyone would have thought twice about this ordinary young man. Not unless they took a closer look. Then one might see that something was different. Something was wrong.

If Amanda Dale had been watching him, she would have thought *Rock star wanna-be* and dismissed him, but Amanda didn't notice his passing, even though she looked right at him out the big picture window that dominated most of the south facing wall in her living room. Her mind was elsewhere as she listened to the afternoon soap opera with one ear, and listened for the baby to wake up from her nap with the other. She was trying to finish the ironing before Lorna would wake up and demand all of her attention.

What Amanda *was* thinking about at the exact moment the kid strolled by was what time her husband might come home that night. He had been showing up later and later over the last four or five months, and twice didn't bother to come home at all. Working he said. Always working. Fortunately for Amanda Dale these thoughts only took up residence in her mind for a few brief moments before she drifted off to other things. Amanda was well disciplined at not dwelling in places that made her uncomfortable. She had had a lot of practice, being Mrs. Kurt Dale for the last nine years. And she intended to stay that way.

All the books and seminars about relationships preached that communication was the cornerstone for every good union. The authors however, had never been married to Kurt. Amanda subscribed to the belief that too much knowledge, too much communication, could kill a perfectly good marriage.

Six years ago Amanda found lab results from a doctor she never heard of shoved in Kurt's jacket pocket. She knew then if she wanted to continue to love her husband, communication was something she was better off without.

Lately he said he was working on a case. Cops work a lot of overtime, everyone knows that. It was enough information for Amanda. More could only prove counterproductive. Never mind that he was a violent crimes detective, and there hadn't been a crime that could be classified as violent in Alder Lake for over ten years now. Unless you considered Richie Welch shooting out the jukebox at Smokey's Tavern a violent crime.

Besides, things had been a little bit better between them for a few weeks now. Since she went to the doctor and got the prescription. The pills were safely hidden in a drawer. Kurt wouldn't have approved of them. He thought it was all in her mind.

At the same moment his wife was wondering when he might come home that night, Detective Kurt Dale sat at his cluttered desk in the precinct and contemplated how he was going to get himself out of the mess he was embroiled in. He never intended to have an affair, let alone allow it to continue for five months. He hadn't touched a woman other than his wife in six years. Not since that horrible scare with the perfume clerk from the department store. They only slept together once before he received a phone call from her at work. In a tear-choked voice she told him that she had contracted something from an ex-boyfriend. — Something Not Very Nice — And he better go get himself checked. Kurt found himself sitting in a stark doctor's office in another town, sweating as he waited to get the test, and trying to figure out how he was going to tell his wife that she too was at risk if his test proved positive. For three days while Kurt waited for the results, he neither ate nor slept. Several people at work noticed his anxiety and asked him what was wrong. The only person that didn't ask, and didn't seem to notice his nervousness was his wife.

The results were negative, and to the best of Kurt's knowledge Mandy never found out about that infidelity. Or any of the three women prior to that perky little cosmetic counter clerk, who's Something Not Very Nice finally cured his wanderlust.

Kurt never knew his wife also made a doctor's appointment in another town after making a rather unpleasant discovery in his coat pocket.

Kurt met Tina Hilliard after she had fallen victim to a stalker. It was hard to imagine that this arrogant and sharp-tongued blonde could be the victim of anyone. She possessed bigger balls than most of the cops Kurt worked with. She went to a nightclub with some girlfriends on a Friday night and caught the eye of Alonzo Perkins, a two time convicted sex offender with a combined total of eleven years spent in a state penitentiary. Perkins was out on parole for only four months when the lovely Tina caught his fancy.

He followed her home from the club and began watching her building. He left her presents by her front door. Tina found the teddy bear when she arrived home exhausted from work one evening and dismissed it as a joke. The flowers, she assumed must have come from a grateful client or maybe a friend. She was a pretty and successful woman; gifts were not uncommon in her professional or personal life. She had no idea the disturbed Mr. Perkins was watching her until the following week, when he dispensed with the presents and decided to wait for her himself.

She rounded the corner in the hallway of the upscale condominium where she lived, and nearly tripped over his outstretched feet as he sat propped against her front door.

"Who are you?" Tina snapped as she caught herself against the doorframe from tumbling into his lap.

"Aww, you don't remember me. We met last Friday," the stranger pouted.

"I've never met you before in my life, buddy. Now would you mind getting up so I can go inside." Her annoyance was clearly evident.

"Well, can I come in for a drink?" the stranger asked, still making no move to rise.

"No, you can't, and I am really in no mood for this crap. So get your ass up and beat it."

Lightning quick, Perkins grabbed her ankle. Tina tried to kick him with one stiletto heel, but lost her balance and ended up in a tangled heap next to him on the floor. He pinned her arms before she could even catch her breath. When he threw his considerable weight on top of her Tina started screaming for dear life. *God! How can this be happening?* her stunned mind screamed in protest to this sudden and unexpected assault. For the first time since arriving home to find this nutcase waiting for her, Tina was truly terrified.

Neighbors heard the struggle, a few doors were cautiously opening on the deserted hallway and someone called 911.

An elderly man charged down the hallway brandishing a broom and yelling, "Get off of that girl!"

Perkins, realizing this was no longer a private party, floundered to his feet and ran out of the building.

"Fuckin' lunatic," Tina gasped under her breath. She was shaking uncontrollably and tears stung her eyes.

As the other residents started descending on her, asking if she was alright, she muttered, "Yeah, yeah fine." She was breathing in rapid little gasps as the broom-wielding man from down the hall helped her to her feet. She offered him a grateful smile and then unlocked her front door and slammed it on her worried neighbors' curious faces.

The police came along with a sketch artist. Reports and statements were taken and a silent panic alarm was installed in her condominium by quick, efficient uniformed officers. A fingerprint match from her front door was a hit. An APB was issued for Alonzo Perkins. The men on street patrol were directed to cruise by her building every hour. Tina admitted she would feel more comfortable if someone would check in with her in the evenings.

The officers didn't mind checking in at all. Tina was a lovely woman, petite, with long blonde hair and big doe eyes. Her lounge-wear of choice was men's boxers and clinging t-shirts. She would give coffee laced with brandy to the officers who stopped by to check on her welfare. She never mentioned she put the brandy in, and no one ever commented, but they all knew. And that was just fine on a chilly winter's night.

A few tried to get a date. Tina always politely declined. She was a stockbroker by trade, and was happy to pass on a little free invest-ment advice to the officers responsible for her safety. But that was all she was offering. Some followed her advice and they inevitably made money. Tina was very popular with the boys in blue, and many of them secretly hoped Perkins would remain at large so they could hold onto their excuse to visit her for investment counseling, a cup of spiked coffee, and a few stolen glances at her unrestrained breasts be-neath the sheer fabric of her t-shirt.

Perkins didn't show up again for three weeks. It took him that long to figure out how to break into the building superintendent's office and steal the key to Tina's condo.

It was after midnight and she was lying in bed reading a book, her cat curled up on her lap. Half asleep, Tina heard a shuffling noise in the living room. She put down the book and gently pushed the cat away. Her heart banging hard in her chest, Tina grabbed the remote activation to the alarm off the bedside table and climbed silently out of bed. She saw a shadow standing by her kitchen counter, and with a cry of fright bolted into the bathroom on rubbery legs and locked the door, her finger repeatedly stabbing the big red button on the remote activation for the alarm. Perkins was still pounding on the bathroom door seven minutes later when nearly every officer in the city broke down Tina Hilliard's front door and grabbed him.

Kurt Dale was the detective assigned to her case. He came over the following evening to remove the police alarm and take more reports and statements. He completed his paperwork while drinking five or six cups of Tina's famous brandy laced coffee.

Her rejection of the numerous patrol officers that tried to approach her on a social level was legend at the department by now, so Kurt was surprised and secretly quite pleased with himself when Tina invited him to stay for dinner. He ignored the little voice that rose in his mind and said this was maybe not such a hot idea. The voice was easily silenced after five shots of brandy and a two hour view of Tina's erect nipples through the thin cotton of her shirt.

Kurt enjoyed the meal, a spicy Cajun chicken, and he enjoyed Tina's company even more. She regaled him with wild stories from her brokerage firm of millions of dollars gained and lost in a day's time.

Tina was concerned that no one would be checking on her now that Perkins had been caught. She was still understandably very nervous. Kurt volunteered to keep checking on her with no hesitation whatsoever. *Just doing my duty, ma'am.*

And he continued to perform his duty with Tina for five long months after Alonzo Perkins was behind bars for a third stretch, and had ceased being a threat to anyone.

When he met Tina, Kurt Dale sincerely believed his cheating days were well behind him. Unless you count the drunken kiss a couple of years back in the parking garage of an after hours bar he and some of his buddies frequented, he had not gone near a woman other than his wife in a very long time. So how, he wondered as he sat behind his desk, did he land here? Tina pressuring him to tell his wife about their relationship. Pressuring him to leave his comfortable house on Lombard Street, a house on which he was still paying off the remodeling bills, and move into her two bedroom condo with her.

He had known for almost a month that he wanted to break it off, but just couldn't find the right moment to do it. Tina felt him growing distant, and the more aloof he became, the more she pushed him to leave Amanda. She kept reminding him of all the things he told her about his troubled marriage. Tina possessed this uncanny ability to remember, practically verbatim, every complaint Kurt had ever voiced about his wife. She kept them in a verbal arsenal, and would assault him with one every time he told her he was not ready to ask Amanda for a divorce. Kurt wished now he had never told her any of it. Of course, even if he hadn't, Tina knew how close he felt to her and how good they were together.

The sex was incredible, admittedly the best either had ever known, and he could tell her anything. They spent hours and hours in her cozy little condo talking and making love. During those times the rest of the world simply disappeared. They really had a great thing, so to Tina the choice was simple. Just walk away. She couldn't understand why he would stay in a loveless marriage when he could be with her.

She would snuggle up against him, and say in that breezy, nonchalant tone of hers, "What we have is magic, baby. Life is short, and we were meant to be together."

What this translated to in Kurt's head was to turn his back on the last ten years of his life and abandon a daughter who was literally the air he breathed. Not to mention the scorn of everyone at work. The town was small, the police department close knit, and most of the officers were friends.

Everyone loved Amanda. Until the baby came she was always the first one on the committee to plan the Officers Ball, the first one to show up at the hospital with flowers, the first one to bake a pie. Mandy was Alder Lake's sweetheart. Kurt knew what all the guys would think if they separated. He couldn't keep his dick in his pants so he lost sweet, beautiful Amanda.

Kurt's image meant almost as much to him as his well-ordered life did. Few ever knew of his extramarital indiscretions, and no one except his best friend and partner, John Wyatt, knew what life was like at Casa Dale since the birth of Lorna.

Kurt knew he shouldn't have confided all the ugly details about his marriage to his mistress. The horrible depression Amanda went through after the baby was born. The night when things got so out of hand he feared for his own safety. Kurt had taken their daughter without so much as a change of clothes and run out of the house amid the sound of smashing dishes. Mandy was taking plates out of the cabinet and throwing them one by one against the wall. He stopped at the grocery store for formula and diapers, then showed up on the Wyatt's doorstep and asked to spend the night. Neither John nor Ellen asked any questions. They knew how things had been in the Dale household since the baby arrived. Ellen once mentioned something about postpartum depression to him, but Kurt waved his hand at her and told her he didn't want to hear any curbside analysis about his wife's insanity, thank you very much.

What possessed him to tell Tina about that incident, and so many other intimate details of his marriage, was his need to share his life with someone again. He needed someone to talk to and he needed to be loved again. This particular affair was a lot more than just the roving eye he once suffered from. Amanda was a stranger now. She turned into someone he didn't even know after Lorna was born. Kurt thought this hideous change was temporary. Everyone said this postpartum crap only lasted a little while, but Mandy had been like this for over a year. There was no end to her black moods or her violent outbursts anywhere in sight.

After Kurt met Tina and they became close, she turned into more than a lover. She became his confidante and friend. He loved her wit, her strength and her intelligence. Though he never made any promises, in hindsight, he knew he dropped a lot of innuendos about them having a future together. The truth was he did contemplate it. Contemplated it a lot. Tina was right, they were great together. The only thing they ever fought about was his stubborn resistance to getting a divorce. At the height of their affair Kurt didn't believe his marriage was going to survive if things didn't change. But he wasn't going to leave Amanda and invite all the chaos and embarrassment of a divorce into his life unless she became a threat to their daughter — a possibility which was becoming more likely with each passing week.

Most of what Kurt told Tina about his feelings for her came from the heart, until a month ago when he let the words he had never dared utter slip out of his mouth as he was falling into a post-coital doze. Her back was to him and her bottom nestled against his middle.

She whispered, "I love you, babe."

And as he was dropping off to sleep, Kurt muttered the most natural reply in the world. "Love you too."

But in those moments between waking and dreaming, he thought he was somewhere else. In a different house and in a different bed. After Kurt whispered those words, he slipped his hand around to cup the breast of the woman lying beside him. Expecting to feel the comforting curve of his wife's full bosom, he instead felt the slight swell of Tina's smaller breast pressed against his palm. He came fully awake with a start, and looked around at the unfamiliar shadows falling over the dark room. Perhaps not as unfamiliar as they were five months before, but they weren't the soothing nighttime silhouette that laced across the bedroom he had shared with Amanda for ten years. At that moment Kurt knew it was the wrong bedroom, the wrong shadows, the wrong woman, and the wrong breast he still held cupped in one hand. He knew it was time to go home.

That was four weeks ago. Not long after, Mandy's dark night of the soul finally broke and she seemed to notice her husband for the first time in nearly a year and a half. She started asking him when he would be home at night, and if it was late she would keep dinner warming for him. He lamely offered the excuse of working late on a case, even though she never asked him where he'd been. A guilty man makes excuses, whether he is asked to account for his whereabouts or not.

Amanda was interested in sex again, and was taking the baby to daycare two days a week so she could go work out. She never got her figure back after the baby was born and didn't seem to care until now. This was so unlike the woman he married, that innocently vain Amanda who wouldn't go out for the mail unless her nails were manicured.

The truth was Kurt missed his wife's easy smile and fiery spirit a lot more than he missed her twenty-two inch waist. But the fact that she just didn't give a damn how she looked anymore was unnerving. She sometimes went days without showering. Her nails, which she always took such pride in, were now bitten down to the quick. He sometimes watched her as she methodically gnawed at them, staring straight ahead without blinking for minutes at a time. She looked like she belonged in a mental institution during these moments.

Her erratic behavior sent shudders down Kurt's spine. One night when Lorna was three months old, he came home to find Amanda in the upstairs bathroom with scissors in her hand. All around her on the floor were pieces of her shoulder length mane of rich, thick auburn hair. He didn't know where his wife had gone, or who this violent monster was that took her place. After she finished cutting the last ragged piece of hair, she turned around and glared at Kurt standing stunned in the doorway. He looked incredulously from his wife's wild eyes to the pile of hair on the floor. He couldn't even wrap his head around what she had done to herself. It was chopped in huge, uneven pieces, the longest falling just below her ears. Then Amanda pointed the scissors at Kurt and started snipping them in the air inches from his face.

"Need a haircut, sweetheart?" she shrieked in a banshee's voice. She threw the scissors down on the ground and fell to her knees sobbing.

Kurt was too frightened and disgusted to try and comfort her. He closed the bathroom door and walked quietly down the hallway to his daughter.

His wife was living in a private hell where there was no room for him. Truth be told, he didn't want to be a part of it anyway. He didn't want to deal with the insanity. This was not what he signed up for when they got married, so Kurt turned to another woman in his loneliness and desperation.

Before Lorna was born Mandy always had a temper, but she never behaved irrationally or gave him any reason to question her sanity.

He never worried about Lorna's safety until the night of the dish breaking incident. He came home the next morning to find the shards of broken china cleaned up and his wife sitting at the kitchen table in her robe, drinking a cup of coffee. There were deep shadows under her eyes and it was obvious she hadn't slept.

In a small, tired voice Amanda said, "I'm sorry, Kurt. I've decided to go to the doctor today and ask him to put me on antidepressants."

In a foul mood from having to sleep at the Wyatts', his nerves being at the breaking point, Kurt shouted, "They don't make pills for the severe case of the fucking loonies you have!" He grabbed her by the shoulders and pulled her from the chair, spilling her coffee. In a rage he yelled, "This garbage is all in your head, Mandy! Now you listen to me! You aren't getting on any pills that are going to fuck you up even worse than you already are and turn you into some kind of fuckin' junkie taking care of my kid! Pull yourself together and quit this crap! It's all in your head. You got that? ALL IN YOUR HEAD! No pill can fix you." He let go of her arms and stalked out of the house.

The insanity, that in the world according to Kurt Dale "no pill could fix," lasted for three more long and stormy months, until Amanda, seriously contemplating suicide, finally made the doctors appointment without Kurt's knowledge and began taking the little blue pills. Within a week her world slowly began to swim back into focus. She looked at herself in the mirror for the first time in a year and was disgusted at what she saw, believing her appearance to be why Kurt was gone so much. She possessed no conception of how horrible her behavior had been. Didn't even remember hacking off her hair. In Amanda's mind, she had merely been very sad since the baby was born. Now that the drugs started to work, she saw herself in the mirror and nearly fainted from shock and revulsion. "No wonder Kurt's never home," she muttered as she pulled the bath scale out from under the sink, "I look like a pig." After stripping off her clothes she stepped tentatively onto the scale. She cringed when the needle hovered just over 160. At 5'6 Amanda never weighed more than 125 pounds in her entire adult life until the pregnancy. She was horrified. Not just at her weight either, her skin was an unhealthy, nearly gray pallor and there were blemishes on her forehead.

That day she called Ellen Wyatt to ask if she could watch the baby for the afternoon. She then called Kurt to ask if he would come home early so they could have dinner together. Surprised and pleased, he agreed.

When he called Tina to say he wouldn't be stopping by the condo that night, she asked why.

He said simply, "I want to go home and be with my family."

She hung up on him seething. Kurt found he didn't really care.

When he arrived home that night his wife's hair was shiny and newly styled. She wore acrylic tips on her fingernails and they were impeccably manicured. Her pale complexion looked nearly rosy from some artfully applied makeup and a facial that afternoon. She told him she joined the all women's gym in the business park up the street, and she cooked the first meal she had prepared for her husband in over a year. They made tentative, rather nervous love that night, also for the first time in over a year, and finally, the storm had passed.

That was three weeks ago. Amanda was down fifteen pounds and her disposition had done a complete turn around. Kurt liked being home again with his wife and daughter. The sex was improving, and as his wife's spirits improved, so did their relationship. He could talk to her again. If he had a rough day, there was a sympathetic ear and a stiff drink waiting when he came home at night. If something amusing happened during the day he now called Amanda to share it, never even thinking to tell Tina these details anymore. Things were back to normal.

But he still could not break off his affair. He kept waiting for the right moment to tell his mistress it was over, but that moment never seemed to present itself. He was still going to her condo one or two nights a week.

At last he did try to tell her they needed stop seeing each other, and as if Tina knew what he was going to say, she silenced him with a long, wet kiss and guided his hand down her jeans. Kurt Dale was a weak man and easy to distract.

As he made love to Tina right there in her foyer, Kurt Dale was ignorant of the fact that the problem of how to break up with her was very soon going to take care of itself. In a very unpleasant manner.

CHAPTER 2

Kurt and Amanda were just finishing breakfast in their sunny kitchen. The baby sat in her highchair nibbling contentedly on scrambled eggs. Kurt had the paper spread out in front of him.

"Damn teenagers," he grumbled as he read an article.

"Kurt, watch the language in front of the baby," Amanda scolded.

"Sorry, hon."

"What is it?" she asked.

"It's just malicious mischief I suppose, but pretty sick. Some kids dug up a two hundred year old grave a few nights ago. The bones are missing."

"Yep," she agreed, "that's sick. What do you suppose they did with them?"

"Some unsuspecting hiker will probably trip over them in the woods somewhere," he answered with disgust.

Amanda kissed the baby's cheek as she lifted her out of the highchair. "Promise me that when you grow up, your idea of fun on a Friday night won't be to rob a grave, okay?"

"One more cup and then I need to run." Kurt held out his cup for Amanda to fill with the proprietary air of a man used to being waited on.

Turning for the coffee pot, Amanda asked, "Who did the grave belong to? Do they know."

"Some seventeen year old kid."

Amanda wrinkled her brow in the worried way only a mother can achieve. "What did he die of so young?"

"Hell, I don't know. Back then it was probably polio or something. They had no vaccines for anything yet, I don't think." Kurt refolded the paper.

Amanda gave an involuntary little shudder and changed the subject. "I was going to invite Darlene to come over for dinner tonight. Will you be home early?"

"I can be." He nodded in the direction of the neighbor's house. "Things going okay over there?"

"I don't think so."

"Let me know if you need me to bring anything home. I'll try to get here around 6:30." Kurt rose from the table, not wanting to hear the details of his dysfunctional neighbor's problems.

Perching Lorna on one hip, Amanda walked him to the door. Kurt kissed both her and the baby goodbye. She stood at the picture window and watched him walk down the front steps — a tall, good looking man with dark, wavy hair and a powerful body. Kurt was pushing forty, but still made women's hearts speed up when they saw him. She watched their dark green Jeep Cherokee back out of the driveway and disappear down the street.

Amanda Dale was still looking out the window when the boy walked by. This time she did notice him.

She looked at the baby and asked, "What do you think, little one? Should we invite him for dinner too? Poor kid looks like he hasn't eaten a decent meal in awhile." Then she dismissed the skinny young man in the army fatigue jacket from her mind and went upstairs to take a little blue pill and change the baby's diaper.

The boy walked up the street and stopped at the corner. The town had changed a lot since he last walked these same streets. It was the field behind the row of houses on Lombard Street he remembered best. It was now a fraction of the size it had been when he last saw it, last ran for his life through it. Most of it was now the backyards of the neat suburban houses lining the street.

He walked up to a waist-high brick wall with planter boxes built in on either side. He sat down heavily, with the sigh of a much older man, carrying a great and worrisome burden. There were deep pink carnations standing tall in the planter boxes. Their colors were rich, their scent fragrant. The boy leaned back, looking up at the clear summer sky. A light breeze blew his hair back from his face and revealed milk white skin. His complexion looked nearly translucent and his eyes were a deep and disturbing blue, utterly startling in their intensity. Death dwelt in this boy, though one would have to look closely to see it.

A moment after he sat down the carnations began to wilt, as though some unwholesome vile force was killing them. The stalks trembled briefly, then lost their valiant effort to stay upright and collapsed. Within moments the flower's edges were singed and smoking. When the boy rose from the wall a few minutes later the carnations resembled shriveled, brown fall leaves drifting lazily in the breeze. It was impossible to tell they were ever once flowers at all.

The boy took no notice of this. He walked back up the street and stood in front of Kurt and Amanda Dale's house. He stood with the tips of his dirty sneakers touching their front lawn. A faint hissing noise began at his feet and thin tendrils of smoke rose from the small patch of grass where his filthy shoes rested. It turned instantly brown. *Soon,* he thought. *Very, very soon.*

When Kurt arrived at his desk and checked his voicemail, there were two messages from Tina. The first asking what time he would be by tonight. The second informing him she was going shopping at Victoria's Secret this afternoon, and if he was a good boy there would be a surprise waiting for him. He deleted both without calling her back.

She called again just as he was leaving for lunch with John Wyatt. He picked up the phone in his usual brisk manor, "Dale here."

"Hi, baby, it's me," Tina cooed into his ear.

Kurt glanced uncomfortably at John sitting across the desk from him. "Now isn't a good time. Can I call you later?"

His partner looked at him questioningly and Kurt averted his eyes.

"Yeah," she sighed, "You are coming over tonight?" Her tone was more demand than question.

He hesitated, then covered the mouth-piece of the phone with his hand. "Hey, John, go ahead and get us a table. I'll catch up."

John rose, tapped his watch as if to say 'hurry' and walked out.

Kurt waited until the door clicked shut to put the phone back to his ear. "Tina, we need to talk."

Her voice turned instantly to ice. "I don't want to have the conversation that goes something like — Hey, baby, it's been real but the party is over — If that's the talk you want to have, I'm not having it. You can't just throw away what we have, Kurt."

"I don't want to throw it away. I want us to stay friends. But I have to try and figure things out at home, Tina. I owe her that much," he sighed.

"And what about me? Don't you owe me anything?" She was getting angry, he could hear the familiar edge that crept into her voice every time they discussed his marriage.

"I can't talk about this now, okay? Not at work."

"So, come over tonight and we can talk then. I might even model my new nightie for you if you want."

Kurt closed his eyes and felt a headache forming at his temples. He thought, *It's like she doesn't even hear me.* "I can't tonight. We are having dinner with the neighbors. I have to be home early."

"Well how very fucking Ward Cleaver of you," Tina snapped, and slammed the phone down hard enough to make him jump.

"Gee, that went well," Kurt muttered as he dry-swallowed three aspirin from the big bottle kept in his desk drawer.

It was time for a little man to man discussion. He planned to ask his partner exactly how he should go about dislodging his ass from the rather tight sling it was currently trapped in. John would know what to do. It wouldn't be the first time he helped Kurt navigate his way out of trouble.

Amanda changed into sweats and put her hair back in a ponytail. With Lorna buckled into the baby jogger, she headed next door. She planned to invite the Coombs over for dinner before she went for a run.

She never noticed the two by two patch of dead front lawn, even as she walked right over it onto the sidewalk. It stood out in sharp contrast to the rest of their lawn, which was lush green.

Kurt was obsessive about the grass. He sometimes reminded her of Mr. Green Jeans when he went outside after work and stood with the hose, watering the lawn as the sun was going down.

Amanda arrived next door and knocked. Darlene opened the door on the chain and pushed her haggard face into the crack. She smiled when she saw Amanda, unhooked the chain and stepped outside.

"Hi, honey," she cooed at the baby.

"Hi, Arween," Lorna cooed back.

"It's nice to see you, Mandy. Sorry I haven't been by. Things have been..." Darlene trailed off.

"Is the drinking really bad again?" Amanda asked, not unkindly.

Darlene didn't answer, just nodded her head and looked down.

"Is he going to go back into rehab?"

Darlene shook her head. "No, we can't afford it since he lost the last job. No more benefits. Besides who ever said three was a charm never had a drinking problem right?"

"I'm really sorry, Darlene," Amanda said sympathetically. "Is there anything I can do?"

Again, Darlene shook her head.

"I thought maybe you and Russ would like to come for dinner tonight. Or just you, if Russ isn't... isn't feeling well," she finished awkwardly. "We haven't talked in awhile, and I thought we could get caught up."

"Actually, we just did, there isn't much more to tell. Thanks anyway, Mandy, but today's not a good day." She smiled wistfully and went back inside, closing the front door.

The Dales had lived next door to Russell and Darlene Coombs for eight years. Darlene married her high school sweetheart, and inherited the house from her grandmother. The house was now run down and in need of paint. Much the same could be said about her husband. Their home stood out in stark contrast to the Dale's impeccably maintained house.

Russell Coombs's drinking problem wreaked havoc over most of his adult life. He'd gone through treatment three times. The longest he ever managed to stay on the wagon was eighteen months — Which was twelve months longer than he ever managed to hold onto a job. He spent most days in an alcohol blurred haze. His one and only prized possession was a Golden Retriever named Samantha. Darlene was relatively sure that given a choice of being able to keep only one of them, his wife or his dog, Russell's choice would be an easy one. Darlene would be packing.

Russell walked Samantha every night after the news. It was the only time he left the house. Darlene wasn't sure he would even leave then if he didn't have to, but she worked the late shift at the diner in the bowling alley and wasn't home to do it.

Russell was a man convinced that his neighbors spent most of their time laughing at him behind his back. He was sure he was the butt of every neighborhood joke. He would have been surprised to learn that most of the residents on Lombard Street moved in only over the last few years, when the drinking got really bad, and the jobs fewer and farther between. Few of their neighbors had ever even seen Russell. Many thought Darlene was single and lived alone.

Amanda and Darlene had forged an odd bond. A friendship based on their less than perfect marriages. Many hours were spent over coffee or by the mailboxes discussing Kurt's infidelities and Russell's alcoholism. They often in the privacy of their own thoughts wondered which was worse, the drunk or the philanderer.

Kurt found John in a corner booth of the crowded café and slid in across from him. Once the waitress took their order, he said simply, "I need some help."

John eyed him levelly for a moment before replying, "Who is she?"

"Who isn't important. What's important is that I can't seem to break it off."

"How long has it been going on?" John asked.

Kurt knew he wasn't judging. Just fact finding, like any seasoned detective would. "Too long," he remarked, "For nearly six months. And… and, well, she thinks she loves me."

John's considering gaze did not waver. "Yeah? Have you given her a reason to think you love her back?" he asked in the same neutral tone.

"I suppose I did," Kurt sighed miserably and started playing with the silverware. "See, I thought I might have loved her for awhile, but things are better at home now. Truth is, I think maybe I just made a colossal mistake here." Kurt finally looked up and met John's eyes.

"So what's the problem? Just tell her the usual — It's not you, it's me — and stop seeing her." John shrugged.

That was easy for him to say, he had never cheated on Ellen one day in eleven years of marriage.

"I can't." He looked away again. "I mean, I tried, but it's more complicated than that now." Kurt looked up again with haunted eyes. "She isn't letting me go that easily. I can't just leave this one on the side of the road with a torn dress and smeared lipstick. You understand what I'm trying to say, John?"

"You think she is going to make trouble for you?" The seasoned detective hits pay-dirt.

"She gets furious every time I breathe one word about breaking up. She might make trouble, plenty of it. Hell hath no fury and all that." Kurt tried to laugh, but it sounded false and tinny in his own ears.

John was frowning at him. "What kind of trouble?"

"I think she might call Amanda, or tell someone in the department. She told every officer on night patrol where to invest their extra pennies a few months back. She knows too many people. That's why I haven't just cut it off. I don't trust her to keep her mouth shut."

"Christ, Kurt not that woman Perkins was after?" John cried disbelievingly, "You couldn't have picked up on another anonymous perfume clerk? Did you have to choose a victim of a crime we investigated? One that became friends with half of the department, no less?"

Kurt ignored this. "You know Amanda just started feeling better. I can't risk anything screwing her up again. I have the baby to worry about too."

But they both knew what Kurt was most worried about wasn't the baby at that moment, and it certainly wasn't his wife. It was his reputation, and not letting Tina Hilliard screw up his neat and tidy life. He didn't want Mandy to find out, that was true. But it wasn't because of her mental health. It was because if she found out, Kurt knew he would pay a hundred different kinds of hell before his infidelity was considered atoned for.

Kurt liked his life just fine now that Amanda was acting normal again. He liked his marriage, his home, his perfectly green grass, and he loved his baby. Tina was an extracurricular activity which had ceased being necessary, and was in fact becoming decidedly inconvenient. Kurt was a man very used to getting things his own way. Relationships ended when Kurt said they ended. No one else was supposed to have a say in the matter. No one else was supposed to make the rules. He just didn't know how to make his mistress understand that.

They arrived back at the precinct and Kurt checked his messages. Amanda called to tell him dinner was off. He called her back and she recounted her conversation with Darlene to him on the phone.

"So, it's bad again over there. Guess that means I have to keep mowing their grass for them," Kurt commented.

"Your sympathy is touching, dear," Amanda said dryly.

"Nothing we can do for them, Mandy."

"Yeah, I know. But I am still going to bring her a lasagna to-night."

Of course you are, he thought. *I am married to Mother fucking Theresa. As long as you don't give birth to anymore babies and get hit with that postpartum whammy stick, you are a regular card-carrying saint, my love.* He wisely didn't say this out loud.

He made a decision while they were talking to go break things off with Tina tonight. Why put off the inevitable. Now that he didn't have to be home for dinner, he could take care of this problem once and for all.

He told Amanda he was going to work late after all. As usual she made no argument and asked no questions.

When they hung up he called Tina and told her he would come by tonight so they could talk. She was, of course, delighted. She was a woman also very accustomed to getting everything her own way. She apologized for hanging up on him earlier and said she was looking forward to their kissing and making up.

Kurt shook three more aspirin out of the big bottle in the desk.

Tina answered the door in her latest acquisition from Victoria's Se-cret. A little red lace number which nearly brought Kurt to his knees, and made him forget why he came over in the first place. It came back to him an hour or so later in her bedroom. But breaking up didn't seem like a very good idea just then. Not with his balls all ex-posed and unprotected like that.

Later, in the living room drinking a glass of wine, Tina commented, "I have something for you."

Kurt smiled, "Didn't you just give it to me?"

"Not that, silly," she giggled.

He looked at her with mild curiosity, and she asked, "Do you remember a couple months back when you gave me two thousand dollars and told me to invest it for you?"

Actually he had forgotten about it. He took the money out of their savings account and told Tina to put it in something that would make enough to pay off the last of the remodeling costs on his house. Amanda noticed it was missing from their account, but never asked him why he withdrew it. He needed close to $25,000 to pay off the balance of the second mortgage they used to cover the remodeling job.

Tina rose from the couch and rummaged through her handbag. When she returned, she was holding out a plain white envelope. He took the envelope and pulled the check from inside. It was cut from the brokerage house she worked for, in the amount of $26,700.

"Tina!" he exclaimed happily, "How the hell did you do that so fast?" He grabbed her, and gave her a long wine-tasting kiss.

She leaned her head on his shoulder. "Because I'm good, baby. Very good."

As he was walking to the door to leave, Tina took Kurt's arm and looked up into his eyes. "So, are we okay?"

He felt the check in his pocket and had a fleeting vision of her putting a stop payment on it on behalf of her company. He replied, "Of course we are, baby. I'll call you tomorrow."

The remodeling was done six years ago. It wasn't something they sat down and discussed. One day he came home from work to find that Amanda had taken out a second mortgage on the house and hired contractors.

One of the benefits of small town life, where everyone knows everyone, is the ability to walk into your bank, sympathize with the bank rep over her recent surgery, talk about last Sunday's sermon, and get a second mortgage by signing your husband's name and giving some vague explanation about how he was too busy working on a case to come down and sign the paperwork himself. After all, everyone knows cops work a lot of overtime.

Amanda did this right after her own test results from the anonymous clinic had proven negative.

Kurt came home from work one evening, and she simply told him what she had done. The contractors would be in and out for the next several months. Kurt started to argue about the money, about her taking out the loan without his permission. The look in her eyes caused him to back up a step, and his mouth clamped shut with a snap.

He knew something at that moment. Amanda's eyes told him that somehow she found out about the cheating. Maybe even about the Something Not Very Nice. He didn't know how, but the look in her furious eyes told him very clearly that every sin had its price. The price of Kurt Dale's latest infidelity was his wife getting the house she always wanted. The look also said that if he chose to argue about this, his life could become very unpleasant, very quickly. He uttered not another word.

Kurt made the additional mortgage payment faithfully every month for the last six years, and never said a word about it to Amanda. In truth, she did one hell of a job on the place. His home was indeed his castle and he secretly loved it, though he would never admit this to his wife. He was afraid if he did she would come up with some new and interesting way to further punish him. But he really wanted that second mortgage to go away. Not because he couldn't afford the payment, but because it was a monthly reminder of a very painful time in his life that he wanted to forget. Every time he wrote the check, the memories of a cold little clinic in another town came flooding back. Just as his wife knew they would.

He heard the guys at work all saying the tips Tina gave them panned out. So, on impulse he gave her the two thousand dollars to see if she could make the money for him to get rid of that annoying reminder of some very bad days.

By the time he arrived home from Tina's, Kurt had already worked out the story he was going to tell Amanda. Lenny Marks, a cop he worked with, gave him the investment tip. Lenny was a bachelor teetering on the edge of retirement. He never went to the department picnics, never showed up in anyone's backyard for a barbeque. It was unlikely Amanda would ever cross his path.

Had Kurt known his wife a little better, he would have known she would never ask Lenny. In fact, she didn't even ask Kurt where the money came from. The only thing Amanda thought when her husband told her he had enough money to pay off the second mortgage was, *So that's where that two grand went to. He's been late all these months because he found a new vice. Out at the Indian reservation gambling, or up to Westin Hill playing the ponies.*

Kurt handed her his carefully crafted story, because a guilty man knows the trail to his wife discovering his infidelity begins with but a single bread crumb. The guilty man believes in his heart, as long as there is a map that leads in the other direction from where he spends his nights, as long as there is a carefully detailed story, one that can account for every moment away, every penny spent, the trail would never begin.

CHAPTER 3

In Kurt's dream, Tina was wearing his shirt. The one she donned after they last made love. She was cringing in her bathtub. Her hair was in a sweaty tangle around her frightened face. She was screaming over and over again, "THIS IS ALL YOUR FAULT, KURT! ALL YOUR FAULT!" Her finger kept pressing the panic button that controlled the alarm, which had been in her apartment all those months ago when Alonzo Perkins was still loose. In his dream the alarm wasn't silent, sounding only at the dispatch desk of the precinct, as it had been when it was installed. It was emitting great, braying beeps that sounded like some kind of nuclear attack warning.

He kept trying to tell her Perkins was in jail, he couldn't hurt her now, but she wouldn't listen, wouldn't stop screaming that one accusatory statement over and over, and she wouldn't stop hitting the button on the alarm. Kurt didn't know how the alarm taken out of Tina's condo nearly six months before could be back, but it was, and he needed to make it shut up before the police started showing up, and everyone would know about the affair. He needed to get his shirt off of her too. They would recognize it as his. And he must get the hell out of there. Why wouldn't she listen to him? What was all his fault?

In the dream, he saw himself running out of the bathroom and trying to make it to the front door. Tina's elegant, and normally neat as a pin condo, looked like a bomb exploded in there. There were bloody tracks leading to the bathroom and broken glass everywhere. The furniture was knocked over. Kurt was throwing things aside trying to clear a path to the front door. The check Tina gave him earlier in the evening was stuck underneath the side of her overturned stereo cabinet. The check was huge, nearly three feet long now, and the only part visible was his name. Instead of being neatly typewritten in the Pay to the Order space, it was now crudely handwritten in big, sprawling red letters. He tried to grab the unnaturally large check and couldn't dislodge it from under the cabinet. When he pulled, the damn thing wouldn't come free. Instead it ripped in half, and the part remaining pinned under the stereo cabinet still bore his name written in those giant, glaring, and somehow accusatory crimson letters.

That was when he heard the sirens coming, and he knew it was too late.

After Kurt left her, Tina took a long, hot bath and watched a movie on TV. She loved the classics. Tonight it was Gaslight. She smiled a little at the irony. She wondered if Kurt shouldn't take some lessons from Charles Boyer about how to drive his wife crazy. Then she reminded herself Amanda was already nuts without any help from him at all. She stifled a giggle and felt a small pang of remorse for being so evil.

Tina was glad she made Kurt happy by giving him the check. His two thousand dollars didn't exactly make *all* the money he needed in just two months, but where she chose to invest it did make over half of it. The rest she took from her own account. He never needed to know, and she wasn't hurting for money.

Tina never loved a man like she loved Kurt. She figured the happier she made him, the less likely he was to keep making noise about them breaking up. Eleven grand was a small price to pay to silence that conversation once and for all. God, she hated when he talked about that. It scared her. She just couldn't imagine her life without him anymore. Desperate times called for desperate measures. Besides, if he didn't have a second mortgage, it would be one less bill his wife could smack him with when they finally got the divorce.

His stupid wife was psycho-woman from hell, the way Kurt described her. That time he found her in the bathroom whacking off all her hair sounded like something out of a horror movie. But of course he couldn't walk out on his child. Tina knew that. Eventually though, Kurt would figure out what to do and how to make it so they could be together. There was no doubt in Tina's mind of this. She knew she was nearly ten years younger than his wife, and at least forty pounds lighter if Kurt's description was accurate. (He naturally hadn't mentioned that Amanda was getting back into shape, or that they had resumed relations.) In the end he would choose Tina. Since the time she was fifteen, the men always chose Tina.

She fell asleep on the couch toward the end of the movie. She was awakened sometime later by someone shaking her. In Tina's confusion she thought it was Alonzo Perkins, come back to finish the job, and she started to scream. The man clamped his hand over her mouth tightly. The smell coming from him was deep and swampy. She reached over her head and jammed the switch on the table lamp sitting next to the couch. The man wasn't Alonzo Perkins, in fact, it wasn't a man at all. *Just a boy*, Tina thought. *What is he, maybe sixteen? He's just a kid who really needs a bath.* She grabbed the lamp and tried to hit him, but her angle was bad. Tina missed the intruder and the lamp crashed into the glass coffee table, shattering it. She started kicking and scratching to get away. The garbagy smell from that hand over her mouth was making her gag. She grabbed the hand and bit down on it as hard as she could. It tasted like gone over meat. The boy yanked it away, with a cry of pain very satisfying to Tina's ears. What was oozing from the wound was a black oily substance that looked nothing like blood. Tina glared in stunned horror at this, but only for a moment. Most of her mind was occupied with self-preservation and getting away from this smelly kid who broke into her house. She couldn't have cared less at that moment if the intruder was bleeding rose petals onto her Persian carpet.

She scrambled over the sofa. "Shit! Didn't I go through enough this year?" she muttered as she ran for the front door. "I survive Perkins only to get my ass raped by a twelve year old that smells like a backed up sewer line?"

The kid leapt over the couch with surprising dexterity. He grabbed Tina around the waist, throwing her onto the floor. She kicked out with her right foot and it landed squarely in his ribs. He went over sideways, taking Tina's nearly ceiling-high stereo cabinet with him. The stereo equipment and the rack of compact discs tumbled out with a loud crash. The bathroom was only two feet from her now. If she could grab her purse by the strap, she could, for the second time this year, lock herself in the bathroom and call 911. Only this time from her cell phone, instead of a little remote activated key chain with a big red button on it.

Tina stumbled to the Queen Anne chair in the corner of her living room where her purse hung. She cut her feet on the broken glass from the coffee table, with too much adrenaline pumping to even feel the razor sharp shards dig into her flesh. Her fingers just brushed the strap of the purse, when the kid stuck out his leg and tripped her. She crashed into the chair and nearly went sprawling. She caught herself on the corner of a plant stand, but couldn't grab her handbag before it slid from the overturned chair, spilling the contents all over the floor. The kid was nearly on top of her now, there was no time to try and get the phone.

Tina went for the bathroom anyway. She was out of options and scared to death. It was obvious this kid meant to kill her. *God, why the hell does this keep happening to me?* Tina's horrified mind screamed. She made it to the bathroom, and was turning to slam the door when her bloody feet skidded on the tile floor. Before she could regain her balance and slam the door closed, her assailant grabbed her by the hair and yanked.

"Owwwwwww! You son of a bitch!" she screamed, "LET GO!" She was pummeling him uselessly with her fists, kicking at him ineffectually with her bloody feet. He threw Tina back into the bathroom by her long hair. She flew across the room and landed half way in the bathtub, cracking her head hard against the tile, and pulling the shower curtain down on top of her.

"Why?" she asked, just as the world was beginning to fade before her eyes, "Why?"

"Because you are a Hilliard. Because my mother's blood is on your hands too." His voice sounded like an old, rusted piece of machinery left out in the rain too long. His mouth creaked like a door hinge in need of oil when he opened it to speak.

Tina lost consciousness just as Francis Barclay descended on her, his lips parted in a hungry grin. It was a blessing she lost consciousness when she did.

The phone was ringing. Kurt woke up with his heart thundering in his chest, thinking the shrill sound of the telephone was the sound of the sirens in his nightmare.

Oh no, he thought crazily, *They're coming.*

Amanda was starting to stir beside him as he reached over her to answer the phone. The digital display on the bedside clock glowed 3:04 AM.

It's true Kurt was a violent crime detective, but in Alder Lake there wasn't much violent crime to speak of. Every few years they had a homicide, but it was usually a domestic thing. It was rare to have anything significant enough happen to warrant a pre-dawn phone call.

"H'lo," he mumbled, the last threads of the dream slipping away.

"Kurt, it's Fitz, we need you down to the Wood River Condominiums. There's been a homicide," Captain Fitzgerald growled, the tension in his voice evident.

Kurt's heart leapt in his chest. He closed his eyes and tried to steady his trembling hands. Tina lived in Wood River.

"Kurt, man, wake up. Did you hear me?" Fitz asked impatiently.

"Yeah. On my way."

Amanda was looking at him in the dark, her eyes huge and frightened. "What is it?"

"A murder. I have to go." His voice sounded too high in his own ears.

"Murder?" Amanda gasped, startled. She looked as though she was going to ask something else, thought better of it, and said simply, "Be careful. Call later if you can."

It was like Kurt was still in the grip of the nightmare as he drove the familiar route to Tina's building through the light rain. How many times had he made this same trip? His hands were shaking on the steering wheel, his heart pounding to the steady rhythm of the windshield wipers. The voice of reason piped up in the back of his head, telling him it could be anyone. Anyone at all. There were over forty units in Tina's building. But he knew it was her. Somehow he knew.

Fragments of the dream were drifting back to him. Tina cringing in the bathtub. The sound of the obnoxious alarm that wasn't even supposed to be there, blatting incessantly. He didn't notice the tears coursing down his cheeks until he was only a block away from the building. Kurt stopped the car and wiped at his face with disgust.

He said out loud, "Gonna look real good if you show up at the crime scene crying there, buddy. Not suspicious at all."

He opened the window, letting the cool night breeze into the Jeep, then slowly drove the last block like a man going to his own execution. He could see the flashing lights up ahead. Could see the crime scene tape looped around the building. A handful of people still in night clothes stood clustered in a tight group whispering to each other.

Kurt parked the Cherokee. He froze his face into a professional mask as he approached the first uniformed officer guarding the scene; a kid named Taylor who was barely out of the police academy.

Climbing under the tape, Kurt asked, "What have we got here?"

The officer looked both very young and very scared. "Female, twenty-five. Looks like someone broke in and she put up a hell of a fight. The place is all smashed up," he replied, unable to hide the wonder from his voice.

"What unit?"

"202, second floor," Taylor answered. Then he added in a hushed tone, "Kurt, it's that gal from a few months back. The one that Perkins broke into her place."

Kurt felt the world start to swim out of focus and thought with horror that he was going to faint right in front of this one year veteran of the force, practically fresh out of high school. He bit his tongue hard enough to draw blood. It worked. The gray, swimmy feeling left him and he knew he wouldn't pass out. At least not yet.

Kurt began to ascend the staircase to the second floor. Twice he needed to grab the railing for support. *This just can't be happening*, he thought. *Not Tina, no way can it really be happening.*

When Kurt arrived at the front door of Tina's condo, John Wyatt and Captain Fitzgerald were talking in the hall. Wyatt looked at him with one raised eyebrow, and Kurt felt an overwhelming impulse to scream out, "I didn't do it! It wasn't me." Fortunately, he restrained himself and the urge passed.

"Kurt, do you remember Tina Hilliard? Woman from about six months ago who was a stalking victim?" Fitz asked.

John Wyatt's raised eyebrow went up even higher.

"Yeah, I do. Is she the DOA?" He was relieved to hear his voice sounded steady in his own ears.

"Yes. We've got a mess in there. I have people dusting for prints, but I am afraid all they are going to find are the prints of half the night patrol squad, not to mention yours, buddy."

Kurt swallowed hard. "Mine? How do you know mine are in there?" His voice was rising and taking on a whining, panicky tone.

John's eyes opened wide with alarm. He shook his head at Kurt.

Fitz looked at him with a puzzled frown. "As I recall, you *were* assigned to the case after Perkins broke in. You *did* take the report, and you *did* take out the alarm system, didn't you?"

"Yeah. Right. Forgot about that," Kurt mumbled uncomfortably and looked away.

"Well, it was a long time ago. Hard to remember back that far I suppose," Fitz's questioning gaze stayed a little too long on Kurt's guilty face. Then he turned and walked back into Tina's condo.

Kurt started to follow him and John grabbed his arm. "Wait."

Kurt turned to look at him, but said nothing.

"You okay, Kurt?"

"I have to be, don't I?" he answered shortly.

"You don't have to be anything except not guilty of whatever the hell happened here tonight," his partner said barely above a whisper.

"Do you think I'm guilty, John?"

"No, man, I don't. But I don't want anyone else to think you are either. Does anyone else know about you two?"

Kurt felt himself growing angry and took a deep breath. John was just looking out for him. He knew that. "No one knows. Just you."

"You are positive she didn't tell anybody else?" Wyatt persisted.

"I wasn't with her twenty-four hours a day. I don't know if she confided it in a girlfriend or something. I doubt it. She wasn't exactly proud of running around with a married man," Kurt snapped.

John nodded. "For what it's worth, man, I'm sorry."

Kurt fought back the tears again. "What happened to her?"

"Don't know yet. And no obvious suspects. One neighbor thought she saw someone with long, black hair and a big coat walking down the street a little after the neighbors heard the place being busted up. But she couldn't be sure if it was a male or a female. Too dark out."

They walked inside and Fitz motioned them over to the couch. He was crouched in front of a small, tacky pool of black fluid that had seeped into Tina's white Persian rug.

"What is this do you think?" Fitz asked the two detectives.

John Wyatt bent down and touched the tarry substance with the tip of his fingers. "Looks like motor oil or something." He brought his fingers up to his nose and sniffed, then curled his lip in disgust. "That's not oil, but I don't know what it is. Smells like someone's forgotten athletic socks six months after the big game." He wiped his fingers on his jeans with unease.

Kurt walked into the bathroom, careful to avoid the bloody footprints smeared across the floor. Tina's body lay still in the bathtub. Someone had covered her face with the shower curtain. There were people crawling all over the place. One taking scrapes from under her nails, another dusting for prints, and still another taking photographs.

Kurt knelt over the tub and pulled the shower curtain back from Tina's face. He remembered how lovely she looked, flushed with pleasure, when she handed him the check several hours ago. He couldn't believe it was only last night. It felt like years ago. Her long legs were splayed at a weird angle over the rim of the tub and her feet were all cut up. *That's where all the blood came from,* he thought, and had a disquieting moment of déjà vu when he remembered that same haunting detail from his dream.

He asked the woman doing the scrapes beneath her nails, "What do you think the cause of death is?"

The woman shrugged. "Nothing evident. The coroner will be able to tell us more tomorrow, I'm sure."

"Sexual assault?"

"Doesn't look that way, she's still got her panties on, but again, won't know 'til the autopsy," the woman answered shortly, then went back to work on Tina's nails.

Kurt gently brushed Tina's blonde hair from her face and silently mouthed, "I'm so sorry, Tina. So very sorry." He wanted to kiss her waxy cheek, but knew if any of the people working saw him do it, they would be surprised enough to remember that detail later when the hunt for a motive began. He let the shower curtain fall back over his mistress's face and walked out of the bathroom, those unwelcome tears stinging his eyes again.

The coroner took the body a few hours later. Tina's family was notified and the condo sealed off.

One of the officers took Tina's cat home. He invested a little money where Tina told him to, and made the money to buy his fiancé a half-carat larger stone than she was expecting. His new bride accepted the cat like family.

Half an hour after they left the crime scene, Kurt and John sat in a coffee shop where they had spent many hours talking over the years. It was a known and somehow comforting surrounding for both of them.

John cleared his throat. "I know this is uncomfortable, but there are some things you need to think about."

"Such as?" Kurt grumbled.

"Such as, do you have an alibi for last night between the hours of roughly eleven and two?"

"I was home but…" Kurt trailed off.

"But what, Kurt?"

"I was with her last night. I left her place around ten."

John threw a sugar packet down in disgust. "Oh that's just beautiful, Kurt."

"I didn't hurt her, John. I'd never hurt her," he cried helplessly.

"Do you know how bad this looks, Kurt? Do you have any idea?"

"Aren't there any suspects? I mean besides me?" he asked.

"Don't know. Haven't questioned her friends and family yet. Frankly, man, I am scared for when we do. Scared as hell where it's going to point. Right now the only person I know who has a motive to kill that girl is you." John's voice rose in anger.

Kurt chewed on his upper lip, his face visibly paled. "So? Am I on this case? It's your call, John."

"Yeah, of course you are. Going to look pretty damn strange if one of the two violent crime detectives Alder Lake employs isn't part of the investigation, now isn't it?"

"Are you going to tell…" Kurt faltered, and couldn't finish.

"I'm not telling anyone anything… For now. But one word of advice. If you see the wind blowing this thing in your direction, you better go have yourself a little talk with Fitz. And with Mandy too for that matter." John rose and threw a couple of crumpled dollar bills on the table. He walked out without a backward glance.

When Kurt returned home, he found Amanda in the kitchen doing dishes. The baby was playing on the floor with some blocks by her feet. He kissed Lorna on the top of the head and gave Mandy a hug.

"Who is it?" she asked him anxiously.

He sat down at the table. "Young woman from uptown. No one you know."

"Was it a lovers thing?"

Kurt winced. "Don't know yet."

"You hungry?" she asked.

"No, thanks. Just want to go take a nap."

"So, what happened?" Amanda pressed.

Kurt looked away uncomfortably, "Looks like someone broke into her place."

Amanda waited. When he didn't add anything more, she turned back to the sink. "Go upstairs and lay down. I will wake you up in a few hours."

Kurt rose from the table and kissed her on the cheek. "Thanks… And Amanda?"

"Hm?"

"Make sure if John calls with the autopsy report that you wake me up right away, okay? I… I need the information."

She looked momentarily puzzled, then nodded her head.

As he walked upstairs, Amanda thought with some bitterness, *Who was she Kurt? Friend of yours?*

CHAPTER 4

He lie in bed remembering. Remembering her smile. Her touch. The way she laughed, deep and throaty, almost musical. She was so damn sexy when she got mad. She was probably the strongest woman he ever met in his life. It was inconceivable that this was the same woman he saw sprawled lifeless in a bathtub just a few short hours ago. How could that be the same woman who answered the door to him last night wearing nothing but a negligee and a wicked smile? God, he loved that smile. It was true he wanted to break things off. He had to. He wasn't going to lose everything he built over the last ten years. And he loved Amanda. Loved her fiercely. But no one knew the hell he had been through after Lorna was born. He never knew what he was going to find when he walked through his front door at night for the solid year and a half that the storm raged at home. After those first twelve months he was a desperate and lonely man. He needed someone during that time and he grabbed onto Tina for dear life. She was easy to confide in and easy to be with. There was no yelling, no erratic behavior and no stress. She was always constant, always happy to see him. He was sorry he was going to hurt her. He naively hoped they would continue to be friends once he called it off. Mostly he was sorry she fell in love with him but,

"Oh God!" he cried suddenly to the empty room, his musing cut short. "Was I the last person who saw her alive before the monster that did this to her?" *Who could have done it? And Why?* His overtaxed mind asked.

John would direct the investigation, but would Kurt's being a part of it help or hinder it? He didn't know. *Better to just wait and see what the coroner comes up with before I make any decisions. How much trouble am I in?* He wondered with horror. Then his strained mind finally drifted into uneasy sleep.

Kurt was dreaming again. This time he wasn't in Tina's overturned apartment. He was in a dark, unfamiliar room, fumbling along the wall trying to find a light switch. Across the room the baby was crying. Where the hell was Amanda? Lorna needed her.

He felt hot, stale breath in his ear and nearly screamed.

"Who's there?" he whispered, his voice a harsh gasp. No one answered. When he turned around he could see only a glowing pair of deep aquamarine eyes staring at him from a few inches away. They appeared to be floating in midair. The two glowing disembodied orbs didn't seem to be attached to a body. And Lorna had moved. He couldn't see her in the pitch black room, but her sobs were now coming from directly in front of him. Seemed to be coming from the same place those ghostly eyes were hovering.

Somehow he knew the thing with the glowing eyes had his daughter, and the thing was grinning at him. He couldn't see its mouth, but he knew it was grinning just the same.

He reached out blindly into the darkness for his sobbing little girl. From the direction of the glowing eyes came a voice that sounded as if it hadn't been used in a very, very long time.

In a croaky whisper the thing barked, "What a pretty baby."

Then Kurt did scream. A high-pitched wail that was nothing like his own voice at all.

He woke up to Amanda's pounding footsteps on the stairs. He sat up in bed, drenched in sweat, as she ran into their room.

"Kurt, what is it? What's wrong?" Amanda gasped, winded from running.

"I had a bad dream. Is the baby okay? I… I thought I heard her crying," he panted.

She looked at him, worry etched on her brow. "Hon, you were just downstairs with us twenty minutes ago. Of course she's alright. Hasn't cried a tear all day."

Amanda sat down on the corner of the bed and took his hand. "Kurt, who was the lady that got killed? Will you tell me?"

He looked away from her and rolled over on his side. "I don't want to talk about it. I need to get some sleep."

His wife replied, "That's fine… if whatever demons you've got over this thing will let you sleep." She rose to leave.

He stopped her as she was walking out into the hallway. "Mandy?"

"Yeah?"

"She was the victim of a stalker about six months ago. I worked on the case. I… I knew her."

"I read about that in the paper. You never talked about that case. Isn't he in jail?"

"Someone else did it. It wasn't the same guy."

"Any leads, or can't you talk about it?"

"I'd rather not right now. I'm… I'm very tired," Kurt sighed, still averting his wife's eyes.

Amanda nodded and walked out of the room, closing the door behind her.

Exhaustion finally overtook him and his sleep was dreamless for the next two hours.

Amanda lie on the couch reading a magazine while the baby napped. There was a knock at the door and she rose to answer it.

"Hey, you," she said warmly, reaching up to give John Wyatt a hug. "How's El?"

"She's fine, Mandy. Um… how are you feeling these days?" he asked a little nervously. They hadn't had much interaction since Lorna's birth. John still felt a little like he was walking on eggshells around her.

"Doing great," Amanda smiled, as she ushered him inside. "I'll go get Kurt. He's lying down."

"Yeah. Been a long day for everyone," John remarked.

Amanda had been a cop's wife long enough to know not ask questions.

She disappeared up the stairs. A few minutes later Kurt descended, looking bleary eyed and pale.

"Lets go for a drive." John held the front door open.

Wordlessly, Kurt allowed himself to be ushered outside.

Once inside Wyatt's nondescript, police-issue Chevrolet, Kurt asked, "So what have you got?"

"Coroners report shows cause of death as toxic poisoning."

"What the fuck?" Kurt croaked.

John held up a hand, "Let me finish before you say anything."

Kurt nodded for him to go ahead.

"No sign that she was raped, but there was semen found in her vagina, so it's clear that she did have sex within four or five hours before she was killed."

At this, Kurt closed his eyes and pinched the bridge of his nose.

John appeared not to notice and added, “Again, there is no sign that the sex wasn’t consensual. No bruising, no tearing. Nothing like that.”

“Go on,” Kurt mumbled.

“It also appears that she bathed after having intercourse because there was no hair or trace evidence anywhere around her pubic area or on her body. There were also traces of some type of bath oil found in her vagina along with the semen.”

“Was there any physical evidence besides the semen found linking someone to this?” Kurt asked.

“The only thing they found were some long black hairs on her shirt and around the living room that clearly don’t match… Don’t match anyone we know,” John finished lamely.

Kurt let out a long, slow breath. “Anything else?”

"A couple things. That stain by her couch.”

“The one that looked like motor oil?” Kurt looked up curiously.

“Was human blood,” John replied.

“What? It was black!”

“That’s right. Black as tar and smelled like your worst nightmare.”

“Then how could it be blood? Are they sure?” Kurt asked.

John shrugged. “The lab report says it’s blood.”

They drove in silence while John let Kurt absorb everything.

Finally Kurt asked, “Do they know what the toxin was that killed her or how she got it? Was it ingested?”

John shook his head. “No I.D. on it yet. They have run a hundred tests and come up with nothing. The only thing they found were two pinhead size holes just under her jawline, on the left side of the throat. So whoever did this probably injected it there. They probably wouldn’t have even found them, but the coroner noticed some dried blood on that area of her neck. No needles found in her house, in the trash, or in any of the dumpsters around her place. The only contents in her stomach was some residue from red wine. The poison was in her blood stream."

Kurt didn't answer. He was beginning to cry again. Red wine. He had shared that wine with her.

"There's one more thing, Kurt. This is tough."

"What?" Kurt swiped at his eyes with his sleeve.

"There were two wine glasses on the kitchen counter. They both had her prints on them." John hesitated and then went on, "But one of them had another partial set as well."

"Do they know it's me?" Kurt blurted out. He was past the point of playing games.

"Me and Mike in the lab know it's you. He ran it through NCIC and got the match. I haven't given the results to Fitz yet. I wanted to give you a chance to talk to him first."

Kurt Dale felt his whole world spinning out of control. Now he would have to tell his Captain about the affair. How long before the breadcrumb trail was long enough for Amanda to follow it, and his marriage destroyed? How long before they thought he was a suspect in Tina's murder? *Not long. Not long at all,* he thought miserably.

"John, can't you just… Can't you maybe keep that set of prints out of things for now? Mike, he's a good guy, he knows how to keep his mouth shut." Kurt hated the panicky wail that had crept into his voice, but was helpless to stop it.

His partner exploded, "Listen, you asshole, Fitz is going to read the coroner's report and know Tina Hilliard had sex before she died. He is going to wonder why the concerned boyfriend didn't come forward to make a statement and to clear himself. This is going to prompt a blood analysis on anyone who's prints they identify anywhere in that apartment, and will probably include every man on our department that so much as waved to Tina Hilliard from his patrol car as he drove by. When they compare that blood analysis to the semen found inside of her who is it going to point to, Kurt? Use your fucking head!"

"But couldn't you just wait..." Kurt pleaded.

Wyatt cut him off, his voice rising even louder, "I am not suppressing evidence in a homicide investigation and putting my ass on the line for you! And you are an even bigger fool than I thought if you think Mike is going to risk his career because your dick wandered where it shouldn't have. All I am offering you is a grace period to do the right thing. Take it or leave it. That file stays with me until nine A.M. tomorrow morning and then it's on Fitz's desk. You dig?"

Kurt walked nervously through the double doors of the precinct. Taylor, the young patrol officer who had been guarding the crime scene tape waved him over.

"Hey, Taylor, I can't talk right now. Need to go see Fitz."

"Just thought you might want to know what I found out from my canvas of the neighbors." Taylor held up his notebook.

Kurt walked over to the desk where the young man sat, and said, "Shoot."

"Well, several of the neighbors saw a green Jeep Cherokee parked across the street from the building a few nights a week. Usually just stayed a few hours. It was there last night before she was killed."

Great, Kurt thought, a*nother nail in my coffin*. "Anyone get a plate on it?"

Taylor shook his head. "No one thought it was suspicious. Probably the boyfriend's rig."

"Boyfriend?"

"Yeah, some guy they say was there a lot. Tall, dark hair, mid thirties to early forties." Taylor glanced down at his notes.

Kurt paled.

Taylor noticing the other man's unease, asked, "You okay, man?"

"Yeah. Anything else?"

"Yeah. The boyfriend might be a cop," Taylor said.

Kurt swallowed. "How… Why do you think that?"

"The DOA told the woman in the unit across from her that she was seeing a cop. But she didn't give a name or anything. Not real surprising though. She got friendly with a lot of us back when Perkins was loose. But the word was that she wasn't interested. I know some guys that tried to make time with her, and she never bit," Taylor commented.

Kurt dropped into a chair across from the younger officer. He didn't think his legs were going to support him much longer. "Did you talk to any of her friends or family?"

"No, man," Taylor laughed, "That's your job."

"Right." Kurt forced a not very believable laugh from his own lips.

"You would have thought the guy would've bragged about it if it was someone from around here, wouldn't you, Kurt? I mean why keep a babe like that a secret?"

"I gotta go see the Captain." Kurt rose abruptly on unsteady legs. He walked toward the back of the station house and Captain Fitzgerald's office. One thought kept repeating itself over and over in his head, as he walked down that long corridor toward his demise, *The jig is up… The jig is up… The jig is up.*

Kurt rapped tentatively on the half closed door. Fitz looked up from the papers on his desk and waved Kurt to a chair. "How you doing? You don't look so good." His clear brown eyes looked at Kurt appraisingly.

Kurt took a deep breath and began, "There are some things I need to tell you. Things that are not going to look real good, but I need for you to know them."

Fitz nodded toward the half open door. "Then you better close that."

Kurt kicked the door shut with his foot.

Fitz leaned back in his chair and opened a desk drawer. He extracted a bottle of bourbon and two Dixie cups. Without asking if Kurt wanted the drink, he poured a healthy belt and slid the cup across the desk.

"Go ahead, Kurt. I'm listening."

Kurt downed the burning liquid in one gulp, then told the Captain his story. He spoke for the better part of an hour, and he finished by telling him about the fingerprints on the wine glass and who's DNA the semen taken from Tina's body was going to be a perfect match with.

Captain Fitzgerald interrupted only once. With a wry smile, he said more to himself than to Kurt, "Explains your memory lapse outside her apartment last night, doesn't it?" His calm expression never changed during the telling of Kurt's tale. When Kurt was through Fitz said nothing for several minutes. He poured them another drink and sat looking out his office window onto the grassy common area outside.

"I don't think you killed that girl, Kurt. I have known you too long to think you capable of that. However, I can't let you be part of the investigation. And I can't cover this up for you. You understand that?"

Kurt nodded miserably.

"I'm going to need DNA samples from you and a statement from your wife that says you were safely tucked away in your bed between the hours of midnight and two, when they put the time of death at."

Kurt looked at him with alarm. Before he could object Fitz held up his hand. “It’s futile for you to think you can keep this from your wife, Kurt. She will be questioned just like everyone else in this department’s effort to clear your name. Frankly, I wish we had another witness that could put you at home besides your spouse, but she will have to do.”

Kurt could no longer control the tears that had been threatening since his late night drive for the last time to Tina’s. He broke down sobbing in Captain Fitzgerald’s office. He cried for his marriage, for his soon to be shattered reputation, for his career and for Tina. He cried until he was an empty husk.

During it all Captain Fitzgerald sat with the same placid expression on his face, looking serenely out the window of his office and nursing his drink.

When Kurt had finished the last few hitching sobs, Fitz handed him a box of Kleenex and refilled his Dixie cup a third time.

CHAPTER 5

Richie Welch, town bad boy, sat under the sweltering lights, and the even more scorching gaze of John Wyatt in interrogation room 4. Despite the heat in the unairconditioned room, he still wore his signature leather jacket as if he thought he'd be leaving soon. He kept tapping his foot in a nervous rhythm which made the many buckles on his jacket jingle. They jangled like that when he walked too. People often commented that you could hear Richie when he was still a block away. The guy never took off that ridiculous jacket. His long, dark hair was slicked back and worn in a ponytail. And the attitude he carried was twice as tall as he was.

"I told you, man, I wasn't anywhere near Wood River last night. You can ask me the same question, but keep phrasing it a hundred different ways, dude. Answer will still be the same. Wasn't me."

"So, where were you last night, Richie?" John Wyatt asked for the umpteenth time.

"I told you. I was out. I was lots of places."

"Name them, and give me times." Wyatt was getting tired. He felt in his gut that talking to Richie was a waste of time. But the questioning had to be done. Whenever there was any crime committed in Alder Lake, Richie Welch was automatically questioned. And seven times out of ten he was involved.

Richie was no stranger to interrogation room 4. He knew rooms 2 and 3 pretty well too. He'd done time for breaking and entering in his late teens, then graduated to grand theft auto in his early twenties. His most memorable crime being the attempted hold up of a 7-11 store while wearing a clown mask. He forgot however, to take off his leather jacket and was caught jangling just beautifully on the convenience store's surveillance camera.

John was pretty sure Richie lacked both the imagination and the brains to kill someone by injecting some exotic poison into their neck, but he matched the vague description of the only lead they had — the neighbor's recollection of a long-haired stranger in a big jacket, who was seen walking down the street around the time of Tina Hilliard's murder.

If Richie were smart he'd have gotten rid of the jacket a long time ago. He was nailed on the grand theft auto charge because someone remembered all those buckles. John was pretty sure that someday that jacket was going to get Richie life in prison, whether he was guilty or not.

"So, where were you, Richie? It's not a tough question," John asked again patiently.

"I told you. I was a lot of places. Got plenty of eyewitnesses."

"Give me your itinerary. Start from when you stood in front of your mirror and put that handful of grease in your hair so all the ladies would love you, then stepped from your bathroom out into the cool night air."

Richie sighed and leaned back in his chair. He was relishing the fact that for once in his life he knew he wasn't guilty of anything. "What's my crime supposed to be this time, Wyatt? Some old lady lose her pension check?"

"Nope. This time you're in the big leagues. Someone was murdered last night. Know anything about that, Richie?"

Richie's eyes widened for a minute and he reached into his pocket for his pack of Camels. Realizing where he was, he let the cigarettes drop back. He decided it was a good time to become very cooperative. "I was at Smokey's Tavern shooting pool."

"What time?"

"Got there just after nine, I think. Stayed 'til around twelve-thirty, then went over to the diner at the bowling alley with Bobby and Hootch for a hamburger. Was there 'til two."

"And if I ask Darlene if you were there, what's she going to tell me?" John asked.

"Why don't you go ask her and stop busting my balls. I didn't do nothing," Richie snapped irritably, glaring at the detective and challenging him to say anything further.

"What time did you get home?" Wyatt sighed.

"Around three. I gave Hootch a ride home."

"What route did you take back?" The time frame was too close for John to let this go.

"Oh man, you are really a piece of work," Richie laughed, "Next you gonna wanna know what time I pissed and how many beers I had at the bar too?"

"What route, Richie?"

Richie tilted the chair back upright and slammed his feet on the ground. He muttered something that sounded like, "Fuckin' unbelievable." Then spat, "Water Street all the way back into town. You satisfied?"

"Did you see anyone when you were driving home?"

"Aw, Jesus, if you are gonna try to find someone to verify my whereabouts during the drive home, I'm shit out of luck. The only witness I have is the fuckin' radio. You want to know what songs they played?"

John frowned at him. "No one walking on the sidewalks? No one hanging around on a corner?" he persisted.

"No. I wasn't looking for an alibi, and if I need one I ain't answering anymore questions 'til I call my fuckin' lawyer."

John sighed. "Get out of here, Richie. As long as your alibi checks out, you won't hear from me again until you and your jacket there decide to hold up another convenience store."

John Wyatt emerged from the brightly lit interrogation room into the dimmer hallway of the station house. He was surprised to see Fitz waiting for him outside the door.

"He know anything?" Fitz asked, nodding at the jangling figure stalking toward the front door.

"No. For once in his life I think he's innocent."

"What's next?"

"Friends and family. Try to find someone that might have had a motive," John answered.

Captain Fitzgerald looked at the detective levelly. "You already have one. Better clear that lead up before you look anywhere else. Do we understand each other?"

"You talked to Kurt," John sighed with relief.

"He is on his way to give some DNA samples and get a statement from his wife verifying he was home last night. Before you question the girl's people I want you to talk to Kurt's neighbors. See if anyone saw him out for a late night drive or anything."

"Fitz you don't…"

"No," Fitz interrupted, "I don't think he did it." He paused, "But I want to know that for sure come this time tomorrow."

John nodded. "I will do what I can, you know that. Meantime the real killer is out there and we don't have jack."

"You have the file from the lab?" Fitz asked.

John handed over the file that could potentially destroy his best friend's career, not to mention his marriage, and maybe even his life. Fitz took it without comment and strode down the hall.

Lombard Street was quiet when John parked at the corner. Most of the residents were probably just finishing dinner and watching Wheel of Fortune. He hated the idea of canvassing Kurt's neighbors, but it had to be done. He strode up the walkway leading to Darlene Coombs's dilapidated house just as she emerged from the front door in her pink waitress uniform.

"Hello, Darlene, how are you?" he asked somewhat stiffly.

She looked at him with narrow suspicion. "Is this about Russ?" She started pulling at the hem of her sweater with nervous fingers.

"No. Not at all, Darlene. I just need to ask you a couple questions. But it's nothing to do with Russell at all. He doing alright?"

"He's just fine. Ask your questions, I have to go to work."

"What time did you get home last night?" John flipped open his pad to take notes.

"Two-thirty, two-forty, same as always."

"Darlene, was Kurt's car in his driveway when you got home?"

"Kurt?" she asked surprised, "Why you want to know if Kurt was there?"

"Darlene, please just answer the question, okay?"

She nodded. "Yeah the Jeep was there. Same as always."

"You're sure?"

"Positive, why?" she pressed.

"One more thing," John continued, "Did you see Richie Welch last night."

Darlene gave a rueful laugh. "Yeah, drunk off his ass with two of his buddies. He came in real late, after the bars shut down. Bastard didn't tip me."

"Thanks, Darlene. You have been a big help," John said. And thought to himself, *bigger than you know. You might have just saved Kurt's ass.*

He was just turning to leave when a thought occurred to him and he turned back. "Hey, Darlene? Was Russ home last night?"

"Yeah, of course. He don't get out much." she looked away.

"Can I talk to him?" he asked mildly.

"Why? You said he's not in any trouble," Darlene cried, alarm creeping into her voice.

"He's not, Darlene. None at all," John soothed, "I just want to know if he saw what time Kurt might have gotten home last night."

"What is it you think Kurt did, Detective?" she asked, exasperated.

"Darlene, I can't talk about this. But it's important. Go get Russ okay? You don't want to be late for work."

"I will ask him for you, he's not feeling up to company right now. Is that okay?" Then she hurriedly added, "But he probably doesn't know. He doesn't pay much attention to people's comings and goings."

Wyatt thought about it a minute and told her to go ahead and ask.

Darlene went inside and returned a few minutes later.

"He said he saw Kurt drive up when he was walking the dog. He walks the dog when I'm at work. Does it right after the news, so it's probably somewhere between ten-thirty and eleven. Okay?"

"Yeah, Darlene, that's great. Really great." John sounded very relieved. He could have kissed her.

She looked puzzled, but also pleased that she had been able to help. She made a mental note to ask Amanda tomorrow what the heck was going on.

John wished her a good evening and started back for his car. He would have liked it if he could find someone else to verify when Kurt arrived home. He wasn't sure the word of an alcoholic that barely stepped out his front door would hold up in court, but it was better than nothing. His step was much lighter as he walked back to his car and started for home.

Richie Welch didn't like being questioned in connection with a murder. Besides a few bar fights, he had never actually hurt anyone a day in his life. The convenience store robbery had been pulled off with a toy gun.

The only person he had ever even contemplated killing was his mother's third husband, a man now long dead. Richie's moral code allowed for crimes against property, but not human beings. That was just wrong.

He drove home chain smoking, wondering if somehow he was going to find himself involved in yet another mess.

Richie had tried to clean up his life over the last year. He held a job in an auto body shop and he hadn't done anything that stepped too far outside of the law in over six months. Part of the reason for this mending of his ways was his on again – off again girlfriend, Charity Ash, the Baptist Minister's daughter.

Like most children brought up under the rules of a too tightly wound man of the cloth, Charity rebelled. She started liking bad boys at the age of twelve. The more trouble they got into, the more she liked them. By the time Charity was sixteen, she had the kind of reputation that was built one boy at a time, in the back seat of numerous hotrods with the windows fogged up.

When she met Richie at age seventeen and found out about his rap sheet, Charity fell hopelessly in love. Richie was older and had a record. He wore his hair long and he smoked unfiltered Camels. She knew Daddy would detest him, and she wasn't disappointed.

Her father, the Reverend Wilbur Ash, did everything in his power to try and dissuade her from this romance. The more he protested, the more Charity liked it. Finally at his wits end, the Reverend Ash decided to pay Richie's mother a visit and see if he could put a stop to it that way.

Reverend Ash showed up on the doorstep of space seventeen of The Happy Wheels Mobile Estates, the single-wide home of four time divorcee, Rachel Burns-Welch-Carter-Ginsburg. He explained to the woman how completely unsuited for one another their children were. He sited religious differences, background differences, age differences, and any other difference, real or imagined, he could think of.

Rachel listened patiently, while nursing her fourth vodka tonic of the day. Somehow she misunderstood the reason for the minister's visit and thought he was hitting on her. When Rachel suggested they move their little party to the bedroom of her trailer, the man seemed clearly repulsed at the idea. Rachel was insulted.

What ensued was a verbal argument, so loud and so violent, that her neighbors called the police.

The reverend required three stitches in his head to sew up the wound from an ashtray the lady of the manor hurled at him. No charges were filed.

After this fiasco Charity was positively gleeful, and she loved Richie all the more. The relationship was a volatile one for the first several months, punctuated with a lot of yelling, and a lot of kissing and making up.

They had been kissed and made up now for the better part of eight months, and Richie was thinking maybe it was time for both of them to settle down. The word marriage even crept into his mind from time to time.

He was not totally ignorant to the fact that he made a bad criminal. Felonies, Richie decided, were only for those that were very detail oriented. Richie was just not a detail kind of guy.

He found something he was good at — fixing cars. The owner of the body shop he worked for had his own previous run-ins with the law, and gave Richie a chance. So far he hadn't regretted the decision.

Richie picked up Charity later that night and told her about being hauled in and questioned about a murder. Her eyes positively sparkled. She seemed oddly disappointed when he told her he wasn't involved.

"Not even a little bit?" she asked, her lips going all pouty.

"You mean you want me to be guilty?" he asked her.

"Well, it would sure piss Daddy off if you were," she replied, with just the hint of a smile.

Now settled happily into her fifth marriage, Richie's mother Rachel had moved out of Happy Wheels. She met Leroy Clovis at an AA meeting. Twelve steps and one year later they were married.

Her luck with men in the past had been dreadful at best. Her first husband, Richie's father, ran off with a cocktail waitress when the boy was four. Her second husband managed to get himself killed at the racetrack over a wager. Her third was only referred to as "the bad husband," and sometimes "the Anti-Christ." He beat her with her son's little league bat. After his arrest she was forced to sit in court and defend herself against his attorney, a short, balding man she was certain was a pedophile. This was before the bruises were even healed.

That husband ended up dying in his prison cell at the hand of a disgruntled fellow inmate. Neither Rachel nor Richie shed a single tear.

Husband number four claimed to be a psychic, and went by the name Donovan. Just Donovan. No last name. His driver's license, however, said he was Norman Ginsburg of Decatur Alabama. And the unemployment office that sent him his only income was unaware he possessed any skills, psychic or otherwise.

That union ended when Rachel came home one afternoon to find Donovan on the couch with the woman from space number 24. He was reading more than her palm. Rachel predicted the future at this moment better than Donavan ever could have. It included a serious ass-kicking and a hasty divorce. It was then that Rachel decided to straighten out her life.

She began attending AA meetings and met Leroy Clovis, one of very few black residents in Alder Lake. They dated briefly and fell in love. When they announced their engagement, Charity was beside herself with joy. She told Richie, "Daddy is going to go just batshit!"

Despite the brief courtship, the marriage seemed to be a good one. Richie noticed no bruising anywhere on his mother at family gatherings. He took this as a positive sign. She was now living on a quiet suburban street in Leroy's neat little A frame house.

Leroy had even once bailed Richie out of jail.

It was a particularly nasty arrest, the result of a drunken barroom brawl in which the arresting officer used a tazer on him. When Leroy picked him up, Richie showed him the tazer burn, and Leroy said, "You are tazed and confused." He followed that with a "You Are Breaking Your Mother's Heart" speech that actually made Richie feel guilty. He tried hard to dislike his mother's fifth husband, but found it difficult. The guy really was pretty cool.

Leroy was tall and thin, his neat afro cut close to the head and entirely gray. He once told Richie he had been drafted by the Nicks, but his drinking destroyed his basketball career. Richie wasn't sure if he believed that or not, but there was something about the guy he liked, and he moved with an odd grace that leant the story credibility. Leroy was quiet and content. The world just didn't seem to faze him much. He never lost his temper no matter how hard Richie tried to piss him off. And Richie tried a lot.

Leroy was a mailman. He was a hard worker, and it was clearly obvious that he loved Richie's mother. Seeing her settled and happy for the first time in his entire life made Richie want the same thing. Leroy was a good influence.

Richie dropped Charity off after their date and decided to stop by his mother's house. He wanted to talk to Leroy about this murder business. He didn't like it. Not even Charity's excitement made him feel any better.

His mother let him in and offered him a soda. There was no alcohol in the Clovis home. Leroy was sitting in the living room watching a football game when Richie walked in and sat down next to him on the couch.

"Hey, Richie," Leroy smiled, "Come to watch the game?"

"Actually, I wondered if I could talk to you about something?"

Leroy glanced over at Rachel in the kitchen. "You want to go for a walk?"

Richie nodded. He waited on the porch while Leroy pulled on a light jacket and told Rachel they were going out.

When they began walking up the street, Leroy asked, "You in trouble again, son?"

"I'm not sure," Richie answered truthfully. He told him about his conversation with John Wyatt.

When he was through, Leroy looked at him speculatively. "Were you where you told him you were last night?"

"Yeah. But what if Darlene says I didn't go to the diner or something?"

"You forget to tip her again, Richie?" Leroy asked with narrowed eyes. When Richie didn't answer, he said, "How many times have I got to tell you? You never know when you are gonna need something from somebody. You got to do right by people, Richie."

Richie mumbled something under his breath that Leroy couldn't hear.

"So, who got killed, Richie?"

The younger man shrugged. "Don't know. Wyatt didn't say."

"Well, you just keep your nose clean. If they want to talk to you again, you call me first. I'll go with you."

Richie nodded. "Hey, Leroy, don't say nothing to Ma, okay?"

Leroy promised not to. "Would just break her heart," he replied.

Richie winced.

CHAPTER 6

Kurt walked out of the clinic where he gave his blood and hair sample. He was surprised to see it was nearly dark. He was grateful not to have his car with him. He was in no hurry to go home and face Amanda.

He started in the general direction of Lombard Street, walking slowly up the nearly deserted road and lingering at shop windows. When he reached the end of the commercial district he crossed the street and went into the park. He sat for awhile on a bench and wondered how different his life was going to be after tonight.

Was he going to be indicted for murder? Was he going to stay married? Was he even going to be a cop anymore? Everything seemed so surrealistic. It was like watching someone else's life from the outside.

He thought about calling his only sibling, a sister in San Francisco, but decided against it. They sent Christmas and birthday cards. Beyond that, there was little relationship.

Both of his parents were dead. They had died in an automobile accident twelve years earlier. They drove into the city to purchase a washer and dryer. On the way back they got into an argument.

According to witnesses, Kurt's father tried to backhand his mother while negotiating a hairpin turn. He lost control of the car and went over an embankment into the river below. It was a sad, but not terribly surprising end to anyone that knew of their long and tumultuous relationship.

Kurt's only real family was his wife and daughter. Losing them was losing everything.

Lost in thought, he noticed none of the people around him. A few couples strolled through the park hand in hand. A couple kids were tossing a ball around. And a lone figure with long, stringy hair, wearing an army fatigue jacket shambled by.

Fighting the most intense wave of loneliness he had ever known, Kurt rose from the bench and walked home.

Amanda was sitting on the floor playing with the baby. She smiled when he came in, but the smile faded when she saw how haggard he looked. Concerned, she rose and went to him.

"Are you okay?" Her eyes were widening in alarm.

"No. I'm not."

"What is it?" She took his hand and lead him to the couch.

Kurt looked at the baby playing with her blocks and scrubbed his face with his hands. "Mandy, you know how much I love you. How much I love Lorna don't you?"

"Kurt, you're scaring me. What's going on?" Her eyes were beginning to narrow in a glint of suspicion.

He sighed, and his voice sounded weary. "The murder of that girl. They think maybe I was involved."

"What! Why in the world would they think you…" Amanda's voice trailed off. She put her hand over her mouth and whispered, "Oh god, Kurt, you were sleeping with her, weren't you? That's where you were all those nights."

He nodded and looked at the floor, unable to meet his wife's stare.

In a flat, toneless voice, Amanda demanded, "Did you do it?"

Startled, he looked up, "You mean did I kill her?"

"Well, did you?" Amanda screeched, her voice rising.

"No! Of course I didn't. I was trying to break it off… Had been trying to for weeks and…"

"SHUT UP, KURT! JUST SHUT UP!" Amanda roared, holding her hand up in a warding off gesture. "DON'T YOU SAY ANOTHER WORD!"

The baby started to cry when she heard her mother yelling. Amanda Dale glared at her husband, her face pulled into a grimace of disgust and hatred. Her eyes filled with tears, and she wiped at them furiously with the back of one hand. She rose and went to the baby. Choking back sobs, she picked her up and carried her upstairs.

Kurt sat on the couch, sad and defeated. He waited for his wife to come back. After a half hour passed he realized she wasn't going to. With a heavy sigh he began climbing the stairs. He looked in the baby's room. Lorna was asleep in her crib. He kissed her on the cheek, walked to his bedroom and slowly opened the door. Amanda lay in the dark room facing the wall.

"Mandy?" he whispered tentatively.

She didn't answer.

Kurt sat down on the corner of the bed and put his hand on her shoulder. She didn't pull away, but she still wouldn't look at him. "Do you want some kind of explanation or something? Do you want to talk about this?"

"No, Kurt, I don't," she spat.

"Mandy, I might be in a lot of trouble. I really need your help."

She rolled over and looked at him, eyes blazing. "My help? You want me to help you?" Her voice was tinged with both sarcasm and shock. “Well you know what, you lying, cheating bastard? I don’t think I am in much of a mood to help you just now.”

“Don’t you think I know that?” Kurt hung his head miserably. “But do you want us to lose everything? I know you are mad. You have every right to hate me, but you can lose as much as I can if I get blamed for this.”

Amanda was quiet for a few minutes thinking about his words. Finally she asked, “Why do they think you did it? Is that where you were before you came home that night?”

He nodded and looked away.

She wrenched her shoulder out of his grasp. “What do you want you son of a bitch? What?” she barked through clenched teeth, tears shimmering in her eyes.

“I need a statement from you that says what time I got home, and that I was here with you until the phone call came in from Fitz.”

“Did you have sex with her that night? Is that what you did? Had sex with her then came home and had sex with me? Who does that? What kind of a sick bastard does that?” Her voice was shrill, the tears now spilling down her face.

Kurt put his face in his hands and started to cry. “I’m sorry.”

“Sorry? You’re sorry? Amanda screamed.

He took a deep breath. “Look, Amanda, there isn’t anything I can say. Just give me the damn statement and I will leave, alright? I’ll go stay at a hotel or something.”

She twisted her face into a horrible smile. In a voice so cold it made the hairs on the back of Kurt’s neck stand up, she laughed, “No. No statement. You’re on your own, Romeo.” She rose from the bed and ran downstairs.

Kurt sat on the bed wondering if he should go after her and try to talk to her. While he was trying to decide what to do he heard the front door slam. He looked out the window and saw Amanda climb into the Cherokee.

She backed out of the driveway so fast she nearly took out a lamp-post.

He stared out the window for a few minutes then went to the phone and dialed John Wyatt's number.

"Hello," Ellen answered.

"Hi, El. It's Kurt."

There was a long pause before she asked rather stiffly, "How are you doing?"

"Mandy just left. I don't know where she went."

"Did she take the baby?" Ellen sounded concerned.

"No. Baby's here. Mandy just ran out… We had a… Well, a pretty bad fight, I guess you could say," he replied uncomfortably.

"Yeah, I'm sure you did. Hold on, I'll get John." Ellen's voice had turned chilly.

Kurt heard some whispers, then his partner came on the line. "Hey, man."

"Hey, John. Any leads on Tina? I mean other than me?" He tried a chuckle that fell flat.

John ignored it. "I have a little good news there. Your neighbor confirmed you got home before eleven and the car was in the driveway 'til morning. As long as you have the statement from Amanda, you should be cleared."

"You talked to my neighbors?" Kurt asked, his voice rising.

"I had to. You know that," John replied defensively. "Fitz's orders."

"Yeah, of course. Sorry. I've never been a suspect in a homicide before." Kurt paused. "About that statement from Mandy… Well, I don't have it. She left. I don't know where the hell she's gone. She's pretty pissed off right now."

"Yeah, I don't doubt it. She'll calm down, Kurt. Give her some time. If she shows up here, we'll let you know."

"Appreciate it," Kurt mumbled. "Anything else on the investigation?"

"Not much. Will talk to friends and family tomorrow. We still have that long black hair and another set of prints taken off her stereo cabinet. No I.D. on those yet."

"Will you keep me posted?" Kurt asked.

"As much as I can."

"Thanks."

"Sure. Take care, Kurt."

John Wyatt hung up the phone and turned to his wife. "You want to know what I think the two unluckiest things in this town are?"

"What?" she asked, smiling a little.

"Kurt Dale's penis and Richie Welch's jacket."

Russell Coombs switched off the news and finished the last swallow of beer from the can propped between his thighs. There was a pile of crushed cans by his feet. He rose on unsteady legs and carried the empties into the recycle bin in the garage. Grabbing the dog's leash off the hook in the garage, he called in a slurred, but surprisingly sweet voice, "Where's Daddy's girl? Want to go out, baby?" Then he burped and mumbled, "S'cuse me." Even though there was no one in the house to hear him except the dog.

Samantha bounded into the garage, thrusting her neck forward to allow Russell to fasten the leash.

He took the flashlight off the kitchen table and a plastic garbage bag out of the cabinet for Samantha's "business," as he called it.

Everyone would have agreed that for a drunkard, Russell was an extremely responsible pet owner and avid environmentalist.

They walked outside and took their customary route through the field behind the house.

As they were walking back home the flashlight died. The field was not illuminated by any streetlight. Without the flashlight it was completely black.

"Goddamn thing," Russell muttered, smacking the flashlight a couple of times against the heel of his hand.

When it didn't come back on, he shoved it into his pocket and started making his careful way back through the pitch-black field, in what he hoped was the direction of home.

They had gone only a few feet when Samantha stopped and began to growl low in her throat.

"Wazza-matta girl?" Russell slurred. He had never heard Samantha growl like that. She was normally the friendliest of dogs. He tried to pull her forward, but she refused to budge. She growled again and began to bark wildly at something off in the field to their left.

Russell squinted into the darkness, but could make out nothing. Samantha was straining against the leash. Russell's heart was bumping hard in his chest, as he looked around the vacant field. "What is it, girl? A squirrel or somethin'?"

She continued to strain at her leash and growl.

"Anyone there?" Russell called out. He was wrestling Samantha toward the edge of the field when he heard footsteps and froze. He looked up and could see a pair of bright, baleful blue eyes staring at him. They were hovering about five and a half feet off the ground. Glowing eyes, seemingly unattached to anything.

"What the fuck!" Russell cried, and yanked Samantha's leash as hard as he could. He took off running, sucking in harsh, panicky breaths. Stumbling from the field, he pulled the wildly barking dog with him. On shaky legs he walked quickly back toward the house.

Samantha was still looking behind her into the field and whining.

When Russell got them safely inside the locked garage he looked at the dog and told her earnestly, "I really have to quit drinking."

Amanda drove through the sleeping city screaming obscenities at her husband and banging her fists against the steering wheel. When she was pretty well screamed out, she drove to the bowling alley and pulled into one of the diagonal spaces in front of the diner. She checked her appearance in the visor mirror and crinkled her nose. She let her hair out of the elastic band holding it back and brushed it out. She applied some lipstick and walked into the diner.

If Kurt had seen her, he would have thought, *How very Amanda.* No matter what the situation, she simply must look her best.

The diner was quiet. Two men sat in a booth finishing sandwiches and a lone woman hunched over the counter reading a paperback. Darlene was behind the counter refilling the woman's coffee when she saw Amanda walk in. She looked surprised.

"What are you doing out after bedtime, lady?"

Amanda gave an awkward smile and sat down at the end of the counter as far from the other patrons as she could. Darlene held up the coffee pot and Amanda nodded.

"I'd take something stronger if you had it," she remarked.

Pulling a cup from the rack behind the counter, Darlene filled it and placed it in front of her neighbor.

"Can you join me?" Amanda asked.

Darlene looked around at the nearly empty restaurant and grabbed another cup. She sat down beside Amanda. "So what's up? You and Kurt have a fight or something?"

"Well, gee, let's see. Where do I start? My husband the policeman was having an affair with a woman that was murdered, and they think he may have killed her. All in all hasn't been a great night," Amanda answered sarcastically.

Darlene looked at her, shocked. When she realized she wasn't kidding, she nodded. "Okay, the affair part I can buy. That's a road well traveled. But the murder part? No way, not Kurt."

"Oh, it gets better," Amanda continued. "He wants I should alibi him. Give him a letter or something that says he was home safe in his bed when the adulterous, little bitch got herself whacked."

Darlene shook her head in disbelief. "That explains why John Wyatt was sniffing around earlier anyway."

Amanda looked at her puzzled, "Sniffing around what?"

"He came over before I went to work. Wanted to know when Kurt got home last night."

Amanda looked down, embarrassed. "What did you tell him?"

"Told him the Jeep was in the driveway same as always. He wanted to talk to Russell too."

Amanda nodded for her to go on, and Darlene said, "I told him no, but I asked Russ, and he saw Kurt get home when he took the dog out, so I told Wyatt that."

"And did that satisfy him?" Amanda's voice sounded uneasy and a little scared.

"Yeah, seemed to. So who was she?"

"Did you hear about a woman that was stalked by some guy that saw her in a bar awhile back? He ended up breaking into her house one night and got arrested there. She wasn't hurt. At least not then."

"Yeah, vaguely. Several months ago, wasn't it?" Darlene asked, sipping her coffee.

"Yep. Well, that's her."

"She has worse luck with her men than we do, Toots," Darlene smirked.

Amanda gave a sardonic little laugh. "Yeah, guess so. Little tramp won't be sleeping with anyone else's husband now, will she?"

They sat drinking their coffee for a few minutes, then Darlene asked, "So what are you going to do?"

"I don't know. It would serve him right if I said he wasn't home that night."

"Maybe, but where would that leave you and Lorna?" Darlene was always the pragmatist.

"Yeah, I know. Kurt was real quick to point that out before I left tonight. I suppose I will give him his precious note. But he can sweat about it for tonight at least, the prick."

"What makes them think Kurt could have done it?"

Amanda didn't answer. After a long pause she finally said, "I have more motive than he does, don't I? She was banging my husband for months. Maybe next they will be asking you where I was that night."

Darlene patted her arm. "Are you going home, Mandy?"

She shrugged. "Eventually."

"So, you want to know what I think?" Darlene asked hesitantly.

"Yeah, sure. I need all the advice I can get," Amanda nodded.

"I think he fucked up royally. And I suspect he knows it too. If you can get past this one — and I'm not saying you should — but if you can, you may finally have the husband you always wanted. The one that doesn't run around. This may prove to be the wake-up call he needed."

"Not much running around he can do from prison," Amanda said bitterly.

Darlene rolled her eyes. "Hell, he's a cop and he's innocent. It will never get that far. You have to know that."

"Why are you so sure he didn't do it, Darlene? He told me he was trying to dump her. Maybe things got out of hand."

"You don't believe that anymore than I do," Darlene said, and in a soft voice, added, "The hardest thing is standing by your man when you know he's wrong. No one would blame you if you didn't. But I don't think he should go to jail for something he didn't do. The punishment wouldn't exactly fit the crime."

"Oh, really? I think it would fit perfectly," Amanda spat.

"I can see where you would. But think about what would become of you and your daughter if that's the way it went. You want to work the late shift here with me? Besides… the best revenge can be had while he's right there at home, hon. You know that." A wicked, little smile played at the corner of Darlene's lips.

Amanda thought about her house. Her beautifully remodeled house. She thought about spending her afternoons at the gym or shopping, and never having to worry about where the money was coming from. She thought about the cashiers check she still carried in her purse. Though she doubted he had come by the money from a stock tip from Lenny Marks, he had gotten it somewhere, and it was snuggled safely in her purse. She hadn't yet gone to the bank to take care of the second mortgage.

Amanda sighed, "Be glad you at least know where your man is at night, Darlene."

"Yeah, on the bathroom floor. And if I'm lucky he will have gotten at least half of it where he was aiming for before he passed out, and I won't have too big of a mess to clean up when I get home."

Amanda winced. Not at Darlene's words, but at the matter of fact way she said them. Startled, she asked, "It's really that bad?"

Darlene rose to get the coffee pot, and avoided eye contact. "Actually, it's worse."

Sensing it was probably a good time to change the subject, Amanda remarked, "Well, all I have to say for my sorry son of a bitch of a husband, is if he so much as has the nerve to get an erection, he better not try and bring it anywhere near me."

Darlene stopped pouring their coffee and her eyes opened in comic surprise. Thinking of her husband's broken down, alcohol abused body, she laughed, "Well, I'd offer to let him bring it next door, but that's what got him in all this trouble in the first place."

For a second she thought Amanda was going to take offense at the joke, but she gave a hearty laugh. "Hell, he'd probably take you up on it."

"Hah. Somehow I don't think I'm Kurt's type," Darlene smiled.

Draining her coffee cup, Amanda shook her head. "You know what, hon? I don't think I am either." But the humor had left her voice. As she rose to leave, there were tears standing in her green eyes. "Thanks, Darlene. Guess I will go on home."

Darlene gave her friend a hug. "If there is anything I can do, just ask, okay?"

Amanda nodded and thanked her again. She walked out into the dark parking lot, letting the tears spill down her cheeks.

When Amanda let herself inside the house, Kurt was asleep on the sofa. She went into the den and rummaged through the desk for a pad of paper and a pen. In her flowing hand, she wrote:

To Whom It May Concern:

My husband, Detective Kurt Dale, returned home from working late on June 10, 2004 at approximately 10:30 PM. He was here until after 3:00 AM when Captain Fitzgerald called and summoned him to a crime scene.

She signed it "Sincerely," and tore the piece of paper from the pad.

Amanda walked back into the living room, dropped the note on her sleeping husband's face, and went upstairs to bed, locking the bedroom door behind her.

CHAPTER 7

By eight o'clock the following morning most of Alder Lake's residents had read the newspaper and the glaring front-page headline about Tina's murder. Unfortunately, due to a late night dispatcher at the police department with nothing better to do than talk to an inquisitive reporter, they also knew that Detective Kurt Dale was the one and only suspect.

The dispatcher in question was the wife of Mike from the lab. She had once won a Dolly Parton look-alike contest. That was before the Krispy Kreme addiction got the better of her. The nice reporter showed up with a whole box of cream filled chocolate, and asked her if she and Dolly were sisters. She felt she owed him something.

Kurt work up sometime in the middle of the night and found Amanda's hand-written statement on his forehead. He read it with a grimace, then stood up and stretched his aching back. He was a tall man and the couch had left him stiff and sore. When he climbed the stairs to his bedroom and met the locked door, he contemplated picking the lock for a minute. Then shaking his head, he mumbled,

"Damn lucky to be in the house at all." And he went back down the stairs.

He awoke again at seven AM and took a shower. His back was aching, his head pounding. He saw the small bottle of blue pills sitting on the sink. Amanda hadn't bothered to hide them in the drawer after taking one last night. Kurt picked up the bottle and read the label. He shook one into his hand. He knew immediately what they were. Of course he did. They were the explanation for his wife's rejoining the land of the living not long ago. The pills he insisted would never help her. Yesterday, Kurt knew he would have thrown them down the toilet and ripped Amanda's head off. Today, however, was a very different day, and Kurt Dale was a very changed man. He put the pill back in the bottle and left them on the sink where he found them. "Hope you take two this morning, babe," he mumbled to himself as he climbed into the shower.

Amanda heard the shower. She donned a robe and checked on the still sleeping Lorna. Yawning, she started down the stairs to make a pot of coffee and face this miserable day. She opened the door in her loosely tied robe to retrieve the newspaper off the step. As she bent down to pick it up, she was blinded by a flashbulb exploding in her face. Someone shoved a microphone under her chin and loud, obnoxious voices volleyed questions at her.

"Mrs. Dale, a statement?"

"Was your husband involved with her?"

"How do you feel about your husband being a suspect?"

Amanda froze for a second, then yanked closed the front of her gaping robe. With a cry of outrage, she slammed the door shut and burst into tears. She threw the newspaper on the floor and the headline screamed up at her:

WOMAN FOUND MURDERED
POLICE DETECTIVE ONLY SUSPECT

Horrified, she reached down with shaking fingers to pick up the paper. She ignored the repeated ringing of the doorbell and sat down on the couch to read the story.

It was filled with innuendo and "unnamed sources." Amanda finished it and stormed upstairs. Furious, she marched into the bathroom and threw the newspaper into the shower, then turned on her heel and slammed the bathroom door so hard the wood at the top splintered. She marched back downstairs, leaving a shaken Kurt with a face full of soap, staring after her in shock.

When he felt something hit him in the head, he had thrown his arms up instinctively in a protective gesture. The soap ran into his eyes and stung. He reached for the towel hanging on the hook outside the shower and wiped his eyes. He looked down and picked up the drenched newspaper, his stinging eyes riveted by the headline.

"Oh shit," he moaned. He quickly rinsed off and got out of the shower. He ran down the hallway calling her name, "Mandy? Honey?"

She didn't answer.

Kurt threw a towel around his waist and raced downstairs.

His wife was in the kitchen brandishing a frying pan in her hand like a weapon. "You make them go away, Kurt! You get them the fuck off my lawn right now!" Her eyes were huge and panicked.

He looked out the picture window in the living room and saw dozens of reporters standing in his yard. One actually took a picture of him in his towel through the glass window. News vans lined the street. His neighbors were standing outside and a few were talking to the reporters.

He went to the phone and called Captain Fitzgerald, the worst migraine headache of his life pounding at his temples.

"Who did this to me? No one outside of the department knew," Kurt yelled.

"Kurt, calm down. I'll send officers over there right now to clear the reporters from your house, but you need to know they are here too."

"Who did it, Fitz? Who talked?"

"That's not important right now, Kurt. Listen to me. I am scheduling a press conference. I am going to say that there is no evidence against you and you have a solid alibi. I hate to tell them anything about the real evidence, but I have to say something about the hairs we found, and the neighbor's recollection of the long-haired stranger. They need to see we have some kind of leads that don't point directly at you."

"But who…" Kurt persisted.

Fitz cut him off, "I think you should be there to make a statement, and I think Amanda should be with you."

"No. No way."

"Detective Dale, we need to do some damage control. It's an order, not a request. I will send officers there now. Once they have gotten rid of those reporters, they are to bring you and your wife down here." Fitz's voice was stern and defied argument.

"She won't… she won't go," Kurt cried helplessly.

Amanda grabbed the phone out of his hand, "Fitz, it's Mandy. Tell me what we need to do?" Her voice sounded calm and silky.

Kurt looked at her, open-mouthed and stunned. She still held the frying pan in one clenched fist.

Fitz told her about the press conference. Amanda assured him they would be there and hung up the phone.

She looked coldly at Kurt. “I’m going upstairs to get dressed.” She eyed the loose towel around his waist with disgust. “I suggest you do the same, loverboy.”

An hour later they were standing in the crowded lobby of the station house. Taylor took the baby from Amanda’s arms as she stood gawking at the reporters, her hand wrapped tightly in Kurt’s. She appeared calm and composed, though the strain was evident around her eyes, which were still swollen and tired looking.

There was a bank of microphones and Captain Fitzgerald stood in front of them making his prepared speech. When he finished, he said, “I will answer a few questions.”

“Were you having an affair with Tina Hilliard, Detective?” someone shouted from the crowd.

Captain Fitzgerald cut in before Kurt could answer, “My officer’s private life is not up for discussion. Let me clarify. I will answer questions regarding the investigation. Anyone else?”

“Mrs. Dale, how do you feel about your husband being a suspect?”

Amanda stepped forward and looked lovingly at Kurt, then dipped her head toward the microphone. “My husband and Ms. Hilliard were friends. It was unfortunate that he visited her on the night this terrible crime occurred. But as Captain Fitzgerald has told you, he was at home with me well before the time she was murdered, and he really isn’t a suspect. I believe fully in my husband’s innocence.”

“Detective, why were you at Tina Hilliard’s house that night?” someone else yelled out.

Again, Captain Fitzgerald stepped to the microphone. He was getting annoyed. “If there are no questions regarding the murder investigation, then this press conference is over.”

"Who did it, Captain?" another voice from the crowd yelled. "If it wasn't Detective Dale, then who did it?"

"We don't know that yet. We are following several leads."

"Are you looking at Detective Dale as a suspect?"

Exasperated, Fitz growled, "Last time, people. Neighbors confirm that Detective Dale's car was in his driveway at the time of the crime. His wife has given a sworn statement that he was home with her at that time as well. There is evidence that points to someone else being in the victim's apartment that night. Given these facts, it is highly improbable Detective Dale had anything to do with this crime. I am convinced he did not, just as his wife is."

Someone else began to shout a question, and Captain Fitzgerald put his hand out to silence him. "I'm not finished yet. However, in order to be thorough, we have to examine all possibilities. Since Detective Dale was admittedly at Ms. Hilliard's home that night, we would have been remiss in doing our jobs if we hadn't investigated any possible, though unlikely connection, he may have had to her murder. Anyone else?"

"Was it a crime of passion? Did you do it, Kurt?" someone from the mob shouted.

Before a red-faced and angry Fitz could get to the microphone, Kurt bent forward and yelled, "No. I had nothing to do with this."

The flashbulbs continued to go off in dizzying bursts of light and they were peppered with more questions. The newspaper the next day would show Amanda looking adoringly at her husband, as he shouted his admonition of innocence.

What felt like an eternity later, Kurt and Amanda were ushered down the hallway away from the chaos. Amanda kept her husband's hand locked in hers until they were out of sight of the reporters, then with a grimace of disgust, shook it off like it was a spider.

Kurt put his arm around her shoulder. "Thanks, babe. Thanks for standing by me."

She bent his fingers back hard enough for him to yelp in pain, and spat, "Go fuck yourself." And stormed down the hallway to find their daughter.

Miserable, Kurt waited in the hallway for Captain Fitzgerald to emerge from the crowd. When he did, Kurt thanked him and shook his hand.

"Where's your wife?" Fitz asked.

"She uh… She went to find the baby I think."

Fitz nodded. "Lets see if John is in yet. I'm hoping for some more lab results. The sooner we get them, the sooner the heat will come off of you." Then in an offhand voice, he wondered, "Did you get an attorney yet, Kurt?"

Surprised, Kurt shook his head. "No, I didn't think I was going to need one."

"Well, you may not. But it's not a bad idea to have one, just in case."

They found John Wyatt sitting at his desk in the cramped little office he and Kurt shared. He was reading the lab results he had received that morning. Kurt sat down across from him and Fitz went and got a cup of coffee. John looked up smiling a little.

"What is it?" Kurt asked anxious.

John waited for Fitz to come back and sit down before saying, "They found skin and more of that black blood under her nails. Also, a broken off piece of long black hair. She must have fought like hell. The blood matches the stain by her couch. Neither matches you, buddy. Totally different blood types."

Kurt breathed a long sigh of relief, and Fitz clapped him on the back. "That's good enough for me. I'm releasing it to the media."

"Am I still a suspect, Captain?" Kurt asked, unable to keep the anxiousness out of his voice.

Fitz thought about it for a minute. "As far as I'm concerned no, but we gotta find this long-haired stranger."

"Let me back on the case then, Cap. Okay?"

"Officially I need to say no. Unofficially if you wanted to ask some questions and do some digging, well, that would be up to you. I am giving you a couple of days off. Administrative leave. Do what you want with them. But if you find anything, I want to know."

Kurt smiled. "Deal," he said, and got up to go find his wife.

Amanda Dale sat with her hip perched on the corner of the dispatcher's desk. She bounced the baby on her lap and listened with disgust, while Rita, the day dispatcher, told her who leaked the story about Kurt to the press.

When Kurt walked in, he looked tentatively at his wife.

She gave him a sweet smile. "Ready to go home, dear?"

"Yeah. Just coming to find you."

Rita looked at him sympathetically, and Amanda gave her a hug.

She handed Kurt the baby and linked her arm through his. With her head held high, they walked past the media frenzy still gathered in the lobby and out to the parking lot, ignoring the shouted questions and accusations.

Without a word, Kurt buckled the baby into her car seat and held the passenger door open for Amanda.

Once he was settled in the driver's seat Amanda growled with contempt, "It was that fat bitch, Natalie, who blabbed to the press."

Kurt looked at her, surprised. "Did Rita tell you that?"

"No, stupid. The man in the moon did."

Kurt pinched the bridge of his nose, as his headache escalated yet another notch.

They drove in silence for awhile, then his wife said almost conversationally, "Maybe that cow will choke on her doughnut one of these days and put her poor husband out of his misery."

"I will talk to Fitz tomorrow about her leaking confidential information like that to the media," Kurt said, hoping to find something that would appease Amanda. She scared him when she got like this.

"Well, maybe next time you will keep that sorry excuse for a dick of yours in your pants and she won't have anything to talk about." Her voice dripped with sarcasm.

Kurt didn't answer. They drove the rest of the way home in silence.

Leroy Clovis sat at the kitchen table drinking coffee and reading the morning paper while his wife cooked breakfast. *What the hell do they think Richie had to do with Tina Hilliard's murder?* He wondered to himself. He delivered mail to the police station and had for the last ten years. He decided to ask some questions on his rounds today.

Richie Welch sat at the small table in his apartment, wearing a pair of drooping briefs. He read the story a second time. "Shit!" he cried out loud to the empty apartment. "Didn't even know the high-town bitch, why the hell would I kill her?" He crumpled the paper up and threw it in the corner.

In a burned out, abandoned mobile home, one that Rachel Clovis would have recognized, a boy with sallow skin and long dirty hair slept. He had a busy night planned ahead of him, and he needed his rest.

Leroy's mail route brought him to the police station around noon. The secretary greeted him with her usual warmth, “Leroy, baby, what’s shakin'?”

“Hiya, beautiful,” his customary reply. He handed her the stack of mail, and in as conversational a tone as he could muster, said, “I hear they questioned my stepson on this murder thing.”

The secretary looked up at him through narrowed eyes. “You know I can’t talk about that.”

“Of course, of course,” he said hurriedly, “I just wondered if you knew why they thought Richie had anything to do with this?”

“C’mon, Leroy, give me a break.” She rolled her eyes. “Richie has something to do with every felony, and most of the misdemeanors that happen in this town.”

He chuckled, hiding his annoyance. “Not this one he doesn’t.”

“Tell it to Wyatt. Not my department, hon.”

“And where might Wyatt be?” he asked, the sunny smile still flashing.

She pointed toward the back, indicating the bullpen of desks and offices in the rear of the station.

He walked down the corridor and tapped on the door of John Wyatt’s office, where the detective sat mulling over lab results.

John looked up and smiled at him, “Morning, Leroy. Come on in.”

“John, man, where you been? We need to shoot some hoops again.”

John laughed, “Yeah, but it may have to wait until I can answer the sixty-four-thousand dollar question.”

"And what's that, my friend?"

"You mean you don't know? Who killed Tina Hilliard?"

Leroy sat down across from John. "I hope it wasn't your partner, like the paper said."

"It wasn't." John waved the lab report.

"And I hope you don't think Richie is messed up in this either," Leroy said, not wasting time getting to the point of his visit.

John looked at him appraisingly. "His alibi checked out. He's not a suspect, Leroy. At least not right now."

Leroy nodded and got up. "You will let me know if that should change, right, man?"

"Sure, you'll be the first."

Leroy started to walk out, and John called, "Hey, Leroy?"

He stopped and turned back. "Hmm?"

"You ever see anyone around? Long dark hair and a big jacket."

Leroy thought about it for a minute. "You know you just described Richie, right?"

"Yeah, but I mean anyone else."

"No. Not that I can think of. I'll keep my eyes open though."

"Thanks, man."

And John knew he would too. Leroy noticed more than most people did, that he was sure of. He was also sure that if Leroy paid him a visit, he was convinced that Richie had nothing to do with this. And if Leroy Clovis was convinced, then so was John Wyatt. Leroy didn't miss much. In fact, John was pretty sure that Leroy didn't miss anything.

CHAPTER 8

Charity Ash sat in her backyard smoking a joint. Her parents had left after dinner to go to some function at the church and she was home by herself. Her walkman blared Marilyn Manson in her ears, her bare feet tapped a ragged jig on the ground.

Richie wouldn't be coming over until later. She planned to be good and high by the time he got there. While she puffed on the joint, she thought that it wasn't as good as the stuff Richie used to get, but he wouldn't buy it anymore.

In Charity's opinion Richie was becoming a big fat bore. He only wanted to have sex at his place. She liked to sneak him upstairs and do it when her parents were asleep in the next room. Richie wouldn't do that anymore. He said there was no reason to when they had all the privacy they could want at his place. It wasn't privacy Charity wanted. What she wanted was to drive her daddy crazy. And nothing made him crazier than when the two of them were locked up in her bedroom.

She didn't know what to do about Richie anymore. She would have broken up with him already if her father didn't hate him so damn much. He'd stopped smoking weed altogether, and he kept talking about getting older and settling down. What was that shit about? Charity didn't want to settle down and she didn't want Richie to settle down either. *If he stops drinking*, she thought, *I am so dumping him.*

When she finished the joint she took a beer out of a cooler hidden in the shed and lit a cigarette. By the time she was through with both it was full dark out. Her eyes were red-rimmed and she felt the beginning of a headache at her temples. Charity yanked the headphones to the walkman off and carried the empty can and jar lid she used for an ashtray over to the garbage bins at the side of the house.

She had just tossed the beer can in when someone touched her shoulder. Startled, Charity jumped and whirled around to see a boy about her own age standing behind her. He had long dark hair and was wearing an army fatigue jacket that was way too big on him.

With a nervous laugh, she stammered, "Man, you scared the crap outta me."

He mumbled something she couldn't hear, and Charity asked, "Do you live around here? I haven't seen you before."

The boy shook his head and looked at her.

She thought his eyes were a little creepy. They were the deepest blue she ever saw, and they reminded her of those baby toys called Glow Worms. They had the same incandescent light. They looked like they were lit up from behind.

"You new around here? Want a beer?" she asked him.

He nodded and followed her into the backyard.

"You don't talk much, do you?" she commented while rummaging in the shed for two more beers. "So, what's your name?" Charity asked, handing him a can.

"Frank," he muttered.

"You got a cold or something? You sound funny?"

The guy didn't answer, just looked at her with those intense, weird eyes.

"Well, nice to meetcha. I'm Charity." Had she been a little less stoned, she may have noticed how off the kid was, but she was very stoned and entering the land of drunk as well. All Charity saw was long dirty hair, and what she thought was probably a bad boy. A *very* bad boy — one her daddy wouldn't approve of at all.

When her attempts at conversation were met with only grunts, she gave up. "We don't have to talk if you don't want to," she said coyly, finishing her beer. "Let's go inside, it's getting cold."

Charity's strange new friend followed her into the house. She closed the door behind them and pressed up against him, resting her hand on the front of his jeans. "So, if you don't wanna talk what do you wanna do?" Charity purred. She undid the top two buttons of her blouse and tilted her head to kiss him. When his lips met hers she jumped backwards.

"Whew!" she cried, "Okay, nothing personal, dude, but how 'bout you use the shower and maybe brush your teeth before we go any further, okay? It smells like maybe you've been on the road awhile."

She unzipped his jacket and pulled it off his narrow shoulders, leaving it in a heap on the carpet.

"Man, you're skinny," she commented.

Francis Barclay was feeling stirrings he hadn't felt for — well, for two hundred years. And though he still needed to kill her, not only to fulfill what had brought him back to Alder Lake, but also to keep his strength up, for the moment his lust had become a more pressing urge.

He followed her up the stairs and into the bathroom. Charity grabbed her toothbrush from the holder and handed it to her dirty companion. "Here, you can use mine," she said. She put a fresh towel on the sink. "Shampoo and everything is in the shower. My room is the first door on the right. I'll wait there for you. Don't be too long, Richie is going to be here in about an hour so we won't have much time."

As she started walking out of the bathroom, the kid grabbed her arm.

"What?" Charity asked impatiently.

When he didn't say anything, just looked uneasily toward the bathtub, she laughed, "Oh, the shower's really easy," and reached toward the fixtures. "Here, you just pull up this knob and adjust the temperature like this."

She turned on the shower and admonished again, "Hurry up, okay?" She walked out of the bathroom, closing the door firmly behind her and leaving him standing in the middle of the floor looking confused.

He vaguely reminded Charity of Frankenstein's monster and she suppressed a giggle behind her hands.

After a few minutes, Francis Barclay put his hand out tentatively into the spray from the shower. It felt hot and it felt good. He kicked off his battered tennis shoes and stripped out of the ragged clothes, then stepped under the water. Immediately the water running off his body turned filthy brown. He put his head under the tap. As the water rinsed through his long grimy hair, small bugs, a few leaves and mud ran down into the tub. After awhile the water running off of him turned gray and eventually ran clear. He didn't use soap or shampoo, just stood under the hot water enjoying the feel of it until the water was up to his shins.

The drain was clogged from all the dirt and debris that washed off his skinny, loathsome body. He stepped out of the shower and cranked the faucet to the left. Successful in stopping the water on his own, his lips parted in an inhuman grin, showing the two teeth next to his front ones. They were about three inches long and looked nothing like teeth at all. Stained dull yellow, his fangs didn't look like any vampire you heard about in stories. They were shaped like toothpicks, and as thin as sewing needles. They came to a razor sharp point at the end.

Barclay took the towel off the sink and dried himself, then picked up the toothbrush off the sink. He managed to figure out the sink on his own and turned on the water. Not knowing what the toothpaste that was sitting on the side of the sink was for, he ignored it and plunged the toothbrush into his mouth, rubbing it over his grit-caked teeth. The bristles were a dull and sickly gray color when he removed the brush from his mouth. He left it lying in the sink. Dropping the towel, he walked out of the bathroom.

"Oh, Frankie," Charity called in a sing-song voice.

He started toward the sound of her voice. She was lying on her bed naked, waiting for him.

He walked into the room, and she reached out her hand. He took it, as she pulled him onto the bed.

"Ohhhh, much better," she sighed. When she pushed her tongue into his mouth and started to kiss him she felt something sharp. "Ouch," she yelped. "Do you have braces? Something just cut me." She put her fingers too her mouth and they came away with a fine rivulet of blood. Something had stabbed her tongue.

Francis's breathing was labored and sounded like a piece of rusty machinery. To Charity it sounded as if something was rumbling in his chest.

"I hope I don't catch your cold." she sounded worried.

Barclay rolled on top of her, his body feeling like a bag of loose rocks. He was trying roughly to push himself inside of her. He grabbed crudely at one of her breasts and put his mouth to it.

"Owww!" Charity screamed. "What the hell do you have in your mouth? You keep cutting me!"

She tried to push him away, as he was still trying to force her legs apart. She stopped struggling, realizing for the first time that maybe having this stranger up in her room was not a very good idea. She didn't want to make him mad, he was creepy. The pot and the beer were wearing off, and as Charity became more aware of her companion's oddness, she was starting to feel a little frightened of him. A nervous shiver ran up her spine.

She took a deep breath. "Okay, lets forget the foreplay, huh, and just do it, but can you keep your mouth to yourself." And with a sigh of resignation, she opened her legs for him. This wasn't any fun anymore. She was running out of time. When Charity tried to tell this weirdo to hurry again, she saw that his eyes were glowing in the dark room — literally glowing, and casting their own eerie bluish shadow over her flesh. Her voice died in her throat. *Oh god, what have I gotten myself into?* She wondered.

A comforting voice spoke up in her mind, reminding her that she was both drunk and stoned, and that combination could make anything glow in the dark. A little more of that shit she smoked and he'd probably be levitating too. The voice further reminded her that she had a lot more to worry about than a marijuana induced hallucination. If Richie found this guy here he was going to kill her. Charity figured she would just get this over with and hustle him out of the house as fast as possible. If she was lucky, she would have enough time to get cleaned up before Richie arrived. It wouldn't be the first undesirable guy she had slept with.

Despite the fact that he had brushed his teeth, his breath still smelled like garbage. Charity thought he must be homeless or something.

He was squirming on top of her but nothing was happening. His equipment was, after all, two hundred years old, and was apparently not working too well.

Barclay grunted in frustration and Charity shoved him off of her.

Naturally, she thought. *The creep just has to be freakin' impudent too, doesn't he?* "Here, let me…" She pushed him onto his back and bent her head over his lap, avoiding looking at his eyes. Her hair fell sideways and exposed the back of her pale neck to him. She took his flaccid and shriveled penis into her mouth with a grimace of disgust.

After a few minutes, when he realized that his body wasn't going to cooperate, with a cry of frustration and rage he shoved the two needle sharp fangs into the skin at the base of Charity's neck. Blood sprayed out over the sheets.

Charity's body went rigid and she let out an agonizing howl of pain. "Wh… why, why did you do that?" she stammered. Dropping his lifeless penis, she reached up and slapped at her neck with panicky fingers.

Francis replied, "Ask your murderous great-grandfather when you meet him in hell." Then he drove his fangs into her again and again.

The Reverened Wilber Ash and his wife Carla arrived home just after 8:30 P.M. When they came in the house was quiet. Mrs. Ash saw the jacket lying on the floor in the family room and remarked, "Well, will wonders never cease. Looks like Richie finally got a new jacket." She picked it up and draped it neatly over a chair.

"Well, where are they?" an annoyed Reverend Ash grumbled. "She better not have him in her room."

"Charity?" her mother called.

When she didn't answer, Reverend Ash started for the stairs.

"Oh, Will, leave her be," Carla scolded.

"She is not going to have that hoodlum in her bedroom, Carla. I have told her that a hundred times." He climbed the stairs and stopped at the bathroom, taking in the filthy towel crumpled on the floor. He looked in and saw the bathtub full of dirt and debris, the stained toothbrush lying in the sink.

"Charity," he yelled, "What the hell happened to the bathroom? It looks like a pig sty." The reverend walked out of the bathroom and into his daughter's open bedroom door. He flipped on the light switch. As he was taking in her crumpled body and the blood spattered sheets, a hand fell over his mouth and he was thrown against the wall. He had only enough time to see a ghost white face with blood caked around the mouth and tangled wet hair, before something sharp pierced him in the middle of the throat and he saw no more.

Carla was in the kitchen making tea when she heard the footsteps coming down the stairs.

"Were they in there, Wilbur?" she asked.

When her husband didn't answer, she turned around and found herself face to face with a scraggly looking, painfully thin, naked teenager with matted wet black hair and blood running down his chin. Absurdly, she said, "You're not Wilbur."

The monster descended upon her, knocking the tea kettle out of her hand.

Minutes later Barclay returned to the bathroom and stepped back into his soiled clothes. He used the towel Charity had given him for his shower to wipe the blood from his face. He took his jacket and left through the back door.

Just as he was rounding the side of the house where the garbage bins were, Richie's Camaro pulled up to the curb in front of the house.

Richie blipped the horn once and waited for Charity to emerge. He didn't like to go to the door when he knew the reverend was home. Had he looked in his rearview mirror he would have seen Francis Barclay retreating down the street. But he never looked.

After a few minutes when Charity still hadn't come out, Richie honked the horn again, this time two long insistent beeps.

Annoyed, he shoved the car in park and turned off the engine. Pocketing the keys, he walked up to the front door and knocked. Receiving no answer, he rang the doorbell. He muttered under his breath, "Where the hell is everyone?"

Richie walked around to the side of the house. Through cupped hands he peered in the living room window. He saw the tea kettle lying on the floor between the dining room and the kitchen. Mrs. Ash's body was on the kitchen floor out of view. Unsure what to do, Richie walked around to the back of the house. Seeing the door standing ajar, a cold finger of unease pressed against his spine, he called, "Hello, anyone home?"

When no one answered, he almost went back to his car and was going to drive home, but that kettle lying there wouldn't let him. Something about the sight of it lying abandoned on the floor made Richie's stomach tie into a knot.

He pushed the door open with just the tips of his fingers and tiptoed a few feet into the living room.

"Hello," he called again, starting to feel the first tinges of real fright.

He walked up to the fallen kettle and bent down to pick it up. His hand froze when he saw a pair of feet sticking out behind the kitchen counter. Richie quickly walked around the counter and saw Carla Ash lying on her back. Her eyes were open and staring. Richie gasped, bending down next to her.

"Miz Ash?" he lightly shook her arm.

Her head lolled to one side. Richie jumped to his feet. “Oh, no,” he whispered horrified. “Ch…Charity,” he yelled into the house. He ran to the base of the stairs and called again, “Rev’rund? Charity? Anyone?”

Getting no answer he fought the urge to run out of the house. Instead, he nervously walked up the stairs. Richie saw the bloody towel lying in the bathroom. With heart pounding, he turned toward Charity’s bedroom. He got one look at his girlfriend’s twisted, naked body on the bed and her dead staring eyes, before some uncontrollable urge possessed him to reach out with frantic fingers and slam off the light switch. He bolted back down the stairs and out the front door.

In his terror he nearly dropped his keys as he fumbled them from his pocket and leapt into the car. He pulled away, tires squealing, and took the corner so fast he nearly lost control of the car. He thought, *They are gonna think I did this. They are gonna think I killed everyone!*

He knew he should call the police, but instead drove straight to his mother’s house, gripped by the worst fear of his life.

Rachel and Leroy were in the kitchen doing the dinner dishes when they heard a car screech to a halt in front of their house. Seconds later someone was hammering rapidly on the door.

Leroy opened it to a pale and terrified Richie. His mother was standing behind Leroy. When she saw it was Richie, she cried, “Good God, boy, what have you done now?”

“Leroy,” Richie stammered. “Please, Leroy, you gotta help me.” He collapsed against the door frame.

Leroy gripped Richie’s elbow and steered him into the house, closing the door behind him. “Rachel, get the boy a glass of water.”

When she didn’t move, he snapped, “Rachel, go on now, get him something to drink.” Leroy led him into the living room and deposited him in an arm chair.

"Get hold of yourself, son. Tell me what's happened."

With an effort, Richie pulled in two hitching breaths. "Someone killed Charity and her mother." He hadn't seen the Reverend Ash's body hidden behind Charity's bedroom door.

Rachel had just walked into the living room with the water. When she heard this she dropped the glass to the carpet, spraying water all down the front of her shirt.

"OH CHRIST, RICHIE!" she shrieked.

"I didn't do it, Mom. I didn't do anything!" he yelled.

Leroy shot an irritated — Shut Up Woman — look at his wife. "Tell me exactly what happened."

"Oh, this time you really did it, Richie," Rachel moaned.

"Rachel, hush and let the boy talk." Leroy glared at her.

She fell onto the couch and sat ringing her hands.

Richie told how he saw the tea kettle through the window, found the back door open and went inside. When he got to the part about the bloody towel, Leroy interrupted with, "Was the blood dry?"

"I don't know, I didn't pick it up," Richie said, irritated.

"Why didn't you call 911?"

"I was scared. I just left and came straight here. If I call the police they are going to think I did this. They think I commit every fucking crime in this town."

"No one is going to think you did anything if you stop acting like you're guilty. I'm calling the police." Leroy started toward the phone.

"NO!" Richie screamed and grabbed his stepfather's elbow, "No, you can't do that. They will arrest me. I have to get out of town."

"Let him go, Leroy, he's right," Rachel cried. "They think everything that goes bad in this town is his fault. Dammit, Richie, I knew that girl was nothing but trouble."

Leroy spun on her, furious. “Rachel, this ain’t the girl’s fault, or Richie’s. You both need to calm down. Richie, if you run out of town like you are guilty, you WILL get in trouble. Plenty of it.”

Rachel and Richie started to argue. Ignoring them, Leroy went to the phone. He called 911 and explained what his stepson had seen to the dispatcher. He answered a few questions, then told her the boy had panicked and ran to his house. The dispatcher told Leroy they were to wait there for the police.

“If I go to jail for this, Leroy, I swear to God…” Richie moaned. Putting his face in his hands, his voice trailed off.

Leroy gripped his shoulder. He walked outside and sat on the front steps to wait for the police.

Another murder, he thought. *Town that gets maybe one homicide every five years, and now we got two in the space of three days. What the hell is going on?* He wondered.

Kurt and Amanda had settled into chilly silence in the house. He tried to talk to her a couple of times, but received only a harsh stare or a sarcastic comment for his efforts. He finally gave up.

When the phone rang, Amanda was sitting on the couch folding laundry and Kurt was upstairs reading to the baby. She grabbed the phone off the side table, “Hello?” Her voice sounded cautious.

“Mandy, it’s John. I need to talk to Kurt right away.”

“Hang on.” She called upstairs, “Telephone.”

She was about to hang up when she heard Kurt pick up the extension, but instead put her hand over the mouth of the receiver and listened.

“Kurt, there’s been another murder. Possibly two,” John said, then told him about Richie’s findings at the Ash home. He told Kurt to go to the crime scene and he would meet him later. He was going to the Clovis home to talk to Richie.

Kurt hung up and came downstairs. “I have to go out. Someone else was killed, Mandy.”

She nodded to him, saw how pale he looked, and bit back a comment about, was it another one of his girlfriends. She said instead, “Call later if you can. If you want to I mean.” She shrugged.

He nodded. “I’ll try. Make sure the doors are locked.”

This sent a chill through her. Amanda rose from the couch to check the locks after he went out.

Kurt arrived on the crime scene as they were taping it off. Captain Fitzgerald pulled in right behind him. “What the hell is going on in this town, Kurt?” Fitz asked, shaking his head. “Ann and I settled here because it was such a quiet place. What’s happening?”

They went into the house and saw the body of Carla Ash. An officer called from upstairs, “We got two more up here in a bedroom.”

“Two more?” Kurt wondered, unable to conceal the shock from his voice. He and Fitz trudged upstairs and looked at the bodies of Charity and her father.

A uniformed officer came up behind them. “Look in the bathroom. Looks like a swamp alligator took a bath in there.”

Kurt went in and looked at the bloody towel. He picked it up between two fingers and dropped it into an evidence bag that the officer was holding open for him. Then he did the same thing with the toothbrush. The officer carefully labeled a piece of adhesive tape with the date and time, added his initials, ripped the tape with his teeth and affixed it to the bag. He stood behind Kurt as he knelt down next to the bathtub. The shower had drained. What was left was a ring of dirt, a bed of leaves, and several dead bugs on the floor of the tub. There was a rank odor coming from there that seemed vaguely familiar to Kurt, but he couldn’t immediately place it.

Fitz walked in behind them. “Bathroom stinks like Tina Hilliard’s place did. And look at this.” He lifted a long black hair from the edge of the sink.

Kurt straightened up as the officer produced yet another evidence bag, and asked, “So, tell me what this family and Tina Hilliard have in common?”

Captain Fitzgerald shrugged. “No sign of struggle or forced entry, and no obvious cause of death. Not much blood. Just some spatters on the sheet and on the wall, and whatever is on that towel.”

“How could one person have done this?” Kurt wondered. “Do you think there are more than one?”

Fitz shrugged. “I don’t know what to think. Why the Ash family? Why Tina Hilliard? If there is a connection, I can’t see it.”

John sat on the front steps next to Leroy listening to the story of how Richie found the bodies and fled to their house.

“John, is there a connection to the other woman that was murdered?” Leroy asked.

“It’s too soon to tell. Where’s Richie?”

Leroy nodded toward the house. They got up together and went inside.

As soon as Richie saw John come through the door, he jumped to his feet, hollering, “I didn’t do nothing! You hear me? Nothing!”

“Settle down, Richie. I just want to talk to you. Find out what you saw.”

Forgetting the no-smoking rule of his mother’s house, Richie lit a Camel with shaking fingers, and again told the story of Charity not coming downstairs when he honked the horn, and going around to the back of the house and seeing the tea kettle through the window.

“Did you touch anything?” the detective asked.

"I just shook Missuz Ash's arm. I didn't know she was..." he swallowed hard. "I didn't know she was dead."

"Then what?"

"Went upstairs and saw Charity on the bed. That's when I ran out and came here."

"Why didn't you call 911?"

"I panicked. I got scared. I thought if I called, I'd get blamed for this. Hell, I get blamed for everything," he ranted, waving his cigarette wildly. "You just were asking me questions about that woman a couple days ago. Now I find this. I thought you'd think I did it."

John couldn't argue with that logic.

"Do you think he did it, John?" Rachel asked in an accusatory tone.

The detective didn't answer. He rose to his feet and told them he'd be in touch. "Not planning on taking any trips, now are you, Richie?"

Richie shook his head, and muttered again, "I didn't do nothing."

CHAPTER 9

A few days after the murder of the Ash family, Kurt and John sat at the table in Kurt's kitchen reviewing lab results.

"This is unreal," John said. "Same cause of death as Tina. Toxic poisoning."

Kurt looked at a report in front of him. "They don't know what it is, but it is similar to snake venom. Has the same properties in it. Have you ever heard of anything like that, John?"

"Since when can't they figure out what a poison is?" John asked, disgusted. "They have now sent samples of it to some lab in Arlington Virginia to try and identify it."

Kurt was troubled by the stain that looked like motor oil from Tina's apartment, and the samples taken from under her fingernails that the lab had identified as blood. When he voiced this to John, his response was, "Yeah. It was weird, but there was nothing like that at this crime scene." He seemed to be dismissing it.

It still left Kurt feeling uneasy, but John was right. There was no point in dwelling on it right now.

"What we have from the Ash home," John summarized, "Is the girl. She was naked, black hairs all over her and the bed. Then there are those punctures. One in her left breast, eight in the back of her neck, and a laceration on her tongue. We got the parents, two holes in their necks, just like Tina. Those little, teeny holes."

"And," Kurt remarked, "We got blood on the towel that matches all three of them, and a bathroom and a toothbrush covered in filth. Presumably the suspect's filth."

"We got a killer with bad grooming habits?" John shook his head, perplexed.

"Do you think Charity was planning on having sex with the perp?"

"Maybe. It would explain why she was naked. But if she was, it never happened. No semen in her, or anywhere on the bed," John said, glancing at the lab report.

They were quiet for a few minutes, both lost in their own thoughts.

"You want to hear something crazy?" Kurt asked, taking a photo of Charity's body from the stack on the table.

"What?"

"What if those holes aren't from a syringe? What if something bit them?"

John raised one eyebrow. "Bit them? What do you think we have here? An animal with very thin, little teeth?"

They both laughed uneasily.

"What did you get off the neighbors? Any dark haired strangers?" Kurt wondered.

"Nope. Just Richie beating feet to his car and burning rubber around the block. Consistent with what he told me."

Kurt nodded.

"I don't like Richie for this. No way he would kill Charity. His prints were on the front and back doors and the light switch in the girl's bedroom, consistent with his story. I almost feel sorry for him," John said.

"He does have a knack for being in the wrong place at the wrong time, doesn't he?"

John looked at his partner thoughtfully. "He's not the only one."

Kurt lowered his head, "No. I guess not."

"How are things between you and Amanda? Can I ask?"

Kurt shrugged. "She won't talk. You know how she is. She stopped with the barbed tongue the night the Ashs' were killed, but I'm still sleeping on the couch and Natalie from dispatch better hope she never meets my wife in a dark alley."

"Or you for that matter, I would think. She was suspended for a week without pay for leaking department business," John remarked.

"Yeah, I heard. But meanwhile the whole town still knows I was cheating on my wife, and half of them think I killed Tina. The other half probably think I whacked Reverend Ash and his family while I was at it." Kurt grimaced and shook his head.

"Do you think you and Mandy are going to be okay?"

"I hope so. I count every day that she doesn't ask me to pack my bags as a good one."

Leroy hadn't been sleeping well. He was tired and preoccupied while he made his rounds. He was walking up the steps to Mrs. Tipple's mailbox when she pulled into her driveway and waved him over.

"Can you help me with these groceries?" she called, motioning Leroy to the trunk of her car.

Leroy laid down his big leather mail pouch. He picked up the grocery bags and followed her into the house.

"Care for a cup of tea, Leroy? You look a little peaked," the old woman asked.

He nodded. "Yes, thanks. That would be good."

As they sat in Mrs. Tipple's kitchen sipping tea and eating cookies she had baked that morning, she asked, "Did you see the paper today, Leroy?"

"Yeah. Some nut loose in the city."

"You know… it reminded me of a story I heard when I was a little girl," Mrs. Tipple said rather hesitantly.

"What was that?"

"Well, it really has nothing to do with this. I don't even know why it reminded me of it at all. But it jogged something in my memory."

"So what's the story, Mrs. Tipple?" Leroy gave her an encouraging smile.

"You won't think I'm a dotty old woman?"

"Of course not. Go on tell me."

"Well, my grandmother told me about this family that got killed a long time ago here in Alder Lake. It's an awful story really. The townspeople all thought they were some kind of vampires or some such thing, and went and burned down their house. The way the story was told to me, supposedly, the son in this family vowed revenge on the ancestors of the men that killed them. Maybe… Maybe this is the revenge."

Leroy laughed. "That's pretty farfetched, don't you think? When was this supposed to have happened?"

The old woman shrugged. "I don't know exactly. At least a hundred years, I think. And it might be farfetched, but it would certainly be a plausible motive for murder, now wouldn't it?"

Leroy shrugged, still smiling. "Yes, ma'am, I'm sure it would be."

Mildred Tipple studied Leroy's face for a few moments, then said, "There's more."

Leroy raised his eyebrows in curiosity, "Really? What else?"

Now that she was finally voicing this story, she was determined to unburden herself with every detail, "Well you see, I also remembered my grandmother telling me that the story had been written up in some book on the town history. So I went to the library and I found the book. There isn't that many history books on Alder Lake, so it wasn't hard to locate." She reached into one of the grocery bags and pulled out an old brown book. The cover was faded and the binding frayed. "The story is in here, Leroy, I marked it." Handing it across the table to him, she said, "It made for very interesting reading."

"Why's that?" Leroy sounded amused as he took the book from her outstretched hand.

"The last names of a couple of the men that were responsible for killing that family were Hilliard and Ash. How's that for a coincidence?"

Leroy felt like he had the wind knocked out of him. The amused and mildly patronizing smile faded from his lips.

"Read it if you want. Just bring it back to me tomorrow or the next day so I can take it back to the library," Mrs. Tipple said.

Leroy promised to do just that. He thanked her for the tea and left. He walked over to the park and sat down on a bench.

A shiver of dread rolled through his body as he opened the book and began reading the page the old woman had marked. The shiver quickly turned to a dagger of panic that pierced his heart as he read about the rash of unsolved murders that occurred in Alder Lake some two hundred years before. The similarity to the recent murders was unmistakable. The hair on the back of Leroy's neck rose up when he read the names of the men responsible for torching the Barclay home and murdering them. Wyatt and Dale were among them. He knew their families had been here for generations, and knew both detectives came from a long line of lawmen.

Suddenly Leroy was transported back two hundred years. He was there. He could see the men discussing the Barclay family's fate in a cramped, dimly lit room. Watched them mount their horses and ride through town, the silver stars pinned to their shirt breasts glittering in the moonlight. He heard the horses drumming hooves, and saw them kick up dust from the hard-pack earth as they galloped. He saw the blaze as the Barclay home was engulfed in flames and felt the heat baking his skin, smelled the burning wood, heard the screams.

According to the story, the two elder Barclay's succumbed to the fire, but their son, seventeen year old Francis, fled the burning home through a back door. He was chased through a field adjacent to the property and gunned down in a gully by the riverbank. His final words were a vow of vengeance and a curse upon the men responsible for the murder of his parents.

Leroy shook his head, trying to clear the vision from his mind. He had a sick feeling in his stomach.

"That's impossible," he said out loud.

Two teenage girls walking by giggled at the man talking to himself in the park.

He never even noticed them. He was too busy picturing the look on John Wyatt's face if he went to him with this information.

A vampire. How ridiculous is that? Leroy forced himself off the bench and went to finish his rounds, but he was like a man in a daze. His mind had become a hated video tape, playing the story he had read over and over until he thought he would lose his mind.

That night over dinner, Rachel noticed her husband's preoccupation and asked him what was bothering him. For a minute he thought about lying to her. He changed his mind and told her the whole story. He got the book out and showed her the marked pages.

Rachel donned her reading glasses and read it quietly. She closed the book, and said rather breathlessly, “Well, I’ll be damned.”

“It’s just a freaky coincidence, right, hon?”

She didn’t answer right away. In a cautious tone, she replied, “Well, I guess it has to be. But if something happens to the Wyatts’ or the Dales’ how do we live with ourselves if we don’t say anything about this?”

“Say what? That a two-hundred year old vampire is up out of the ground and going around killing folks. They’d think I was drinking again. Or worse, trying to cover for Richie. We don’t even know for sure that it really happened. Just because some stuff in that old book might be accurate, doesn’t mean all of it is. Maybe they just put that story in for the dramatic effect.”

Rachel looked at him doubtfully. “Do you think Mrs. Tipple will say anything, Leroy?”

He shook his head. “I doubt it. She doesn’t want to be thought an old fool. And frankly, neither do I.”

“It’s crazy, right? I mean even if that family was killed, an old dead vampire going around murdering people just isn’t possible. Stuff like that only happens in the pages of a Stephen King book. It can’t actually be real.” Rachel laughed nervously.

“Who are you trying to convince? Me or yourself, dear?” Leroy asked.

Kurt was having nightmares again. This time it was the same one he had right after Tina was killed. Same dark room with the baby crying, and the weird pair of eyes glaring at him. Only this time there were fangs, dripping black oily blood a few inches below the glowing blue eyes.

He woke with a start and barely stifled a scream behind one clenched fist. He sat up on the couch. The sofa was murder on his back. Stiff and sore, not able to stand lying on its narrow surface a minute longer, he rose, putting his hands to the aching small of his back and stretched.

He knew Amanda would probably be mad, but he couldn't get back to sleep on the sofa. That nightmare had left him disconcerted and his back was screaming agony. He went upstairs and tried the doorknob to his bedroom. To his surprise, he found it unlocked. He silently padded across the carpet and carefully lowered himself onto his side of the bed, trying very hard not to make any noise. He noticed, with some satisfaction, that Amanda was asleep on her side, and hadn't moved into the middle of the bed during his imposed absence from their bedroom. He didn't know why, but he took that as some small sign of hope for his marriage.

He jumped when she said, "You don't have to sneak, Kurt. I knew you were there."

"I wasn't sneaking. I just didn't want to wake you."

When she didn't say anything, he asked, "Can I stay?"

"You can stay," she sighed and rolled away from him.

He lay there for a few minutes, then asked, "Are we going to be okay, Mandy?"

When enough time passed that he didn't think she was going to answer, he rolled onto his side.

Several minutes later, as he was just dozing off, she said, "I know why you cheated."

Snapping fully awake, he chose his words carefully. "There is no excuse for what I did, Mandy. I know that."

"No. You're right, there isn't one. But I guess I can understand why you did it this time."

"The pills helped you. I shouldn't have been so hard on you about wanting to get some help. I guess I should have trusted that you knew what you needed to do."

"Yes, you should have," Mandy agreed.

"I really was trying to end things with her when..."

"Kurt, I don't want to talk about that. Not now. Not ever," she cut him off, a sharp edge creeping back into her voice.

"Are you going to forgive me?" he asked miserably.

After awhile, she sighed, "I'm going to try."

He rolled over and put his arm around her. She stiffened for a minute, then relaxed against him and he fell asleep with no more dreams that night.

CHAPTER 10

Rachel Clovis sat in the Beauty Spot listening to the women chatter around her. Amy, the girl that did her hair, was talking about the murders. Of course everyone was.

Rachel hadn't slept well last night. It was the story her husband had showed her in that ancient book.

The police were no closer to catching whoever had killed Tina Hilliard and the Ash family. Against Rachel's wishes, her husband had not gone to the authorities with what they learned. He returned the book to Mrs. Tipple and told her it was just a weird coincidence and nothing more. The old woman seemed relieved that he thought so. Leroy didn't think she would pursue it any further.

While Rachel sat under the dryer, she thumbed through a well-read copy of People Magazine and tried to think about something else. The Jolie-Pitts were always a good distraction.

The woman sitting next to her commented to Amy, "You know this all started right after those kids stole the bones out of that old grave."

Rachel lifted the dryer up with a bang, and cried, "What did you say?"

The woman looked at her, surprised. "It was in the paper a few weeks ago. Some kids stole the bones out of a grave. Belonged to some teenager that died back in the 1800's. The first murder was just a few days after that, I think."

Rachel jumped out of the chair casting the Jolie-Pitts aside and screaming, "Oh my God! I have to go find Leroy!" She raced out of the Beauty Spot, her wet hair still wrapped in aluminum can sized rollers.

The woman watched her run out with a puzzled expression, then turned to Amy. "Is she drinking again?"

Ellen Wyatt worked two nights a week at the same auto body shop that employed Richie Welch. She did the accounting and bookkeeping for Craig the owner, and had done it for Tom, the owner before him. Tonight she was going to do the time consuming job of payroll.

Her husband and Kurt had gone to the triple funeral for the Ash family. They were going to be spending some time with the relatives tonight, part investigating and part community service. They wouldn't be home until late.

Ellen liked working for the garage. Her father and two older brothers were racecar drivers. She was raised around the strong smells of gasoline and oil, and they always brought back fond memories.

Ellen met John Wyatt when he pulled over her red Corvette for speeding. She offered to cook him dinner if he wouldn't give her a ticket.

It was the only bribe he ever accepted during his career in law enforcement. And one he never regretted.

John did not have the same good looks that Kurt Dale possessed, but he was a solidly built man, with an open, friendly face. He also did not share his partner's love of attention from pretty women. He seemed oblivious to the numerous young ladies that found men in uniform captivating. Most of his evenings while he was a bachelor were spent in his apartment reading true crime books. It wasn't that he didn't want to date, it was more that he didn't like the kind of women that chased after policemen. They reminded him of the groupies that hung around stage doors waiting for rock and roll singers. The attention made him uncomfortable. Flashy women made him uncomfortable too. He was by nature a shy man. His personal opinion of Amanda Dale was that she was pretty, but too made up looking and he didn't know how she got anything done with those ridiculously long fingernails of hers. The words high maintenance came to mind.

Ellen rarely wore makeup. She had a naturally pretty face and dark blonde hair that fell straight to her shoulders. She was tall and slender, usually seen wearing faded Levi's.

When John first met Ellen James, the word that came to his mind was "earthy."

She had already received a fair number of speeding violations by the time John pulled her over. Her family was well known in Alder Lake because her father had earned some small-town notoriety from his racecar driving career.

Ellen had impulsively extended the dinner invitation. She was not usually that forward, and John sensed that. He had just as impulsively accepted, and Ellen drove off without another traffic citation to add to the growing pile stuffed in her glove box, and a date with a man who she thought had kind eyes.

During that first date, she jokingly told John she should marry a police officer so she wouldn't get anymore speeding tickets. John thought that was a real good idea.

It was a warm evening and the garage was only six blocks from where the Wyatts lived. Her husband told her to take the car to work until this lunatic that was going around poisoning people was found. He didn't want her walking home in the dark. But Ellen honestly believed no one would be stupid enough to hurt a policeman's wife. Besides that, she had lived in this town all her life. Some psychopathic stranger that blew into town wasn't going to make her start changing her routines. She decided to obey her false sense of security and walk.

When she got to the shop, the last of the employees were just going home. She let herself into the big garage through a side door and walked across the oil stained floor to the back, and up a narrow wooden staircase to the tiny office overlooking the whole operation.

Craig waved to her from downstairs. "I'll lock you in, Ellen. Make sure you shoot the bolt on the side door when you leave tonight."

She waved back. "Will do, Craig. Have a good night."

She liked to work after everyone was gone. She cranked up the radio and made herself a pot of coffee, then settled in behind the desk and got to work.

The check printer was an ancient thing of the dot matrix variety. It was annoyingly loud while it printed. She did the checks last because the printer sound grated on her nerves so bad she couldn't concentrate on the books while it ran. Also, it had to be babysat because it had the aggravating habit of jamming the paper when your back was turned. If she wasn't paying attention, it could crumple ten checks in a minute's time. After the first experience she had with the printer jamming, and having to spend an hour reprinting checks, she always gave the printer her undivided attention while it worked.

Ellen's fingers ran deftly over the calculator keys as she double checked her addition. She wrote up the deposit slip and paper clipped it to the checks the garage had taken in this week. She put the deposit in her purse to take to the bank for Craig tomorrow and finished writing everything in the ledger books.

She checked her watch and frowned. She promised Amanda she would try and come by for a visit since both their husbands were working late tonight. She picked up the phone and dialed the Dale's number.

"Hello."

"Hi, Mandy. Sorry to say I haven't even gotten the payroll started yet. Can I take a rain check?"

"Sure, no problem," Amanda said. "You didn't walk to work did you? It's getting dark."

"Uh… No, of course not," Ellen lied.

"Well, be careful when you leave there, El."

"You sound just like my husband," she laughed.

They hung up and Ellen opened the computer program that calculated the payroll. She began the tedious job of going through each employee's time cards, tallying the totals and inputting them into the computer so it could calculate taxes and overtime.

Once finished, she stretched, and fed the perforated stack of blank payroll checks into the printer and fastened the plastic clips over the sides of the holes. She keyed the start print button. It immediately began to make the screetchy, nerve-grating noise. Ellen reached behind her and turned up the radio even louder to be heard above the machine's racket.

She didn't hear the footsteps begin to climb the creaky staircase, and her back was turned on the big glass window that looked down over the garage.

Ellen got up from the desk. Still keeping one eye on the worrisome printer, she poured herself another cup of coffee. As she was dumping a sugar packet into the cup, a reflection in the glass caught her attention. She dropped the sugar on the floor. She was an athletic and graceful woman, gifted with uncanny reflexes. In one gazelle-like movement, she jumped to the office door and sprang the lock, a split second before a hand reached the knob.

Rachel pulled into her driveway and jammed the car in park. She jumped out without turning off the ignition and sprinted for the door. It was locked. She began banging on it with her fists, yelling at the top of her lungs, "LEROY, OPEN UP!!"

When Leroy opened the door, his wife was wild-eyed and frantic, huge pink rollers bobbing on her head.

"Rachel, what the…" he began.

She charged past him into the house and slammed the door. "OH MY GOD, LEROY!" she screamed, "IT'S TRUE! IT'S ALL TRUE!"

"Rachel, calm down. What's true?" he tried to take her hands.

She pulled away, sobbing, "The vampire! It's him! He's doing this! He killed those people! You have to call John Wyatt right away!"

"Rachel, what the hell happened? Why is your hair in those things?"

"Forget my hair, Leroy. Don't you get it? Those officers are in trouble!" she shrieked, ran into the living room and picked up the phone.

Leroy grabbed it out of her hand. "Whoa. Wait a minute. Just take a breath and tell me what happened first."

With a huge effort, she pulled herself together enough to tell her husband what she heard in the Beauty Spot.

"Honey, I'm not going to call John Wyatt because some busybody in a beauty parlor said that some bones are missing from an old grave. We don't even know that it's true. Did you see the story? I don't remember anything about it."

"Well, no," she reluctantly admitted, "But how many coincidences do we need before you say something?"

Though she was probably right, his rational mind was still having a lot of trouble accepting that anything so incredible could be happening. "Do you realize how crazy this sounds, Rachel? How hard it is going to be for anyone to believe? Hell, I don't even believe it myself."

"I don't care how crazy it sounds. It's true. Somehow it's true, Leroy," she said stubbornly.

He drummed his fingers on the table restlessly. "Okay, tomorrow morning I will go to the library and look at the newspapers from a few weeks back. They have them on microfiche. If I find any story about a grave robbery, then I will call Wyatt, okay? I promise."

Rachel knew it was the most she was going to get out of him. "I guess one more day won't make any difference," she sighed.

"Honey?"

"Yeah?"

"Do you think you should go back to the beauty parlor? I don't think your hair is quite done."

The office door shook in its thin frame and Ellen backed away from it. She grabbed for the telephone. In her terror, she knocked it off the desk. It fell to the floor with a loud clang.

She looked around for anything she could use as a weapon if whoever was trying to break in succeeded. She spied one of Craig's bowling trophies on a shelf and grabbed it. Out the window was a kid with dirty long black hair and a big jacket. A perfect match to the vague description of the suspect given by one of Tina Hilliard's neighbors. Ellen's heart took a giant lurch in her chest.

The intruder was throwing his body against the flimsy door, trying to break it down.

Ellen scrambled back around the desk and grabbed the telephone cord. She was trying to yank the phone back up, when the kid, with one last powerful slam, came crashing into the office.

Without thinking she swung the bowling trophy in a wide arc. The sound it made when it connected with the kid's face was like a sack of flour being thrown onto a hard surface. The top of the trophy cut a chunk of his flesh at the hairline. A black viscous fluid poured from the wound in a gush.

He screamed with rage. The sound of that hellish wail reminded Ellen of a rusty door hinge. One that hadn't been opened in fifty years.

Knocked off balance, he fell over onto the little metal cart that held the dot matrix check printer and sent it skittering to the floor. The cart and the overturned printer trapped Ellen behind the desk in the cramped office. The sound of jamming chewed paper filled the office as the printer soldiered on.

Ellen was trying to climb over the desk and reach the door. The kid was wiping that weird black blood out of his eyes. When Ellen looked into those dark glowing orbs she froze.

"Your eyes," she whispered. "Your eyes."

The boy smiled, and the evil in that smile broke her paralysis. She let loose a piercing scream.

Without thinking about what she was doing, Ellen swung the trophy again with all her might. This time it hit him in the arm, a corner hooking into his jacket. She tried to jerk the trophy back, and the kid grabbed the other end and pulled hard.

Ellen went flying on top of him, never giving up her death-grip on the trophy locked in her hand. She wrenched it free of his jacket and heard the sound of ripping cloth.

The kid was trying to bend his head around to get his mouth to her neck.

Oh shit, he's trying to bite me! Why the fuck is he trying to bite me? Her mind screamed in fear and confusion. Ellen thrust the trophy forward as hard as she could. There was that flour sack connecting with the hard surface sound again, and the kid howled in pain. More dark, oily blood spilled from his nose. Ellen was no more aware of the strange color of his blood than Tina had been when she saw it.

Ellen grabbed the edge of the desk while the kid was preoccupied with his wounded nose. She pulled herself up in one cat-like movement, and backed out of the office while her assailant struggled to his feet.

Halfway down the stairs the heel of her sandal caught under a riser and she fell the rest of the way to the bottom. She landed on her stomach and heard something in her arm crack. With the wind knocked out of her, it took her a minute to scramble to her feet again.

The kid was stumbling down the last three steps as Ellen pulled herself up, his face a gory mess.

Holding her hurt arm cradled against her side, she ran for the back of one of the service bays and grabbed a wrench from an open drawer. The kid was right behind her. As she turned to strike him with the wrench, his feet slid on the oil stained floor and he went down to his knees. Ellen flung the wrench at him, missing his head by bare inches, as she reached the side door.

He grabbed for her ankle, but wasn't fast enough. His hand closed on nothing but thin air.

She fumbled open the bolt and stumbled blindly out into the dark street yelling for help. Hearing the boy's footsteps behind her, a terrified Ellen sprinted as fast as she could, her long legs pumping and her sandals slapping the pavement. Her aching arm throbbed against her. The sandals were digging into her feet, slowing her down. She looked over her shoulder and saw her attacker less than five yards behind her in the deserted industrial area. Ellen pulled her sandals off and dropped them. She ran for several blocks, maintaining her narrow lead on her assailant, before she turned a corner and sobbed with relief when she entered a residential neighborhood. As she opened her mouth to scream for help again, something sharp stabbed her bare foot. The scream turned into a sharp intake of breath from the pain. She was forced to a limp, and unable to stop long enough to find the razor-sharp object and pull it out of her tortured foot. Ellen was winded and tired, her foot screaming agony and she realized there were no yells left in her throat. All that was coming out were barely audible wheezing gasps for air. Looking over her shoulder again, she saw the kid had gained ground and was now just a few feet behind her.

Ellen knocked over a metal trash can to try and slow down her attacker.

He tripped over it and howled in frustration when he hit the ground.

Lights came on outside a few houses, as people started coming out to see what all the noise was about.

Ellen limped up the front lawn of the house closest to her. An elderly couple stood huddled in the doorway. Taking in her frightened face, her limp arm hanging at her side, and her grease and oil stained clothes, the man ran down the porch steps and seized Ellen's arm. He pulled her inside, closing the door behind her.

CHAPTER 11

Fury buzzed in Francis Barclay's head like an angry insect. The events of the previous night whirled through his mind like a tornado. He had nearly been caught. The woman got away. Worse, she had seen him, and now a crudely drawn sketch of his likeness was tacked up on every telephone pole and shop window in town.

He had returned to the abandoned trailer after the woman escaped by running into the house of that old couple. His legs ached from running after her. They were barely accustomed to walking, let alone charging after someone like that. His head and nose throbbed where she nailed him with the trophy. The bleeding was down to a trickle now, but his body had no healing powers, and the flap of skin at his hairline hung like a gaping mouth.

He fell asleep, his head still pounding with a murderous anger unlike anything he had ever known.

He had stolen food or pulled it from garbage cans since his return to Alder Lake. Now he was hungry and sore, but too scared to leave the trailer during daylight hours for fear someone would recognize him from that sketch.

Worse, he needed human blood if he had any hope of healing at all. He was becoming more and more sensitive to light with each passing day and the sun hurt his eyes. He seemed to need more sleep with each passing day as well. He didn't notice that his skin was growing paler, and was now nearly translucent, or that his eyes, an intense and inhuman deep blue to start with, now glowed like oil lamps on a foggy night.

He had ventured out in the early morning hours and found the wanted posters of him hanging everywhere. That uncontrollable rage flared up at the sight of the first one. He pulled down every one he came across, crumpled them into balls and threw them into the gutter. Then he skulked through the alley back to the trailer to await darkness. He suddenly felt very exposed. It was no longer safe for him to be outside during the day, even if it would have been tolerable for him physically.

Leroy awoke early to go to the library as promised, but in the light of day the idea now seemed mostly ludicrous.

He had just about convinced himself the whole thing was a huge coincidence, until he was driving to the library and saw someone putting up a wanted poster. Curious, he pulled his car over and climbed out to read it.

A black and white penciled likeness of what looked like a teenager with long dark hair and strange eyes, which reminded Leroy vaguely of Charles Manson, stared back at him from the paper.

WANTED FOR QUESTIONING
IN THE ATTACK OF ELLEN WYATT

Last night during 9:30PM and 10:00PM a person matching this description attacked Ellen Wyatt at the Alder Lake Auto Body Shop on Murphy Ave. Anyone with information regarding this suspect should contact Detective John Wyatt with the Alder Lake Police Department. He should be considered dangerous and should not be approached.

Leroy felt like someone just dumped a bucket of icy water over him. He climbed back into his car and drove the rest of the way to the library with shaking hands.

The microfiche confirmed his worst fear. The woman at the beauty parlor had been wrong. The murder of Tina Hilliard wasn't a few days after that grave was found empty. It was the very next night. Besides that, the theory that kids had robbed the grave was just that — a theory. No one knew for sure how the bones had come to be missing. There were no witnesses, no clues and no suspects. Leroy was pretty sure no one assumed that the bones had up and walked out under their own steam.

Ellen looked tired. The cast on her arm itched. Her entire sense of life-long security had been shattered in a few short seconds by a dirty teenager.

John was notified and hurried to Alder Lake Memorial Hospital where his wife was having her arm set.

He listened to the story with mounting horror and phoned the police station to have them wake the sketch artist and send him to the hospital.

His wife was insistent that the assailant's eyes were like nothing human she had ever seen before. She argued bitterly with the artist because he couldn't make the eyes more intense and frightening.

John chalked up his wife's reaction to the stress of what happened. He figured it would be tough to think of someone that just tried to kill you as a fellow human being. Ellen had always been practical. In a day or two, he thought, she would probably start to feel better and maybe the experience wouldn't seem so Twilight Zone to her. Once the shock wore off he was sure it would be easier for her to accept that this was just a psychopathic kid, and not some ominous mythical monster.

After several hours, the artist finally came up with a rendering that Ellen felt accurately displayed this ogre's evil nature. John thought the artist had turned the kid's eyes into something you would be most apt to see in a comic book, and not on a Wanted poster. A quickly assembled team worked through the night to create the poster, get copies xeroxed, and have them up all over the city by dawn the following morning. John was reluctant to go to work, not wanting to leave her home alone. Ellen insisted she was fine, but as soon as he left she called Amanda and asked her to come over.

They sat in Ellen's living room eating breakfast sandwiches Amanda brought over from a take-out place. Ellen just picked at hers and said little. She didn't want to talk about what had happened. She just wanted someone to be in the house with her.

Amanda didn't push for any details. "Do you think you will be going back to work soon?" she asked.

Ellen shrugged. "I can't work with my arm in this thing. Not sure I could work in there alone anymore anyway." Tears were standing in her eyes.

"I'm sorry, hon. Well, I can come over during the day while John's at work if you like. You know, just until you are feeling better."

Ellen gave her a small, grateful smile. "Yes. That would help. At least until we get the dog."

Amanda looked surprised. "Dog? What dog?"

"We are going to the pound and getting the biggest, meanest one we can find."

"Who's idea was this?" Amanda asked.

"John's. He is away at work so much he thought it would be better if I had some kind of protection. Also, we are having an alarm system installed tomorrow."

Amanda was stunned into silence. The Ellen she knew wasn't afraid of anything and would have balked at ever having an alarm in her house or owning a dog for protection. The Ellen she knew never even locked her front door. It hurt her heart, and somehow made her more aware of her own vulnerability, seeing her friend like this.

"Of course," Ellen went on, almost to herself, "I'm pretty sure anything with eyes like that could probably get through a dog or an alarm system. Probably rip them both to shreds with his bare hands. I don't think he was human," she whispered and shuddered.

Amanda looked at her friend. This silent and brooding woman that was so unlike the woman she had just talked to on the phone the night before. "What do you mean not human, El?"

"I mean his eyes weren't like a person. They were like some kind of ghoul. John doesn't believe me. But it's true. He wasn't human,

Mandy." Her voice was shaky and edging toward hysteria. She shuddered once again, then rose abruptly and stalked out of the room.

Leroy stopped at Mrs. Tipple's house on his way to see John Wyatt. He wanted to retrieve that book of the town history so he could show it to the detective. He figured he would need every available ounce of proof he could lay his hands on just to convince the good detective that he hadn't lost his mind or started drinking again. Leroy knew the tale he needed to tell was going to be hard enough to swallow, even with that book in his hands and the information he neatly copied about the disappearance of those bones and when the killing started.

Mrs. Tipple said she returned the book to the library a couple days before. She wrote the name of it down on a scrap of paper for him and he drove back to the library.

Leroy handed the woman at the desk the sheet of paper. She punched something into the computer in front of her.

"I'm sorry, we don't have it in stock right now. We only have the one copy, and it's out."

Leroy shook his head in frustration. "Can you tell me who checked it out?"

"Mildred Tipple," the librarian said.

"No, no. That's not right." Leroy shook his head. "She just returned it a day or two ago."

"I'm sorry, but I don't show it back yet," the woman responded, clearly annoyed at his questioning her computer.

"Well, where would it be? Let me look for it." His voice sounded a little too panicky for his own comfort.

The librarian sensed him edging toward making a scene and looked at him over the rim of her glasses. "If it's that important I can see if I can locate a copy for you at another branch."

"Yes. Would you please do that."

He searched row after row of books while the librarian went about trying to find him another copy. The book wasn't on any of the shelves or on the cart of books waiting to be put away.

When he walked back up to the librarian, she smiled. "I found one copy. It's at the Parkland branch. Do you want me to have them send it here, or do you want to go pick it up?"

Parkland was two hours away, but Leroy didn't have the time to wait for it to be mailed. "I will go get it. If you would just have them hold it."

She nodded, relieved that he appeared to have calmed down. "Your name?"

"Clovis. Leroy Clovis. Thanks for your help," he mumbled, and walked dispiritedly out of the library and back to his car. He needed to call work and let them know he wasn't going to make it in today. He somehow felt responsible for Ellen Wyatt's attack because he hadn't gone to John sooner with what he knew.

He called his wife at home to tell her about the wanted poster and about what happened to Ellen Wyatt.

Rachel sounded as sick as he felt. She wisely didn't say 'I told you so.' She offered to drive to Parkland and get the book for him.

Meanwhile, he knew it was time to make a long overdue visit to the police station.

After convincing John Wyatt that what he had to say was important, Leroy walked out of the big double doors of the police station and waited outside on the grass for John to wade through the sea of people that kept stopping him and asking after Ellen.

They walked a little way in silence, and John asked, "What's so important we couldn't talk about it inside?"

Haltingly at first, and then faster, the story poured out. Leroy told him everything. Starting with Mrs. Tipple and ending by handing him the copies he had made of the news articles that showed the dates when it all started.

"Rachel is on her way to the library in Parkland to get the book with the story about the boy's family being killed and how he vowed to come back and avenge the murders. I told her to drop it off at the station for you so you can read it." He hadn't looked John in the eye once during the telling of this magnificent tale. When he finished, he kept walking with his eyes down, waiting for John to say something.

John was thinking about Kurt looking at the marks on the photo of Charity Ash's neck, and telling him he thought it might have been an animal. He was thinking about his wife's unreasonable insistence that the boy wasn't human. He was quiet for several minutes.

Coming from anyone but Leroy, John would have written it off as pure fantasy or stress induced hysteria. But he had known Leroy a long time, and if there was anyone in town even more cynical, and less likely to believe this kind of wild story than himself, it was Leroy Clovis.

"A vampire, Leroy? A two-hundred year old one, no less?" John shook his head.

"Look, I know how it sounds. Believe me, I do. If your wife hadn't been attacked, I never would have even said anything. I read that story in the book I told you about a week ago already. Rachel was convinced long before me and pestered the hell out of me to tell you, but I refused. Hell, I talked myself into believing it was nothing but a damn coincidence. But now, after what happened last night to Ellen, I had to say something. As amazing as it sounds, I believe it's true, man. Every word of it." He looked at John with earnest and unblinking eyes.

"When will Rachel be back with that book, Leroy?"

"Not for a few hours. Copy was clear up in Parkland. Will you call me after you read it?"

The detective nodded, unable to hide the doubt he felt from his face.

After Leroy left him, John didn't go back to work. He needed to think. Everything in him rebelled against what Leroy had told him. He was a problem solver by nature, and a believer in the theory that everything that happened, no matter how unexplainable, had a perfectly reasonable explanation somewhere behind it if you just looked close enough. But this? This one he couldn't even get his head wrapped around. He knew that Leroy believed this story. That alone gave him good reason to examine it. But he also thought that if he just had enough pieces of this difficult puzzle, he could make it all make sense and come up with that fabled "Reasonable Explanation."

Still his mind kept circling things that couldn't be explained no matter what angle you looked at them from. All that dirt in the Ash's bathroom. Was it graveyard dirt? John barked a nervous laugh, and a passerby looked at him with unease.

He had virtually ignored those stains that looked like motor oil and the lab said was blood. He disregarded that evidence at Tina Hilliard's because blood simply wasn't black, and it didn't smell like that stuff did. He ignored it because it couldn't be explained. That's just how his mind worked. If it was inexplicable then don't deal with it until it became explicable. It wasn't something he did on purpose, it was just how he was wired.

Now there was a puddle of the same black, tarry substance at Craig's garage, spatters of it on the staircase and more on the road where Ellen ran from the guy. A huge smudge of it was still on the bowling trophy Ellen used to clobber her assailant with. The lab report again came back insisting it was human blood. The same blood type as the stain in Tina's apartment.

A long black hair was found on the torn piece of green fabric from his jacket. The lab results were slower coming back on the hair from the crime scenes. When they finally did come in, the lab said the strands were from the head of a very old man. Yet his wife said the kid looked like he couldn't have been older than twenty, and wouldn't very old hair be gray?

A very old man, John thought. *Like two hundred years old maybe?*

A completely unwelcome thought entered his mind — One that would have made Leroy very happy. *No one knows how the hell those bones were removed from that grave. No one knows for sure that it was kids, or that it was a robbery at all. People just assumed that, because hell, what else could it be?*

Slowly, just as it had for Leroy, the unthinkable began to seem possible. John headed back to the police station to talk to Kurt and to read a story about one of his ancestors burning down a house and killing an entire family.

CHAPTER 12

A woman sat on the window seat in her living room. The blinds were drawn. She peered through narrowed eyes, between two dusty slats held open with a nicotine stained finger. She clutched a bottle of Jim Beam in one hand and a cigarette dangled from her lower lip. A long cylinder of ash suspended from the end of it, threatening to topple off at any moment. The front of her ample bosom and the lap of her green polyester pants were littered with a dusty gray coat of ashes from the pack she was halfway through chain-smoking.

She had been watching the boy for the last few days, but not with much interest until she saw the Wanted poster this morning. She knew he was stealing from her garbage and from a few others as well, but took him for a homeless bum, as opposed to a wanted fugitive.

Norma Krueger, of space 24, didn't miss much that happened at the Happy Wheels Mobile Estates. She'd been living there for the last seventeen years and had helped to break up more marriages than just Rachel Clovis's fourth, to the wayward Donovan. She knew everyone's secrets. The cushion of the window seat where she sat was clearly indented with the outline of her hefty rear-end from all the hours she spent over the years watching her neighbors through those two slats in her yellowed and faded blinds.

Norma Krueger had blackmailed a few, gotten drunk with a few, and slept with more than a few. And there was very little she ever missed at Happy Wheels.

With Norma, nothing was sacred. One month when she was a little short of cash and there was no one to blackmail, she stole a pension check from an old widow's mailbox and cashed it in another town. She felt no guilt over this. A girl's gotta do what a girl's gotta do, right?

The boy walked out the front door of the abandoned trailer that once upon a time Donovan and Rachel shared. After Rachel moved out the Morgans lived there briefly. That was before an electrical fire in the wall burned down the back half of the trailer. The Morgans weren't insured and the trailer was never repaired or replaced. It sat there, abandoned and desolate ever since.

The kid had been holed up there for days now. He walked out this morning slouched over, and though his head was hanging down and that dirty black hair obscured most of his face, Norma was able to see the swollen nose and the flap of ragged skin hanging at his hairline. She saw the rip in the arm of his jacket as well. *Bar fight*, she thought.

Nothing interesting about his movements, until he came hurrying back ten minutes later, his hands clenched into fists and a crumpled piece of paper held tightly in one. She watched him throw the balled up wad of paper out into the street and slink back into the trailer. She waited a few minutes. When he didn't come back out, she stepped outside. Glancing up and down the street to make sure no one was watching, Norma walked at a brisk pace toward the bank of mailboxes at the front of the trailer park. As she strolled, she stooped down for just a mili-second and scooped up the crumpled, discarded flyer, slipping it deftly into her pocket.

Once she was back in her own trailer, Norma lit another cigarette and studied the poster for several minutes. *Attacked a cop's wife. How stupid did you get?* She thought. She wondered if just maybe the kid might have had something to do with those murders too. She seemed to recall something from the newspaper article about a long-haired stranger walking up the street after the Hilliard woman was killed.

The prospect of having a psychopathic killer camping out just twenty-five feet from her front door didn't cross Norma's mind. The only thing that did was, *How much will the reward be if I turn him in?* Pretty good she figured for attacking a cop's wife. But if he actually whacked those people too, why it would be that much heftier.

She absentmindedly picked up a doughnut from the box resting by her feet and mused over the poster some more, dropping bits of crumbs onto it while she read it over and over again.

With each reading, the dollar signs grew larger in her mind. Norma was thinking. A plan was being hatched. She wasn't going to hand the kid over for nothing, that was for sure. If they wanted him they would have to come play on Norma's field and play by Norma's rules. And of course, pay Norma's asking price.

Rachel Clovis blew a tire when she was still forty miles out of Alder Lake on her way back home from the Parkland library. Cussing under her breath, she gently guided her Buick off to the side of the road. Leaving the windows down in the summer heat, she slammed the door and started up the road on foot. She walked for over a mile before finally coming to a gas station. She was hot and sweaty, and stopped in the ladies room to freshen up and for a swig of cool water from the ancient drinking fountain bolted to the wall.

Rachel approached the man behind the counter. He was a nice enough fellow who offered to drive her back to her car and put the spare on for her. For the duration of the drive, which he was making at well under the recognized speed limit, the man talked non-stop. Rachel tried to cut in once or twice and explain that she was on an errand for her husband and really needed to get back to Alder Lake as soon as possible, but there was no way to get a word in edgewise to the man's incessant chatter. She gave up and just let him talk.

After what felt like hours, he changed her tire, pausing numerous times in between to gesture with his hands during one story or another. It was nearly three in the afternoon before Rachel was back on the road again. She thanked the man and waved as she was pulling away from the curb.

She reached down between the seats for her cell phone to call Leroy and explain her delay in getting back.

Not finding the phone in its usual place, she felt around between the seats for a few seconds without taking her eyes from the road. When her fingers didn't locate it, she finally looked down, and froze. The cell phone was gone. So was the library book she was supposed to deliver to John Wyatt, as well as three other books she checked out on the history and defenses against vampires and placed on the passenger seat. Also missing was the half consumed Slurpee she bought from a 7-11 store on the way up. Someone helped himself to everything that wasn't nailed down from her unlocked car while she walked up the road for help. This time when Rachel cussed, it wasn't under her breath.

John checked to see if anyone had dropped off a book for him yet. The secretary said no, but that he had about a hundred phone messages from people calling in tips about the black haired stranger. He assigned Taylor to call everyone back and document it all, then he left the station again.

He told the secretary to page him immediately if someone left a book for him. He wasn't going to tell Kurt this insane story until he read what it was that had the normally very level-headed Leroy so convinced anything this amazing could be happening.

He went home to check on Ellen, and found Amanda Dale sitting on his couch reading a magazine when he walked in.

"Hi," he said, surprised to see her there. "Where's El?"

Amanda set the magazine aside and stretched. "Upstairs taking a nap. You want some coffee? I was just going to make some."

He nodded. "So, how is she doing?"

Amanda shrugged. "Honestly, she is still pretty upset. She asked me to stay while she laid down."

John sat down heavily in his easy chair. "Did she tell you we are getting a dog?"

"Yeah, she did. And an alarm system. But she said that if that guy wanted to, he could probably get through anything. She doesn't think he's… Well, she said she didn't think the guy was even human, John."

There it was again. Not human.

When he didn't answer her, Amanda asked, "You alright? You look funny?"

John looked appraisingly at Amanda. "Do you believe Ellen?"

Amanda looked startled. "About what exactly?"

"That maybe this guy isn't quite human."

"Well, what kind of a human being goes around killing people, John? I believe that he is an evil creep."

He cleared his throat and tried again, "Mandy, do you think it's possible that something less than completely human, I mean really, literally *not* human attacked her?"

Amanda looked at him, speechless. Finally she asked, "Like what exactly?"

"I don't know. I'm just asking hypothetically if you think it's possible that someone could look like a person, but not be one."

Amanda was completely rattled. The tough, take no shit from anyone, Ellen Wyatt, turned into a silent and brooding zombie. Now her husband, the one man you could always count on to show you why two plus two equals four, and give you the exact reason why it didn't if there was a mistake in the math, was asking her if she believed in the boogey man. "John, what the hell are you talking about?"

"Never mind. I gotta go. You'll stay with her, right?" He rose from the chair.

"Yeah, I will. If you see Kurt tell him where I am, okay?"

John didn't care much for that look in Amanda Dale's eyes. The one that said she thought a few of his oars may have slipped.

Norma Krueger fixed herself a ham sandwich, then on impulse made a second one and put it on a paper plate. She checked the street, making sure she was alone, and gingerly walked across the narrow road to the abandoned trailer where the kid was hiding. She figured if he didn't have to go out foraging for food, there would be less chance of any of her nosy neighbors seeing him and reporting him to the cops. She knew most everyone must have seen those wanted posters by now. And Norma didn't want the boy turned over to the authorities until she was ready to present him, all wrapped up with a bow.

She walked carefully up the broken steps and laid the sandwich on the leaning, dilapidated porch. She rapped sharply on the door three times, and with surprising speed for such a large woman, ran back across the street. She hurried inside her own home, slid onto her window seat and parted the blinds just an inch. She watched for fifteen minutes, still as a statue, and the boy finally opened the door a sliver. He looked around furtively and grabbed the sandwich off the stoop, slamming the door as soon as it was in his hand.

Satisfied, Norma settled into her own sandwich, her eyes never leaving the front door of the trailer across the street.

With nothing to do but wait, Leroy went home. He paced the floor, anxious to hear from John Wyatt. Now that he had told his incredible tale he thought he would feel some relief. But all he felt was foolish. He knew John didn't believe him. Hell, he didn't want to believe this himself.

He was lost in thought when Rachel quietly let herself in the front door. He saw she was crying and went to her.

"Honey? What is it? Did you deliver the book to the police station?"

Between hitching sobs she told him what happened.

Leroy loved his wife, and though he was desperate to figure out how to get his hands on another copy of that book, he took the time to soothe Rachel and tell her it wasn't her fault. He didn't mention that leaving the car unlocked wasn't the brightest thing she had ever done. He shuddered when he thought of telling John Wyatt about this. If the detective didn't think he was a raving lunatic already, he surely would now.

Mildred Tipple was dusting her sideboard when something fell to the floor with a loud thunk. She put aside the feather duster and bent down. Groping behind the sideboard, she retrieved a fallen book. A puzzled frown creased her forehead.

"Thought I returned you," she said to the book, and put it aside to take back to the library later.

CHAPTER 13

After spending the better part of the day wading through dozens of phone messages from people who thought they spotted the boy, Kurt determined the last time anyone had actually seen him was when he ran from the residential neighborhood that he chased Ellen Wyatt into from the garage.

Kurt was disturbed when Amanda told him she thought she saw the kid walking down their own street just before the killings started.

Taylor methodically interrogated every single caller who thought they saw their suspect. It was evident he was sticking to the South side of town. He was spotted behind a grocery store foraging in a dumpster, and had been seen slouched over shambling through the park. But since the night of Ellen's attack, nothing. Not one person had reported seeing him since then.

Taylor informed Kurt that a woman called several times wanting to know what kind of reward was being offered for information leading to his capture, but she refused to give her name and refused to speak to anyone but John Wyatt.

And just where the hell is John anyway? Kurt wondered, while he sifted through the mountain of paper in front of him, trying to track their suspect's movements. He hadn't seen his partner since he walked out the front door hours before with Leroy Clovis. He was getting annoyed that John wasn't there helping him. Kurt figured he probably went home to check on Ellen, and he really couldn't blame him. If it had been Amanda that was attacked, he didn't think he would have even left the house this morning. He knew Ellen wasn't handling things well. He felt sorry for John. Kurt knew what it was like to try to deal with the pressures of work, and have a wife that was freaking out at the same time. Of course, neither of them had ever had to deal with a serial killer at large before.

Captain Fitzgerald was debating whether or not to bring in the State cops, or even the FBI. Neither John nor Kurt wanted that. This was their town and they would handle it themselves.

He tried to call Amanda at home to remind her to keep the doors locked, but got the answering machine and hung up. Kurt's mind automatically saw his wife in the clutches of some maniac, and an involuntary shudder went through him. He chided himself for worrying like that. He knew she was probably at the gym or out somewhere with the baby. He wondered if anyone who lived in Alder Lake would ever be the same again, even after this monster was caught. He had no doubt they would catch him. He just hoped it would be before he killed again.

Francis Barclay felt stronger. It was easier to think with his belly full. Someone left a sandwich for him outside on the porch steps. This was bad because it meant someone knew he was there. Why would someone do that? Who would feed him?

Feeling better, he went through the cabinets in the kitchen and found an old bottle of whiskey. He took several deep swallows. Eventually he fell into a deep restful sleep and waited for night to fall.

Norma made a pot roast for dinner. She took great pains with the planning of the meal. She was acting like a woman newly in love. She wondered if the boy would rather have roasted potatoes or mashed. She hoped he liked peas. She prepared the feast and sealed it all in a Tupperware container. Making sure the street was free of people, she tiptoed across the lane and left the meal with a carton of milk and a huge hunk of freshly baked chocolate cake on the steps. She rapped sharply on the door, then slid back across the narrow road and into her own house, flushed and breathless.

Barclay was startled out of his sleep by the banging on the door. He froze in terror. When the knocking wasn't repeated, he rose from the stained sofa and peered between the dirty curtains. He saw no one on the street. As he was just about to let the drape fall back, he noticed the slats of the blinds askew in the trailer across the road. He could see pale light behind them. He squinted in the near darkness, and could just make out a plume of cigarette smoke curling up behind the crooked blinds.

Norma knew the boy was looking out the window, but she didn't think he'd spotted her. She saw the curtain begin to fall back, and abruptly rise again. She sensed the boy staring right at her. She remained perfectly still, waiting for him to let the drapes drop back before she dared even breathe. She was completely unaware of dragging on her cigarette and blowing the smoke out of her nostrils while she waited. She was also completely unaware that the boy was grinning at her in the dark, behind the heavy curtains shielding his face.

John Wyatt was more troubled than he could ever recall being in his life. Rachel Clovis never delivered the book. Leroy gave him some story about her car being prowled, while she went off to find help for a flat tire on her way back to town from the Parkland library.

The hardest thing to deal with, was that he found himself actually starting to entertain Clovis's story, and spent several hours walking through town trying to figure out how he was going to tell Kurt about this. Now he felt like a fool. He wasted almost an entire day on Leroy's fantasy, instead of doing what the city paid him to, and finding this monster. He knew Kurt was probably pissed at him for being AWOL all day, but now he was too embarrassed to even face him. Kurt saw him walk out of the station with Leroy this morning. John knew he would probably ask what was so urgent that he had to talk to Leroy right in the middle of an investigation? What was so Secret Squirrel that they needed to leave the station to discuss? Knew he was going to ask him where the hell he was all day too. What was he going to say? That Leroy thought their killer was a two-hundred year old vampire their ancestors had murdered, and maybe just for a minute or two, he believed that story himself? He didn't think he could handle Kurt looking at him the way Amanda did when he tried to talk to her about it.

He called his house. Ellen answered in a tired and listless voice that hurt his heart. She asked if there were any leads, and he felt like a complete failure when he had to tell her there were none. He never mentioned Leroy's story.

Leroy was exhausted. He went into every bookstore within a hundred mile radius. No one had even heard of a book called "Alder Lake: Its History; Its Ghosts," much less carried it in stock. Many laughed at him for even suggesting someone would have written such a thing, or that it would have ever been published. He felt like he used to when he was still drinking and everyone thought the alcohol had muddled his brains. Back then they were usually right.

Leroy thought he could never have used a drink so badly in his life as he could now. He also knew that if he let himself take that drink he probably would never stop, and he didn't think he could live with himself if anymore people wound up dead because he went back on the booze in a grand effort to run away from this madness.

As the sun was setting he pulled into the parking lot of the library. His last hope was that somehow they found the copy Mrs. Tipple returned. He walked up to the librarian, steeled for her reaction when he told her his wife lost what was probably the only other copy in existence of this book.

The librarian was busy looking up something for a young boy, so Leroy wandered over to the section where the book should have been the first time he came looking for it. He thought he must be hallucinating when he saw it sitting on the shelf. He blinked and rubbed his eyes. When it didn't disappear, he reached up and pulled it down.

The urge to drink was stronger than ever now. He should have been elated to find that nearly extinct book, but all he could think about was stopping at a bar and feeling that warm heat slide down his throat, igniting the old familiar fire in his belly. All he wanted was to make this whole nightmare go away.

Leroy checked the book out and threw it unceremoniously in the back of his car. His hands shook as he started the engine. He hadn't eaten all day and knew he'd be wise to get something in his stomach. He thought about going to find John Wyatt. He thought about going to find an AA meeting. Instead, he left the library and drove in the gloom to Smokey's Tavern.

Several hours later, red eyed and unsteady, Leroy tottered to the men's room. The book was completely forgotten, drowned out of his mind by several shots of Jim Beam and a few beer chasers. He told himself he would just order a burger and maybe one drink to settle his nerves. Just the one, then he would go find Wyatt and give him the damn book. He skipped the burger entirely and had just swallowed his sixth shot of whiskey.

Leroy weaved to the bathroom on wobbly legs and pushed open the door. His stepson was just finishing his business at the urinal and zipping his fly when Leroy stumbled in.

Richie's eyes opened wide in shock. "Leroy, man, what the fuck are you doin' here?"

"Leave me alone, Richie. It's been a bad day."

Richie stared at him, wide-eyed, not sure what to say. "Okay, man. I can see that. Do you want to get out of here? Get a cup of coffee or something?"

Richie spent most every night since Charity's funeral at Smokey's. He was just starting to realize that drinking wasn't making the grief and pain any better. It was only making it worse.

Leroy shrugged him off and wavered over to the row of urinals against the wall. He leaned on one for support. Retching violently, he threw up. Richie grabbed his arm to keep him from falling over sideways.

Wiping his mouth, and bathing his stepson in a warm mist of whiskey fumes, Leroy whispered, "Don't you dare tell your momma about this, boy, you hear me?"

Richie smiled for the first time in days, and said, "I wouldn't dream of it… It would just break her heart."

Francis Barclay thought he had never tasted such wonderful food. He didn't know why the woman was feeding him, but he intended to find out.

When darkness fell, and he saw her blinds settle back into place, he silently let himself out the door and snuck across the lane. He slunk to the side of Norma's trailer and peered in the window. That pale light was still on. He could see no one in the cluttered living room. He walked to the back, tried the doorknob. It slid easily in his hand and squeaked as he pushed it open onto a darkened hallway.

Norma charged down the street winded and panting. She saw the boy emerge from the trailer and start across the road toward her place. The moment he was around the side of her house, she slid open the glass doors that opened off her little dining area, and ran as fast as she could down the street. She left her purse behind, and didn't dare take the time to get in her car. If that kid heard the car door slam or heard the engine start, she was dead. She knew it.

Norma made it to the entrance of the Happy Wheels Mobile Estates. She was sprinting out the gates when Jerry Harper from space #4 pulled in. Norma leapt in front of his truck, waving her arms in frantic circles. Jerry slammed on the brakes to avoid hitting her.

He opened his window, and yelled, "Norma, are you nuts? What are you trying to do? Get yourself killed?"

She was so out of breath she couldn't speak in full sentences. She yanked the driver's door open. "Out," she panted. "Need the truck," she gasped.

"Hell, woman, you can't have my truck," Jerry chuckled, and tried to pull the door handle closed.

"Out, asshole! Right now! Or I tell your wife about last summer."

That got him moving. Jerry meekly jumped from the driver's seat and surrendered the truck with no more argument. The story he would tell his wife was that he loaned it to Norma because her car broke down. A guilty man always has his story in order.

Mixed with the mildew and smoke odors permeating the fat lady's trailer, was also the more pleasant aroma of recently cooked pot roast. Barclay walked slowly down the hallway and looked in the bedroom.

He knew the woman wasn't there anymore. He hadn't seen her leave, but the house felt empty now. He walked into her bedroom and looked through her closet trying to get some sense of who she was. He even wondered if maybe she was like him, a creature of the dark. But, if that were true, he knew the woman wouldn't have fled the trailer in such a hurry. He could still smell her fear. When he opened her closet all he could determine was that she was a fat woman who favored bright colored clothes. He looked on her dresser and saw a single photograph of a much younger Norma, (though Barclay didn't know this,) holding up a pie with a blue ribbon dangling from it.

Norma had once won the Pillsbury bakeoff. This was the only photograph anywhere in the house. There was no family, no pets. The walls were decorated with cheap paintings of fruit and flowers. A huge, gaudy picture of Elvis Presley, done in oil paint against a black velvet background dominated the wall in the middle of the living room.

Francis wandered into the kitchen and helped himself to another piece of chocolate cake. He wanted to wait for the woman to return home, but there was work to do. And if he didn't do it while it was dark it wouldn't get done at all.

Norma tore through town, tires squealing, heart racing, to the police station. The doors were locked and it was dark inside. She drove to a gas station around the corner and used the payphone to dial 911.

An operator answered, "911 state your emergency."

"I need to talk to John Wyatt right away," Norma yelled.

"He's gone home for the day, ma'am."

"Well, call him up and get him the hell back there, this is urgent!" Norma shrieked.

"What is this regarding?"

"None of your damn business. I need to talk to Wyatt now, you dumb bitch, so give me his number."

The now irate operator told Norma she didn't have to listen to such language and to call back in the morning during business hours. She hung up in her ear.

Would it surprise anyone to learn that the operator on duty was none other than the Krispy Kreme Queen, Natalie?

Norma slammed the phone down hard enough to crack the plastic casing on the receiver and tried to figure out what to do next.

Taking the rest of the chocolate cake and a pack of Norma's cigarettes, Francis Barclay left her trailer. He wandered through dark alleys and bushes until he found himself in the field behind Kurt and Amanda's house.

This was the same field where a very drunk Russell Coombs and his dog Samantha encountered Francis not too long ago.

The same field where centuries past, Francis Barclay fled, frightened for his life.

There were lights on in the house he stared at. His aqua eyes glowed with bestial hatred. He sat down in the field to wait. He lit one of Norma's cigarettes and coughed. The sound was dry and rusty. He wished he had something to drink — preferably Kurt Dale's blood. He stamped out the cigarette after just two puffs and watched the house.

Amanda was in a mood. She had spent a morose afternoon with Ellen, and now she thought John was losing his mind too. She recounted to Kurt over dinner what the Wyatts both said about this moron not being human. She was surprised when Kurt didn't laugh or find the concept as foolish as she did.

"Hon, you didn't see the pictures. I swear those little holes in Charity Ash's neck could be a bite of some kind. I mentioned to John myself that maybe it was an animal or something."

"Oh come on, Kurt. People saw the little scumbag chasing Ellen. They *saw* him. It was a person. Not an animal, not a ghost, just a whacked out, skinny kid on crack or something," she said, exasperated.

Kurt shrugged, but she liked the look in his eyes no better than the one she saw in Ellen's this afternoon. *Is everyone losing their minds?* She wondered.

She was upstairs giving the baby a bath, when she leaned over and slid open the bathroom window to let in the evening breeze. It was a warm summer night and the bathroom felt stuffy. As Amanda leaned over to take Lorna out of the tub something caught her eye in the field behind the house. Peering out the window, she saw what looked like twin circles of light off in the distance. They were a deep aquamarine color. She stood hypnotized, staring at them. *Holy crap,* she thought, *I am witnessing a UFO.*

With a huge effort Amanda pulled her gaze from the window and slammed it shut. "What we have here, friends and neighbors," she said to the baby, "Is a group hallucination caused by a whacked out teenager. And I guess I am no more immune than Mr. and Mrs. Rational Wyatt, now am I? Let's just keep this our little secret, okay, honey? Not a word to Daddy."

Lorna giggled at her mother.

Amanda dismissed what she imagined she saw without another thought. She was, after all, well practiced and good at this skill after so many years as Mrs. Kurt Dale.

She dried the baby off and put a fresh diaper on her. She popped a little blue pill just before she walked out of the bathroom to hand the baby off to Kurt so he could read her a bedtime story.

CHAPTER 14

With some effort, Richie managed to haul Leroy out of Smokey's and into the shotgun seat of his car. He backed out of the parking lot and started slowly down the road.

He didn't know if he should take Leroy home to his mother in this condition or try and sober him up first.

"What the hell were you thinkin', man?" he asked his stepfather.

"I wasn't," Leroy grumbled.

"You wanna go home?"

"Hell, no. Get me over to the diner for a cup of joe, and stop your yammerin'. I got a bad enough headache already."

They had to stop once so Leroy could stumble from the car to throw up into the gutter. The world tilted sideways and he grabbed the hood of Richie's Camaro for support.

Richie once again loaded Leroy into the passenger seat.

They walked into the nearly empty diner, Richie holding up his stepfather. Darlene looked with mild disproval at Leroy, and outright contempt at Richie.

"When did you start drinking again, Leroy?" she scowled, walking around the side of the counter with the coffee pot and two menus in her hand.

"Darlene, why don't you. . ." Richie started to say.

Leroy cut him off. "I got the flu, Darlene. Just the flu."

"Yeah, right. My husband has the flu a lot these days too." She dropped the menus onto the table as they slid into a booth. "Coffee?"

They both nodded and she poured, never taking her critical gaze from Leroy's haggard face.

Richie went to the payphone by the restroom and called his mother. He told her that he ran into Leroy and they went for a bite to eat. She sounded worried. He somehow managed to dodge her questions and hang up the phone.

"I gotta call your mother," Leroy groaned when Richie sat back down.

"Already done. She knows you are with me."

Leroy looked up alarmed. "You didn't tell her. . ."

"No. Just said I ran into you and we were grabbing a burger."

Leroy nodded and picked up his coffee cup with trembling fingers.

Lorna was asleep in the crook of Kurt's arm by the time he finished reading Winnie the Pooh.

He carried her to her crib, kissed her softly on the temple and turned out the light.

Amanda was in bed half asleep when he climbed beneath the covers. He reached out and began stroking her hip. After a few minutes she moaned, rolling toward him. He slid his hand up her stomach to cup her breast. She reached for his stiffening penis beneath the sheet and rolled on top of him. She guided him inside of her and began rocking her hips back and forth. She was moving faster and faster, starting to reach orgasm, when Kurt suddenly pushed her off of him and scrambled out of bed.

"What the hell was that?" he sounded alarmed.

"What was what?" Amanda groaned, "Kurt, come back to…"

"SHHHHH," he hissed, yanking open a dresser drawer. He fumbled a pair of sweats out and climbed into them, leaving the drawer open and clothes spilling out.

"Kurt, what…"

"Amanda, shut up, there is someone in the house," he whispered, grabbing his service revolver from the metal box on the dresser.

Terrified, Amanda pulled the sheet up to her chin. Kurt padded out of the room, gun drawn, and started down the stairs.

Amanda's eyes flew open wide, as she thought, *The baby!* She jumped from the bed and ran naked down the hallway to Lorna's room. She picked up the still sleeping child, and hurried back into her own bedroom. Closing the door, she twisted the lock, then gently laid Lorna on the bed. Amanda donned a robe and tied it tight around her waist. She didn't know if she should call John or dial 911, or just let Kurt handle whatever was going on. She hadn't heard a thing and wondered if maybe his nerves were so frayed from the murders that he just imagined it. She pressed her ear to the locked bedroom door straining to listen for any noise.

When the last light was turned off and the house he watched finally dark, Francis Barclay made his quiet way through the pitch black field. He needed no light to help him see. His eyes glowed like blue tinged fog lamps lighting his path. He reached the slumbering house and pried a screen out of one of the windows in the breakfast nook.

Amanda had cracked the window earlier while she cooked dinner. She forgot to close it before they went up to bed.

Careful not to make any noise Barclay removed the screen, slid the window open and climbed onto the tile floor. He crept silent across the kitchen on tiptoes. He was reaching the stairs just as Amanda was reaching her orgasm. The riser creaked beneath his filthy tennis shoe and he froze.

Kurt knew all the sounds of his house. That first stair only creaked when someone stepped on it.

Barclay heard the commotion of Kurt interrupting their love-making. He scrambled into the den off the living room. Looking around in a panic, he spied a tiny closet against the far wall. Climbing in, he closed the door behind him without a sound. He flattened himself against the wall, as Kurt came pounding down the stairs with his gun drawn, and his heart thudding in his ears.

The remains of Richie's burger and Leroy's grilled cheese sat on the table between them. Leroy hadn't been able to eat much. His stomach was still rumbling, but at least he wasn't dizzy anymore. And more important, he wasn't drunk anymore. He felt ashamed and self-conscious, sitting in the diner with his stepson under Darlene's insolent stare.

"So what happened, Leroy? Why tonight after ten years on the wagon?" Richie asked, lighting a cigarette.

"It's a long story, and a pretty unbelievable one."

"Well, I just lost my girlfriend to a psychopath that at one point the cops thought might have been me, so I'm pretty open to unbelievable right now."

Leroy chuckled. It was a bitter sound, even to his own ears. "You believe in monsters, Richie? Specifically vampires?"

Richie took a long drag off his cigarette. He looked at Leroy through a cloud of smoke. "Like Dracula?"

"Yeah, like Dracula."

"I never really thought about it. Why? Did you meet a vampire, Leroy?"

"Haven't met him, no. But he's here. Right in Alder Lake."

Richie knew it would take something pretty horrible to dismantle Leroy enough to fall back on the sauce. But a vampire? He hoped he wasn't cracking up. After everything Richie just went through, he didn't have the energy to see his mother through a fifth divorce right now. "A vampire. Here in Alder Lake?"

Leroy nodded. He told Richie about his talk with Mrs. Tipple and about the book, "Alder Lake: It's History, It's Ghosts." The one his mother lost from one library and the one he found at the other. He hoped it was still in the back of his car. Told him that he actually worked up the nerve to tell John Wyatt about it.

Richie listened to the whole story without interrupting. He knew Leroy must believe what he was saying. The guy was normally so stable. *What the hell happened to get this shit in his head?* He wondered.

"You told my mom about this?"

"I told you," Leroy responded patiently, "She's the one that insisted I go to Wyatt with it."

Richie could see his mother buying into this crap. Hell, she was always buying those newspapers at the market with headlines like, **UFO KIDNAPS BABYSITTER WHO GIVES BIRTH TO ALIEN TWINS. SEE PHOTOS INSIDE**. The woman was addicted to reruns of the Outer Limits. He could definitely see his mother pouring fuel on this very twisted fire. But Leroy? Stable, calm, don't let the shit get you down, Leroy? No way. He couldn't believe what he was hearing. "And you believe this old, dead vampire is responsible for killing Charity and the others. That right?"

"Boy, don't look at me like I got dipshit written on my forehead. You think I want to believe this? You think I would have gone off on a bender tonight if I thought it all made perfect sense? Use your head, Richie. You know me better than that." Leroy massaged his temples. He looked at Darlene glowering at him behind the counter, and asked, "You got any Excedrin back there, dear? I could swallow a whole bottle just about now."

Darlene brought over a bottle of pills and placed it on the edge of the table. She dropped the check and slunk away, her disapproving eyes never leaving Leroy's bloodshot ones.

"Great," he said to Richie out of the side of his mouth, "I think she overheard everything. By morning the whole town is gonna think I'm drinking again and all my brain cells got fried."

Richie started to dig his wallet out, wondering if maybe that wasn't so far from the truth.

Leroy took out his own wallet, and said. "I got it. You can leave the tip though."

A telephone book swung from a cord bolted to the bottom of the payphone. Norma Krueger hoisted it up on one plump knee and flipped through the pages until she came to the W's. She ran one nicotine stained finger down the page, then slammed the book shut in frustration.

"Fuckin' cop thinks he's Elvis. God forbid the asshole should put his number in the freakin' book," she cried in frustration.

A young couple walking by looked at her wide-eyed, and she spat, "What the fuck you lookin' at?"

They quickened their step and hurried away with their eyes down.

What now? She wondered. She couldn't very well go home.

She drove Jerry's truck to Smokey's. She was walking in just as Leroy and Richie were leaving. Richie's arm brushed her shoulder on his way out, and she snapped, "Watch where you're going, nimrod."

Too worried about Leroy to even notice much, he mumbled, "Sorry," and continued walking his stepfather out the door, without a second glance at the overweight lady with the bad attitude.

Norma approached the cocky group of men at the billiard tables and made a few bets. She shot three games of pool and won enough money to buy herself a bottle of Beam and a room at a motel downtown for the night.

She planned to pay a visit to John Wyatt tomorrow morning, first thing. And if anyone tried to stop her, well God help them.

Wouldn't be the first ass I had to kick to get someone's attention, now would it? She thought as she pulled into the parking lot of the Oaktree Motel.

Kurt stopped at the bottom of the stairs and listened. Hearing nothing but his own rapid breathing, he flipped the light switch illuminating the living room. With his back to the wall, he brought the gun around in a smooth arc that swept the whole room, and yelled, "Get out where I can see you! Now! I'm armed."

He waited and heard nothing. His nerves were like live wire. Hearing a branch scrape against the picture window in the wind, he nearly shot out the glass. He took a deep breath to try and steady his nerves and walked backwards into the kitchen, arms outstretched, finger resting against the trigger of his gun.

Francis Barclay heard the man yell for him to come out. He flattened himself even further into the corner of the closet. He held his breath when he heard footsteps retreating in the other direction.

Kurt walked into his kitchen and flipped the switches on the inside wall. The bright overhead lights illuminated the kitchen and breakfast nook. He trained his pistol on the area behind the island that was hidden from his view. "If you are in here, get up now and put your hands where I can see them."

Nothing.

The killer heard the man's voice, this time from farther away. He raced out of the closet. Throwing the narrow window in the den open, he punched out the screen and wriggled out.

Kurt heard the intruder's noisy exit. He ran into the den just as Francis Barclay was disappearing out the window. He grabbed for his foot. Barclay lifted his leg and brought his foot down hard on Kurt's hand, mashing his fingers against the window sill. Kurt let go with a grimace of pain.

Barclay wasted no time squirming out the narrow window and took off running.

Kurt put his hurt fingers into his mouth then leaned out the window. He aimed his pistol at the jogging figure and fired once. The bullet blew up dirt and grass just inches from the intruder's retreating feet.

Amanda heard the gunshot and screamed. The baby woke up and screamed with her.

Next door, Russell Coombs, his hair disheveled, a beer clamped in one fist, opened his front door to see what all the racket was. Francis Barclay fled past, glaring at him with bright murderous eyes. Russell backed into his house and slammed the front door.

His dog sat in the foyer with a puzzled expression on her face. His voice blurry with alcohol, Russell patted her head, and said, "Sammy, baby, I really gotta quit drinking."

Kurt ran out his front door, unmindful of his screaming wife and daughter. He tried to catch the intruder, but he was gone by the time

Kurt arrived at the end of the block. He walked back to his house winded and panting, to find Amanda already on the phone with John Wyatt.

Alder Lake's one and only K9 unit was dispatched. Within fifteen minutes Lombard Street was awash in flashing red and blue lights. A perimeter was set up around the surrounding two blocks and the police German Shepard, wearing a reflective orange vest with the Alder Lake Police Department logo on it, sniffed his way through the field behind the Dale house. The dog lost the intruder's scent half way into the park. It was all just a little too late.

The killer had managed to escape once again.

CHAPTER 15

He felt like his head was going to explode. That feeling like there were wasps trapped and buzzing in his skull was back. The uncontrollable fury that went with it hammered away inside his head. First the woman gets away and now this. He narrowly escaped capture this time, and he knew it.

"Careful," Barclay muttered to himself. "Must be more careful."

He ran through the field, then cut south through the park into downtown. He collapsed in an alley behind Smokey's Tavern, gasping for breath and punching his open palm with a balled up fist. Rock and Roll music that sounded like only insane noise blared from the bar's open back door. It made his head pound even worse. Sweat was pouring into his eyes and he tasted blood in his mouth. His still sensitive nose was bleeding freely again and warm blood was trickling down his throat.

After awhile, Barclay tried to get up and found that his legs wouldn't support him. He slid back down the dirty brick wall of the alley, sobbing in frustration.

Norma gunned the engine of Jerry's truck and backed out of Smokey's. She needed to talk to that damn cop and was seriously pissed off she couldn't do it tonight.

She drove past the alley where Francis Barclay sat trying to get his wind back, both of them unmindful of the other.

The time for playing games was over. Now that the kid had found her out, she knew it was time to turn him in. Her plan was to go back to Happy Wheels in the morning and make sure the little freak hadn't skipped out. If he was still there and needing to hide, as she suspected he probably would be, Norma would go straight to the police station, confront Wyatt, and demand twenty-five thousand dollars in cash to lead them right to the little snot's doorstep. She knew they would probably never give her that much. Hell, a little shit town like Alder Lake probably didn't even have that much in the whole damned treasury account. The amount she decided she would be willing to settle for was ten grand. But, Norma would open with twenty-five just to show them she meant business. If they wouldn't cough up the ten, then let the little bastard keep going around attacking cop's wives for all she cared.

Apparently Norma had never heard of a little thing called Obstruction of Justice. Nor did she know that it carried not only a fine, but jail time as well.

Richie drove Leroy back to Smokey's with an awkward silence between them. Richie wanted to say something to try and make his stepfather feel better. Something to talk some sense into him. But he really didn't know what to say, so he remained quiet. *I am not a fuckin' shrink. This Tales From the Crypt crap is way out of my league.* He thought.

Leroy knew exactly what his stepson was thinking, and he too remained silent. He stared out the car window for the duration of the drive lost in his own thoughts.

When Richie dropped Leroy back off at his car, they exchanged clumsy goodnights and Leroy watched Richie's taillights disappear down the road. He was relieved to see the book was still in the back seat where it had been carelessly thrown. He looked up once at the flickering neon sign of the bar and scowled. He was feeling more self loathing then he had in ten years. He climbed behind the wheel of his car and drove home.

Taking the book with him — he wasn't willing to let it out of his sight again, Leroy let himself in the front door as quietly as possible. He didn't want to wake Rachel up and have to talk to her just yet. All he wanted to do was go to sleep and try and get rid of the mammoth headache he had drank himself into. It was painfully obvious that Richie bought not one word of the wild tale he told him, which made him all the more sure John Wyatt wouldn't buy it either. If he couldn't convince Richie, there was no way in hell he was going to convince a cop.

As Leroy eased the door closed the light came on in the entry hall. He was met with the disapproving glare of his wife. Leroy closed his eyes against the light and leaned against the door.

"Just where the hell have you been?" Rachel asked in a tight voice.

"I thought Richie called you," Leroy answered, not wanting to meet his wife's eyes.

She peered at him closely. "He did. Said you ran into each other and stopped for something to eat, but seeing as the only place Richie goes these days is Smokey's, I wasn't sure how it was you happened to just bump into him." She paused, and in a low voice said, "Unless of course you were drinking. You weren't drinking were you, Leroy?"

A million lies went through his head, all of which he knew she wouldn't believe. After all, she too was a recovering alcoholic. He knew that after you have been sober long enough you develop a sixth sense about other people's sobriety, especially your own spouse's. In the end he told her the truth. He braced himself for the yelling and the recriminations, but none came.

Her silence was much, much worse. Her mouth pinched into a thin line. She said only, "I am very disappointed, dear." And walked into the kitchen to get him some aspirin and a glass of water.

Rachel went to bed without another word and Leroy lay beside her, tears sliding down his cheeks, until he too fell into restless and uneasy slumber.

Amanda sat in her breakfast nook shivering. Her teeth were chattering, a blanket was wrapped around her shoulders. It took several minutes to settle Lorna down and rock her back to sleep. She was fighting an urge to keep checking on the baby every five minutes. She was drinking a cup of tea and waiting for Kurt to come back in the house. An open brandy bottle sat on the table next to her. She could hear Kurt out on the front step talking to John and Bill Smitty, the K9 officer.

After a few minutes she heard car doors slam, ignitions start, and Kurt walked into the kitchen. He pulled a tea bag from the drawer. Dumping a healthy shot of brandy from the open bottle into his cup, he added the hot water from the simmering kettle and sat down next to his wife.

"You alright?" he asked.

"I don't want to be scared in my own damn house, Kurt. Why can't you catch him?"

He had no answer.

"What is he, a ghost? Just vanishes in the night?" she said, disgusted.

"We will get him. It's only a matter of time."

"A matter of time? How many people will he attack and terrorize before you find him, Kurt? The little bastard has the luck of the devil."

Kurt drank his spiked tea and put an arm around his shivering wife's shoulder.

She started crying. "I'm sorry. I know you are doing the best you can. It's just so frightening. How could he be so bold as to walk right into our house like that?"

Kurt didn't mention the window she forgot to close. He had already made a mental note to double check all the windows and doors at night from here on out. He should have been doing it anyway. He knew how forgetful Amanda was. Of course, to say anything to her about the open window would have been inviting a nasty fight. This was no more Amanda's fault than it was his.

Having no words of comfort for her, he held her close and waited for the tears to stop. When they finally did, she pulled away from him, and said, "You shot at him. Were you trying to kill him?"

"I don't know. I guess I was, but I missed." An uneasy laugh escaped his lips.

"Is that what you are going to put on the Shots Fired by an Officer report when you fill it out, Kurt?"

He thought about that for a minute. She was right of course. Whenever an officer discharged his weapon outside of a firing range, he had to fill out a form explaining why it had been fired.

"Maybe it's a good thing you didn't hit him. Not that I think the little bastard deserves to live, but you would have shot him in the back while he was fleeing you know," she reminded him.

"Yeah, I know. I wasn't thinking like a cop just then, I guess I was thinking more like a man trying to protect his family."

"Well, that's very noble, but start thinking like a cop again. You need to explain that bullet on a report first thing tomorrow and hand it to Fitz. We have had enough trouble already without your getting tossed into the middle of an internal investigation."

"I know, hon," he soothed, his mind going over how he would explain firing his weapon. He knew he would have to lie, and Amanda knew it too. Not that it surprised her all that much —she knew from experience what an accomplished liar he was.

Kurt and John were now thinking seriously of telling Fitz to go ahead and call in the State cops. The little monster had hit too close to home for both of them.

Little did they know that once Fitz got wind of the break-in at the Dale's, he was already on the phone calling in the cavalry.

After what felt like hours to Barclay, he was able to pull himself up from the cold cement. On shaking legs he walked out of the alley into downtown. He didn't know where to go. He knew he would have to find another hiding place. The abandoned trailer wouldn't be safe anymore now that the big woman knew he was staying there.

"Careless," he said again to himself, "I was too damn careless."

His mind was still preoccupied with why the woman would have left food for him, but none of that mattered anymore. All that mattered was extracting his revenge so he could go back to his eternal rest. He was so very tired. He knew on some deep, primitive level that once avenging the murder of his family was taken care of, he would no longer be forced to walk the earth in this broken body. He would be at peace.

Barclay turned a corner, watching as a hefty woman jumped from the cab of a pickup truck in front of a motel. She slammed the door closed with one meaty hip. He was several yards away from her, but caught her scent on the breeze. A mixture of cheap perfume, booze and cigarettes. He recognized that scent. He had smelled it lingering on his porch when he found the food there and had smelled it much stronger inside her trailer. It was his personal chef.

Barclay hid in the shadow of a large tree, watching as the woman stalked into the office. She emerged a few minutes later with a key dangling from one plump hand. She walked down a row of closed doors. He watched as she let herself into one of the rooms.

All at once the buzzing in his head stopped and that evil, not quite human grin, surfaced on his lips.

Norma stripped down to her no nonsense, size 16 cotton underwear from Sears. She climbed under the threadbare covers of the Oaktree Motel's double bed. She lit a cigarette, grabbed the remote control, and settled in with her bottle of Jim Beam to watch sitcoms until sleep overtook her.

"Careful. Must be very careful. Must wait until she is asleep. No more mistakes," Barclay whispered to himself.

He was sitting cross-legged behind the motel. He waited and waited. An hour passed. Then another. Finally, he rose.

Pins and needles shot through his legs and he clutched the corner of a trash dumpster to keep from falling. He shook out his legs and stamped his feet a few times, trying to get the feeling back in them.

When he felt steadier, and was sure his legs would support him, Barclay cautiously peered around the corner of the building. His eyes slid over the abandoned street. When he was sure he was alone, he crept to the room he watched the woman go into and tried to turn the knob. Locked of course.

Prying the window screen off, he gained access to the room the same way he forced his way into the Dale residence. Francis Barclay did indeed seem to have the luck of the devil. The thin window's catch was broken. It opened easily. The window screeched in its tracks. Barclay froze, listening to see if the noise would awaken the woman.

Satisfied, after listening to her braying snores for a few seconds, he dropped down into the seedy motel room through the billowing drapes. He stood over her for a few moments, watching her sleep. Her mouth sagged open and a thin line of drool hung from the corner of her lips.

He placed one hand over the drooping mouth, and she woke up with a start. Before the killer knew what was happening, Norma was bucking and thrashing. She scissored her meaty legs and jumped from the bed on the opposite side from where Barclay positioned himself. Norma leapt for the door with unsuspected speed, her huge and pendulous breasts, flopping on her stomach. She tried to scream, but her throat locked up. All that emerged was a startled squawk.

Barclay scrambled over the bed reaching for her. He hooked a finger inside the back of her extra large cotton panties. She came reeling backwards, pinwheeling her arms for balance and snorting with shock.

He spun her around and drove his fangs into the hollow at the base of her fleshy neck. Her punctured jugular sprayed hot blood into his mouth. He drank hungrily.

It was over in seconds.

As the sun rose over Alder Lake the next morning, the only person who knew where the murderer was, now lay dead in a cheap motel room.

It would be two days before her body was discovered.

CHAPTER 16

It seemed a small furry animal had crawled into Leroy's mouth and died while he slept.

He rose up from the depths of unconsciousness and winced in disgust at the taste inside his mouth. His tongue felt like it had been coated with bird feathers and glued to the roof of his mouth. As he sat up, a huge bolt of pain shot through his head. His stomach performed a lurching somersault. Leroy groaned and massaged his temples. Through heavy eyelids, he looked next to him and heaved a sigh of relief when he saw Rachel's side of the bed empty. Throwing the covers off and sitting up, Leroy closed his eyes against the pain that walloped him in the skull again. He rose slowly, holding onto the night table for support. His stomach was rolling again. He barely made it to the bathroom before throwing up the grilled cheese and whatever booze hadn't made it into the gutter outside of Richie's car the night before.

It was the granddaddy of all hangovers. The light seemed ten times brighter than normal, and made Leroy's eyes water. Every sound seemed magnified to a hundred times its normal volume.

Leroy found it hard to believe he had spent most mornings of his life for nearly fifteen years feeling like this.

"No wonder I stopped drinking." he muttered to himself, "Now I remember why."

Splashing cold water into his stale, sandpapery mouth and over his face, he looked at his bloodshot eyes in the mirror. His skin was sallow and he thought he looked just like the boozehound he once used to be.

"Yep, John Wyatt's sure to believe a wild tale about a vampire wreaking revenge on a small town from an upstanding citizen such as myself. Hell, I ought to just run for mayor," he said to the sickly image in the mirror.

Leroy brushed his teeth and went downstairs to find his wife, and the strongest cup of coffee he could lay his not quite steady hands on.

Rachel wasn't home. She left a note saying she was out running errands and that she turned off the alarm clock so he could sleep. She took the liberty of calling him in sick at work. There was an AA meeting schedule next to the note. She had left a pot of coffee brewing on the counter. Leroy drained most of it, while forcing himself to eat a piece of dry toast. He swallowed a couple of aspirin. Eventually his stomach settled and the dull thudding in his head receded a little. He opened the morning paper Rachel had left folded on the kitchen table.

Leroy felt some trepidation as his fingers began smoothing out the paper. He hoped that while he tied one on last night at Smokey's, someone wasn't being murdered by Alder Lake's version of Count Dracula.

Leroy started shaking violently when he saw the headline.

"Aw, Christ! Aw, shit!" he shouted to his empty house.

The front page screamed with the story of the break in at the Dale home.

'Still at large and still dangerous,' the paper quoted an official saying of the suspect.

"You have no idea," Leroy muttered.

It would be another twenty-four hours before Norma's corpse was discovered. Leroy blessedly didn't know about her demise yet.

It's okay, it's alright. Nobody got killed this time, nobody even got hurt. He didn't do nothin' but break in and bust out a window, Leroy's mind insisted.

Oh no, didn't do nothin', you drunk fool. Nothin' but terrorize a family with a little baby in the house. And what worse would he have done if Dale hadn't woke up and chased him out? What worse! His mind screamed back in protest.

Leroy pounded a fist on the table. "Well, what the hell am I supposed to do about this? How the hell can I fix it? I'm a mailman, for chrisakes!"

And the hated voice in his mind, replied, *Why nothin' — Nothin' at all, Ace. Why don't you just head on down to Smokey's and have yourself a little hair of the dog that bit you. Leave the fixin' to the law. Don't even worry your pretty, little head about it.*

"Oh shut the fuck up why don't you," Leroy said to the voice, and headed upstairs to the shower.

Another day in paradise. The voice replied.

Phones were ringing, people were scurrying in every direction, and John Wyatt couldn't even hear himself think.

The normally sleepy police station was alive and buzzing. Captain Fitzgerald called in the State cops before the sun was even up. The State cops had summoned the FBI. They all converged on Alder Lake, proverbial guns blazing within hours.

All the evidence had been turned over to men (and one woman) in nondescript gray suits. John now felt like a bit player in his own investigation.

The press was herded outside and pounced on anyone that walked into or out of the front doors.

"Who are all these people?" Kurt asked, as he arrived at the chaotic police station and saw the milling bodies everywhere.

John waved his hand at the room in general, "Welcome to the world of real crime fighting, my friend. Apparently you and I are just amateurs, and these here are the professionals. The tall balding guy there in the corner is Superman, and that frigid looking woman with no lips, wearing a man's suit, would be Wonder Woman. Anymore questions?"

Kurt whistled. "Damn, that was fast. Didn't know they would send over so many state cops."

"They aren't all state. Some are FBI, Kurt."

"Damn! Really?"

John nodded. "They took all the files, and I believe that fellow there with the Harry Potter glasses said something to the effect of, 'We'll take it from here, son'."

Kurt looked numb with shock. "Son? He actually called you, son? Okay, so what do we do now? Suck our thumbs and watch them work?"

John smiled with little humor. "I made copies before I turned the files over," he grinned, tapping his briefcase with one finger. "Lets go catch us a killer, buddy. Show these superheroes how it's done."

"Well, sure. Lets go do that. After all, we certainly have done wonders up to now. Haven't we, son?" Kurt replied with his own humorless grin and clapped John on the back.

They skirted past the mob and walked out of the frenzied police department, avoiding the clustered press. They drove to Kurt's house, where they could fight crime in peace.

Amanda and Ellen sat at the Wyatt's kitchen table playing cards. Lorna napped on the couch in the living room. Ellen's cards were propped between the tips of the fingers poking out of her cast. There was a half eaten cheesecake and two forks between them on the table.

"The walls are still covered in that black powder they use to dust for fingerprints," Amanda was saying. "And this morning when I got up, this rather tense woman who looks like she was never properly acquainted with a lipstick, was crawling under the desk in the den with a magnifying glass."

"Was she a cop?" Ellen asked.

"Apparently. She didn't answer me when I asked who she was. Just pulled her jacket back and flashed a badge at me. Not from around here."

"Anyone ever figure out how the little bastard knew where you live? Or where I worked for that matter?"

"Can't catch him long enough to ask him." Amanda sounded disgusted.

"Why us, Mandy? You think he's targeting cops now or something?"

Her friend shrugged and took another bite of cheesecake.

"Gin," Ellen said, and laid her cards out.

Amanda tossed her own hand into the pile on the table. "Well, I've been beaten enough for one day. What do you want to do now? We could finish the rest of the cheese cake." She pushed her fork against the crust in lazy little jabs.

"Maybe we ought to go find the little bastard ourselves. Our husbands aren't doing such a bang up job."

"Yeah. My hero," Amanda laughed, her voice dripping sarcasm.

"No. I'm serious," Ellen said, never taking her intense gaze from her friend's eyes.

"Find him ourselves? How do you propose we do that, El?" She didn't much care for the storm clouds of madness she saw brewing in her friend's eyes.

"We look. That's how."

"Look where? And what do we do if we find him?"

Frustrated, Ellen replied, "We look everywhere. Our husband's are wasting time shuffling papers, statistics and crime scene photos. They aren't out LOOKING," she insisted. "I mean turning over garbage cans and looking in bars and strip joints for the little weasel. He's gotta be somewhere."

Amanda looked at her, stunned. "Alright, Ellen. So we find the lunatic ourselves, say at a titty bar for instance. What do we do then? Buy him a drink or offer him a lap dance?"

"We kill him," Ellen replied simply, the thunderheads Amanda saw winking in her eyes grew more ominous still.

"Huh? We do what?"

"Kill him, Mandy. I have a gun."

Amanda knew her friend was serious. It made her feel cold all over.

"Honey, we'd go to jail." Her tone sounding like she was dealing with a three year old.

"No! No we wouldn't!" Ellen whipped her head back and forth in negation. "He's a mass murderer and we are police officer's wives. They… they couldn't send us to jail. John and Kurt wouldn't let them," she stammered and started to cry. "I can't just sit here and do nothing, Mandy. I can't."

Amanda understood the helplessness she felt, but she also knew that the good fabric of Ellen's psyche had unraveled a little since she had been attacked. Amanda knew she was walking on dangerous ground even discussing this with her. Though troubled by the events of the previous night, she didn't feel the same wild desperation Ellen was displaying. Amanda Dale's only nodding acquaintance with that type of insanity had been her postpartum depression, which was long forgotten and buried under many months of little blue pills.

"Ellen, if we walked into a public place, or even if we found the asshole in a deserted alley and we shot him, they would send us to prison. Period. They wouldn't care who we were married to. Kurt and John wouldn't be able to stop them. Don't you see that?"

Ellen shook her head stubbornly, the lightning in her eyes flashing violently once more. "We have to do something. We can't just keep letting him kill people. We… We could say it was self defense. I mean, my god, it probably would be!"

"Forget it, El. Let's just let our husbands, inept as they may be, do what they get paid to do, and we will stay safe and sound right here in your house. Okay?"

"NO!" Ellen spat. "You can stay here if you want to, but I am going to go looking for him. Maybe we can't kill him, but we sure as hell could look for him. And if we find him we could call in the posse couldn't we?"

Amanda thought about this. Maybe it would be better if she humored her. They could drive around a little, then come back home. No harm done, and maybe it would knock that weird stormy gleam out of Ellen's eyes. A little fresh air might help restore some sanity. Besides, Ellen was determined to go find the killer whether Amanda went with her or not, and short of physically restraining her, Amanda didn't know how to stop her.

“Okay, we can look. We can do that much. But you leave your damn gun at home.” Their husbands had left them with strict instructions not to wander any further than the grocery store, but she’d deal with that later.

Ellen agreed not take the gun readily enough, but when Amanda went to get the baby, she quickly slid it from the cabinet where it was stored, checked to make sure it was loaded and dropped it in her purse.

Clean, shaved and dressed, Leroy felt a little better. He took the AA meeting schedule Rachel left for him and put it in his back pocket. He rummaged through the desk in the living room and found a manila envelope. In his careful hand he wrote John Wyatt’s name on the front in block letters. He slid “Alder Lake: Its History; Its Ghosts” into the envelope and sealed it.

At the police station, he asked the extremely harried secretary if he could speak to John Wyatt.

“I haven’t seen him, Leroy. Don’t even know if he’s here. We’ve been a bit… Uh… Busy this morning.” she waved a hand toward the bustling room.

Leroy looked around at all the unfamiliar faces. “Who are all these people?”

“State cops, some FBI. They got here this morning,” she answered, a frown creasing her brow.

State cops! FBI! The voice was back barking at him from his brain. *Oh that’s just beautiful, Leroy, baby. Why don’t you sit yourself down and tell one of those gray suits there all about the vampire. I bet they’d really get a kick out of this. Might even deputize you.*

Leroy felt his jaw slam shut, as the powerful urge for a drink hit him again like a fist in his gut. He handed the secretary the manila envelope. "Give this to Wyatt when you see him, would you?"

She took it from his outstretched hand. "Why aren't you delivering the mail today, Leroy? You sick or something? You don't look so good."

He turned his back and walked out the doors without answering.

The secretary shrugged and went to give John Wyatt the bulky envelope. Not seeing him in his office, she dropped it in his IN basket.

Phones were ringing off the hook, people were shouting, a copy machine was jammed, and Captain Fitzgerald was yelling at a uniformed officer, who kept mumbling, "Yes, sir."

The envelope and Leroy were both forgotten seconds later.

Leroy sat in his car in the parking lot of the police station. He pulled the AA meeting schedule from his back pocket. He would be a little late for the meeting at the church across the river, but he thought that would be okay. There was another one at the Masonic Lodge starting in twenty minutes. But that was right across the street from Smokey's, and Leroy didn't think it was a wise idea for him to be anywhere near a tavern right now. The urge for a drink was clambering in his head. The lying voice purring in its soft, persuasive tone, *Just one to steady your nerves. It would be just the one.*

He planned on spending the entire day locked in one smoky AA meeting after another if he had to, until that powerful, all consuming desire passed, and that miserable, fibbing voice was silenced.

He drove across the bridge and swung into the parking lot of the church. He walked into the meeting as a man was saying, "My name is Gordon, and I'm an alcoholic."

He slid into a folding chair and joined the group in saying, "Hello, Gordon."

Gordon had been a five martinis at lunch, three at cocktail hour, and four with dinner bank executive, up until he found out his wife was having an affair with his best friend. The subsequent divorce sent his life spiraling out of control. Finally, he and a bottle of expensive Russian vodka drove off the road, and through someone's garage door in the middle of Thanksgiving dinner.

Gordon inevitably lost his cushy bank job. He showed up for job interviews well into his cups, alcohol reeking on his breath. Even without the DUI charge and the night spent in county lock-up, no financial institution in the state would touch him.

He lost his cushy suburban house next, and that was followed by his cushy suburban Cadillac being repossessed. Finding him passed out naked on the front lawn, his cushy suburban kids thought he was a disgusting lush. They wanted nothing further to do with him.

It was now a year later. Sober for the last six and a half months, the fifteen months of community service he was sentenced to well underway, and really the soup kitchen wasn't so bad.

Gordon never got another bank job again. His framed masters degree sat dusty in a drawer. He was currently a clerk in one of those places that offer loans until payday with outrageous fees attached. He drove a 1981 Pinto with ignition problems. His children returned the Christmas presents he sent them unopened.

Leroy shuddered as he listened to Gordon talk about his life and where the martinis had led him.

Just like that, the urge to drink was gone. Utterly and completely gone, and the only thing the committee in his head had to say was, *Damn I'm hungry. How about a good steak?* He left the church half way through the meeting and called his wife on her cell phone to see if they could meet for lunch.

Rachel sounded relieved to hear his voice.

They met at the Colonial Inn for a couple of medium-rare porterhouses. He drank apple juice with the meal, and nothing had ever tasted so good.

CHAPTER 17

Amanda and Ellen dropped the baby off at the sitter. They headed for a section of town that would have made their husbands cringe if they knew. Not only were they wandering a whole lot farther than the grocery store, they were going to a neighborhood that even Richie Welch wouldn't venture into after dark.

"What makes you think he goes to these strip joints, Ellen? He's probably under-age and couldn't get in anyway," Amanda said, guiding Ellen's Mustang smoothly up the hill past downtown.

"Where else are we going to look? Besides, he's just the sleazy sort to hang out in places like that, that's all."

"Yeah, so is my husband," Amanda remarked, straight-faced, never taking her eyes from the road.

Ellen looked at her with a wan smile and laughed. It wasn't much, but Amanda was relieved to see the slightly mad gleam her eyes held all morning, was for the time being extinguished.

The first and only club they went into was fronted by a glass door that had been shattered. Taped over the gaping hole was what appeared to be a large green, plastic trash bag.

They walked into a dim, smoke filled room with faded red shag carpet. Circa the 70's Ellen guessed. Cigarette burns punctuated it every few feet. They were greeted to deep, sensuous instrumental music. The bass was turned up so high they could feel it reverberating under their feet.

They took out the now famous Wanted Poster, and approached a doorman smoking a cigar.

He looked at Amanda speculatively for a moment. "You are a little too old to apply for a job here." Then he turned to Ellen, and said, "And you are a little too… Well… Er… You ain't quite big enough, if you catch my drift." And he turned his eyes back to the stage, where a woman with incredibly long legs, and incredibly large breasts was wrapped around a blue strobe-lit pole like a contortionist.

Amanda and Ellen looked at each other with comic surprise.

"We aren't here to apply for a job. We are looking for someone," Ellen yelled over the music. She pushed the poster into the man's face.

Without even glancing at it, he waved it aside. "Never seen the guy before in my life."

Amanda grabbed his arm. "Hey, this guy is wanted for assaulting a woman, and maybe even for murder. You might want to just look at the damn thing before you dismiss it, okay, pal?"

The man looked at Amanda's hand resting on his arm like it was something just discovered stuck to his shoe, and smirked. "Which one are you? Starsky or Hutch?"

Amanda pulled her hand away.

"Look, I told you I never seen him before in my life. Now if you two… Er… Lovely ladies ain't here to enjoy the show, then I suggest you leave."

"Well, could we at least ask your bartender and the waitress if they might have seen him?" Ellen asked.

"Pay the three dollar cover and buy the two drink minimum, and you can stay till midnight and ask them if they found Jesus for all I care," he replied.

Amanda paid him.

Feeling extremely self-conscious, the two women sat down on hard splintered chairs, at a small round table in the back of the bar. There were only a few men dotting the other tables. One very old gentleman appeared to be passed out over a bowl of pretzels at the bar. No one looked their way.

A tired looking topless woman, with a gorgeous mane of curly brown hair, put down two coasters before them. "You trying to ambush your boyfriends? Or are you lesbians?"

Again, that look of comic surprise crossed between them. Amanda said, "Neither. We are trying to find somebody."

"Yeah, honey, aren't we all. But trust me this isn't the place to find him."

Neither woman had ever been in a place like this before. The whole afternoon all of a sudden took on a very surrealistic, nearly dreamlike quality. *What,* they both silently wondered, *were two suburban housewives, cops wives no less, doing in a joint like this?*

Tearing her eyes from Amanda's, Ellen held up the wanted poster. "Have you seen this guy?"

The waitress took the poster and glanced at it. "Just tacked up on telephone poles all over town." She handed it back. "What are you drinking? You gotta buy two apiece."

They ordered four diet colas. Not wanting to get any closer to the stage then they already were, and certainly not wanting to walk by any of the occupied tables, they asked the waitress if she would show the bartender the poster for them.

She plucked it from Ellen's hand. "Yeah, but in a place like this, even if he had seen him, he wouldn't admit it. You two don't look like cops."

"We aren't. Our husbands are," Ellen said.

Amanda smacked her good arm.

"What?" Ellen asked.

"Don't tell anyone that. We don't want them to find out where we went today, remember?"

"Oh yeah. Sorry."

While they waited for the waitress to return, their eyes were drawn to the girl on the stage.

"You don't suppose those are real do you?" Ellen whispered doubtfully.

"Nah. But she's definitely double jointed. If I threw my leg up that far, I'd need surgery to get it back down again."

"Hell, Amanda, if your legs could do that I don't think Kurt would ever cheat again."

She was just about to apologize for saying such a thoughtless comment, when Amanda barked a noisy chuckle.

The laugh was so loud it caused a few heads to turn and give them a curious glance, before returning their vacant gazes to the woman on stage.

They both fell into a fit of giggles, wiping at their streaming eyes with tissue that Amanda fished out of her purse. They snorted a few more times before getting themselves under control.

The waitress returned with four flat diet colas. She handed back the poster. "Sorry. He says he's never seen him."

They thanked the waitress, left her a five dollar tip, and hurried out of the gloomy club.

The doorman called after them in a sarcastic tone, "Hope you girls enjoyed the show."

Squinting into the sunlight, Amanda said, "Are you satisfied now? We aren't going to find him this way. I was crazy to ever let you talk me into this." Secretly, she thought it had been a good idea after all, though. Ellen looked completely sane again.

Ellen sighed, "No, I guess this isn't the way to find him." She paused, and in a completely serious voice, asked, "Mandy, what the hell did he mean I'm not big enough? Have you any idea how perky these things are for a woman my age?" She looked down at her chest.

Amanda laughed, "Yeah, and mine are apparently big enough, but they wouldn't want to see a geriatric old bag like me swinging around that blue pole, I suppose."

"No, you might land wrong and break something, you old fart," Ellen howled.

They were nearly doubled over in hysterics at their rejection by the strip club's sleazy doorman, and his outrageous assumption that they showed up there looking for employment. Hanging onto each other, they started walking in the direction of the car.

"Do you remember where I parked?" Amanda's smile faded, and was replaced by a puzzled frown.

Ellen stopped and peered down the block. "I thought we were right there, weren't we?" She pointed a finger toward an empty parking space against the curb.

Then, with dawning horror, Ellen gasped, "Oh, shit. The car is gone."

Amanda stared at the vacant stall as if the car was just invisible, and if she looked long and hard enough without blinking, it would somehow materialize again.

"Did you hear me? Someone stole the car!"

"I heard you," Amanda sighed. "What should we…"

Ellen slammed her fist into her cast, and yelled, "That bastard! This is all that bastard's fault." Those horrible thunderclouds were instantly back, and her eyes flashed with fury.

Amanda's jaw fell open in shock. She tried to grab for Ellen's pounding fist. "Ellen, what? Whose fault? Stop hitting yourself like that!"

Ellen's eyes blazed. "Whose fault? Who the hell do you think! The prick we came here looking for."

Ellen's behavior was scaring her. Just a moment ago she seemed her old self again. Now the crazy storm was brewing just over the horizon again, and madness flashed in her eyes.

Amanda wasn't about to argue with her about anything when she looked like this. "Okay, Ellen. Fine, whatever. But right now we need to call Kurt or John and have them pick us up."

"No! No, we can't! John will be furious if he knows we came down here. We'll have to call a cab or something."

"How are you going to explain the car being missing?"

Ellen didn't answer. Just stared at where the car should have been and started crying. "I'm going to get him," Ellen muttered under her breath.

Neither woman noticed the shadows descending over them, as they stood on the dirty street looking at the empty parking stall.

While their women scrutinized a naked dancer in a strip club halfway across town, detectives Kurt Dale and John Wyatt sat poring over crime scene photos. Of particular interest were the neck wounds of the victims.

In Kurt's mind, the glossy black and white blow up of Tina's slender and graceful neck was no longer that of his former lover. It was now just a wound on victim number one's throat. He had grieved for an amazingly short period of time and then put it behind him. He found a way to detach himself from the terrible fate that had befallen her in much the same way he had detached himself from all of his previous lovers once the relationships ended. For Kurt Dale, once a romance was severed there was no point in dwelling on it, no point in suffering the pangs of a guilty conscience over someone else's broken heart. Whatever emotional attachment may have warmed his heart while the relationship endured, simply disappeared once it was over. No fuss and no muss, no looking back.

It was truly remarkable how quickly and efficiently Kurt Dale was able to wash the stain of guilt from his soul.

Kurt thought with some wonder, that he couldn't even fully remember what Tina looked like anymore. When he tried to summon her face in his mind, all that emerged was a blurred, grainy image, like an old and faded photograph.

At this point what bothered Kurt more than Tina's untimely demise was that his home had been invaded and the punk got away. What bothered him even more was that the investigation had been unceremoniously yanked from their grasp and handed over to strangers.

John called the police station and tried to speak to Fitz a few times throughout the afternoon. "Sorry, John, he's in a meeting," was what he was told every time. He left messages and none were returned. They wondered if their captain was just busy, or if he was avoiding them.

"So, exactly what kind of a wound is this? What caused it? I'm just not convinced that it was done by a syringe. Look at the holes, John. Must have been one hell of a thick needle to do that." Kurt was peering at the small puncture wounds circled in red grease pencil.

For just a moment John thought of telling Kurt about Leroy's incredible story. He changed his mind and asked instead, "Well, what do you think it is then?"

"I don't mean to sound stupid, I've been a detective as long as you have, John, but doesn't it look a little like some kind of bite? Some kind of really sharp teeth?"

"You back to that again?" John shifted uncomfortably in his chair. He had to remind himself that Leroy didn't produce the legendary history book that was supposed to substantiate his crazy fable. The "Rachel's car got prowled" story was just too hard for him to swallow. It was way too convenient. He was a trained detective, and he refused to focus on anything but the logical for the duration of this investigation. He knew Leroy Clovis to be of sound mind, but how many perfectly sound people had snapped under pressure before?

John's own overtaxed mind forgot all about Leroy telling him that both the Dale family and his own were targets of this monster if the story in that old book was true. He believed Ellen's attack and the Dale's house being burgled was either a very large coincidence, or the killer was now targeting cops. It didn't matter. They would find him, and then they would find that ever popular Rational Explanation, and it would all make perfect sense. If they just looked close enough. If they just located the right pieces of this baffling puzzle.

Unfortunately, the detectives drew no closer to Francis Barclay that afternoon than their wives did. It would probably have come as small consolation to them if they knew that the state cops and the FBI detectives, (what John had dubbed The Gray People) milling around their police station were no closer either.

By five o'clock both men were hungry and frustrated. They put the grisly photos away.

Kurt took two beers from the fridge while John went to the kitchen phone to call his wife. The machine picked up and he left her a message to call him at Kurt's.

They waited a half hour before he tried again. When he heard Ellen's mechanical voice say, "You have reached the Wyatts. We can't come to the…" he hung up the phone.

"Where do you suppose they are?" he asked, a ghost of disquiet creeping into his voice.

"Probably at the grocery store," Kurt answered. But he felt that same small ripple of unease travel up his own spine.

CHAPTER 18

The night Francis Barclay killed Norma Krueger was the best night of his miserable new life. He went back to Happy Wheels. Instead of staying in the abandoned trailer with no food, no electricity, and no running water, he stayed at Norma's place.

The bed was big and comfortable. The shower worked, and the refrigerator and pantry were fully stocked. For now, Norma's blood had satiated his other primal appetite.

He was somewhat inhibited by his lack of knowledge in the operation of modern conveniences, such as the microwave oven, or even the stove, but there were plenty of potato chips, doughnuts and other snacks to keep him full and happy. There was also left over roast in the fridge that was just as tasty cold as it had been hot.

He opened canned goods with a steak knife found in a drawer, ignoring the electric can opener sitting on the counter. He didn't know what it was or how to use it. He avoided most of the appliances in the kitchen. They made his very outdated brain nervous, looking more like mechanical monsters than anything useful.

He knew he couldn't stay here for much longer. Just before sunrise he carried as much food as he could back to the abandoned trailer. There was no fat meddlesome woman to turn him in to the authorities anymore.

He assumed if any of the other people living around here saw him the place would have been crawling with lawmen by now. Those posters were everywhere. He knew most of the people who lived in the trailer park must have seen them. He just had to make sure that they didn't see him.

Barclay figured the big woman's body would be found the next day and people would begin showing up at her house soon after. He didn't know it would be another twenty-four hours before a housekeeper made the grisly discovery.

He stood under the hot shower in her bathroom until the water ran cold, then dried himself off with a towel and left it on the floor of the bathroom. The mess wasn't as bad as what was left behind in the Ash's bathroom, but it was a long way from clean. He had been out of the ground for a much longer time now, but the shower was still coated with filth when he emerged.

From Norma's bureau he pulled some baggy sweat pants and a gray sweatshirt, several sizes too big for him. He left behind his jeans, now stiff with grime.

He found a down parka, also far too big for his scrawny frame, hanging in a closet in the hallway. The army fatigue jacket he'd been wearing went through a lot in the last week. It was ready for retirement. Confiscated from the abandoned trailer he had been lodging in, none of his attire was exactly fresh to start with.

Despite the summer heat, Francis Barclay was cold all the time. He kept the down parka zipped up to his chin. He took some warm blankets from a cabinet and a carton of cigarettes before returning to his temporary residence across the street.

He figured he filched enough food from the big lady's trailer to last him until this nightmare was over and his revenge was, at last, complete.

Though his flagging strength had been renewed by Norma's blood, he knew that if he couldn't get his hands (and teeth) onto Dale and Wyatt soon, he would need to kill someone else to keep his strength up. His body's need for human blood hadn't changed much in two-hundred years it seemed. And the longer he was here, the faster he weakened.

He wrapped himself in the blankets he took from Norma's trailer and settled back onto the worn, threadbare couch of the abandoned trailer. He fell asleep just as the first state officers and FBI agents were descending on Alder Lake.

Francis slept the entire next day while Amanda and Ellen went looking for him in a strip club, where the pulsing lights, loud music, and shamelessly naked women probably would have scared him into a heart attack if he'd been there.

When the phone rang at 6:15, a nervous John Wyatt jumped up and grabbed it. "Hello, Ellen?"

"Uh, no this is Karen from down the street. I was just wondering if someone was going to pick up Lorna soon? She's been here all day, and Amanda said she would only be gone a couple of hours."

"Oh, man. Hang on."

He covered the mouthpiece of the phone with his hand. As he relayed the message to Kurt, the color drained from his face. He took the phone from John and spoke to the babysitter. She told him that Ellen and Amanda dropped the baby off before noon. They promised to be back no later than three. They didn't tell her where they were going.

"Karen, I might have an emergency here. Do you think you could keep Lorna for a little while longer? Give her dinner?"

She sounded worried when she replied, "Sure, Kurt. I hope everything will be okay. Call and let me know when you are going to come for her."

"Will do, Karen. Thanks."

John was running his hands through his hair. "If that bastard has them…"

"Stop it, John. We don't know anything yet. Let me try Amanda's cell phone."

The call went straight to voicemail. Kurt left a message and turned back to John. "Try Ellen's cell."

"Voicemail," John replied miserably.

"Let's get over to your house."

They raced to the Wyatt residence.

Once in the front door Kurt called over his shoulder, "I'm going to check the garage for Ellen's car." He went toward the kitchen where there was a door leading out to the garage, as John called upstairs. Kurt stopped in the kitchen and took in the half eaten cheesecake and the scattered spray of playing cards on the table. He opened the garage door. "They're not here. Ellen's car is gone."

Both men looked like little boys, as they stood helpless, unsure what to do.

"Call the gym, maybe they worked out today," Kurt said.

"Ellen isn't working out until her busted wing is healed. Would Mandy have gone today after what happened at your place last night?" John asked doubtfully.

Kurt shook his head. "No, they were going to be together all day. They were supposed to be here. Only thing they were going to do was go to the grocery."

"Did Amanda say she was going to take Lorna to the sitter?"

"No. She was going to keep her here with her."

"Well, then where the hell are they? This isn't like Ellen," John said.

Annoyed at the unspoken reference that disappearing and leaving their daughter at the sitter was normal behavior for his wife, Kurt was about to snap at John. But when he saw him gnawing on his thumb nail, looking lost and tired, he let it pass. Kurt sat down hard on one of the kitchen chairs and put his face in his hands.

"Come on lets go," John sighed.

"Go where?"

"To the station. We need the patrol units out looking for the car."

Kurt nodded and followed his partner outside.

There were three of them. Not a one looked over sixteen years old. But they were tall, and they were obviously mean. They dressed identically in black baggy clothing and stocking caps pulled down nearly to their eyes. One had brass knuckles and an enormous tattoo running busily up his forearm.

Amanda turned around and drew in a sharp breath when they surrounded them on the street.

"Someone took our car," Ellen blurted out when she realized they were there.

Amanda stared at the boys in frightened silence.

They spoke rapidly in Spanish for a few seconds. A kid sporting a rather pathetic Fu Manchu moustache turned toward Ellen. His voice bore a thick Latino accent. "Yeah, man. Red Mustang, chrome wheels, totally cherry. That one?"

Ellen nodded her head. "Yes! That's mine. Did you see who did it?"

This caused them all to laugh. The kid grinned to reveal one gold front tooth. "Yeah, man. I did it."

They closed in then, and things got out of hand quickly.

Amanda grabbed Ellen's elbow, steering her back down the sidewalk. The boy with the brass knuckles grabbed her hand and tore it from Ellen's arm. When he saw the diamond in her wedding band catch the sunlight, he bent her fingers back and tried to yank the ring off. Amanda's fingernail broke with an audible snap.

"Hey. Ow. Don't!" she yelled, trying to twist her hand away. The kid tightened his grip. Amanda stumbled back a couple steps and dropped her purse in the scuffle. The third boy swept it off the pavement before Amanda even realized where it landed. He took off running down the block, disappearing around a corner.

Ellen tried to scream but her lips felt numb with shock. All that emerged was a mouse-like squeak.

Amanda was struggling with the kid and yelling for help. The neighborhood was oddly quiet. A Hispanic girl looked out a third story window from a tenement across the street. She peered at Amanda with frightened eyes, then quickly pulled her head back and slammed the window shut.

"Call the police!" Amanda cried. The kid had managed to work her ring half way over the knuckle in the center of her finger. It would budge no further. She thought if the creep didn't stop pulling, he was going to rip her whole finger off.

Ellen was trying to reason with the kid with the Fu Manchu in an oddly irritating voice.

Amanda yelled, "A little help here, Ellen!"

The kid Ellen was talking to turned his attention to Amanda and his buddy wrestling. He sauntered up to them and closed one barrel sized fist over the other kid's fingers in an effort to help him seize the ring. For one terrible bone-crushing instant, Amanda was sure her finger was going to snap like a twig. Suddenly the pressure disappeared and Amanda looked up to see both boys gawking wide-eyed at Ellen, her ring forgotten.

Ellen was holding her gun pointed at them, the barrel stuttering up and down in a hand that shook violently. Her purse was on the ground at her feet, the contents scattered on the dirty sidewalk.

"You get away from her right now," Ellen shrieked in a banshee's voice. Her hair hung in her face like a sweaty helmet and tears rolled down her face. Those awful storm clouds of insanity Amanda had seen winking on and off in Ellen's eyes all day were back. Her face was twisted into a hag's mask.

"Oh shit, Ellen! You brought the gun!" Amanda gasped. She looked back and forth from Ellen to the two punks, who now looked no more menacing than a pair of toy poodles.

"Easy, lady," Fu Manchu soothed, raising his hands up in front of him. "Easy, okay." He cast a nervous glance at his buddy who was staring with rapt attention at the jittering barrel of Ellen's pistol. His mouth stood open in an astonished little O.

Amanda tried to push her ring back into place, but her finger was swelled and it wouldn't budge. She winced in pain. She couldn't bend her finger with the ring wedged over the knuckle like that. Underneath the broken and bleeding nail was turning a disquieting blue. All in all she figured it was still better than getting her wedding set stolen.

"Where the hell is my car, you little thief?" Ellen spat.

"Well, uh, lady, you see…

"I SAID, WHERE THE FUCK IS MY CAR?" she roared in a torrent of spittle. The gun was jumping viciously in her hand, her finger resting on the trigger. Ellen's cast lay against her stomach. With a grimace, she raised it a little to steady the gun. She leveled it at the two kids before her.

"Okay, okay, Jesus, lady, just calm down will you."

Amanda was looking at Ellen with stark amazement. She was horror-struck as she thought, *This is what it feels like before something really bad happens. This is what it must feel like before you witness someone get killed, or a really bad car crash. Tthis is what it must feel like when...*

"Mandy, get my purse."

"What?" she gasped, knocked from her dark musing. She felt sluggish and slow, like she was moving underwater.

"The fucking purse, girl! Get it!" Ellen gestured at the ground where it fell.

Amanda quickly kneeled down, shoved the scattered contents into Ellen's shoulder bag, and clutched it against her chest.

"Now, my car. Where?" Ellen growled through gritted teeth.

The boy with the brass knuckles started to whine. "Tell her, Julio! Tell her! She gonna shoot us if you don't tell her! The bitch is crazy, can't you see that?"

The other one pointed down the block. "Down there, two blocks. But it's not... It's not..." He trailed off and looked at his feet.

"Not what?" Ellen barked.

"It's... It's missing some stuff now, you know," he mumbled and shifted uneasily from foot to foot.

"What did you take off my car?" Ellen demanded.

With a huge effort Amanda spoke. "Christ, Ellen, forget it! Let's just get out of here, okay?"

Ellen looked at her. "But he..."

Amanda said through gritted teeth, "We are standing in the middle of the street with two juvenile delinquents, who I have no doubt at this moment you are preparing to gun down in broad daylight. This isn't good, Ellen. Not good at all." Her voice was rising to near hysteria.

"Yeah, alright, okay," Ellen stammered, her eyes clearing a little. She waved the pistol at the kids. "Get out of here before I change my mind."

They bolted down the street and rounded a corner out of sight.

Ellen exhaled a shaky breath and let the hand holding the gun drop to her side.

"Put that away, okay, El?" Amanda asked in a gentle voice, the kind reserved for the very young and the very crazy. She cast a wary glance at the gun.

With a bewildered expression Ellen thumbed the safety and handed it to her. Amanda stowed it in the other woman's purse, with a fleeting look up the deserted street.

"C'mon, let's go." She wrapped an arm around Ellen's shoulder and they started up the road, neither of them talking.

"Oh, no," Ellen cried, when they found the car.

Two tires were slashed, all the hubcaps gone, as was the stereo system and both front seats. A screwdriver stuck rudely out of the driver's side door and another poked out of the steering column. The trunk stood open, lock demolished. The Mustang looked like a dead dog left by the side of the road.

Tears sprang to Ellen's eyes, and Amanda tightened her arm around her shoulder. "It's okay, El. I know you love the car, but I think we are damn lucky to be in one piece right now."

Ellen swiped at her eyes with her good arm. "It's all that son of a bitch's fault."

Amanda nearly asked who, but bit it back. In the world according to Ellen today, everything that happened was now the fault of the psychopath stalking their town. Global warming? The killer's fault. World hunger? The killer's fault. Bush being in office? The killer's fault. Ellen had a one track mind. And that too was the killer's fault.

Ellen sighed. “Better call Kurt on your cell phone, Mandy. Have them come get us.”

“What cell phone? That bastard with the gold tooth took off with my purse. Where’s yours?”

Ellen smacked her forehead. “It was in the fucking car. Aw, shit. What now?”

“We go find a payphone,” Amanda groaned. “Come on.”

The police station had settled down from the hubbub that greeted the detectives earlier in the day. The press was gone and the dayshift people had long since gone home. Left were some of The Gray People, working busily at desks in the bullpen or talking on the phone.

They walked into their office. John was startled by a man sitting behind his desk.

“Who are you?” Wyatt asked, annoyed.

“Oh, sorry is this your desk?” The man started gathering an armload of papers.

“Yeah, it is. Who are you?”

“I’m the profiler from the FBI.” He rose, extending a hand, “Lance Honeywell.”

John shook it briefly. “Well can you excuse us please.”

“Yeah, I was just finishing up. I’ve left a copy of the profile I composed on your perp in your IN basket for you, Detective Wyatt. I thought it might be of some interest.”

John nodded his thanks and kicked the office door shut behind him.

“Profiler?” Kurt wondered.

John shook his head. Ignoring his IN box entirely he reached into a file cabinet drawer behind him and retrieved a missing persons report. He and Kurt painstakingly filled it out. They took photos of their missing wives from frames on their desks and paper-clipped them to the missing persons report.

Captain Fitzgerald's office was closed and locked. No light under the door. Fitz must have left for the day.

They made copies of the report, brought it into the patrol briefing room and dropped it in the Shift Lieutenants box. The lieutenant looked at them with a puzzled expression.

"Is this a joke?" he asked.

"No. Just pass them out at briefing, okay?"

"Yeah, guys, will do. Let me know if they turn up."

He wanted to say more. Had about a million questions, but the look in both of the detective's weary eyes silenced the unanswered questions in his throat.

They walked back into their office and John swept the pile of papers overflowing from his IN box into his briefcase while Kurt rummaged through his own box of accumulated papers. They decided to drive through downtown and see if they could spot Ellen's car. Maybe their wives went for dinner or to see a movie. They were grasping at straws, both men knowing that Amanda and Ellen wouldn't have gone out without telling them, or abandoned Lorna with a sitter. Neither had ever felt so helpless in their lives. Worry ate at them, the strain showing clearly on their troubled faces.

Amanda's heels were blistered and she was limping by the time they found a working payphone. Her left ring finger was an angry dark purple and the flesh was puffed up grotesquely around her ring now. The back of her hand was caked with dried blood from her torn fingernail.

Ellen's arm was a dull ache and a vicious itch inside her cast. There was a stitch in her side and she was out of breath.

This wasn't the first phone they stopped at. They tried many. Some missing the receivers, others with large out of order signs hanging on them. Mostly from kids trying to smash them open for the change they held. They found one a few blocks back outside of a coffee shop that might have worked, but when Amanda picked up the receiver, a large fresh wad of wet snot dripped onto her palm. Dropping it with a cry of disgust, she wiped her hand on the back of her slacks.

They went into the coffee shop and split a tasteless hamburger, before realizing Ellen's wallet was lost when she dropped her purse to pull the gun on the kids who accosted them. Neither had eaten anything since their cheesecake, which now seemed like a lifetime ago, and they were both growing faint with hunger. The manager wanted to call the police when the women couldn't pay for their burger, but somehow Amanda convinced him to let them go, with a promise that she would send the money plus a healthy tip tomorrow. The sight of her ruined finger helped.

They had no idea how many miles they walked. An unknown amount of time later, they stood crammed together in a phone booth outside of a liquor store. It was growing dark, the sky above turning a glowing orange. The color of bad dreams, Amanda thought, as the sunlight fled west. Already another cluster of tough looking boys were glaring at them from across the street. There was a small pile of change, dug from the bottom of Ellen's handbag. It was neatly separated into two stacks on the little silver shelf under the phone. Ellen called the main number to the police department and an unfamiliar voice answered, "Alder Lake Police."

"Who is this?" she asked.

"Inspector Burke with the Regional Justice Center. What can I do for you?"

Amanda saw a funny look cross Ellen's face, and mouthed "What?"

Ellen shook her head. "I am looking for Detective Wyatt."

"He's not here."

"Is Detective Dale there?"

"Never heard of him."

"You never heard... Oh never mind." She slammed the phone down.

Amanda jumped at the sound of the receiver smacking the cradle. "What happened?"

"Some inspector with a regional something or other answered the phone. Said John wasn't there and he never even heard of Kurt."

"Beautiful. Must be a close relative of the lipless bitch that was crawling around my den this morning." Amanda sighed and reached for the phone.

They called both of their homes and got the answering machines. They hung up without leaving messages. Both calls gobbling up thirty-five precious cents from the quickly dwindling stack of coins. They dug enough change from the bottom of Ellen's bag for one more phone call, then they were completely broke. Ellen called John's cell phone and tears sprang to her eyes when it went to voicemail. She hung up without leaving a message.

John had switched the phone to the vibrate mode earlier in the day. Too preoccupied with finding their wives, he never bothered to switch it back when he threw it in his briefcase with the contents of his IN basket.

Buried under a bulky manila envelope, containing "Alder Lake: Its History; Its Ghosts," the phone quivered, unheard.

"What should we do, Mandy? I don't have anymore change?" Ellen breathed a weary sigh.

"I guess we better ask the liquor store clerk to call us a cab and get out of here before it gets dark. We don't need anymore trouble." Her tired voice matched Ellen's.

"You go. I'm just gonna sit out here on the curb. I'm tired."

Amanda shook her head. "No way. We stay together. You aren't staying out here alone." She didn't think Ellen had noticed the kids eyeing them from across the street and didn't want to alarm her, but she wasn't letting her out of her sight. She still couldn't shake the image of her friend holding the gun on those two punks.

"Come on, Ellen." She took her friend's hand and they walked into the brightly lit liquor store.

The call that Ellen's car was found came in at just after 8:00 PM. They were sitting in John's living room, neither talking. Kurt called the babysitter earlier and asked if Lorna could stay the night.

John pounced on the phone when it rang and listened to the news that his wife's stripped Mustang was found abandoned in Hell's Kitchen. They were having it impounded and brought to the station for examination and to be dusted for prints. Quietly John replaced the receiver. Through numb lips he told Kurt about the car.

"Call Fitz," Kurt grumbled, his face crumbling with anguish.

John dialed Captain Fitzgerald's home telephone number. When Fitz's wife answered, he identified himself and asked to speak to the Captain.

"Is it important, John? He's had a pretty hard day." "Haven't we all, Ann. My wife is missing, so please put him on the phone."

"Oh, dear," she said, "Just a moment."

"What do you mean she's missing?" Fitz asked in a gruff voice when he picked up the phone.

John recounted the evening's events. Fitz told them he would meet them at the station to help with the search and to pull credit card and bank account transactions. John thanked him, said he was grateful, and the detectives headed back to the police station for the third time in what was fast becoming the longest day in both of their lives.

CHAPTER 19

Amanda and Ellen waited for the taxi inside the doors of the brightly lit liquor store. By now it was completely dark outside. Arc sodium lights snapped on some twenty minutes earlier, casting the parking lot in a sickly yellow glow. Small clusters of teenagers, unmistakably gang members, were hanging out in the parking lot and on the street. They glared inside at the two women through the glass like they were some kind of exotic fish in an aquarium.

It took the cab over an hour to arrive. The surly liquor store clerk allowed them to use the phone to call the cab, but refused to allow them to make anymore calls. Amanda felt sick having not gotten in touch with Lorna's babysitter.

Finally they were settled into the back seat of a taxi and watching the miserable neighborhood disappear behind them.

The driver took in the women's haggard appearance and asked what they were doing in such a rough neighborhood. They exchanged a look, but didn't answer him. Amanda saw the driver's puzzled eyes looking at them in the rear view mirror. He looked as though he was about to say something else, but then decided he would like to get a tip from this fare, and his eyes fastened on the road ahead.

Ellen picked up Amanda's injured hand. "That looks really gross. Must hurt like hell."

"Actually, I lost all the feeling in it a couple of hours ago. Just feels like a piece of stone hanging from the end of my hand now."

"You realize it's all that bastard's fault, don't you?" Ellen snarled.

"Yeah, it was both of them. The other one was trying to help him. Damn near broke my finger off."

"Noooo. Not them. The other one. The one we were looking for. It's his fault. All of this is his fault and I want to kill him for what he's done." Ellen's voice cracked as she started crying again.

Amanda thought if those thunderheads she'd watched brewing in her friend's eyes ever since this morning grew together and didn't wink out again, as they had done all day, there was going to be one hell of a storm — one hell of a *crazy* storm. And she sincerely hoped she wouldn't be there to watch it.

They were on their way to the Dale house where Amanda kept a small stash of cash in her jewelry box and a spare front door key under a potted plant in the backyard. The Dales kept an extra set of keys to the Jeep hanging on a hook in the kitchen. If Kurt was still riding with John, then both the keys and the jeep should be there.

"The guys are probably really worried." Ellen was gnawing on a cuticle.

"I guess we should have left a message on the answering machine. I just didn't think everything was going to take so long. Crap, I hope Kurt picked up Lorna."

"I bet Karen called him by now." Ellen remarked.

Amanda glanced at the cabbie and lowered her voice to a whisper. "El, how much are you going to tell John about what happened?"

Ellen looked out the window and plucked at some imaginary lint on her jeans. She cupped a hand over her mouth and leaned toward Amanda's ear. "I don't think I have ever outright lied to him," she whispered. "And I am going to have to tell him where we went and what happened to the car, but I may… Well… I may just leave out the part about bringing the gun. You won't mention that will you, Mandy?"

Amanda shook her head and patted her friend's shoulder. "It wasn't loaded anyway, right?" she murmured.

Ellen looked at her dumbfounded and leaned toward her again. Amanda felt her friend's hot stale breath in a rush against her ear, as she hissed, "Of course it was loaded. And if the little shit hadn't let go of your hand I would have happily shot his foot off."

The cabbie glanced in the mirror again at the sound of Ellen's heated whispers.

Amanda stared at her friend in silence. In that moment, looking into Ellen Wyatt's fiery eyes, the ominous clouds dancing briefly before flickering out again, she had no doubt that she really would have shot those kids. Ellen had changed since being attacked. Amanda was just now beginning to see how much. Right after the assault at the garage Ellen had seemed frightened and vulnerable, maybe even in shock. But in the past day her fear had been replaced by a barely caged and very dangerous fury. Amanda doubted if Ellen even realized how volatile and irrational she was acting. Ellen Wyatt wasn't the same woman she had been a week ago. She probably never would be again.

Kurt sat before a dully glowing computer monitor with John leaning over his shoulder. "This makes no sense," he cried in frustration.

"It does if Mandy isn't the one using the card, Kurt."

They were scanning the activity on their credit cards. The Wyatt accounts showed no activity in the past twenty-four hours at all. On the Dale's Visa card seventy dollars was charged at a video arcade and another eight bucks at a fast food joint not three blocks from where Ellen's car was found. A purchase for two thousand dollars and change was attempted and declined at a stereo and electronics shop, where the card was at last confiscated.

Captain Fitzgerald walked up behind the detectives, shirt sleeves rolled up, face haggard. "I've got a couple men enroute to the stereo store to canvas. They will pick up the card, Kurt. I called in a favor to get the prints we found on the Mustang run tonight, and we got back a match."

"Oh god, just tell me it isn't the killer's prints, Fitz. Tell me it isn't," John choked in an anguished voice.

"No, not him. Just a couple small time hoods from Hell's Kitchen. My guess is they are the ones using the credit card."

Both men sighed with relief. By now they had nearly convinced themselves that the serial killer terrorizing Alder Lake was behind their wives disappearance.

Fitz handed them two mug shots with rap sheets attached. Mostly petty theft and one commercial burglary. Richie Welch had a longer sheet than the two punks combined.

"Why don't you go pick them up and bring them in for questioning. I can't get you an arrest warrant until morning, but the prints are sufficient enough probable cause to bring them in. Not going to do either of you any good hanging around here. I'll call you if we get any news on the women."

The detectives looked at each other and John shrugged, "He's right, let's go. Maybe they can give us a clue about where to look."

Kurt rose from the chair. The worry that the homicidal maniac they were tracking was behind Amanda and Ellen's mysterious vanishing act had gnawed at him like a disease until it became a near certainty in his heart. When the prints came back on Ellen's Mustang and matched two suspects with a history of auto crimes — two suspects who so far hadn't killed anyone, the relief left Kurt weak and shaking. He was having a hard time staying focused now. His stomach grumbled with hunger, his mind whirled in a hundred different directions trying to figure out where the two women could possibly be. He knew if there were any way his wife was physically able, she would have picked up their daughter from the sitter, or at the very least called. This one fact troubled him more than anything else. Amanda just wouldn't leave the baby like that. Anxiety was eating away at his senses. Invasive and horrid thoughts about finding Amanda dead played over and over in his mind. God! Having to raise Lorna alone. Lost in his dark reverie, he stumbled into a wastepaper basket on their way out.

John grabbed his shoulder to steady him.

"You alright, man?" He didn't like the way Kurt looked. "Don't fade on me now, okay?"

Kurt nodded, grunted that he was fine. Head down, shoulders slumped he walked out of the police department into the mild summer breeze.

"I am going to have to cut the ring off, Mrs. Dale." The doctor was peering at her finger through bifocals.

"Am I going to lose my finger?"

The doctor managed a small reassuring smile. "No, just the nail. And it looks like you will need two or three stitches at the cuticle. I warn you, there is going to be a great deal of pain when the blood flow returns and feeling comes back. I will prescribe both painkillers and an antibiotic. It looks like it's already infected. Mind if I ask how this happened?"

"Yeah, actually I do mind," Amanda snapped irritably.

The doctor gave an affronted sniff, but continued working in silence.

Amanda looked away and closed her eyes as a nurse wheeled in implements on a tray. Next there came a sound that reminded her of Kurt's power screwdriver. She winced when she felt the sting of a hypodermic needle. When she opened her eyes again she was looking directly at her wedding ring, lying broken and blood soaked on the table next to the doctor's tools. It was only then, when she saw the cloudy diamond lying there like a crushed insect, that she allowed herself to cry.

John pulled into a parking space and was immediately greeted with suspicious eyes by the people on the street. In this part of town everyone could spot a cop. Even when they were in an unmarked car and not in uniform. Ignoring the hostile stares, he and Kurt strode into the video arcade where the charges were made on Kurt's credit card. They had already been to both of the last known street addresses for the thugs whose prints were taken from Ellen's car and didn't find them.

At one, a whip thin woman with hair pulled back into a severe gray bun kept repeating "No se, No se" over and over again. Spanish for, "I don't know." Kurt and John's Spanish wasn't good enough to find out what it was the old woman didn't know, and felt too pressed for time to try all that hard. At the other address no one answered the door.

They decided they would check out a couple of local hang-outs, and if they came up dry they would go back home and face the long night ahead. They had both been cops long enough to get an instinct about the crimes they investigated, and this one was no different. Intuition told them Ellen's car was most likely stolen while it was parked and their wives were elsewhere. The two kids they were looking for were guilty of auto theft, but probably nothing more. And at this moment the theft of Ellen's Mustang was the least of their worries. They didn't honestly believe the hoods who gutted it had any better idea of where Amanda and Ellen were than they did.

The detectives went to a few gathering holes where they flashed their badges and showed the mug shots around. Few gave the photos more than a cursory glance before shaking their heads. Within moments of Kurt and John entering an establishment, most everyone present lost their ability to comprehend the English language, which they had appeared to be quite fluent in when the detectives first walked in. Neither man was very surprised.

Ellen dozed in the emergency room waiting area. When Amanda emerged from a long corridor, her hand completely swaddled in a big white bandage, she jumped to her feet. Dark circles ringed Amanda's eyes and they looked swollen and puffy as though she'd been crying. Ellen hurried down the hallway to her. They exchanged a brief one-armed hug with their good arms, and Amanda managed a small, wan smile.

"Well I guess I'll live." She waved her bandaged hand in the air.

"Did they hurt you?" Ellen asked, concerned.

"Not too bad. My wedding ring took a worse beating than I did. It's going to have to be reset. Did you reach the guys?"

She shook her head. "Tried both of our houses, John's cell and the station. Left messages all over. It's like they disappeared."

"They are probably thinking the same thing about us. I need to stop at the all night pharmacy and get a couple of prescriptions filled, then we can go home." Amanda yawned.

"Do you want to go pick up Lorna?"

"Not at this hour. I imagine Kurt has her, or he arranged for her to stay the night at Karen's. She's probably already sleeping." Amanda glanced at her watch and was surprised to see it was after midnight.

They pulled into Ellen's driveway just as John was rolling up to the curb in front of the house. The men raced from the car. John yanked open the passenger door before Ellen could even finish fumbling the seatbelt unbuckled with her good arm.

"Where the hell have you been?" he hollered.

Kurt was rounding the driver's side. Seeing Amanda's bandage, he reached over her to unbuckle the seatbelt. "Your hand! What did you do? Are you alright? You look like hell." He smoothed her hair.

"Thank you, sweetheart. You don't look so good yourself." Amanda smiled, her voice sounded sleepy. She kissed his stubbly cheek. The relief in his voice was unmistakable. She hadn't been very convinced of her husband's love in recent months, but in that single moment, and by that simple act of smoothing her hair, she held no doubts at all.

Ellen and Amanda promised to explain everything, but insisted they needed to eat something first. They walked in front of their husbands up the walkway to the Wyatt's front door. Kurt and John exchanged worried glances as they followed their wives into the house.

John phoned Captain Fitzgerald and notified the department to call off the search.

Kurt followed the women into the kitchen.

"So, where were you?" he demanded, leaning against a counter with his arms folded and glaring at Amanda.

"I told you, I will tell you all about it after we eat something, okay? Please, honey, I am starving and I just took a painkiller on an empty stomach." She turned her back on him and busied herself pulling a pan from a cabinet. She mouthed something silently to Ellen that Kurt didn't catch and the other woman nodded. The two of them working with only one hand would have been amusing under different circumstances.

Kurt grunted and walked back into the living room where John was still on the phone talking to Fitz. He heard Ellen and Amanda whispering in the kitchen and shot a nervous glance in their direction.

Ellen boiled some spaghetti noodles and Amanda poured a bottle of red sauce into a pan. They heated up a loaf of French bread. The four of them ate in complete silence. The men shot irritated looks at their wives, but were too hungry themselves to say much yet.

While cooking their late supper, Amanda and Ellen agreed they wanted to tell their husbands the story about what happened separately. Both had their own idea of how it should be told to cause the least amount of damage with their respective spouses.

After the meal Amanda told Kurt she would explain everything in the car on the way home. Kurt and John exchanged puzzled frowns, and goodbyes were said at the door.

The painkiller was making Amanda groggy. She could hear herself talking, but it was like listening to someone else. She felt the fog roll in, dulling her senses, and the pain in her finger receded to a far away throb by the time they arrived home.

She told Kurt the whole story and began crying again when she pulled her ring out of the pocket of her slacks to show him the broken pieces of the band and the filthy, blood encrusted diamond. To her surprise, he wasn't angry. Not about the ring, and not about the fool's errand she and Ellen had embarked on. Amanda did not know how truly worried her husband had been for her safety during those long hours she was missing. She was only relieved that he wasn't chastising her for going to the roughest neighborhood in the city to look for a dangerous criminal. If it wasn't all so ludicrous, she would have laughed.

Kurt was strangely quiet. He told her only that she would need to contact the bank and credit card companies to report everything stolen, and to call a locksmith to change the locks on the house.

Amanda gave him a grateful smile through her tears when he said they would go pick out a new setting for her diamond once her finger healed. He was so relieved that she was home safely he didn't have the heart to be mad. Though in the privacy of his own mind he thought what his wife and Ellen had done was incredibly stupid and potentially dangerous as well. He would need to remind her tomorrow that this was no game.

Amanda never mentioned the gun. She promised Ellen she wouldn't. Though she did say she'd have to be careful because maybe Ellen's insanity was catching.

She didn't hear Kurt when he asked, "What insanity?"

She just kept on talking in a slightly slurred and muzzy voice, without even acknowledging that Kurt had spoken.

Kurt thought those must have been some mighty strong pain killers the doctor gave her, because his wife was quite obviously stoned.

She got to the part about the doorman saying she was too old to work in the strip club as they climbed the stairs to their bedroom.

As Kurt helped her undress, he remarked, "You know, if it's that important to you, you can do a lap dance for me when your finger feels better."

"You're on, big guy. As long as you remember to tip." Amanda yawned and fell asleep in his arms.

Ellen's version of the day's events wasn't quite as straightforward as Amanda's. She had a less captive audience.

John's reaction to the story she was telling was very out of character. He was normally the gentlest and most rational of husbands, willing to listen and try to understand any transgression.

But not now. Now he was furious, pacing the carpet and yelling. Firing questions at her and not waiting for an answer before barking another one. How could she take off and not let him know? How could she go to that horrible neighborhood? What was she thinking?

Ellen thought he didn't seem very relieved that she was home safely. Just angry. Angrier than she had ever seen him. She felt foolish and humiliated.

"What the hell do you mean you went looking for the kid that attacked you, Ellen? Have you lost your mind?" John ranted, stalking back and forth across the floor.

His wife sat on the couch with her legs tucked under her watching him apprehensively. "I told you. We just didn't think that anyone was really out looking for him, so we thought we would just… You know, check around a little."

"No one out looking for him? Are you crazy? We have a police station full of FBI agents!" His eyes were incredulous in disbelief. "Let me get this straight. You go unarmed to the worst, seediest part of town, and go into a strip club to find him? What on earth possessed you to do something that stupid?"

John didn't see Ellen's eyes flicker at the word "unarmed." Didn't see the dull hurt or the slightly mad gaze in those eyes either. Back and forth he marched the carpet. "Well? Tell me! Who's idea was this? Was it Amanda's? I can see her thinking she's Wonder Woman. But you? You are much smarter than that, Ellen. At least I thought you were."

Still she didn't answer.

"Have you any idea what we went through tonight trying to find you? Any idea at all of the hell you put me through?"

"I tried to call." Her voice was small and defeated.

"You didn't even have the sense to leave me a message on the answering machine. Why the hell didn't you call my cell phone?"

She tried to tell him that she *had* left a message, left several in fact, but he was beyond listening. She tried to tell him that she called his cell phone over and over, but her words fell on deaf ears.

"I asked you a question. Was this Amanda's idea?"

For the first time Ellen could remember in ten years, she knowingly lied to her husband. "Yeah," she breathed through thin lips.

John threw his hands in the air. "Of course! I knew it had to be. How could you let her manipulate you like this? I swear you spend too damn much time with her. She's a bad influence." Ranting and marching up and down the carpet as his wife disappeared further and further into herself, and he became someone she did not know.

Ellen closed her eyes. "I'm tired. I am going to bed."

"Fine. I will be up in awhile. I need to look through some work papers. I meant to look at them earlier, but I was too busy looking for you."

Ellen rose from the couch with a heavy heart and started for the stairs, tears standing in her eyes.

John called to her when she was halfway up the steps. "Ellen?"

She stopped, but didn't turn toward him. She didn't want to see the stranger standing there.

"Tomorrow we will go find those punks that took the Mustang. I'll see that they pay for this."

A shiver of fright ran through her. *The gun! They'll tell him about the gun and he'll take it away from me!*

She walked back into the living room, alarm creeping into her voice. "No! Um...No, John, don't do that. The insurance will take care of it."

He looked at her with flat suspicion. She thought this must be the look he saved for the interrogation room. Never once had it been turned on her until today.

"You don't want me to arrest the son of a bitches that stole our car? Why?"

"Be...Because I think your time is better spent working on the murder cases and trying to find that bastard who hurt me," Ellen stammered.

His eyes glittered like a hateful rat. Ellen felt like they were boring into her skull and seeing a neon sign flashing, LIAR, LIAR.

'I don't believe you. You want the guy that attacked you arrested, but not the ones that stole your car and landed Amanda in the emergency room? That doesn't make sense, Ellen. It doesn't wash. What are you afraid of? What happened out there today?" he badgered.

She stood speechless, thinking wildly, *good cop-bad cop-good cop-bad cop. Where the hell is good-cop to give me a minute to think?* Her damn investigator husband was nailing her like she was a criminal. Ellen nervously chewed at the side of her mouth. Her ears started ringing and her husband's voice grew distant in her head. She looked away from his murderous eyes, drilling into her like......like what? They reminded her of something. Something horrible. What was it? What did those horrible accusing eyes remind her of? *Oh, God! EYES! The eyes of the monster that attacked her at the garage!*

Inside Ellen's head, a loud and anguished voice shrieked, "NOOOOO!"

And just like that, after threatening to happen all day, Amanda's fear came true. The dark and menacing clouds shifting across Ellen

Wyatt's tortured mind grew together, and in one awful instant, the last of her remaining sanity slid quietly and completely off its moorings and into the abyss.

There was no great clap of thunder to mark its passing, no silvery sliver of lightning to illuminate the dark sky. John never saw the last of his wife's sanity wink out of existence like a falling star right in front of him. He never saw the hard and watchful look that flooded her face, replacing the desperation she showed only a moment before.

Tell him something. A callous, but eerily calm voice inside of Ellen's head spoke up. *If you don't tell him something, he's never going to let you go. And it better be good enough to get that ugly cop-in-the-interrogation-room look off his face.*

"Mandy did something," Ellen replied in a cool voice. "She could get in trouble for it and I don't want her to, because she was only trying to defend us." She looked into her husband's watchful eyes to see if this would be good enough. She saw it wasn't. *Meddling bastard!* The cool voice inside her head spat.

"What did she do?" A knowing, smug look came into John's face, and the new, but not very improved Ellen, fought a strong urge to slap it off.

With an effort, she softened her tone. "I don't want to say. Just let what happened today go, okay? Please, John, let it go."

"No! I won't let it go. Tell me what the hell that woman did that is so bad you don't want me to prosecute those bastards."

With a hollow sigh, Ellen looked hatefully at the man she had been married to for the last ten years. *Who are you? She wondered.*

She offered a perverse grin. "Fine, Detective. You want to know. I'll tell you. I'll tell you everything, Detective, just turn off the bright light, okay. Amanda pointed a gun at them to make them go away. She had to. There was no choice."

Ellen listened dispassionately as her husband exploded again. "Is she crazy? She brought a pistol with her?"

His wife looked at him with bright hate, waiting unmoved for the latest tirade to pass. When it did, she asked in a voice barely loud enough to hear, "John, did you ever love me?"

He looked at her with a blank, bewildered expression, the anger suddenly gone. "What? What kind of a question is..."

"Because if you ever did, you will let this go and you won't say a word about it to anyone. Especially Kurt."

"But, Ellen..."

"But, that's only if you ever did love me, John. And tonight, I'm really not sure that you ever did."

John recoiled as if she slapped him.

Ellen turned on her heel and walked quietly up the stairs, leaving John looking after her, hurt and totally confused. He was not the only one who had become a stranger.

As Ellen lay in bed she carried on a long and satisfying discussion with the new voice living inside her head. The voice insisted that the lie she told John was not her fault. (When did he become such a relentless prick anyway?) Really, it wasn't John's fault either, the voice continued. Nor were the lowlifes that stole her car to blame. No, the responsibility lay solely at the feet of only one — the murderer. The monster who killed those people and tried to kill her. Something must be done, the voice told her. Something must be done to stop him.

Ellen agreed. The voice was rational and it made perfect sense.

Her face felt hot and flushed with a blinding rage one moment, cool and calculating the next, as she thought of what she must do. It was as if two very separate people were now inhabiting her mind and discussing what steps needed to be taken to resolve a difficult issue.

When someone blows the neat orderly world a woman dwells in straight to Hell, then he must be blown to Hell too. There is no other way to right this, the voice said.

Ellen understood. She tasted the bitter tang of revenge, like copper on her tongue. She fell asleep with the image of her pulling the trigger and watching as the bullet slammed into his skinny chest, knocking him from this world over and over again. Her lips stretched in an eerie smile before sleep finally stole that frightening grin from her lips.

CHAPTER 20

Kurt and John stayed out of the way as the state cops and the FBI inspected Norma Krueger's two day old corpse.

A tearful maid sat in an interrogation room explaining that she had been sick the day before, or the room would have been turned and the body found sooner. She could offer little help with the investigation. Nor could Jerry Harper, the man whose truck Norma made her escape from Happy Wheels in. He sat in the interrogation room next door to the maid going over his story with one of the state cops, a man who made him feel as though he wanted to make a full confession and ask for the death penalty, even though his only crime had been arriving home at the exact moment the unfortunate Norma was fleeing down the street. While he was being questioned, his angry wife sat in a hard plastic chair in the lobby glaring at every woman that walked by. Jerry would have preferred lethal injection rather than have to ride home with his wife, a temperamental shrew convinced that he slept with other women every chance he could. If she had known the truth about her husband's one and only indiscretion, it was that he liked to play poker. A pastime at which he was neither very good nor very lucky. Last summer he lost three hundred dollars to Norma in one hand of seven card stud, one eyed jacks wild. Jerry's wife guarded the checkbook as though it were the Holy Grail, so Jerry had an arrangement with his boss to get paid in cash for overtime. Given his talent for losing at cards he worked many extra hours to support his poker habit, which gave his wife a lot of time to sit home by herself and imagine him in the arms of some anonymous blonde.

After only a cursory glance at the crime scene and the Krueger woman's remains, John and Kurt went back to their respective homes to work independently while they awaited the lab results. They both knew the labs would produce toxic poisoning as the cause of death, and the crime scenes would reveal a few long black hairs and the same set of fingerprints they were no closer to identifying now than they were after Tina Hilliard was murdered.

They were trying to find some next of kin of Norma's to get keys to search her home for any clues, but so far had found no one. They were waiting on a search warrant Fitz promised to hand them before any of the gray people, as soon as it was signed by a judge. They wanted to go through her house before the state cops and the FBI flocked there and took over.

John was quiet and distant most of the morning. Kurt chalked it up to one more victim and not enough sleep. He tried to talk about the stunt their wives pulled yesterday, but John didn't want to discuss it so Kurt let it drop.

When John let himself in the front door the house was quiet. He went upstairs and found Ellen fully clothed asleep on the bed. Her face was a mask of misery and he felt a stab of guilt for being so hard on her the night before. He knew his rage was only a result of the fear that something truly terrible had happened to her. It was much easier for him to blame this on Amanda than on his sainted wife. He knew it was illogical for him to feel angry at Kurt for the actions of his wife but he couldn't help it. He somehow believed that his friend's infidelity contributed to Amanda being as reckless as he perceived her. It was much easier to blame the Dales' for putting him in a position which left him feeling as helpless and scared as he did last night, than to look at the fact that Ellen might have been responsible, even in part, for what occurred. He planned to apologize to her for his outburst and take her out for a nice dinner. He had no idea the depth of her anguish, or the utter derailment her sanity suffered.

In the meanwhile he went downstairs and rifled through his briefcase. His hand bumped the manila envelope Leroy dropped off the day before. He pulled it from the briefcase and tore it open. He studied the book's cover, flipped to the pages Leroy marked with post-it notes and began reading.

Leroy was making his rounds. The day was sunny and mild. He felt better than he had all week. His drunken binge, and subsequent hangover behind him. He believed he had done all he could to help the investigation. He told everything he knew, produced the history book to back up his claim, and was now absolved of any guilt. He would wait to hear from John Wyatt, and if he or Kurt Dale asked him for anything else he would gladly assist them. But for now he had found a high interior shelf on which to store this whole nightmare, had found a way to accept what was happening in Alder Lake. The mind, Leroy decided, could adapt to just about anything given enough time and the right set of circumstances. If accepting the impossible meant he wouldn't hit the bottle again then he would embrace it with open arms. Hell, he'd be the first one in line with a necklace made of garlic and a silver cross at his breast if that's what it took to stay out of Smokey's. He once heard it said that the human psyche was elastic and could stretch to amazing lengths without breaking. He thought believing a very old vampire was out of the grave and going around town killing people was reaching pretty close to the edge of his poor stressed out mind's rubber-band capabilities, but believe it he did. And for now at least, the urge to drink had departed.

Leroy parked his mail truck at the bank of mailboxes just inside the gates of Happy Wheels Mobile Estates and climbed out. He was sorting the mail and placing it in the appropriate slots when Jerry Harper walked up to him. Leroy smiled a greeting, but the smile died on his lips when Harper approached him. He was pale and unshaven, dark crescents ringed his eyes. His hair stood up in spikes on his head.

"Jerry, man, what the hell is wrong?" Leroy asked.

Jerry shook his head. "I loaned my truck to Norma Krueger a couple nights ago and she went off and got herself killed. Just spent the first half of the morning talking to the cops and giving hair samples, and the second half trying to convince my wife I wasn't having an affair with her."

Leroy looked at him wide-eyed. "What? Norma's dead? How? When?" he stuttered

"They think it happened a couple days ago. Some maid found her in a motel room this morning. She must have stayed there the night she went hauling ass out of here in my truck. I told you I loaned it to her, but the truth is she pretty much stole it from me."

"Who did it? Do they know?" Leroy asked, knowing the answer before he even heard it.

"It's gotta be the same asshole that killed the minister's family and that rich woman from uptown. They said the only way to clear myself is if I gave 'em blood and hair samples, so I did. Do you think I need a lawyer, Leroy?"

Numb, Leroy fumbled the rest of the letters into the boxes and locked them. “I don’t know, Jerry.” He mumbled absently.

“I think she must have known someone was after her. She come charging down the street and I damn near ran her over. Then she took off in my truck like a bat out of hell. Never told me what was wrong or nothing, just said if I didn’t give her the truck she’d tell my wife about all the money I lost last... Well never mind. She was just real upset.”

“I gotta go.” Leroy jumped into his mail truck and drove away, leaving a haggard Jerry standing on the curb staring at him.

Leroy's poor strained mind had to stretch yet another inch. He barely saw the road before him as he raced home to talk to Rachel. His mind was a jumble of disjointed and random thoughts. Just when he accepted the whole Vampire With An Axe To Grind conjecture as real, someone turns up dead who has nothing to do with it. Now he really did believe his wild theory was wrong, and he was feeling like a hysterical fishwife for having shared it with John Wyatt. It really was just some sociopathic kid after all. Norma Krueger was in no way related to any of the people who participated in killing Francis Barclay or his family. In one way Leroy found comfort in this thought; no crazy Lovecraftian monster to worry about. However, in another way it brought with it a sense of even deeper horror. No one could seem to catch this teenage killer. No one even knew who he was or why he was preying on the residents of Alder Lake. Leroy knew his hypothesis based on the book Mrs. Tipple showed him was flimsy and even unbelievable, but at least it was something. Without the theory of revenge — the oldest motive in the book, they had nothing. And for Leroy, it was somehow easier to accept the law being ill equipped to deal with a creature of mythological proportions, than with just a mere mortal. Even a homicidal one. He tried to find whatever small comfort he could in this new revelation that none of the Brahm Stoker idea was true after all. But there was little comfort to be found, and the high shelf in his mind where he had stowed Francis Barclay splintered and broke, sending the entire nightmare crashing back into Leroy's lap.

"Oh my god, it's all true," John Wyatt gasped in his empty living room as he laid the book beside him on the couch. He started pacing again. His mind was nearly paralyzed with shock. He had read the story, then reread it another three times until the reality of it finally sunk in.

Unlike Leroy, John was a trained detective, and he didn't believe the murder of Norma Kruger negated the whole theory. There were too many unanswered questions in Norma's death. Why did she run from her house and insist Jerry Harper surrender his truck instead of just driving her own vehicle? Why did she stay at the motel without so much as a toothbrush or a change of clothes? Who she was fleeing from was evident, based on her murder being a carbon copy of the others. The only way in which it differed was that Norma wasn't a blood relation of any of the men who killed Barclay and his parents. So somewhere along the line the Krueger woman became a threat to him, and knowing this, she fled. Barclay found her or followed her to the motel and eliminated her. The fact that the killer murdered Norma didn't negate Leroy's hypothesis one bit. In fact, it served to prove to John Wyatt that Francis Barclay would kill anyone who got in the way of his extracting every last bit of revenge.

For a moment Wyatt forgot Francis Barclay died two-hundred years before. The detective was reveling in the exultation of solving the case. This was no different than a hundred times before when the interior instinct which drove every investigation kicked in and told him they cracked it. His gut knew the motive for the murders was solved, the identity of the killer was revealed, and the next logical step would be his capture. He couldn't wait to tell Kurt.

Then, as though struck by a two by four upside the head, John recoiled. He glanced uneasily at the book lying on the couch.

"But, he's dead!" John cried to the empty living room. And thus the process of stretching to accept the unthinkable began for Detective Wyatt. And it was a painful process for such a rational brain. Somehow this unthinkable and impossible scenario made all the pieces fit. His gut instinct never lied. Not when it came to cracking a case. He'd never been wrong, not even once.

With yet another murder, and his family and Kurt's being at risk, John didn't have the luxury of retreating into the comfortable land of *This Can't Be Happening*. He couldn't refuse to accept it any longer. For the first time he was really seeing the evidence before him. He realized with disgust that he had spent the bulk of this investigation ignoring facts because they didn't fit into his neat and tidy idea of reality. His mind ticked them off one by one; The holes in the victims necks, the deaths by toxic poisoning from an untraceable substance similar to snake venom, hairs which seemingly came from a very old man, the only survivor of one of the attacks, (his wife, for God's sake,) insisting the killer wasn't human, the tacky substance which looked like motor oil but turned out to be human blood.

He had to tell Kurt about this. He didn't feel much trepidation about it. Kurt was the one who brought up the possibility of those puncture wounds being caused by an animal. Kurt had an open mind. Far more open than that of his partner, John realized morosely. Kurt would probably have a much shorter road to travel to accept this remarkable tale. The people John dreaded telling, and didn't think he would ever be able to bring this to, was his Captain and the FBI — those annoying gray people who had taken over his case.

Fitz called him just as he was picking up the phone to call Kurt. He told him that he obtained the search warrant for Norma Krueger's trailer and a locksmith would meet them there. John made arrangements to meet Kurt at the trailer after he picked up the warrant from Fitz.

Kurt was on the steps waiting when John pulled up to the doublewide trailer. The front door was standing open as he walked up. He stopped and looked inside. He glanced at the huge portrait of Elvis Presley done on black velvet, and said to Kurt, "Tasteful decorating I see."

They entered the home together and shut the door. Lying upside down on the floor next to the coffee table was the wrinkled wanted poster Norma had plucked from the street. Snapping on a white cotton glove, John held it up between two fingers and turned it over.

"Looks like someone balled it up like they were going to chuck it and then straightened it out again," he said.

Kurt nodded and held open an evidence bag for John to drop it in. Opening Norma's purse and thumbing through the contents, Kurt remarked, "She sure must have been in a hurry. She didn't even take her purse."

They walked into the kitchen and looked at several snack food wrappers lying in crumpled heaps on the counter and littering the floor. There were two or three cans of fruit cocktail lying on their side with dried juice trickling out the side. The lids were crudely cut into and pried off just enough to allow the contents to pour out. A steak knife, bent and stained with the juice was lying in the sink.

"Looks like Norma had a little company. Why do you suppose he would have tried to cut the lids off the cans when there is a perfectly good electric can opener right here?" Kurt asked, pressing the button on the appliance, sending it whirring briefly to life.

John swallowed, "Maybe he didn't know how to use it."

Kurt gave him a curious glance and walked down the hallway and into the bathroom. “What the hell have we got here?”

John looked in the narrow doorway behind him, and said, “Christ, he took a shower here too?”

Kurt turned and looked at him. “Where do you suppose he goes that gets him so damn muddy? Not a very gracious houseguest, now is he?” He looked back at the dirty bathroom and continued, “Do you think he was in the house with the lady of the manor when she took off?”

“If he was, she must have let him in. There is no sign of forced entry,” John answered, and picked up the soiled towel from the floor.

“He may not have needed to force entry. We didn’t even need the locksmith. The back door was open when I got here,” Kurt said.

“So, what’s the scenario here? The perp came in the back door, freaked Norma out, and she took off running down the street? Ms. Krueger never struck me as the kind of woman who would scare that easy. Frankly, she seemed more the type to clobber any uninvited guest over the head with a baseball bat, rather than run frightened from her own house,” John remarked.

“True, but factor in the wanted poster in her living room, and she would know that the uninvited guest bore a startling resemblance to a kid suspected of killing four people and attacking another one.”

“Yeah, maybe.” John was still unconvinced Norma Krueger would frighten that easily. Given what he knew about her, he thought if presented with a choice of fight or flight, Norma would fight. To the death if necessary.

They continued down the hallway to the bedroom. Their eyes were immediately drawn to the bed. Rumpled sheets and the coverlet lay in an untidy heap on the floor.

“Norma must have been a rough sleeper,” John commented.

"Or Goldilocks that slept in her bed was." Kurt bent down and lifted a long black hair from a pillow and dropped it into an evidence bag.

"You don't think the perp and Norma…?" John asked.

"Uh… I don't think the charming lady liked them quite that young, John."

"Rape?"

"Then why wasn't she killed right here at home? What was she doing in the motel?" Kurt wondered. "No, I think the perp scared her and she took off. He followed her to the Oaktree and whacked her. Then he broke into my house planning to do the same thing to me, and came back here for a midnight snack and a nap," he surmised.

"Brave kid to return to the house of a woman he just murdered, eat her food and sleep in her bed don't you think?"

"He's already proven how bold he is, John. Look at how he waltzed into my house last night. Besides, he knew he didn't have to worry about anyone showing up here if Norma was already dead at the motel. It was an easy guess she wouldn't be found at least until the next morning."

John reached onto the floor and picked up the abandoned army fatigue jacket. "He left behind his signature jacket."

"He and Richie Welch must have graduated from the same crime school," Kurt said. Their eyes met and they both smiled. The distance standing between them all day evaporated a little.

They bagged and tagged all of the evidence they could, just as the state cops began rolling up to the curb and marching through the front door. They handed over what they found and escaped before they were confronted for going through the house by themselves.

"Kurt, can we go to the coffee shop and talk? There is something I need to show you," John asked as the other detective climbed into his car.

"Sure. I'll meet you there."

John nodded, climbed into his own car and drove off.

Neither man noticed the curtain held askew in the abandoned trailer across the street, or the pair of murderous aquamarine eyes that stared malevolently from behind the window.

CHAPTER 21

"No, Leroy, I don't think just because Norma Krueger was killed the presumption of who's committing these crimes is blown all to hell," Rachel said for the umpteenth time.

They sat in their living room, Leroy with his postal uniform shirt unbuttoned and a can of soda in his fist.

"Why? Why would he kill Norma? Her people had nothing to do with the death of his family."

"Honey, it all happened so long ago. Maybe the author of the book didn't know about everyone involved. Maybe Norma's great-great-great Uncle Dufus went along for the ride? Maybe she just got in his way? Who knows!"

Leroy shook his head. "It's no good. Norma's kin is all from Minnesota somewhere. She told me that. She only moved here maybe fifteen years ago, after she divorced that trucker."

"It's possible she crossed Barclay, got in his way somehow." Rachel shrugged.

"I can just see Wyatt and his partner laughing their asses off about the drunken fool who believes in goblins," Leroy moaned.

Rachel rolled her eyes, “No one that knows you would think anything of the sort — least of all John Wyatt. Why don’t you go find him and see what he has to say instead of sitting here imagining the entire police force laughing at you.”

Leroy shook his head. “No. I’m sure I will hear from him soon enough.”

“Fine then,” Rachel rose from the couch, “But do something productive, don’t just sit here and whine. Because so help me, Leroy Clovis, if you work yourself up into another trip to Smokey’s…” She didn’t finish the threat, just glared at her husband until he dropped his eyes.

Kurt closed the book with a snap and stared at John across the booth in the crowded coffee shop. The pretty waitress, a girl who under normal circumstances would have held Kurt’s full attention, went unnoticed while she refilled their coffee cups, her large breasts spilling out of her tight uniform as she bent over.

After an uncomfortably long silence, he finally sighed, “Uh, John, I have a real problem with this.”

“So? Does that mean you don’t think it makes a perverse kind of sense?”

“No, the problem I am having is that it does. Perfect sense in fact. Everything inside of me is going off like it does when an investigation hits pay dirt. What better motive? But it’s impossible, isn’t it?”

“Up until this morning it was impossible. Now I’m not so sure,” John replied, sipping his coffee.

“How did you find out about this book? About the whole thing?”

“Leroy Clovis.”

Kurt's eyes opened wide in shock, "Oh man! Leroy? If anyone in this town is less likely to buy a scenario like this than you are, it's him. Where did he hear about it?"

"Mildred Tipple. That old woman who lives in the restored Victorian on Pine. Her great grammy or someone like that told her the story when she was a kid. When the murders started she remembered it and went to the library and hunted up the book. Then she showed it to Leroy, who felt compelled to share it with me for obvious reasons."

"Yeah, I guess it does make a very sick kind of sense, given the killer's victims. Up until Norma Krueger that is," Kurt sighed. "Where does she fit in?"

"I don't know exactly, but I have some ideas."

"Maybe she was just in the wrong place at the wrong time," Kurt shrugged.

"No, it's got to be more than that. Why did she have the wanted poster in her house?"

"Because she was up to something," Kurt replied. "But who is stupid enough to try and blackmail a serial killer?"

"Maybe not so much stupid as greedy," John suggested.

Kurt looked doubtful. "What could she want from a violent, psychopathic teenager? As far as Norma knew, that's all he was."

John shrugged, "I don't know, but I can guarantee you she was after something. I just feel it. Dispatch told me the night she was killed some woman called trying to get a hold of me. Said she sounded frantic and refused to give her name. Call came in on the 911 line from a payphone just around the corner from the motel where she was found. They sent patrol to do an area check but she was gone by the time they got there. I'm guessing that was Norma. Call that intuition too."

"And does your intuition tell you this story is true?" Kurt asked, holding the book up.

"I hate to admit this, but yeah. It all fits somehow. You know how it is when the puzzle finally comes together. We have been investigating crimes long enough to know when the evidence finally all clicks into place." He paused and said, "Am I wrong?"

"I don't know. I gotta think about this. Can I take the book?"

John nodded. "I've had a few days to get used to the idea. Leroy told me about it awhile ago."

"Why didn't you tell me?" Kurt asked.

"Why do you think? It's not the kind of thing you just lay on someone, now is it? Tell you the truth, I didn't believe it myself until I got around to reading that story today. We were a little preoccupied with finding our spouses most of yesterday," he said, an edge creeping into his voice.

Kurt picked up on it instantly. "Is there something bugging you? I mean about what they did? You've been acting weird all day."

John looked away. "Never mind. It's not important."

"Is it something to do with me? You pissed at me about this?"

"I told you it isn't important. Just drop it," John snapped, the tension evident now.

"It is important if it's going to affect us working on this case. We have to work together, or we have to tell the state cops and the FBI all about this vampire business, and I don't know about you, but I wouldn't want to see the look on their faces if we did."

"Does this mean you believe it?" John asked.

"I don't know yet. But I do know that whatever or whoever our killer is, it's our responsibility to stop him. This is our town. And we can't do that if we can't work together. So, what's the problem, John?"

"Can't you rein in your wife so she doesn't drag Ellen into these wild goose chases with her."

Kurt was dumbfounded. "Rein her in? You think what they did yesterday was Mandy's fault?"

"Well, it sure as hell wasn't Ellen's idea," John answered defensively.

Kurt weighed his words carefully, "Perhaps you don't know your wife as well as you think."

He slid stiffly from the booth. Picking up the book, he said, "I will read this again and take a look at the evidence. We'll talk later." He turned on his heel and walked out of the coffee shop.

Ellen awoke from her nap. She felt anything but rested. Her head felt heavy and muzzy. The upstairs was stuffy and hot. She rose from bed and opened the bedroom window to let in the breeze. She knew she should probably call Amanda and see how her hand was, but she had other things on her mind.

Ellen sat down heavily in a rocking chair by the window in her bedroom and looked outside. The house felt like a prison. Would she ever be able to leave it again without looking over her shoulder or without giving her husband a written itinerary of her whereabouts? With these thoughts came the same hatred which welled up in her last night. Oh how she wanted that little son of a bitch to pay for what he did to her life.

Anger, bright and cold flared in her head and she got up from the rocking chair hard enough to send it crashing back into the wall. She washed her face, ran a comb through her hair and went downstairs. She found her purse and rummaged through it until she found the gun lying in the bottom. She removed a small box of ammunition from a cabinet and dumped the bullets into her handbag next to the gun. Satisfied, she stalked out her front door.

A chastened, and far less whiny Leroy, changed into sweats and was going to the park to shoot some hoops. He decided to take his wife's advice and get some fresh air. Thinking about the vampire and his victims could only lead to one thing — Smokey's.

He was just walking out his front door when the phone rang. He dropped his basketball in the entry hall and walked into the living room. Leroy looked at the phone like it might explode in his hand and then cautiously picked up the receiver.

"Hey, Leroy, it's John Wyatt."

"Hello, John," he said evenly.

"Are you busy right now? Can we talk?"

"Are you wanting to discuss my options? You know, being committed versus an outpatient kind of thing? I would prefer a facility with a good arts and crafts program."

John laughed. "I don't think you're crazy, man. I wish I did. Would make this all a lot easier on me if it were that simple."

Leroy breathed a sigh of relief. "I was just going to the park to shoot some hoops. Why don't you meet me there."

"Okay. I'll go home and change. See you there in about twenty minutes."

Amanda fed the baby and was putting her down for a nap. She whacked her hurt hand against the sink while trying to do the dishes. Seeing a bright bloom of blood soak through the bandage, she was afraid she might have torn her stitches. She hadn't taken a much needed painkiller because they made her so groggy she was afraid she would fall asleep with no one to watch Lorna. With nothing more powerful in her system than a couple of Tylenol, her finger was screaming agony, and her disposition unpleasant.

A stressful morning was spent on the phone dealing with the bank and canceling the credit cards. A locksmith was due over later to change the locks on the front and back doors. She was just plucking at the bandage to see how much damage she'd done by rapping her finger against the sink, and cussing at the pain, when the phone rang.

"Yes?" she barked into the receiver.

"Amanda, where's Ellen?" John Wyatt yelled in her ear.

"Hello, John, nice to talk to you too," she snapped sarcastically.

"Don't play games with me. Where the hell is my wife?" he hollered.

"How should I know?" Amanda bit right back. "I haven't talked to her since last night."

"She isn't home!" The first traces of panic filled his voice.

Because Amanda was overtired, in a great deal of pain, and already quite cranky herself, she was in no mood for John's accusatory tone. Things went from bad to worse.

"Well, Christ, John, it doesn't mean she's run off to a strip club again. Maybe she went to the store or something. She doesn't check in with me and she shouldn't have to with you either for that matter. She's a grown woman for chrissakes."

"That's easy for you to say. You think you can just go wielding a gun around at people and no one would hurt one precious hair on your head. Now you've got my wife acting like she's some kind of fucking heroine in a B movie."

Amanda froze, her throbbing hand temporarily forgotten. "What? What did you say?"

"You heard me," John yelled. "You should be ashamed of yourself for dragging Ellen into your hallucinations about saving this town from that scumbag. This isn't a fucking movie you know, people are getting killed."

"Whoa. Back up a second." Amanda brought her voice back to a calmer level. "What did you say about me wielding a gun around?"

"Give it up, Amanda. Ellen told me what you did. How it was your idea to go look for that bastard and how you brought the gun and pointed it at those juvenile delinquents who stole our car. What the hell's the matter with you? My wife won't even let me press charges against them because she is so worried about protecting you." John spat through clenched teeth.

Amanda was stunned. She felt a terrible sense of betrayal at her friend for having lied about what occurred in Hell's Kitchen yesterday. Then again, she knew how John behaved when they finally arrived home last night. She wondered if maybe Ellen didn't believe she had any other option but to pin this on her.

The post-attack Ellen was not the same woman she had been before. She was no longer playing by the rules established over the ten years of her marriage. It was understandable John wouldn't want to accept that Ellen could have done anything so reckless on her own. If Ellen admitted it was her idea or that she was the one toting a gun around, she very well could have written her own divorce papers. But why not just leave out the part about the gun altogether? Why tell John about it at all? She had sworn Amanda to secrecy so why would she have said anything?

Not wanting to make the situation even worse, Amanda said in a chilly voice, "I have no idea where Ellen is. If she calls me, I'll tell her you are looking for her."

Still feeling angry and provoked, John ranted, "I see you aren't denying what you did. I hope you realize the danger you put Ellen and yourself in by your escapades."

"Goodbye, John," she said softly and hung up the phone.

Alder Lake Auto Body and Repair was busy. A few people looked up from their work when Ellen walked into the garage. They were happy to see her.

"Hey, Ellen! How's the arm?" someone called.

The smile on her lips felt forced and insincere. "Doing better, thanks."

"Hey El, you back to work?" another asked.

"No. Not yet. Has anyone seen Richie Welch?" she asked.

A guy pointed to a pair of splayed legs clad in grease stained overalls, sticking out from underneath a sports car.

Ellen approached the bay where he was working, and said, "Hello, Richie."

He climbed from beneath the car and rose to his feet. Wiping his hands on a dirty rag, he smiled. "Hey, Ellen. How are you?"

"I wondered if we could talk for a minute outside." She looked away nervously.

"Uh… Yeah, sure." A puzzled frown creased Richie's brow. He followed Ellen out the same door she ran for her life from just the week before.

"What's up?" he asked, as he lit a cigarette from the pack in his pocket.

"I want your help with something. I don't… I don't know who else to ask. Who else would understand." Ellen bit her lip to keep from crying.

Needless to say, Ellen Wyatt and Richie Welch ran in very different circles. Over the years her husband had arrested him at least twice. They exchanged guarded pleasantries since Richie came to work for the garage, but had never shared a conversation that ran much deeper than the weather. To have her standing in front of him, near tears and enlisting his help scared him a little. He wondered if she was trying to score some weed or something.

"What do you need?" His tone was wary.

"I want to find the guy that hurt me. The one that killed Charity. I want to find him and I want to kill him. Will you help me?" Ellen sobbed in a rush.

Richie stared at her through a cloud of smoke. "You've got to be joking, lady. Does your husband know you are thinking about this?" He was trying, but not succeeding too well in keeping the shock from his voice.

"Of course he doesn't know. He doesn't know anything! He doesn't even know me anymore!" she screamed. "He can't catch the monster and I can't have my life back until he's dead and buried. Will you help me?" The tears were flowing freely now.

Uncomfortable, Richie handed her a stained bandana from his pocket and offered her a cigarette. She waved the pack away, but took the bandana and dabbed at her streaming eyes. He looked away until she composed herself a little.

"Ellen, I know what happened to you was a bad deal. What happened to my girl was even worse. But I can't go look for this asshole and help you kill him. That's just… Well, it's just nuts!"

She started to protest, and he cut her off. "Listen to me. You have never seen the inside of a prison. I have. More times than I care to remember. Trust me, you don't want to end up there. And if you kill this son of a bitch that's where you'll go. Justifiable homicide or not."

Again Ellen started to argue, and Richie held up his hand. "Let me finish. What's worse, if you actually found him, he could end up killing you instead. In fact, he probably would. He already tried once. I don't like to admit it, but your husband is a good cop, Ellen. Or maybe I was just a really bad crook — but either way this is his ballgame. I have committed my fair share of crimes, and believe me when I tell you I sucked at robbing gas stations. I don't think I could get away with murder, even if I wanted to." Richie dropped the butt of his cigarette to the cement and ground it out underneath the heel of one boot.

"Even though he killed Charity?" Ellen persisted. "You wouldn't want justice for that?"

"I want him to pay for what he did. But I'm not the high court and executioner, and you ain't either," Richie replied. "Just chill out a little. Let your husband and his pals nail him. They will, you know. You gotta believe that."

He reached out and squeezed her shoulder. "Look, I gotta get back to work. I'm sorry about what you're going through — What this whole town is going through. But this isn't the way to fix it. You gotta trust me about this."

Richie left Ellen Wyatt standing behind the garage and walked back inside thinking, *Everyone is going crazy. My nice normal stepfather thinks it's a vampire and Mrs. Cop thinks she's Clint Eastwood now and can just go find him and dust him.* He shook his head and climbed back under the sports car he was working on.

Ellen stood outside the body shop for several minutes. She couldn't believe Richie Welch wouldn't want to nail the son of a bitch who killed his girlfriend. She didn't know where else to turn, and she had no intention of just sitting idly by while this bastard continued his killing spree, and her husband sat around fuming and studying charts and graphs. Even the state cops and the FBI were clueless, doing nothing more than scurrying around town like lost sheep. It had to be her. She would get him even if she must do it alone. She would find him and she would eliminate him. In Ellen's rapidly unraveling mind there was no other choice. She really didn't have any faith that her husband or any of the state police they called in even knew what they were dealing with. They hadn't faced him and lived to tell about it. She had.

Ellen walked slowly back to her house trying to think of where she could look for him next.

She strode up her driveway, and was startled from her thoughts when her husband came bounding out of the house and down the steps.

"My god! Where were you? You scared the crap out of me? No note? No nothing? Ellen, what's gotten into you?" John yelled.

She looked at him like he was some odd insect she had never seen before, and said in a voice, both calm and chilling, "I went for a walk."

"Why didn't you leave a note?"

"A note?" she asked, in a very annoyed tone. "I have to leave notes now if I walk outside? I was gone maybe fifteen minutes. Why the fuck don't you just give me one of those metal ankle bracelets you put on the drug dealers that are under house arrest?" Ellen elbowed past him and marched into the house.

"I… I was worried," he replied uncertainly.

"WELL QUIT WORRYING ABOUT ME AND GO CATCH THAT MOTHER FUCKER THAT TRIED TO KILL ME!" she screamed in a voice unlike any that John ever heard come from her lips before. He glanced nervously up the street wondering if the neighbors heard.

"Ellen, what's wrong with you?" He sounded completely bewildered.

"Just leave me alone, John, will you." Her voice was suddenly weary. She raced upstairs, slamming the bedroom door behind her.

CHAPTER 22

Amanda decided not to tell Kurt about her conversation with John. He had enough to worry about with a murderer on the loose, his wife being assaulted by gang members, his house being broken into, and a bunch of humorless special agents taking over his case. He didn't need anymore bad news.

She changed her mind when he arrived home, and asked, "Did you know John thinks that mission to find our town psycho you and Ellen embarked on yesterday was your idea? Why the hell he thinks you orchestrated the whole thing, I have no clue. But in the world according to John Wyatt, the sainted Ellen was merely your puppet."

"Because that's what Ellen told him," Amanda answered, and proceeded to relay her phone conversation with John. Out of a sense of loyalty to her friend she still never mentioned the gun.

"Ellen told him that? You mean Saint Ellen told a lie to her beloved husband?" Kurt snorted.

"You saw how he was acting last night. I'm not sure she had a choice," Amanda replied. "He would have gone ballistic if she told him it was her idea."

"You aren't mad she blamed it all on you?" Kurt asked.

"No. Not really. I can understand why she did it. I'm sorry it caused a problem between you two though."

"He'll get over it." Kurt shrugged.

Amanda could tell he was still bothered by the conversation which took place between the two of them at the coffee shop, however.

"I want to call her, but I'm afraid John will answer the phone, and the last thing I need right now is another confrontation with him myself," she said.

Kurt picked up her bandaged hand. "Did you take a pain pill? You look a little pale."

"I wanted to wait 'til you got home. They make me so woozy that I was afraid I'd conk out and Lorna would have to fix her own lunch."

"Actually, I'm glad you're fully conscious. There's something I want to run by you. And believe me you will want to be wide awake for this. How long will Lorna be asleep?"

"She's only been down about twenty minutes or so. We have time. What's on your mind?" Amanda cast a curious glance at her husband as he handed her the book.

Kurt replied, "Read the marked pages. I'm going to run up and take a shower."

Amanda took the book from his outstretched hand. Examining the cover, she laughed, "A book about Alder Lake's history? Oh that must make fascinating reading."

"You'd be surprised," Kurt replied.

"What's this all about?"

"It's a theory on who our killer is. Just read it. I'll be back down in a few minutes."

Amanda brought the book into the breakfast nook and put the tea kettle up to boil. So engrossed in the story was she, that when the kettle began whistling, she absently moved it from the burner and turned off the stove. Her cup with the teabag inside sat on the counter forgotten.

When Kurt returned downstairs, she looked up at him stunned. "So, maybe it wasn't kids who robbed that grave after all. He just climbed out of it! Dear God, Kurt, this can't be!" Amanda's eyes were two round saucers of shock.

Smacking a palm against his forehead, Kurt cried, "Oh man, I forgot all about that. One more goddamn piece of this insane puzzle. Maybe it was kids, and they… I don't know, by disturbing it they woke him up or something. I can't believe I am even talking this way," he hesitated, and asked, "So, do you believe it, Amanda?"

She looked at him, chewing the side of her lip before nodding hesitantly. "It's the only thing that makes any sense, weirdly enough. Who else would choose the victims he has? Or this town?"

"True, but shit like this just doesn't happen. It can't." Kurt shook his head.

Amanda looked at him thoughtfully. "You know, strange things do happen sometimes. I mean… Well, do you remember when we were first dating and I worked with that little mousy girl named Sandy?"

"Yeah, I vaguely remember her, but what has she got to do with this?" Kurt asked.

"She used to tell me these wild stories about seeing people out of the corner of her eye at this summer home that had been in her family for decades. There were weird noises all the time, doors slamming, sounds in the walls, and things would turn up lost, then be found a month later in a totally different part of the house. She was convinced the house was haunted. I thought she was either a little loopy or making it up. Then a friend of mine, someone I knew wasn't given to this kind of nonsense, and frankly didn't have the imagination to make it up, spent a week with Sandy in that house. By the time she got back she had lost like five pounds and for weeks afterward she jumped through the ceiling every time she heard a noise. She told me she couldn't fall asleep anymore without the bathroom light on. I asked her what the hell had spooked her so bad, but she wouldn't tell me. Then one night about six months later, after a couple glasses of wine I finally pried it out of her. She told me she didn't think I'd believe her and she really didn't care. She said she woke up one night while she was at the summer place and there was some guy standing next to her bed. She asked him who he was and he said his name was Gavin, I think. She said she was just about to scream for help when the guy just disappeared like smoke. She was really shaken up but figured she must have dreamt the whole thing."

"That'd be my guess," Kurt offered.

Amanda held a hand up. "Let me finish. Then the next day when Sandy's mom was showing her some old family photo albums, the guy she saw by her bed the night before was in them. Sandy's mother told her his name was Gavin and he died about twenty years before in a boating accident when he was seventeen and living in that house. She swore she'd never go back there." Amanda finished.

"Fascinating story, love, really, but your point?" Kurt asked mildly.

Amanda rolled her eyes. "Yo detective, isn't it obvious? If there are haunted houses — if those can be real, then why not vampires? Why not ghosts? Who's to say this couldn't happen? It's not common, I'm sure, but how common are true haunted houses? And I believe beyond a shadow of a doubt that at least one of those exists. This girl I told you about went on to become a state prosecutor. In fact she has probably tried some of the cases you busted. She was no crackpot, and wouldn't believe you if you told her the sky was blue unless you proved it. So, against my better judgment I will say that this vampire thing is possible. Not likely, not definite, not congratulations Sherlock Holmes you have solved the case, but possible." Amanda shuddered.

"There's more," Kurt said.

"Okay, go on."

He laid out all the evidence to her that had finally clicked into place for John Wyatt just hours before. Amanda absorbed it all.

"John told you about this?" The surprise evident in her eyes.

Kurt nodded. "And you will never believe who his source was. Leroy Clovis."

Amanda gasped. "Well, then it has to be true. You know Leroy is the sanest person in this entire town, Kurt. Does John believe it?"

"Yeah, he does. Amazing isn't it?"

"So, let's assume this is true. We have to assume that, I think. How do you find him? How do you stop him? Do we even know what kind of powers he might have if this is all for real?" Amanda asked, the disquiet evident on her face.

"I don't know any of that yet. I am still not sure I can accept this."

"It's too much to be waved away as a coincidence, Kurt. Who else would want to go around killing people in Alder Lake? We are hardly even a speck on the map. You are the one that always told me there are very few motiveless crimes."

"You know, I was counting on you laughing me out of the house when I showed you this. You were supposed to tell me all the reasons why it couldn't be," Kurt chuckled.

Amanda felt an answering, but nervous smile on her own lips. "Sorry to disappoint you," she said. "Kurt, did you ever hear your family talk about any of this? Did you ever hear that your great-great grandfather, or whoever he was, did such a thing?"

"No. But I do know one of my ancestors was the sheriff here at one point, Sebastian Dale his name was. Never heard anything about a witch hunt or a family of vampires getting slaughtered by the man though."

"Ellen didn't think he was human. She insisted he wasn't and no one believed her," Amanda remarked.

"Well, he sure looked human to me when he was beating feet across the backyard after I shot at him the other night," Kurt said.

Amanda shrugged. "You only saw him from the back though. Anyway, it's good to know he isn't immune to the effects of a .38 special."

"Should I go buy a few silver bullets just in case," Kurt grinned.

"I think that only works on werewolves, dear." Amanda rose to go check on the baby.

Kurt threw his head back and gave his best werewolf howl as she walked away. It was intended to be funny, but the sound made Amanda shudder, and Kurt closed his mouth mid-howl, as the hairs on the back of his neck stood up.

Leroy and John were winded and sweaty from seven games of HORSE. The sun was setting and a light breeze felt good on their heated skin. They played hard, both needing to exercise out their own private demons. They sat down under a large oak tree to catch their breath.

"I never thought I'd hear myself say this, but if our suspect is a mythical creature, how would you suggest we find him? And if we do find him, do we have to run a stake through his heart to stop him?" John asked, then looked away embarrassed.

"Well, first you can take away the make believe part. He's as real as you or I. As for how to stop him, hell, man, I don't know. You're the cop." A small smile played at the corner of Leroy's lips.

"Yeah, well they didn't cover this one in the academy. It's a little out of my league, and I'm not sure the gray boys are up to the challenge either, Leroy. So any opinions you have on how to get him back where he came from, I'd listen to with an open mind. Don't tell me you haven't thought about it. I know you have. You have always struck me as a man that could find a solution to just about any of life's problems."

Leroy sat thoughtful for a few minutes. "Well, my wife got some books on the subject, but the only one she found that wasn't fiction was written by a screwball. Namely, a self-proclaimed Catholic priest who professes to have performed over two hundred exorcisms, a few being vampires. It basically said the same stuff all the lore does. You know, crosses, garlic, holy water, and of course, that ever popular finely honed stake through the heart. Question is, Detective, if you found this bad boy could you kill him that way?" Leroy looked at John with frank curiosity.

John shook his head. "I don't think so. Even after what he did to Ellen. I really don't think I could do that to anyone." Unease was evident on his face.

"Anyone you know that would believe this story who could do it?"

"The only person I shared it with is Kurt. I don't plan on telling anyone else about this, including my wife, who is not feeling too good today as it is. And no, I don't think Kurt could do it either. Could you Leroy?"

"Hell, no. And it ain't my job. You're the lawman, I'm just the consultant," Leroy smiled.

"Right, my resident expert in the field of vampires." John laughed. "This is just sick you know?" He shook his head sadly.

"How the hell did he come back. That's what I want to know."

"I don't know and I don't care. I just want to stop him before he exacts all the revenge he's looking for. Are you sure we have to kill him that way? Can't we just arrest him and lock him up? What he's done is premeditated murder. He could get the death penalty," John said sagely.

Leroy laughed at the hopeful and somewhat innocent look on the detective's face. "Don't think so, man. He's a dead guy already, remember?"

John grimaced. "Dead, right. I keep forgetting that part. But if he's dead how come he bleeds? It's weird blood mind you, black oily shit, but he does bleed. I think my wife broke his nose."

"How do you know what his blood looks like? Your wife tell you when she busted his nose?" Leroy asked.

"This is all privileged information. I can't disclose it. Let's just say he left blood behind at the crime scenes. We didn't even know it was blood until the lab results came back. And even then, I admit I thought they were wrong. Looked just like dirty motor oil." John shook his head in disgust.

Leroy let the whole 'privileged information' thing go. He could almost laugh at how by the book Wyatt still insisted on playing this, in light of their suspect.

Leroy said, "If his nose breaks and he bleeds, maybe it wouldn't take a stake to kill him. Maybe a bullet would stop him. I don't think we can rely too heavily on what the legends say. And just my own advice, man, get any idea you have about arresting him and doing it all nice and legal-like out of your head. This is no normal criminal you're dealing with. You'd do well to remember that. Don't underestimate him, it could prove fatal."

John nodded. "Can the son of a bitch even die again if he's already been killed once?"

Leroy shuddered and felt a sudden tremor run up his spine. "I hope so. If he can't… Oh my God… If he can't…" He didn't finish. Couldn't finish.

John and Leroy shared a look of such utter and complete horror that neither of them could speak.

Ellen went back to bed after her husband left and immediately fell into a deep troubled sleep, scattered with fragmented and frightening dreams. She awoke several hours later with shadows falling across the bedspread, her sweaty hair clinging to her tearstained cheeks.

Why am I so damn tired? Can't keep my eyes open long enough to figure out what to do about that bastard.

The anger had become a part of her now. It was an infection coursing through every vein, every nerve, every organ. The desire to make her attacker pay was a constant and unchanging need with no room for negotiation. With every beat of her heart that need grew stronger.

She peeled off her sweat-stained clothes and took a clumsy shower with her plastered arm suspended just outside the curtain.

She would need to try and act as normal as possible toward her husband. She didn't want him to get wind of anything she was planning. Didn't want him to know what she needed to do until she could produce the little bastard's head on a platter. By then it would be too late for John to stop her. There was no question in her mind she would kill him. She believed that was why she had lived, when the others he went after all died at his hand. She had completely forgotten about his breaking into the Dale's house and escaping without harming anyone. It never entered her mind that what she was planning was murder. It was justice. And despite Richie's horrified reaction when she asked him to help her, she believed the rest of the town would congratulate her once it was over. She didn't think what she planned was a crime. No, it was justice. She did however believe she was on her own. Richie's reaction convinced her that she must share her plan with no one else. No one was supposed to help her, she was supposed to do this alone. She was... *'The Chosen One'* was the phrase which came to mind.

John crept through the front door of his house. He felt like he was on very shaky ground after the incident with his wife earlier. Every word was going to be like walking on eggshells. He wasn't sure what to say to her or what might make her go off on him like that again. He had a brief flickering thought that she was losing her mind, but he slammed the mental door on it before it was ever truly heard. In John's humble opinion his wife burped roses and crapped gold Tiffany boxes with little pink bows on them. There was no room for such a lovely and glorious mind to go off the deep end. That only happened to inferior people — Like Amanda Dale for instance. Not his perfect, carved from heaven Ellen, who never had an impure or devious thought, and who never spoke anything but the gospel truth, Amen.

John was relieved when he walked into the kitchen. Ellen looked up from the table where she tapped the keys of a calculator, their checkbook open in front of her. Her hair was freshly washed and back in a ponytail. She had changed out of her rumpled clothes, and her face devoid of the little makeup she usually wore looked pallid. There was a faint tinge of blue beneath her eyes but she appeared much calmer than when he last saw her. In fact, she looked nearly like her old self again. The frightening look he saw in her eyes this afternoon was gone.

She smiled up at him. "I kind of let things go this last week. Figured I should get caught up on the bills."

The truth was, Ellen hadn't even looked at the bills placed on the table before her. She'd been sitting there for fifteen minutes watching the clock and waiting for her husband to arrive and find her the same way he had found her countless times before, doing the perfectly mundane task of paying the bills. The stage was carefully set for him to walk in on. Calculator, checkbook, a few scattered pieces of mail, and completing the illusion perfectly, her standard can of diet soda.

"Are you alright?" John asked tentatively.

The smile Ellen offered was forced and a little too bright, stopping short of reaching her eyes. This went unnoticed in John's overwhelming need to stop his world from unraveling. His mind was still not stretched far enough to accept Francis Barclay, let alone this stranger his wife had become in the last twenty-four hours.

"Yes, dear. Fine. Sorry about earlier. I think I'm just overtired. I took a nap."

"Yes, of course you're tired. Well, that's to be expected," John said, in this rational, Freudian tone that made Ellen want to rip his patronizing head off. She couldn't remember ever feeling such loathing for the man she married. The smile grew brighter still, as she gritted her teeth against the scream rising in her throat.

"El, I'm sorry about earlier too. I was just worried when you weren't here. Probably over-reacted."

"I know, hon. I was foolish to go out and not let you know where I was after everything that's happened. Let's just forget about it." Ellen's tone was far too light. Her voice, both strained and false, was a weird caricature of her usual one. The complete wrongness of that voice registered for only the briefest moment before being strong-armed out of John Wyatt's mind by his overpowering desire for normalcy. He took Ellen's good hand and kissed it. He didn't see her grimace when his lips made contact with her skin.

In a voice an octave too high, she asked, "Dear, do you have any idea when the car will be fixed? I feel a little confined not having it here you know?" She sounded like she was reciting a script from Ozzie and Harriet.

If her husband had fully accepted what he was hearing, it would have frightened him far more than her outburst this afternoon did. Probably, far more than Francis Barclay ever could have. Seeing someone slide over the edge and into insanity, especially someone you love, is possibly the most terrifying monster ever witnessed.

Ellen's question about the car sent him back to his panic of the night before, and of that very afternoon. He was about to start in on her again about what a bad idea it was for her to leave the house until the murderer was apprehended. But the sheer unnatural quality of his wife's voice and his own mind's unwillingness to accept what he was hearing made him stop. He told himself now while things were better between them he didn't want to set her off again. She was still so fragile.

"Well, since we aren't pressing charges against the kids that took it, we don't need it for evidence anymore. I'll have it towed to the body shop tomorrow and call the insurance company, okay?"

"Thank you, John."

They went to dinner and Ellen did little more than push the food around on her plate. That odd smile stayed in place throughout the meal like it was glued there. Her husband noticed she wasn't eating, but chalked it up to stress. Of course he did.

Later, in their bed, he reached out to her. Though she didn't resist his advances, the first since she'd broken her arm, she lay oddly still and silent beneath him until it was over. This too, John attributed to the stress, and perhaps the awkwardness of having sex while her arm was in a cast. He kept telling himself, *Everything is back to normal. She paid the bills, we went to dinner, we made love. Normal. It's all perfectly normal.*

Beside him, his revolted wife stared at the ceiling, wishing she could wash her husband's sweat off — and thinking about how she was going to find and kill the monster. The hateful life stealing murderer.

CHAPTER 23

Special Agent Greta Fike, also known as the lipless woman who was never properly introduced to the miracle of lipstick, set her alarm for 2:00 A.M. The accommodations she found herself in weren't much higher on the food chain than the Oaktree Motel, but they were clean and marginally comfortable. The bureau was not known for extravagance when putting up its agents on assignments out of town.

Greta Fike had been with the FBI for seventeen years — the past ten of which were spent tracking serial killers. Her track record included the cracking of three of the most notorious and sensational serial crime cases in the United States, and the subsequent conviction of two of the perpetrators. The third committed suicide moments before they broke down his door.

She was forty-something and had had two life partners. The first, a fellow agent she met at a forensics class, was killed during a drug bust turned bad. After eight years of grieving she found Dee Dee, a retired naval officer. They shared a love of gardening and a small farm in Arlington, Virginia. They tried to adopt a child three years ago, but were turned down by the agencies. After much consideration they attempted invitro fertilization. Since Dee Dee lacked the necessary plumbing, it was Greta that underwent the long and exhaustive treatments. After four very painful and expensive attempts that they were still paying for, and not a single missed menstrual cycle, they gave up and adopted an Old English Sheep Dog named Sally.

Greta's fellow agents knew little about her personal life and most didn't care. She was a force to be reckoned with, and commanded a healthy respect of those who ever had the pleasure of working a case with her.

Special Agent Fike found her uncanny ability to catch killers by investigating their crime scenes on her own in the middle of the night. No one ever knew she did this. Greta wasn't sure where the gift came from to figure out the next destination of a twisted mind, but the inspiration only struck well after midnight, standing all by herself in the middle of a murder site.

Her one very feminine feature was a beautiful mane of Lady Godiva-like blonde hair that fell to her waist. No one except Dee Dee ever saw it in anything but a tightly coiled bun at the back of her head. Tonight it was tucked into a black stocking cap.

Greta donned dark clothing and black leather gloves. She tucked her government-issue handgun into the waistband of her slacks. A thin lock-picking kit was folded in a leather case in the pocket of her windbreaker. She checked the motel parking lot to make sure she was alone and then slid cat-like behind the wheel of her rental car.

Greta's first destination was the Oaktree Motel a few blocks away. She parked around the corner and popped the lever to open the trunk. Tiptoeing around the car, Greta rummaged inside and extracted a fresh roll of crime scene tape and a flashlight. On silent, rubber-soled shoes, sticking close to the wall, she glided shadow-like to the room where Norma Krueger had breathed her last. It took less than ten seconds for Greta to tear off the crime scene tape affixed to the door and gain entry into the room.

This case bothered her. The word which crept into her mind repeatedly was *intangible.* There was something about this perp that she just couldn't grasp. It was more than the troubling aspects of the case, like the lab's return on the hair found at the crime scenes. If the perp was as old as the lab thought, then the hair should have been white and gossamer thin.

Greta had little faith in small town law enforcement, having worked enough cases in Podunk towns like this one. The small town detectives always considered the FBI an unwelcome intruder and they were never terribly forthcoming with information. She learned early in her career that when it came to working a case in a small town, they had to start the investigation from scratch. They were lucky to obtain anything from the detectives working on this up until she and the other agents arrived. Neither man, she noted, had been in the stationhouse or bothered to say two words to her since she arrived in Alder Lake. Not even so much as an introduction.

On her own Greta snared a few hairs from the Ash family's home when they went through it. Confident that her friends in Virginia would give her more accurate information than she read in the file, she sent the sample overnight express to a lab there, and was completely dumbfounded when they gave her the exact same results the tiny little two man lab in Alder Lake had come back with. Since nothing else made any sense, Greta decided it must be a very old human hair wig the perp was wearing when he committed his crimes. Of course instinctively she knew that was wrong. It didn't feel right. But for now, she kept the thought in the back of her head. It was at least one tangible idea in this puzzle she could hold onto. One thing that made sense, in a case that was like looking into a bunch of funhouse mirrors with each step closer she took.

Greta never saw such a scattered mess of puzzle pieces in her entire career. No two pieces seemed to fit.

The victims had nothing in common. Nothing she was aware of anyway. Yet there seemed to be a purpose to them being targeted. Until the last one, which Greta thought was the only murder that hadn't been planned.

Greta used her brain like probing fingers, peeling away the mind of those she hunted layer by layer like an onion. Once you peeled far enough you could always see where the killer was most likely to go next. Who he was most likely to target, and occasionally even why the twisted and tortured landscape of his mind felt the need to kill. From the crime scenes Special Agent Fike could often tell if the killer she was tracking was getting ready for a hiatus. Most serial killers who remained at large for long periods of time always took a hiatus from killing. It could last anywhere from a month to as long as seven or ten years before they began a murderous spree again.

This was the first case she ever investigated where her interior probes reached out and couldn't even begin to grasp the first layer to start peeling. This killer was the first true enigma of her career. Greta didn't like the word *intangible*, nothing in her extensive training in the complexity of the human mind prepared her for it. But intangible was exactly what this perp was.

Greta Fike knew everything there was to know about serial killing. She had studied every text ever written on the subject, and written a few well regarded articles of her own. She spent countless hours in stuffy classrooms listening to lectures, and even more hours questioning the killers she caught. Once the jig was up, serial killers were very forthcoming with information. They loved to talk about their misdeeds. She found a very high percentage of them began killing no earlier than their early twenties. In the rare occasions when they killed before then, it was a maiden voyage — never more than one victim.

This suspect was supposedly barely out of his teens according to those who had seen him, and he already racked up a body count of five. Five in less than a month, and two more attempts. His weapon of choice, some exotic poison no one could identify. He didn't fit into any of the molds Greta Fike had seen in ten years of investigating serial crimes.

By nature, serial killers avoided targeting police officers, avoided going anywhere near them in fact. But this kid not only went after a cop's wife, but just days later he actually waltzed right into another officer's house knowing full well the officer was inside at the time.

Greta never saw a perp so young, yet so bold. Or one lucky enough or crafty enough to avoid capture.

The locals insisted he wasn't from around here. So, the question remained, how did he know who the local detectives were? And why was he in such a hurry to make their deadly acquaintance? Were the minister's family and Tina Hilliard just practice before he went for his real targets, the town's two violent crime detectives? What was this kid after? Had these detectives busted his father, or someone he loved?

Greta studied the paperwork for nearly all of the cases the detectives had ever worked on, and nothing came together. This was a small town, the cases were all pretty uninteresting.

Greta Fike sat on the bed in the seedy motel room. The bloodstained sheets had been taken into evidence, but the mattress still gave off the pungent odor of blood and death.

Norma was a big woman. She probably outweighed their suspect by fifty pounds, yet the room showed virtually no signs of a struggle. The assumption of her colleagues was that he killed Krueger while she slept. This theory didn't feel right to Greta. No particular reason, except the body and most of the blood were found on the floor to the left side of the bed, yet a booze bottle and a full ashtray were both found on the night stand on the right. This indicated the victim had probably been in bed around the time she was attacked. In bed on the right side where her booze and smokes were. So, why was her body found on the floor on the other side of the bed if she was asleep when the perp attacked her? Greta figured Norma Krueger probably woke up before she was attacked and tried to run.

Greta looked in the bathroom, under the bed, and through the dresser drawers. Nothing spoke to her. No light bulbs were going off in her head. She didn't think her abilities were anything so grand as to be called psychic, but they were based largely on hunches and thoughts that just resonated when they popped into her mind. Her mental fingers were still struggling for that first purchase on her young suspect's mind.

With a sigh of frustration, Special Agent Fike exited the room. She ripped two fresh lengths of crime scene tape from the roll with her teeth. From memory she affixed them to the door in the exact same criss-cross, at the exact same place she found the tape secured when she arrived. The balled up tape she removed upon entering the seedy room was stuffed into the pocket of her windbreaker.

Greta went through Tina Hilliard's apartment and the Ash family's house on a pre-dawn run the night before. She came up with nothing on those excursions either. She looked at her watch. Finding she had spent less than forty-five minutes in the room, she decided to go to Norma's trailer and have another look there. Generally her feelings came at the murder scenes, but maybe she could get a hold of something on this slippery suspect in a place where he had slept and showered. She thought it was worth a try.

Greta parked at the bottom of the deserted street and jogged up the hill to the entrance of Happy Wheels Mobile Estates. Cutting through the backyards of the slumbering trailers, she gingerly slid her lock-pick kit out of her jacket. She froze when she saw the crime scene tape at the back door of the Krueger woman's trailer hanging in a loose flap on the steps. She crept around the front of the house. Seeing the tape still intact in front and around the perimeter of the small property, she returned slowly up the narrow patch of grass to the back and bent down to study the fallen tape.

Her mind ticked off possibilities, and rejected each one. A strong gust of wind, curious kids, curious neighbors, vandals.

Finally her interior fingers found the first layer of Francis Barclay's mind and grabbed on eagerly.

If he was bold enough to break into a police detective's house at eleven o'clock at night, with said detective inside, then surely he was bold enough to come back to his latest victim's house for a midnight snack and a nap in the big soft bed.

Her suspect made the first miscalculation Greta could see. He never anticipated any late night visits from the FBI. "Hello, darling," She sighed under her breath.

She pressed her ear to a glass panel set into the rear door and listened. There was no movement from inside. Removing her gun from the waistband of her pants, Greta Fike clicked off the safety and cocked the hammer halfway back. She tried the doorknob and it turned easily in her hand. She pushed the door open and stepped backward onto the steps, wincing at the loud squeak the door made as it swung in on its hinges. She tensed, gun drawn, waiting for the murderer to come at her, or to turn on a light, or try and run.

Nothing happened. The trailer remained still and silent. Greta entered the back door leaving it open. Keeping her back to the kitchen counter, she flipped on a light switch, again tensing for some activity or any noise. There was nothing.

Agents had inventoried the contents of the trailer during their initial search. Not because they thought the killer might return and take anything, but because families of victims had a tendency to sue law enforcement agencies if things turned up missing after the fact. It had become standard practice over the years. When a house was to remain vacant and inaccessible to family members during an ongoing investigation the contents were always catalogued. Greta counted the contents of the pantry and kitchen cabinets herself.

She swung open the pantry door with one foot, keeping her eye on, and her gun pointed at the darkened hallway ahead. She glanced quickly inside. Boxes of snack foods and bags of chips were missing. There were no additional wrappers littering the floor that hadn't been there during her last visit. This didn't cause her to relax in the slightest. Though it was possible the killer came back for the food and had simply taken it with him, she wasn't going to take that chance until she made sure the entire trailer was empty. Nor was she going to call for back-up until she made sure it wasn't. If it turned out to be a false alarm, she would rather save herself from having to explain how it was she came to be there all alone in the middle of the night.

Across the street, a bony finger with graveyard dirt still crusted beneath the nail, allowed the curtain to fall back into place when a flashlight beam flickered behind the blinds in Norma's trailer. A silent figure crept outside and approached the crime scene tape surrounding the property. The shadowy figure lifted one long, thin leg over the tape. On quiet feet he padded to the back of the property, where a door had been left standing open like an invitation.

Once Greta made sure the house was secure, she flipped the safety back on her gun and jammed it roughly back into the waistband of her slacks.

Her heart was racing as she walked to the back door. Swinging it shut, she found herself face to face with a pair of incredible glowing, bestial aquamarine eyes. Eyes belonging to her prey.

In an instant, the hunter had just become the hunted. He must have gotten inside while she was investigating the hallway, and was now standing just behind the open door glaring at her.

It took Special Agent Fike only a second to assess the situation and reel backward, grabbing a pot from a rack over the stove next to her.

The wound that had been inflicted to his head by Ellen Wyatt left Francis Barclay very wary of large shiny objects in the hands of women. The ragged hunk of skin left by his previous scalp laceration fell off, but the deep gash was puffy, red and seriously infected. His nose still bled when he so much as rubbed it. He wanted no more injuries. Barclay flinched when the woman grabbed the pot.

Greta used his momentary hesitation to turn and flee down the hallway. She dropped the pan and grabbed for her gun. It caught in her waistband. She looked with horror at her empty hand when she tried to yank it free.

She reached again for the weapon, but it was too late. He was on her, grabbing Greta by both arms and throwing his weight on top of her. Together they sailed to the floor. From underneath him, Greta grunted and pistoned one knee up, jamming it as hard as she could into her attacker's groin. The connection knocked the air from his lungs in a putrid puff, and Greta felt something like small stones being shaken violently in a bag. The repulsive body on top of her felt loose and jello-like. It made her gorge rise. There was an animal like whimpering coming from deep in his throat. *What the fuck is this guy?* She thought.

He collapsed on top of her when her knee connected with his groin, and the hand holding one of her pinned arms released slightly.

As she was trying to wriggle out from under him and push him off with her free hand, Francis brought his hand down on her head and pulled the stocking cap over her eyes. Her sight gone, she instinctively stopped pushing at him, and reached to pull the cap back up.

In that second, she felt the first sharp sting at her throat.

With sick horror, Greta realized her perp was not human. *My killer is a vampire. That explains the throat wounds of the victims.* Her last thoughts were of Dee Dee and her Old English Sheep Dog, Sally.

As the blood poured from her, and her attacker drank it greedily, Greta Fike finally found her foothold on the killer's mind. Sadly, it was a little too late to solve the case.

It had not been Francis Barclay that made the miscalculation. It was Special Agent Greta Fike who did. She made two in fact. The first was assuming the killer was human. The second was assuming if he wasn't in the trailer, then he wasn't nearby, so she put her gun away. Put it away just a little to deeply into her slacks to allow for easy access. That second miscalculation cost Special Agent Fike her life.

CHAPTER 24

Francis Barclay lay for a long time curled into the fetal position, staring with bitter hatred into the open and staring eyes of his latest victim. He cupped his injured testicles. The whimpering Greta Fike heard while she lay dying was still coming in between pants of air from his blood-caked lips.

It took seeing the first slanting rays of sunlight leaking through the blinds in Norma's living room to get him moving. He pulled himself up to his knees and gasped when he saw a thin black oily stain soaking through the crotch of the sweat pants he wore. His body wasn't put together right anymore. It was wobbly and easily broken. Sometimes when he ran he could feel things jarring loose and rolling around inside his stomach.

When the woman kneed him in the groin he felt something tear. He felt a shiver of fear when he saw the stain, knowing it was blood, and thinking one of his balls had been torn off. He was half right. When he summoned the courage to check, he found his left testicle still attached, but ripped loose, lying against his thigh. He threw up violently next to the dead woman's head, tasting the sickly sweet tang of regurgitated chocolate cake, mixed with the woman's blood in his mouth and burning his throat. He wretched until he thought he would puke up his intestines. Unable to stand, he crawled away from the woman and the steaming mound of vomit toward the back door. Hanging onto the kitchen counter, he pulled himself up to a standing position and started down the steps off the kitchen. He felt a sickening sliding feeling coming from his wounded testicle. A bolt of pain that made everything he had been through up to now feel like nothing more than a slap on the wrist shot through his stomach and bowels. Holding onto the wall, he made his unsteady way back toward Norma's bathroom. When he lifted his leg to step over the body he had left sprawled in the hallway, he felt more blood ooze down his crotch. He started whimpering again and limped into the bathroom.

Holding himself up against the sink, Barclay slid open drawers until he located some bandages and tape. He gently eased down his sweat pants. Biting his lip to keep from screaming out, he placed a square of gauze against the torn left testicle and wound the tape around his right one to hold it still. Pocketing the tape and a few more bandages, he edged his way back toward the kitchen door.

The sun was now nearly up. The light was bleeding through the windows and shooting bolts of dizzying pain into his eyes. He was perspiring heavily and didn't know if it was from his latest injury or from the light.

He would need to hurry back to the abandoned trailer, but every step caused fresh agony to explode between his legs. Hurrying wasn't an option right now. He moaned against the light, slamming his hands over his eyes when he stepped outside. Half lurching and half stumbling, he made it across the road, grunting from the ache between his legs at every step. His nose was leaking again, fresh blood coursing over his lips and down his chin. He could feel the warm wetness flowing down his leg by the time he finally stepped inside the abandoned trailer. He collapsed on the floor in a sweaty, panting heap. There he lay unconscious for the next several hours.

Accustomed to having breakfast at a nearby coffee shop and then going into the police station together, Special Agent Lance Honeywell waited in the parking lot of the motel for Greta to emerge from her room. He frowned when he looked around the small parking lot and realized the rental car they shared was gone. He assumed she went to get it gassed up, or to run an errand. An early riser, she was usually down before him in the morning. He checked his watch, his frown growing deeper. It was 8:30. He had been waiting twenty minutes. Knowing she wasn't there because the car was gone, Lance ascended the stairs and knocked on her motel room door anyway.

As expected, there was no answer. Special Agent Honeywell walked back down the stairs to the motel office and called the police station. No one had seen her. Captain Fitzgerald sent a patrol unit to pick Honeywell up from the motel and bring him into the station.

Though it wasn't like her not to let him know if she wasn't going to meet him, Lance was not overly concerned at her absence. Greta liked to work alone. This wouldn't be the first time she flew off solo without telling anyone where she was headed. He hoped she was chasing a lead.

Nobody became too alarmed until nearly two o'clock in the afternoon when she still hadn't shown up. Her description and the make and model of her rental car was put out over the air.

A patrol unit found it down the block from Happy Wheels with the engine cold.

Kurt and John spoke briefly in the morning. The conversation was awkward, the bad blood still unresolved. They didn't plan on working together that day unless there was anything new to go over. Neither had any idea where to look for the killer, and short of arresting him, neither knew what to do with him if they found him.

Kurt asked John to have Ellen call his wife, and John mumbled that he would give her the message.

Ellen was still asleep at noon and John went up to wake her. She said something garbled and unintelligible, then rolled over and continued sleeping.

Still in a major case of denial about Ellen's declining mental health, John reminded himself that anyone under so much stress would need to sleep more. It was all perfectly natural. Nothing wrong. He was worried about leaving her alone, but equally afraid she would go off on him again in a tirade if he showed his concern and didn't go into work. Torn between staying and going, he decided to work in the kitchen until she woke up. There was nothing for him to do now at the station anyway. He had been muscled aside by the gray people, and felt like he was under-foot and in the way whenever he went there, so what was the point. Besides, he knew who the killer was and he couldn't tell anyone. The only person he trusted with the information was angry with him, and though he wouldn't admit it there was a part of John that knew they would have a better chance of finding Francis Barclay if they could work together on it. He was far too stubborn to admit this out loud, but in the privacy of his own mind John thought he picked a pretty lousy time to rag on Kurt about Amanda. For a moment he nearly picked up the phone to call Kurt back, but in the end his pride wouldn't let him.

He opened his briefcase and went over the same material they had been going over for days and waited for his wife, who had now been asleep for a record fourteen hours, to wake up.

Kurt locked himself in the den. He asked Amanda not to bother him. When she asked him what he was doing, he said that he was working and didn't want to be disturbed. She shrugged and left him alone.

Kurt sat in front of the glowing computer screen. He was logged onto a national criminal justice search engine and was pulling data about vampires or murderers that modeled their crimes after vampires. There was far more information on the subject than he ever dreamed he would find.

He found scientific opinion from a court transcript of a woman convicted of killing her boyfriend by biting his neck and severing his jugular. The opinion was that she suffered from an uncommon psychosis that caused her to believe she needed the blood to survive. This diagnosed psychosis was her defense. They locked her up in a maximum security mental facility, where three months later she killed an orderly in the same grisly manner.

There was a documented case of a farm boy in Wisconsin convicted of felony animal cruelty for killing rabbits by slashing their throats and drinking their blood. He was found dead of mysterious causes on his farm four months later. There was speculation that members of an animal rights group outraged at his brutal actions had killed him. This was proven false when the coroner was unable to find a cause of death. There was nothing to substantiate that he had been murdered. His heart just stopped beating it seemed. He was nineteen and in perfect health at the time of his death, but it was ruled as natural causes.

The most notable case was of a man in London convicted of killing three prostitutes by similar means. He was sentenced to life in prison. Upon sentencing, the defendant became hysterical, insisting he would die if incarcerated and not given any blood to drink. He was put into a ward for the criminally insane, and was indeed dead within three weeks. Cause of death unknown. He was thirty-four years old. *Could the mind kill you?* Kurt wondered. *Could you convince yourself you need something so bad that you actually die without it?*

There were three or four cases of people charged with theft or malicious mischief for stealing blood from hospitals and blood banks. One twenty-seven year old male who worked in a blood bank was charged with stealing from them. He too insisted he needed the blood to survive. This was the only common thread in the cases.

Nothing in any of the cases Kurt read about said anything about toxic poisoning being involved in the death of the victims. The murders he found were all bloody and brutal. No neat little pin holes to the throat. Only the woman that killed her boyfriend did so by biting, and had first drugged the man into unconsciousness with several Valiums cooked into his dinner. The rest all used knives to slash the throats of their victims before drinking their blood. And the crimes were all committed by people very much alive. No two-hundred-plus year olds in the lot. None of the cases were anywhere close to what they were dealing with.

After several hours, a bleary-eyed Kurt emerged from the locked den. He and his family sat down to a late lunch.

Kurt told Amanda about the research he had done. When he told her the story about the woman severing her boyfriend's jugular, she threw down her fork in disgust and held up her hand.

"Yuck! Okay enough already, Kurt. Go tell it all to John. He has the stomach for it, I don't. Least of all during lunch, okay?" she grimaced.

But Kurt couldn't tell it to John, he was still mad at him. Now he was feeling frustrated, having no one to share his gruesome research with. Also, he was getting on Amanda's nerves. Since she didn't want to talk about the vampire topic he took to following her around the house recounting every detail of the conversation he had with John the day before. Finally exasperated, Amanda spun around and ordered him out of the house.

"Go do something. Anything! Just get out of here already," she snapped. "I can't get anything done with you following me around like a puppy and whining. You're wasting time complaining about that ridiculous argument," she told him. "Go to John's house and talk about it. If you can't resolve it, then you need to figure out how to work around it. The longer you two stay mad at each other, the worse this is going to be for everyone." She glared at him until he grudgingly agreed with her and left.

He drove to the station to see if there was anything new in the investigation from the state and federal end of it. He was, of course, secretly hoping that they found something to refute the whole vampire theory.

The primary police channel was turned up on the police radio mounted under the dashboard in his jeep. He was only listening with half an ear when he heard a patrol unit ask dispatch to run a license plate. The crackled voice of the dispatcher came back, "SAM51 your plate comes back clear and current on a 2000 Chevy Cavalier registered to Fleet Rental Cars."

The patrol unit asked the dispatcher if this was the car they were looking for belonging to the missing FBI agent. She confirmed it was.

"Missing FBI agent?" Kurt said out loud to the empty Jeep. He felt the hairs on the back of his neck stand up. He pushed down harder on the gas pedal.

When he arrived at the station Fitz was in a closed-door meeting, and the gray people were all very preoccupied with their missing agent. No one wanted to talk to him and they wouldn't answer his questions about who was missing.

Frustrated, he walked down the hallway to the communications room where the dispatcher worked, knowing she could be counted on to tell him any and all the dirt he wanted to know, and probably some he didn't. It wounded his pride having to resort to obtaining his information by these means, but it was better than staying in the dark.

Once the day dispatcher filled him in about the absent Greta Fike, Kurt called John at home.

"No one knows where she might have gone?" John asked.

"No. I think a patrol unit found her car just down the street from Happy Wheels. Engine was cold. Do you think she was nosing around there looking for something?" Kurt asked, the disquiet he felt evident in his voice.

"You don't have a good feeling about this do you?" John asked, their disagreement temporarily forgotten.

Kurt was quiet for a minute, thinking. "No, I don't. I really don't."

John sighed and looked at his watch. "Why don't you pick me up. Maybe we can look around for her. We know the town better than our new gray friends do. Has anyone checked Norma's trailer?"

"I have no idea. No one will tell me anything," Kurt complained, "It's probably a good place to start though. I'm on my way."

When they arrived at Norma's trailer, Kurt didn't immediately open the car door. The vague feeling that something bad had happened to Special Agent Fike was now a full blown certainty gnawing at his gut.

John opened his door to exit the Cherokee, but when he realized Kurt was not moving he stopped. "What's wrong?" he asked.

Kurt swallowed hard. "I don't want to go in there." A cold finger of fear had begun pressing at his spine.

"Now isn't a good time to get squeamish, Kurt."

"It's not that."

"Then what?" John frowned, his annoyance showing. "We don't have all day."

"I think she's in there," Kurt replied.

John paused briefly, before sighing, "Well, we won't know that until we check. Look, you know the seriousness of this situation as well as I do. And you know we have information that we haven't shared with the gray people. We have to go in there, Kurt," he said, pointing at the trailer.

"I know. But if she's in there does that mean we have to come forward with the Barclay story? No one would believe us."

John leaned his head back against the passenger seat, one leg out of the jeep on the sidewalk. "If the bastard killed a federal agent, we have to talk to Fitz. We won't have a choice."

"How do we do that, John, and still maintain one shred of credibility?" Kurt sighed.

John stepped from the car. "Come on. Let's get this over with." He lifted the crime scene tape, and held it up for Kurt to climb under.

They found what they expected to. Both men felt sick with fear and guilt. They did a cursory examination of Greta Fike's body.

John said, "He must have surprised her. She never even had time to pull her weapon."

Kurt bent down over the body. "She tried." He looked miserable.

John looked at him questioningly, and Kurt replied, "Look at the trigger. It's snagged on the waistband of her underwear. She was trying to pull it out and it stuck in the elastic. Lousy fuckin' luck." Kurt shook his head sadly.

"Why the hell wasn't it in a holster? Who carries a weapon jammed into her panties like that? You'd think the FBI would train their agents a little better than that." John's voice was mingled irritation and fear.

"I think bringing the gun was a precautionary measure. I don't think she was actually counting on running into the suspect here. The body looks like it's been here for several hours already. I think she came out in the middle of the night on a fishing expedition. She wasn't expecting company. Least of all a vampire."

John ran his hands through his hair. "Let's get out of here. I'm going to be sick."

They walked out the front door, both men wondering how they were going to tell their chief and Special Agent Fike's fellow agents about Francis Barclay. Both feared it was a conversation that was long over due.

In the end, neither detective could carry out that long over due conversation after all. They didn't even know where to begin. Once they discovered Greta Fike's body, they dutifully called it in, and then quietly crept away. They drove back to John's house where Ellen still slept upstairs. They were both sullen and preoccupied.

"You want coffee?" John asked.

Kurt shook his head. "We have to tell Fitz."

"Not yet. I have an idea."

Kurt looked at him with mild curiosity.

John took a deep breath and let it out slowly. "The perp — this Barclay, I guess, is hanging around that trailer park somewhere. I think he's sleeping at Norma's."

"Maybe he was, but do you think now that he killed an FBI agent he's still going to hang around there? He's going to know we'll be watching her place now."

John was quiet for a few seconds. "Did you see that pile of barf next to her head?"

Kurt grimaced in disgust and nodded.

"Looked like a whole fuckin' bloody chocolate cake. But there was some of that black oily shit that he bleeds in it too, it wasn't just her blood."

Kurt shrugged, "So what?"

"I think he's sick. Maybe can't travel too far. He's gotta be around there somewhere camping out."

"How do you know, John? Maybe he just ate too much sweets and drank too much blood. He could have just thrown up, then went on his merry way after killing Fike."

"Because it fits. He's not of our world, and I think the longer he stays here, the sicker he's becoming, and probably weaker too. Why hasn't he come after either of us again? That's why he's here. He should have made another go at one of us by now. He obviously knows how to find us, so why hasn't he come out for another round?"

"So, if we don't tell Fitz, then what do we do?" Kurt asked miserably.

"We wait until after dark when the gray boys are safely back in their motel and we go look around Happy Wheels."

"John, they are going to have a patrol officer stationed at Norma's trailer now all night."

John shrugged. "So what. It'll be one of our own officers. And I doubt anyone would find it all that strange that the two original detectives on the case went looking around after a federal agent is found dead there. Hell, we were the only ones that had the presence of mind to even look for her there."

"True. No one asked us anything about why we were there when we made the call that we had found her," Kurt answered.

"You just feel guilty because you think we are withholding evidence. But we aren't. Not really."

"Yeah, maybe. I guess it wouldn't be all that suspicious if we went looking around a little."

Kurt cleared his throat, and said, "Uh, John, if we are going to do this after dark, then I want our wives together. I don't want either of them home alone. I know you are still upset about their little joy ride, but I hope you will put that aside for the sake of their safety. And my daughter's."

John looked away and nodded. "I will bring Ellen over and they can stay at your place. Say around ten o'clock tonight?"

Kurt agreed and rose to leave. "Where is Ellen?"

John averted his eyes. "Taking a nap." He never bothered to mention she hadn't made it out of bed yet today. It was 4:30 in the afternoon.

When he saw Kurt out the door, John went up and checked on Ellen. She was still sleeping. It was a record nineteen and a half hours now. He closed the door behind him and went back downstairs.

After deliberating for a few seconds, he picked up the phone and dialed Leroy's number.

"Hello."

"Leroy, it's John. There's been another one."

In a tense voice, Leroy asked, "Who?"

"Federal agent. She was found in Norma's trailer."

"Aw, shit! Little bastard was staying there all along and we missed it!" Leroy cried in frustration.

"Maybe we didn't," John replied. He proceeded to lay out his theory that Francis Barclay was falling apart and not able to get around so good anymore. He told him of their plan to go looking for him at the mobile home park that night, and asked if he wanted to come along.

"Our wives are staying at Kurt's house. You are welcome to have Rachel stay with them," John offered.

"Rachel's got bingo tonight." Leroy replied.

"Are you in?" John asked.

"I'm in. I'll meet you at your house at quarter 'til," Leroy said grimly and hung up the phone.

CHAPTER 25

When she heard her husband hang up the phone, Ellen gently replaced the bedroom extension's receiver and sat up in bed. *So the little bastard is somewhere near that trailer park,* she thought with some satisfaction.

"You're in the big leagues now you fucking scumbag. Wiped out a fed did you?" she whispered to the shadowy room.

Ellen went into the bathroom adjoining their bedroom. Pawing through the medicine chest she found the prescription for Valium the doctor gave her after setting her arm. The attack upset her so badly he thought she would need something for her nerves. She hadn't taken any of the pills, but a plan was forming in her mind and she was very glad she had filled the prescription. She thought a few tranquilizers would come in quite handy tonight.

Ellen heard their bedroom door open and she slipped the bottle of pills into the pocket of her robe.

"Honey, you're up," John said, the relief in his voice unmistakable.

With an effort, she smiled and stepped out of the bathroom. “Nearly slept the day away didn’t I? But I feel much better. Guess I needed the rest.”

“I’m glad you’re better because you are going to need to stay with Amanda for awhile tonight. I have to take care of something.”

She feigned surprise, “Take care of what, dear?”

“It’s about the case. Kurt and I have a lead. We need to check it out and we don’t want either of you staying alone.”

Counterfeit smile firmly in place, Ellen answered brightly, “Alright, dear. Well, I guess I better get cleaned up and start dinner.”

“Let’s just order a pizza.” he turned to leave, stopped in the doorway, and gave her a puzzled look. “No curiosity about what the lead is?”

She stammered, “I just don’t think I can handle another disappointment if it, you know… turns out to be a dead end. Why don’t you just tell me after you catch him, okay?” She tensed, waiting for him to continue grilling her.

“Honey, you are really feeling better, aren’t you? You aren’t just saying that are you?”

The smile grew brighter. She fingered the vial in her pocket. “Of course not, dear. I’m a hundred percent better,” the weird June Cleaver voice replied.

Leroy explained to his wife everything that John Wyatt told him. Rachel threw a fit about his going with them to find the killer.

“You aren’t a cop, Leroy. They can’t drag you into this. It’s too dangerous,” she argued vehemently.

“Rachel, this isn’t about the law anymore. Surely you see that. I am just as capable of dealing with this fiend as they are. Maybe even more so.”

"How? How are you going to deal with him? How are they? Does anyone even know what he is capable of or what it's going to take to stop him?" she cried.

Leroy tried to comfort her, but she pushed him away. "I don't want you to go. You've done your part, now it's up to the cops to deal with him. Please, Leroy, don't go," she begged.

"I have to," Leroy responded in a quiet, but firm voice.

"Why? Isn't it enough that you found out who the murderer is? Why do you have to help them catch him too? That's what they get paid for," Rachel quarreled.

"I told you. This isn't about the law. They aren't going to find him, handcuff him and read him his rights, Rachel. They need someone with them that knows who he is. I mean *really* knows. And that leaves me and thee, darling. And unfortunately you got bingo tonight and can't make it," he smiled.

Rachel posed a few more feeble arguments, but in the end she relented. She said she would stay home from bingo, but he persuaded her that he had enough to worry about without her staying in the house alone. He told her she might as well do something other than sit home and fret about this. He promised to call her cell phone as soon as there was any news, and said he would probably be home before she was.

Rachel liked none of this, but reluctantly agreed.

Leroy waited until she pulled out of the driveway and went to the phone to call Richie.

After listening to his stepfather explain the nature of his call, Richie snarled, "Why the fuck would I want to roam around Happy Wheels and look for a psycho killer, Leroy? Hell, man, I spent enough time wandering through those woods when I was a kid, waiting for mom to sleep off a drunk. Not the fondest of memories, so I think I'll pass."

"That's exactly my point, Richie. You know the terrain much better than any of us. You could probably find places we don't even know exist," Leroy explained patiently.

"When did finding this prick become my responsibility?" Richie argued. "And don't tell me it's because he killed my girlfriend. I know that, but it doesn't mean I have to go get myself killed too does it?" he replied in a gruff voice.

"No, Richie. This has nothing to do with Charity. It has to do with who is next, and when is it going to stop. It's not for the dead that I'm going with them tonight, it's to protect the living," Leroy said in a soft voice.

"How very noble of you," Richie answered, disgusted. "Why the fuck does everyone in this town think I am supposed to help bring this asshole down?"

Bewildered, Leroy asked, "What do you mean everybody?"

"The cop's wife asked me to help her find him too. She was planning on becoming a one-woman vigilante team and scalping the bastard. I think she wanted me to hold him still while she fired her husband's shotgun at him or something," Richie laughed.

"Which cop's wife?" Leroy asked, surprised.

"Wyatt. She looked like a few gears had slipped a little, if you know what I mean. Funny little gleam in her eye I didn't much care for."

"Did John know she talked to you about this?"

"No, and if it's all the same to you, I'd rather you not tell him. I don't need anymore trouble."

Leroy hated himself for it, but replied, "I'll make you a deal. I won't tell him if you come with us tonight and help us find him."

Richie exhaled loudly, "Fuck, man! You blackmailing me? You saying you're gonna tell Wyatt his wife asked me to help her whack the guy if I don't go along with this?"

Leroy closed his eyes and gripped the phone tight. "That's exactly what I'm saying, son. And he ain't gonna like it if I tell him. He especially ain't gonna like it that you didn't bother to tell him yourself."

"Does my mother know what you're up to?" Richie asked suspiciously.

"She knows where I'm going tonight. She doesn't know I am asking her baby boy to come along."

Richie lit a cigarette and blew a great plume of smoke from his nostrils. His hands were shaking with rage. "Fine. I'll go. But if my ass ends up dead, my mother is going to kill you," he spat.

"If you end up dead tonight, she won't have to because I will probably be dead right along side you. I'll pick you up at 9:30." Leroy hung up the phone before Richie could offer any further argument.

"Is it safe for you to go out looking for him without telling Fitz or those federal people what you are doing?" Amanda asked Kurt when he told her about finding Greta Fike in Norma's trailer.

"I think it's safer than telling them who we think the killer really is at this point," he answered defensively.

"I don't see why you have to tell them the whole story. Can't you just say that you have reason to believe the killer is still hanging around that trailer park and have them come along for back-up?" she pressed.

"They would ask too many questions. And besides, what if we can't kill him with a gun, Mandy? What if it comes down to actually having to put a stake through his heart or something? How are we going to explain that?"

Amanda glared at him, "Who's bringing the stake? You or John?"

That caught Kurt off guard. They hadn't discussed bringing anything of the sort, and by the look in Amanda's eyes she guessed that.

He was saved from answering her by the ringing of the telephone. He eagerly grabbed it. It was John asking him if he had shared with Amanda who they thought their killer was.

"Sure I told her. I showed her the book yesterday afternoon," Kurt said, then hastened to add, "She believes it."

"Well, can you tell her not to mention it to Ellen. I haven't talked to her about this. I don't want to upset her anymore than she already is. She's not feeling well," John replied in a faltering voice.

"Yeah, I'll tell her," Kurt said.

"Oh, and Kurt, I invited Leroy Clovis to come with us tonight."

Without thinking, Kurt asked, "Is he bringing a stake with him?"

John laughed as if it were a joke. "Well, he didn't mention that he'd be armed."

"John, do you think it's a good idea for us to bring a civilian?"

"I think it's a good idea to bring this one, yes," he replied evenly, not liking his judgment questioned. "This is no ordinary case."

"And what are *we* armed with? Just guns?" Kurt asked, his voice betraying his nervousness.

"He bleeds, Kurt. If he bleeds he can die from a well-placed bullet wound."

"You don't know that. I think we should bring some other things with us. I mean if he really is a... You know, what you claim he is, we should bring something like a stake with us."

"Hey, I don't *claim* anything," John snapped, that familiar edge back in his voice.

"No offense, John. I just thought maybe we need to be better prepared if it turns out he is Francis Barclay," Kurt answered, trying to smooth things over. He didn't think now was a good time to have another disagreement with John, but he felt like he had to say something, with Amanda standing there staring daggers at him, like he was a five year old planning to go out and play in the snow without his mittens.

John took a deep breath and brought his voice under control. "Look, I don't think we will need much beyond a gun if we find him. I don't think things like holy water or a cross are going to do us any good, if that's the stuff you are talking about. That's just what the myths are made of, not the real thing. But you are welcome to bring anything that makes you feel better. I might even have some garlic in the fridge I can loan you," he chuckled.

"Are you bringing anything with you?" Kurt asked glumly.

"Yeah. My .38 special."

Kurt hung up the phone feeling embarrassed.

"Well?" Amanda demanded.

"Leroy's bringing the stake," Kurt replied without missing a beat, and looked away.

Amanda snorted, "The mailman is coming with you and he's bringing a stake? Please tell me this is all a really bad dream and I am going to wake up soon," she groaned, rolling her eyes.

"You asked who was bringing the stake and I told you." Kurt hated the whiny quality in his voice. A whine that only popped out when he was scared or lying, and right now he was both.

Amanda shook her head, walking out of the room.

Kurt picked up his daughter from her playpen and sat down on the couch with her.

"Daddy eat steak?" Lorna asked, misunderstanding her parents overheard conversation.

Kurt kissed her soft cheek. "No, honey, Daddy eat crow."

Lorna made a funny face, and Kurt smiled down at her.

Amanda returned a few minutes later and placed something in his palm. "Do me a favor and wear this, alright? Even if you think it's silly, just humor me."

He glanced down at his open palm at a small gold cross on a chain. "Was this my mother's?" Kurt asked.

Amanda nodded. "I took it out of the box of her things you keep in the closet."

Kurt handed it back to Amanda to clasp around his neck. The chain was so short that he felt like it was choking him. It barely fell past his Adam's apple.

"How bout I just keep it in my pocket, hon. John might laugh if I show up wearing my mother's jewelry," he commented.

Amanda unclasped it and carried it back upstairs. She returned a few minutes later with the cross hanging from a longer chain that belonged to her. She fastened it around his neck, then reached around and tucked it inside his shirt.

"Okay?" she asked.

"Okay," he smiled, and kissed her softly on the lips.

Kurt didn't know it, but he hadn't lied to his wife after all. As soon as Leroy hung up the phone with Richie he went out to the garage and took a piece of leftover plywood he bought last summer to build a birdhouse. He used his power saw to cut it in half then filed the tips of both pieces to razor sharp points. He put the makeshift stakes, plus a Black and Decker rubber-grip hammer in the trunk of his car.

After completing the last minute stakes, he rummaged through the kitchen cabinets until he found an empty jam jar.

Next, Leroy drove to the Our Lady of Perpetual Sorrows Catholic church. He delivered the mail there and was friendly enough with Father Murphy to knock on the rectory door and ask him if he could go into the sanctuary to pray.

Once inside, he was going to lift some holy water. He had concocted a story about his wife misplacing her wedding ring. It was a tale he thought the old man would buy.

Not too long ago, Leroy told the priest about a watch he lost. Father Murphy suggested he pray to Saint Anthony, the patron saint of lost items, to help him find it. Feeling a little foolish but not wanting to insult the old man, Leroy stopped briefly in the sanctuary and mumbled a hurried prayer to the saint. A few days later Leroy found the watch. He told the priest his saint had come through and gave his church a small donation.

When Leroy arrived at the church luck was with him, and telling the old priest a lie wasn't necessary.

There was a wedding reception in progress in the banquet room downstairs and the sanctuary doors stood open. He slid in unnoticed. Taking the empty jar from his pocket, Leroy dipped it into the font and filled it half full with holy water and screwed the lid on tightly.

When Leroy returned to his house he rummaged through Rachel's jewelry box until he found two silver crucifixes. Both had belonged to her mother. One he put around his neck and tucked under his shirt. The cold weight against his chest was comforting. The other he put in his pocket to give to Richie. Looking at his watch and seeing there was still an hour before he needed to leave, Leroy went into the kitchen and heated up a can of soup. He found he wasn't very hungry and ended up throwing most of it down the garbage disposal.

He sat at his kitchen table feeling restless.

Closing his eyes and clasping his hands in front of him, Leroy prayed, "God, if you can hear me and you ain't laughing too hard at what we are planning to do tonight, I hope that you will help us out. I know I haven't much believed in you and probably don't have a right to ask for anything, but the truth is I am scared shi… I mean I am really scared and could use some help tonight. I'm not even sure what it is we are supposed to do if we find this freak of nature, but I guess you will tell us when we cross that bridge, won't you? Anyway, please don't let Richie get hurt, cause Rachel would whoop my a… Uh, Rachel would be real upset, God. Real upset indeed. Thank you."

He started to rise from the chair, then stopped and clasped his hands in front of him once again. "Oh, and just one more thing, God. If someone has gotta use one of them stakes I put in the trunk, please make it be one of the cops. I just don't think I have the stomach. Amen."

CHAPTER 26

John and Ellen ate their pizza in relative silence, neither wanting to talk, both lost in their own reverie about the fate of Francis Barclay.

As they prepared to drive to the Dale's house, Ellen took her purse from the table in the kitchen and slid the bottle of Valium out of the pocket of her jeans. Making sure John was out of sight, she dropped the small plastic vial into her purse and double checked the gun to be sure it was loaded. She zipped the top of the handbag and tucked the strap down against the zipper.

John came downstairs a few minutes later.

"I can't find my car keys, hon. I'll have to use yours." He was reaching for her purse, when she grabbed it off the table and clutched it to her chest. She backed away a few steps, bumping into the kitchen counter. He gave her a questioning look.

Adopting that irritating cheery voice she had been using for the last two days, she answered, "I'll get them for you, dear, you couldn't find anything in this mess," and turned her back on him.

"What mess? Since when is your purse a mess?" he asked, confused by her reaction. Her purse was always neat as a pin, and she had never minded his retrieving anything from it before.

Not being able to think of a reasonable explanation for her reaction, Ellen didn't answer him. She set her purse on the edge of the counter, blocking it from his view with her body. She unzipped it and began fumbling in the pockets for the keys with her good hand. For one terrifying moment she thought the whole purse was going to tumble right off the counter and spill the contents to the floor. She braced it against her cast and shoved it back from the edge. At last her frantic, searching fingers reached under all the loose bullets she had dumped in her bag and touched the metal keys. She grasped the ring and yanked it out. The pills rattled when she jostled the bottle, and she closed her eyes at the sound, which her mind amplified to an ear-splitting degree.

John stood behind her with a bewildered expression on his face at his wife's peculiar behavior.

Ellen zipped up the bag in one violent movement, and slung it over her shoulder as she turned and handed John the keys. Wearing the too bright smile, and in that too bright voice, she said, "Here you go, dear."

He took the key ring from her hand, his eyes never leaving hers. "El? Are you okay?" he asked in a low, worried voice.

"I'm fine, John. Just fine. You spend too much time worrying about me," she answered, flustered. "Now let's go, we don't want to be late."

"We have to wait for Leroy. He should be here any minute." John's wary eyes still stared at her.

Ellen pushed past him out of the kitchen, "Fine. I'm going to brush my hair." Purse still slung over her shoulder, Ellen marched out of the kitchen and ran up the stairs.

SHE'S NOT OKAY! A voice screamed in John's head. *ALL YOU HAVE TO DO IS LISTEN TO HER TALK AND YOU KNOW SHE'S NOT OKAY. SHE'S NOWHERE NEAR OKAY!*

He mentally strong-armed that voice out of his head. He'd deal with it later. Right now he had Francis Barclay to contend with.

Unfortunately so did his wife. But John had no way of knowing that as he watched her storm out of the kitchen.

Leroy pulled up in front of Richie's apartment and blipped the horn twice. When his stepson didn't immediately appear, he grunted. Impatient to be kept waiting, Leroy leaned on the horn again and someone yelled from a window, "Shut up the racket or I'll call the police." Leroy glared at the window and stepped out of his car. His nerves were like live wire. He was fidgety and edgy.

He was hurrying to Richie's door, ready to read him the riot act for making him wait thirty seconds, when the boy strutted from his apartment, cigarette jutting from his lips, and the many buckles on his jacket jangling wildly. His disposition was sour. By way of greeting, he said, "Hold your horses, pops, I was on the can."

Leroy said nothing and climbed back in the car.

Richie slammed the car door, settling into the shotgun seat and stared straight ahead.

Reaching into his pocket, Leroy removed Rachel's mother's cross and handed it to his stepson. "Don't give me no lip, boy. Just put this around your neck and tuck it down into your shirt. If we find the kid, take it out of your shirt and make sure it's visible."

Richie was too pissed off about this whole mess he had been dragged into to even laugh at what he deemed his stepfather's overactive imagination or declining mental factors, he wasn't sure which. He slung the crucifix over his head and dropped it down into his shirt. Never a good idea to argue with the crazy folks he figured, but couldn't resist at least one crack.

"Where's the stake to drive into his heart, man? Don't tell me you forgot the stake, Leroy. You slippin', dude."

"In the trunk. I made two just in case," Leroy answered, his jaw set. He never even turned sideways to see Richie's mouth hanging open and his wide staring eyes.

Richie knew from his tone that Leroy wasn't just having him on. There really were stakes in his trunk. *Poor Mom.* Richie thought. *Another husband gonna bite the dust. Well she never had one that ended up locked in a loony bin before. What a nice change from the guy who beat her with the bat.*

He turned and faced forward again, chain-smoking as they drove in silence, wondering if his whacked out stepdad really was going to try and kill the kid with a stake through the heart. Wouldn't it be ironic, he thought, if he had to stop Leroy from murdering Charity's killer?

When they arrived at the Wyatt's house, Leroy popped the trunk and walked around to the back of his car.

"Uh, hey, Leroy, man, you ain't gonna show those stakes you made to Wyatt are you?" Richie asked in an alarmed voice. "You know, if the cops don't uh… share your opinion that the dude is Dracula or whatever, they might think it's kinda dangerous you carrying those things around. Don't you think?"

"They know exactly who the boy is, Richie. And exactly *what* he is. The only one that hasn't accepted it in this little party is you."

Richie stared at his stepfather, dumbfounded. "Holy shit! The whole fuckin' town has gone utterly loco. Now you got the cops believing this crap?"

Leroy spun around glaring at him. "Let me tell you something, Richie. This whole mission becomes a lot more dangerous for you the longer you keep holdin' onto the belief that all we are dealing with is a troubled teen here. It becomes a lot more dangerous for all of us.

The kid is a vampire. That's what he is, plain and simple. No one is crazy, no one knows how the hell he climbed up out of the grave, and believe me, no one wants to believe it's happening. Least of all me. So get your head out of your lily-white ass and wrap your mind any way you can around what we gotta do. And do it now, cause there ain't no more adjustment time left. You got it, son?" Leroy raged.

Carrying the stakes in one hand and the hammer in the other, he checked his pocket for the holy water and started up the steps to John and Ellen Wyatt's front door, leaving a frazzled Richie staring open-mouthed at him by the car.

Amanda set out a platter of cheese and crackers for them to nibble on. She opened up a bottle of chardonnay, and set two crystal wine glasses on the coffee table next to the bottle. There were also a few videos out on the coffee table for Ellen to choose from. The night ahead promised to be a long one, and she thought they could use the distraction of a good film.

She argued with Kurt about not telling Ellen the truth regarding Francis Barclay, but agreed that anymore strain between them and John was not a good idea right now, so she promised to remain silent about the killer's suspected identity. It frustrated her not to have Ellen to discuss this with, but when the Wyatts' arrived and she saw how Ellen was acting, she realized early in the evening that even if she could have told her, "Rational Ellen" had gone bye-bye, and the new and not so improved Ellen wouldn't have had much to add to the discussion anyway.

When John rang the doorbell she saw Leroy and Richie standing a few feet away on her front walk, looking nervous with their hands thrust in their pockets like they were waiting to meet the parents of a first date. She cast a worried glance toward Kurt, but he had been growing increasingly restless as the minutes crawled by and was already shrugging into his coat, anxious to get on with the night ahead.

Ellen just stood in the foyer with this loopy grin on her face like they were going to a party. John kissed his wife's slack cheek and Amanda could swear she saw her grimace.

The night began to take on a very surreal quality at that moment for Amanda. She felt like she had just stepped into a funhouse, where the mirrors distort everything. Nothing could possibly be as it seemed. Her husband and the others couldn't possibly be going out tonight looking for the boogie man, and Ellen couldn't possibly be standing in her doorway looking like an escaped mental patient, flinching when her beloved husband kissed her. None of this could really be happening. She shuddered when Kurt told her not to worry and gave her a quick peck on the cheek. She begged him to be careful, but he was already closing the door on her words.

Without a single glance or word of greeting to the baby, which was very unlike her, Ellen walked past Lorna playing on the floor and sat on the couch. She tucked her purse against the sofa pillow next to her and leaned against it.

Amanda sighed and sat down next to her. As she began pouring the wine, Ellen held up a hand. "None for me thanks, but you go ahead."

"Oh, okay. Do you want a soda or something?"

The bright smile that never made it quite to the eyes lit Ellen's face. "Oh, a Diet Coke would be great, Mandy, thanks!"

Amanda gave a small nervous laugh as she rose from the sofa for Ellen's soda. "For a minute there you sounded like a commercial for the stuff."

Ellen's unusually loud laugh caused Amanda to cast a concerned look over her shoulder as she disappeared into the kitchen to get the drink.

Ellen waited until she heard the refrigerator door open, then she opened her purse and removed the pills. Working with only one good hand, the bottle fell and landed on her lap. She checked over her shoulder to make sure Amanda was still in the kitchen, and managed to get the cap off the bottle with her teeth. She shook two of the pills into her palm, hesitated and added one more. She dropped them into Amanda's wine glass. Replacing the lid on the bottle, she shoved it back into her purse. She stuck her finger in the glass and swirled it around a few times, sloshing wine over the rim of the glass onto the coffee table. The pills were fizzing in the pale liquid and Ellen looked on with horrified fascination as they continued to bubble wildly as Amanda walked back into the room, popping the tab on a can of soda. Ellen reached down and made a quick swipe at the spilled liquid with her sleeve, as Amanda plucked the empty wine glass from the table and poured Ellen's soda into it.

The fizzing was still faintly visible in her glass and the wine looked cloudy, but Amanda never even looked at it. She made herself comfortable again on the sofa, tucking her legs under her and began munching on a cracker. She pushed the tray toward Ellen, who shook her head and demurely sipped her soda.

Amanda took a small swallow of wine and replaced it on the table.

"Is it not good?" Ellen asked her, her eyes felt too big in her head.

"No, it's fine. Why?"

"Oh, nothing, you just took such a small little sip I thought maybe it didn't taste right or something," Ellen rambled.

"El, what's the matter? You are acting very strange." Amanda took another small drink from her glass.

"Why does everyone keep asking me that? I mean it's been a tough week, Amanda, you should know that. And now our husbands are out on some secret squirrel mission. I'm just a little stressed is all," she said in an exasperated tone that made the baby stop playing with her doll and look up.

"Stressed," the baby squawked and giggled at Amanda. "Auntie El has stressed, Momma."

Lorna was at the age where she was parroting what people said. Amanda, as her mother, thought it was the cutest thing in the world. She burst out laughing and took another drink of wine.

Ellen grinned like an idiot and watched as Amanda drained half of her glass.

The four men said little as they piled into John's car. Kurt rode up front, Leroy and Richie climbed in the back seat, sitting as far apart from each other as they could manage in the cramped sedan.

Neither John nor Kurt were overjoyed that Leroy dragged Richie along with them. Even after Leroy explained he thought it would be better to have someone along that knew the lay of the land, neither man trusted Richie Welch. And both felt that the fewer people that knew about Francis Barclay the better.

After John pulled away from the curb, Richie said, "So tell me something, Detective Wyatt. Are we looking to kill this kid or just arrest him?"

Kurt and John exchanged alarmed glances. "Richie, how much has Leroy told you about him?" John asked.

"Well, I was afraid if I told you that, you would think he was a lunatic. But when you saw the stakes he made and said that might be a good idea, I figure you don't think he's off his rocker after all. So, why don't you tell me what you think, Detective Wyatt, okay?"

Kurt turned in his seat, and said to Leroy, "You brought stakes? I'm glad. My wife thought we should bring one. I hope we don't need it, but I feel relieved that someone brought one just in case."

Reaching into his pocket and extracting the jam jar, Leroy replied, "I crashed a wedding at Our Lady of Perpetual Sorrow and got us some holy water too. I'm wearing a cross. I would have brought extras for everyone, but my wife only has two and I gave one to Richie."

Kurt reached under his shirt, pulling out the small crucifix Amanda had fastened at his throat, and showed it to Leroy, who nodded approval.

"How about you John?" Leroy asked.

John reached under his jacket and took his gun from the holster. "I brought this. It's all the protection I think we are going to need."

Richie was growing more worried by the second, realizing that whatever the cops believed, they fully intended to kill the kid if they found him.

"Wyatt, you didn't answer my question," Richie snapped.

"What was your question? What do I think? Yes, I think he's a vampire," John nodded, and stared at Richie in the rear view mirror.

"And obviously you think so too, that right, Dale?" Richie demanded, glaring at Kurt.

Kurt nodded, "Yep, pretty much."

"Well I will tell you all right now, I will help you find your way around the trailer park and into the woods behind it, but I will have no part in hurting that kid no matter what he did or who you all think he is. I'm a convicted felon in case you boys have forgotten and I have no intention of going back to the slammer for anyone. I'm just here as a tour guide. I will show you around then I'm outta there. You got that?"

"Fine by me," John said quickly, and Kurt nodded his agreement.

"To be honest, I wouldn't mind taking you home right now, Richie, I think we can manage the terrain okay on our own." John was unable to mask his hostility toward the boy.

"Yeah…" Richie began, but Leroy interrupted him.

Whipping his head back and forth, Leroy fumed, "No way. He's coming. He knows that place like the back of his hand and we need him. If he goes home so do I, and I call your Captain first thing in the morning, John."

Hearing the stubborn insistence in Leroy's voice and seeing it in his eyes as they glowered at him in the rear view mirror, John relented. They drove the rest of the way in tense silence.

Richie was itching for a cigarette, but afraid to light one in the detective's car. He wondered, and not for the first time, why, no matter how hard he tried to avoid it, trouble followed him and clung like a magnet.

CHAPTER 27

Amanda's head felt like it weighed a hundred pounds. Her mind felt stuffed with cotton. Her eyelids heavy, tongue thick, and the room had taken on a greenish cast. Ellen refilled her wine glass twice, depositing two more of the Valium into it when Amanda went to the bathroom.

"Ellen," she mumbled, "I think something's the matter with me. Don't feel right."

Ellen watched her for a few moments and then slid off the couch. "Here, why don't you lay down." She helped Amanda stretch out her long legs onto the sofa and put a pillow behind her head.

"Feel so dizzy," Amanda muttered.

Ellen didn't answer. Just watched her with cold, speculative eyes and glanced at her watch. She was disturbed to see it was already after eleven.

When she was sure Amanda had passed out, she tiptoed toward the kitchen where the Dales' kept the spare keys to their Jeep. Just as Ellen turned her back, Amanda slurred, "El, don't leave me. Don't feel good. The baby. Where Lorna?"

Ellen sighed, exasperated. "This is taking too damn long," she snarled. "Baby's fine, Amanda, everything's fine. Now go to sleep, would you."

"Can't sleep… The baby…" she trailed off, at last losing consciousness.

Ellen looked at the baby playing on the floor and a war of conflicting emotions crossed her face. The last semblance of sanity from somewhere far below the surface told her she couldn't leave the baby alone with a passed out mother and no one to mind her. She stood undecided for a few moments, then swept the baby up in her good arm, striking Lorna's stomach on the hard cast. The baby gave a startled squawk and started crying.

"Momma," she wailed, and held her arms out to the slumbering figure on the couch.

"Mom went night-night. Want to go for a ride with Auntie Ellen?" Ellen crowed in a jovial, loud voice that served only in making the baby cry even harder. She shifted the squalling child on her hip as she walked into the kitchen and plucked the key ring from the hook.

When they arrived at Happy Wheels, the four men sat silent in the idling car. John pulled onto the soft shoulder just outside the gates.

Richie opened his door, grumbling, "Well, come on. Let's get this over with." He climbed from the car, boots crunching on the gravel, and began jingling his way into the mobile home park.

John killed the engine and that got the other two men going. Richie was in the lead and the other three men followed in a tight cluster a few feet behind.

When Richie stopped to light a cigarette, he turned around and glared at his companions. "So, where do you want to start?" He was relieved to see that no one had bothered to take the stakes from the trunk of the detective's car, and he had no intention of reminding them.

John pointed toward the back of the small development. "By Norma's old place."

Richie nodded and started jingling his way down the street again, a glowing Camel clamped between his lips. He stopped a few feet in front of Norma's trailer and waited for the three men to join him.

"We got company," he remarked, nodding toward a patrol car parked against the curb in front of the crime scene tape, with one loose end fluttering in the breeze.

John told the other men to wait there and approached the black and white. He rapped sharply on the window, startling its occupant out of a doze. The young officer was embarrassed to be caught napping by a detective, which suited John just fine. An embarrassed cop wasn't likely to tell anyone about the detective that told him to take off from his assigned post. At least not right away.

Kurt watched uneasily as John and the young officer exchanged a few words. Moments later the patrol car roared to life and pulled away from the curb.

"What did you tell him?" Kurt asked.

"That we were here to go over the crime scene again." "He didn't find that unusual this late at night?" Kurt asked skeptically.

"He's more worried about my telling his lieutenant he was sleeping than he is about what we're doing here. I told him to take a break and go get some coffee and that I'd radio him when we were through."

Kurt nodded, satisfied.

The four men climbed over the flapping crime scene tape and walked single file into Norma's backyard. Kurt shined a flashlight into the kitchen window. He said in a doubtful voice, "He isn't going to be stupid enough to come back here."

Richie barked a nervous cough. "I ain't going in there."

John cast an annoyed glance his way. "No one asked you to. Come on, Kurt, let's make sure it's clean and keep moving." He turned to Leroy. "Wait out here and let us know if anyone shows up."

"Like who?" Leroy looked startled, and noticed for the first time that they forgot to bring the stakes with them.

"Anyone," John answered in a curt tone and produced a small ring from his pocket. On it were three keys marked with tape. He trained his flashlight down, selected the key he wanted and slid it into the doorknob.

As the two detectives disappeared inside, Richie lit another cigarette with hands that weren't quite steady. He offered one to Leroy, who shook his head.

"Who's he expecting?" Richie asked.

"I don't know. The killer I guess. Maybe another cop nosing around. One of those fibbies."

"Fine, you can alert him to any unwanted guests if you like, but we see anyone and I'm hauling ass out of here." Richie pulled a long drag off of his cigarette.

Leroy looked around anxiously and thought maybe Richie had the right idea after all.

Strapping the baby into the SUV's car seat with only one hand was a challenge, and by the time it was accomplished Ellen's arm was throbbing dully in the cast. She was sweating and breathing hard. The baby was crying in big braying whoops that set Ellen's teeth on edge. She scooped up a toy from the floor of the backseat and thrust it into Lorna's hand. It did little to placate the screaming child, who didn't even spare the toy a glance before flinging it hard into the front seat.

Ellen hoisted herself into the driver's side, afraid the baby's cries would wake up the entire neighborhood. She adjusted the seat to accommodate her cast and pulled out of the driveway as fast as she could.

"Quit crying, Lorna. I can't even hear myself think," she yelled.

The baby continued to squall, until finally her troubled cries became little breathy moans and she fell asleep.

Grateful for the quiet, Ellen drove on in silence. She ran the Jeep up over a curb while trying to negotiate a turn, sparing a nervous fleeting look into the rear view mirror, afraid she had woken Lorna. The baby continued to snore softly, tears drying on her cheeks.

As they expected, Norma's trailer was empty. When the two detectives emerged from the back door, Richie walked to the edge of the yard and opened a small wooden gate which opened on to the woods beyond.

"Come on," he groaned in a resigned voice, and led the three men into the thick belt of trees surrounding the mobile home park. "There's a foot path this way."

"Wait," Leroy cried.

They all froze. Kurt whispered, "What is it? You see something?"

"No. We forgot the stakes. I left them in the damn trunk."

John shrugged. "It's too late to worry about that now. There's no time to go back." He started forward again, ignoring Leroy's worried face.

As they walked deeper into the forest, pale circles of light bobbed from the flashlights held out before them. They were unaware that from only a few yards to their right, a silent, brooding figure watched their every step.

When Ellen arrived at Happy Wheels, she swung the Jeep in behind her husband's police issue sedan and doused the headlights. She turned around to look at the sleeping child.

"Christ, what the hell am I going to do now?" she cried in frustration, banging her fist on the steering wheel. "You're gonna sleep, right baby? Just gonna take a nice long nappypoo for Auntie Ellen, aren't you?"

She opened her purse on the seat beside her and shoved a handful of bullets into the front pocket of her jeans. She pulled the bottle of tranquilizers out and considered giving one to Lorna. Shaking her head she dropped the vial back into her purse. Unlocking the safety on the gun, she jammed it into her waistband. One wrong twitch and she could have easily shot off her foot, but the danger of an unlocked pistol shoved in her pants never crossed Ellen's tortured mind. She looked around at the abandoned street and cast a final uncomfortable glance at the baby. Leaving the keys in the ignition and the doors unlocked, she climbed out of the Cherokee.

Francis Barclay waited until the men were far out of sight and down the path leading into the woods before he started back toward the street. He could still see the pale circlets of light cast by their flashlights bobbing ahead, but they were growing fainter. The men's voices grew more distant as they reached Francis's ears in snatches through the trees. With his usual eerily quiet strides, Barclay crossed the darkened street and started for the gates at the entrance to the park.

The sound of approaching footsteps stopped him cold. His head came up like a deer that senses hunters in the woods. He darted quickly behind the trailer just south of the one he was staying in, and waited until the approaching figure was illuminated by a streetlight.

Seeing who it was, he shifted from foot to foot, undecided if he should charge her. He was still frightened of the woman's freakish strength. His hand went absently to the gash at his forehead, a wound inflicted by this very woman. Feeling the raw flap of decomposing skin wasn't reason enough to hesitate. Seeing the gun sticking out of her jeans was.

Ellen stopped in the middle of the roadway and looked around. She had no idea where to begin searching and she didn't want to be confronted by her husband. She was looking almost directly at Francis as he hunkered down on his haunches, trying to avoid being detected. After a moment she set off in the direction of Norma's trailer.

Francis, breathing a sigh of relief, quietly slid back into the shadows and snuck through the backyards of the sleeping residents toward the main gates of the Happy Wheels Mobile Estates, where John's car and Kurt's stolen Jeep with his sleeping child sat on the shoulder of the road.

CHAPTER 28

Russell Coombs switched off the TV and crushed one final can of Budweiser in his fist. Rising from his easy chair, he climbed awkwardly to his feet, stumbling a little.

His dog looked at him with amused eyes. *Poor daddy.*

He took her leash from the hook and fastened it to Samantha's collar. Depositing the can into the recycle bin, Russell led Samantha through the garage and out the side door leading onto the woods behind the house he shared with Darlene.

His previous experience there was long since forgotten, in his nearly continuous drunken haze.

Russell saw his neighbor's taillights receding down the road. The brake lights winked briefly at the stop sign on the corner.

"Li'l late for a drive is'nit?" he asked Samantha.

The dog gave an answering bark, and the two of them went off for their nightly stroll.

In the house next door, Amanda slept on. At one point she thought she heard the front door slam and the sound of their Cherokee's engine idling in the driveway, but these sounds came to her from very far away. Back from somewhere in that same distant land she also heard the disquieting echo of her daughter crying, and in her drugged near-coma, she murmured to the deserted house, "Baby cryin,' Kurt go Lorna." But no one was there to hear her faint whispering voice.

Many minutes later, her left hand slipped from her chest and banged sharply against the coffee table, knocking the half empty wine bottle to the floor. Blood bloomed from beneath the bandage on her ring finger.

And Amanda slept on.

The four men had traveled nearly half a mile into the woods behind Norma's trailer. Leroy was terrified. The way the flashlights jumped on the path in front of them reminded him of a movie he saw a couple years back. The Blair Witch Project, it had been. He started to open his mouth to mention this to his companions, but thought better of it.

They shone their flashlights in great arcs looking for any sign of where Francis Barclay had been keeping camp. A blanket, food wrappers, his jacket. Anything to provide a clue of his whereabouts. They found nothing, and frustrated they turned to go back. They still had a lot of ground to cover and decided if they didn't see some residue of where the boy might be hiding after a half mile then they probably were looking in the wrong direction.

The dense woods surrounded Happy Wheels Mobile Estates on three sides. They were literally looking for a needle in a haystack. Yet none doubted the boy was somewhere close at hand. John especially felt it.

They retraced their steps, Richie pushing his long hair back from his sweaty face, and the rising wind sending it relentlessly back into his eyes. Ellen heard faint voices approaching as she lifted one foot over the loose crime scene tape at the front of Norma's yard. She hastily yanked her leg back over the tape, catching her heel on the unfastened end. She darted across the street, unmindful of the tape now stuck to the bottom of her shoe, following behind, and marking her course better than a trail of breadcrumbs. She dashed around the back of the rundown trailer Richie and Rachel used to call home, blissfully unaware of who it currently housed. Her heart hammering in her chest, Ellen held her breath as she heard her husband's voice from less than twenty feet away.

"What the hell is this?" John asked, bending down to pick up the crime scene tape, now stretched across the narrow lane and disappearing somewhere beyond the side of the trailer where his wife stood pressed against the dirty siding.

Ellen felt a tug on her foot as her husband lifted the tape. Her blood ran cold when she saw what had happened. Tearing the bright yellow tape from her tennis shoe, she tip-toed up the ramshackle back steps.

Seeing the place pitch-black and obviously abandoned, she tried the door. She exhaled a relieved breath when the knob turned easily in her grasp.

Stepping into the tomb-like darkness of the dank trailer, Ellen felt her way through the gloom with an outstretched hand. She scuttled through the darkened hallway into the burned out master bedroom. Groping her way along the wall until she came to a sliding closet door. She slid it open, climbing inside bare seconds before a flashlight shone in through the window.

Four pairs of eyes pressed against the filthy glass. Richie felt long forgotten memories stab at his heart and backed away. Leroy looked at him nervously.

"What's wrong?" he whispered.

"Nothin'," Richie mumbled, turning away as unexpected tears stung his eyes.

In a soft voice, Leroy remarked, "Nothin' like old home week, huh?" He clamped a hand on Richie's shoulder and left him to compose himself.

John's flashlight was trained on the center of the burned out room and Kurt's light swept it from side to side. They saw nothing. Neither man noted the closet door standing half open on its track. They walked around the front of the trailer, everyone's nerves heightened to a sizzle. Each man sure the foot which dragged the loose crime scene tape across the narrow road belonged to none other than Francis Barclay.

Francis Barclay left everyone who was searching for him behind and lurched out from the rear yard of Mr. and Mrs. Jerry Harper's trailer, unmindful of the argument that raged within, regarding exactly where Jerry had been all night.

He saw the two vehicles parked at the shoulder but didn't spare them a second glance. He was several yards up the hill and headed toward the Dale's home. He had no intention of trying to take the two detectives down while they were in a group. Instead, Francis's thoughts turned to Kurt's pretty wife and his young daughter.

Nearly far enough away that he might have missed it, Barclay heard a faint but audible sound carried by the rising wind. A baby crying. It reached his ears, dim but unmistakable. He stopped and turned around. Seeing no one on the deserted street, he knew immediately the sound was coming from one of the two cars which his pursuers left on the shoulder of the road. A small grin parted his lips as he started back down the hill, unaware that his thick mysteriously black blood was once again flowing from his injured testicle. It ran down his leg, pooling in his shoe. He was further unaware that with every breath, he was inhaling and exhaling a black bloody bubble from his right nostril.

Ellen was breathing in short little gasps, terrified they had seen her. From her place in the closet she was blind. She felt like a cornered animal. She took the gun from her waistband and held it in her trembling good hand.

The four men went around each side of the house, looking into the few windows not covered by decaying curtains. Seeing nothing but a sad and dirty forgotten trailer, they tried the front door. Finding it unlocked, they entered.

John was in the lead, his gun drawn. The other three men clustered tight behind him on the leaning steps. Richie was pulling up the rear. When the two detectives and his stepfather turned left into the kitchen, Richie switched off his flashlight and turned right, silently walking down the hallway which led to the bedrooms. He needed no light to chart his course, he knew this hallway intimately.

Once inside his old home, a feeling of loss and sadness so great that it overshadowed his fear of what he might find, carried him down the hall toward old memories. The smells were now damp and moldy but still familiar. Tears began to fall as he navigated the old and well known corridor easily in the dark.

None of his three companions noticed his absence. He stepped into his old bedroom, switching on the flashlight again. Something caught his eye. He ran his hand over a small ripped flap of paper covered in time-yellowed tape, clinging to the dark paneling. It was the corner of an old Harley Davidson poster he displayed above his bed when he was a child. When he took the poster down it ripped, and that one small corner had never been removed. After all these years it was still affixed to the moldering panel. A lonely torn reminder of a childhood better forgotten.

The three men in the front of the house were still unaware that Richie wasn't with them, as they stared astonished at the littered living room and kitchen. Having at last found Francis Barclay's hiding place, they were horrified to learn that he had been right under their noses all along, and probably watching every move that went on in the trailer across the street.

Richie used a fingernail to pry the old tape from the wall. He put the torn corner of the poster into his pocket. He walked slowly down the rest of the hallway to the bedroom his mother once slept in, now nothing but a burnt out putrefying shell. His mind had turned back to a time some fifteen years before when that room smelled of his mother's perfume, stale booze and cigarettes. The tears were flowing freely now.

From her hiding place, Ellen could hear heavy footsteps approaching. She pulled herself up to her knees and wriggled even further into the corner of the closet, terrified that within seconds she would be face to face with her furious husband. Or worse, that he would try and stop her from what she came to do.

The bedroom door squeaked as a hand swung it open. The sound nearly caused Ellen to fire the gun. She saw a flashlight flicker across the wall and nearly screamed. Catching the shadow's figure in the pale light of the flashlight froze the scream in her throat. Ellen leveled the gun against her cast, watching the shadow's long stringy hair and big jacket walk into the room.

Without another thought, she rose from the floor in one lithe movement. A movement that Francis Barclay would have recognized, and emerged from the closet firing the gun repeatedly.

CHAPTER 29

Lorna stopped crying when she saw the deep aquamarine eyes staring at her through the window. She pointed at the boy's face, sniffling.

"Blue." She proclaimed. Then turned her chubby fingers toward her own eyes, and said, "Mine blue too. See?"

Francis's hand was cupped against the glass to block the glare from the brightly lit streetlamp standing directly over the Jeep. He looked with amazement at the unattended child. Trying the rear door handle, he was further amazed to find it unlocked.

He stretched forward, opening his mouth over Lorna's neck when the baby reached her arms up and wiggled her fingers in a "take me outta here" gesture.

"Out," the baby demanded.

Francis paused.

Lorna looked at him with a puzzled expression. One that said, *Don't you know what out means, Bozo?* She wrinkled her nose, and complained, "You need diaper change."

He was so startled that he actually put his hand to his mouth and barked a brief, rusty laugh.

Lorna gave him an answering giggle, and waving her outstretched fingers even more urgently, she commanded the stranger to take her out again.

Barclay knew he should finish this. Time was short. He heard gunfire and knew the sound of approaching sirens couldn't be far behind. He wanted to get out of here. He could take care of the child, then go and take care of Dale's wife. But when he leaned over Lorna again, opening his jaws, he couldn't bring himself to sink his fangs into this tiny trusting being's neck.

As if arguing with himself, trying to justify this uncharacteristic display of emotion he was experiencing, he said out loud, "Don't need to kill the kid. Keep her for insurance."

He fumbled with the clasp of her car seat, but couldn't release it. He threw anxious looks over his shoulder, afraid at any moment someone was going to come back for the baby. Surely no one would leave her for very long in an unlocked and unattended car this late at night. He pressed his thumb repeatedly over the catch, but it stubbornly kept hold.

Exasperated, Lorna said, in a very grown-up impatient voice, "Dat way," and waved her little hand to the left. "Gotta go dat way."

The boy pressed the catch to the left, the direction Lorna indicated with her tiny, chubby fingers. It sprang free.

The moment it unlatched, Lorna reached up and pushed the top of the seat over her head, with the well-practiced ease of a veteran who had performed the maneuver many times before. She climbed easily into the boy's arms.

Francis took off sprinting down the street with the baby holding onto his neck and giggling.

The gunshots were earsplitting in the small trailer, but it took the men several seconds to react, so preoccupied were they with what they had found.

"Oh, sweet Jesus, where's Richie?" Leroy wailed and took off running down the hallway toward the sound of the gunfire.

The woman nearly knocked him over as she barreled out of the rear bedroom.

"I KILLED HIM!" she screamed triumphantly. "I KILLED THE BASTARD!"

She continued yelling as she ran out into the living room and grabbed her husband's arm. "DO YOU HEAR ME, YOU INEPT BASTARD? ME, I DID IT! I KILLED HIM AND HE'S GONE!!"

Like a man waking from a nightmare, John stared into his crazed wife's eyes, and whispered, "Oh, Ellen, what have you done?"

Kurt shoved past both of them and ran down the dark hall. He stopped short, nearly falling over Leroy's kneeling body.

Leroy held his dead stepson in his arms and wept.

Kurt cried, "Oh, no. Oh, dear god, no." He backed away from the dreadful vision of the bullet-riddled form, and the weeping man beside it.

The first bullet nearly took off half of Richie's head, killing him instantly. The four additional bullets Ellen fired into his lifeless corpse weren't even necessary. The room stank of a mixture of gun-powder and blood.

Stunned, Kurt stumbled back into the living room. He looked from his partner to the hysterical woman who kept screaming over and over again, "I DID IT! I KILLED HIM!"

He grabbed her by the shoulders and shook. "You stupid bitch. You killed Richie Welch. That's who you killed. That's what you did," Kurt's voice cracked through her screams.

Ellen's mouth slammed shut in the middle of the chant. She looked at Kurt with frightened uncomprehending eyes.

"Wha?" she whispered.

"Richie Welch, that's who you shot, Ellen. Why? Why did you do this? Why are you even out here?"

She whipped her head back forth wildly, and bellowed, "No, no, no, no, no! It was the killer. It was the filthy, murdering bastard that attacked me."

"No it wasn't, Ellen. It was Richie. Richie Welch is dead. You shot him," Kurt croaked in a voice, barely above a whisper, and sank to his knees on the dirty floor.

Ellen looked at the still smoking gun dangling from her fingers, and dropped it. She backed out of the trailer's front door, staring from her husband's shocked white face to his partner, now crumpled on the floor with his hands covering his face. All the while her head whipped back and forth in that negative gesture of denial, as she kept repeating, "No, no, no," and staggered down the steps.

Emitting an agonized, piercing howl that sounded far less human than anything Francis Barclay could have produced, Ellen Wyatt fled down the street.

John watched her go with dazed eyes. He made no move to stop her or go after her. His knees went out from under him and he landed on the floor next to his partner. He reached out with a shaking hand and grabbed Kurt's shoulder.

"What do we do?" he barked. "A civilian is dead. One that we brought with us on official police business."

Kurt looked at his partner with incredulous eyes, and climbing to his feet, he whispered, "A civilian, John? Official police business? Do you even realize that your wife just murdered Richie Welch in cold blood?"

Kurt was stunned by the completely insane twist this doomed mission had taken. How did everything turn so bad so quickly?

"It was a mistake," John cried, "Just a terrible misunderstanding. Ellen wouldn't do something like this."

Kurt stared at him with loathing and said nothing.

"Don't you see, it was self-defense! She had no choice," John shrieked.

Kurt glared at him with murderous rage and John recoiled as if he'd been struck.

Kurt returned down the hall to Leroy. The first distant wails of police sirens could be heard in the distance.

He pulled Leroy up by the arm. "You gotta get out of here, buddy. Right now, out the back."

Leroy yanked his arm back and buried his face in Richie's blood-soaked chest. "Get away. Get away. I never should have made him come," he wept.

"Listen to me, Leroy. Do you want Rachel to lose a husband as well as a son?"

That quieted his sobs. He glared at Kurt through narrowed eyes. "What are you saying?"

"Do you hear those sirens? That's the entire Alder Lake Police Department responding to probably six or seven calls to 911 from people in this trailer park who heard gunfire. If they find you here with us, and Richie dead, they are going to want a helluva lot of explanations about why he was here in the first place. Do you want to tell them you forced him to come with us? Because of your goddamn insistence he's dead! Leroy, go home, and keep your mouth shut about what happened here tonight."

With dawning horror, Leroy slowly climbed to his feet. Kurt held him by the elbow until he was sure the man could stand on his own.

"Go now. Out the back way, you hear me? No one ever has to know you were here tonight at all," he paused, and said, "Not even Rachel. If you're smart, you will tell her you changed your mind and never went with us at all."

With shaking hands, Leroy swiped at his streaming cheeks. He gave Kurt a final baleful look and hurried out the back door of the trailer without looking back.

Kurt felt sick with shame over what he'd just done. He knew there would come a day when he would have to face the truth. He forced Leroy to run, not for Leroy's sake alone, but to protect himself and John from the repercussions of bringing civilians with them to find Francis Barclay, and the tragic catastrophe the plan had borne.

If anyone found out Leroy and Richie were with them, their careers were over. As it was, they probably already were. But Kurt was going to try and climb out of this as unscathed as he possibly could. And right now, for the first time that Kurt could remember, John had a lot more to lose than he did.

Kurt watched through the window until Leroy was out of sight, then sighed and went back to the living room where John still sat on the floor with dazed and uncomprehending eyes.

"Get up, John. We got company." Kurt grimaced as the first blue and red revolving lights illuminated through the dingy curtains.

He helped John to his feet, hissing, "Don't say one fuckin' word. Just let me do the talking."

"Kurt, please don't say anything about Ellen. Please," John pleaded.

"Just pull yourself together and keep your mouth shut. And for God sakes, get that fuckin' deer caught in the headlights look off your face," Kurt barked.

He bent down and swept up the gun Ellen dropped. He wiped it clean of prints on the back of his sweatshirt and engaged the safety. He shoved it into his left sock and shook his pant leg over it.

He was suddenly furious with John. The comment he had made that day in the coffee shop about not being able to "rein in" Amanda came back to him with bitter irony.

Staring at his partner with cold angry eyes, Kurt spat, "I think this should stamp 'paid in full' to anything you might think I owe you for ever covering for me during one of my extra-marital dalliances, or getting my ass out of a sling. Just remember that when this shit-storm is over, buddy."

John's eyes flashed with hurt.

The first units were arriving. Kurt met them at the front door. It wasn't until several minutes later, after the first string of lies were passed around, that he remembered Ellen was supposed to be in his house with his wife and daughter before she showed up at Happy Wheels to take matters into her own hands. That was when the first traces of real panic started nibbling at the base of Kurt's spine.

Ellen heard the approaching sirens. She hid behind the fence of someone's backyard. The trailer park had sprung to life when the commotion started. Miraculously no one saw her fleeing down the street. But her scream was heard, and people dressed in night clothes were now stepping cautiously onto their front steps to see what all the commotion was about. With puffy tired faces, they watched with fascination as the police cars crowded in front of the old abandoned trailer, revolving lights bathing the street in an eerie red and blue glow.

Ellen sat on her haunches behind the fence watching the activity and listening to the mad cacophony of sirens as they wailed past. For several minutes after the last police car zoomed by, she stayed paralyzed in her hiding place.

What finally got her moving was the porch light coming on above her, and a round frightened face peering into the dark, calling, "Who's out there? Is someone there?"

Ellen slunk back into the shadows. Shaking, she climbed to her hands and knees and crawled out of the yard. She pulled herself up in one very un-Ellenlike, graceless motion, on legs that didn't want to support her weight, and she nearly went down face first. She would have landed in the dirt had she not clung to the fence to steady herself.

After several seconds, Ellen staggered drunkenly from the trailer park's main gates and lurched into the driver's seat of Kurt and Amanda's Cherokee. She flooded the engine on her first two tries to start it. On the third try she kept her foot off the gas and managed to fire the engine. Ellen pulled the Jeep around in a wide arc, driving straight up onto the curb on the other side, before righting the vehicle and facing the direction that would take her back toward Amanda's.

"Sorry, baby," she moaned in a small, tear-choked voice, and looked into the rear view mirror. "We're gonna go home now and see Mommy and…" her words trailed off when she saw the empty car seat.

She slammed on the brakes, and shrieked, "LORNA!!! LORNA, WHERE ARE YOU?"

Ellen jammed the gearshift into park and jumped from the seat. She ran around to the passenger side, yanking open the back door.

Her heart thundering violently, she put her hand on the empty car seat and looked onto the floor, hoping the baby somehow managed to free herself and crawled down there on her own.

She spun around, looking wildly up the well-lit road. On numb, barely functioning legs, Ellen staggered over and looked first into the windows of John's car, then underneath it.

Jerry Harper walked out his front door. Seeing a harried blonde woman in a cast, crouching down and looking under the car, he approached her.

"Did you lose something, Miss? Can I help?"

Ellen screamed and ran from the sound of his voice. She stumbled back to the Jeep.

Burning rubber, she sped away from Happy Wheels. She drove on without seeing where she was going. She knocked over a stop sign and a few blocks later took out a traffic light at an intersection. How fortunate for her that there was not a single officer in the entire city available to cite her. They were all at the trailer park she had just fled, listening to Detective Dale explain the dead man in the back bedroom.

CHAPTER 30

Francis Barclay was breathing laboriously by the time they exited city park into the quiet neighborhood, with its rows of neatly maintained houses. Carrying the additional weight of the child caused his frail legs to become progressively weaker, and a low, dull ache deep in his back added to his torment. He was fighting for every gasp of air. He stopped at the edge of Lombard Street to catch his breath, and shifted the baby's weight to the other side.

"I'm hungry," the baby said when he stopped walking.

He reached into his jacket pocket and extracted a Hostess Twinkie. He tore the cellophane wrapper off and handed it to the child.

She smiled her sunny smile. Finishing all but the last bite, she handed it back to him, saying, "I share. This for you."

He felt tears sting his eyes as he ate the offered piece of cake the baby held in her chubby fist.

They began walking again and Lorna watched the bubble of blood expand out of his nostril and burst. Black oily fluid began to trickle from his nose.

She asked, "You got a owwie?"

He nodded, and croaked, "I got several."

He grimaced at the squishy sound his right shoe made every time it hit the pavement. The viscous fluid poured from his wounded testicle. His pant leg was wet and stuck to his skin. Both his sock and shoe were sodden with blood.

Despite Francis Barclay's pain, he couldn't help but smile when Lorna spoke to him. He couldn't remember feeling any emotion other than hatred since returning to Alder Lake. His fleeting moment of unfulfilled lust toward Charity Ash not withstanding, he was awed to find himself growing more and more attached, and feeling more and more protective of this little girl with each moment that passed.

Lorna leaned forward. "I kiss it better for you," and she smacked a noisy kiss onto the tip of his nose. She reached up and delicately dabbed the smear of inky dark blood from his upper lip, then wiped her fingers on her blouse. Examining her hand and seeing that a small swipe of black still remained, she started to stick her fingers into her mouth.

She gaped in surprise when the boy grabbed her tiny fist in his dirty hand, crying, "Don't do that!"

The alarm in his corroded voice was unmistakable, but she yanked her hand back, and said in that strangely adult tone she could adopt, "It's dirty." And before he could stop her, she jammed the fingers into her mouth and sucked the bloody smudge off.

Francis closed his eyes in horror. "Oh no," he whispered, and lifted the baby's fingers to look at them.

She re-examined her hand with him and nodded. "See, all clean now." She slung her arm back companionably around his shoulder.

Francis began limping up the road again, a troubled frown creasing his brow.

Surely she didn't get enough to hurt her, enough to cause any damage...any change, he thought.

Russell Coombs wove his slow careful way out of the field, stopping occasionally to let Samantha sniff the shrubs and overgrown hedges. He was just stepping onto the little dirt path which led to his backyard when he heard the sound of the neighbor's baby talking. Curious of who would have the little girl out at this late hour, he walked around to the front of his house and stopped at the sidewalk.

When he looked up, his heart froze in his chest. There was a scraggly stranger holding Lorna and walking unsteadily toward the Dale's house. There was a single line of black slimy footprints behind them.

Samantha began to whine low in her throat.

"Hey there," Russell cried. "Hey, you! What are you doing with that baby?"

The stranger turned around to face him and Russell nearly wet his pants when he saw the bloody face, and the eyes glowing like dark blue coals sunk deep into the stranger's sallow flesh.

Samantha charged forward, her leash sliding out of Russell's hand and leaving a deep red burn mark in its wake.

Ellen continued to barrel through town in the general direction of the Dale home, taking down everything in her path. Her road casualties now included a fire hydrant tilted drunkenly and shooting water straight into the air, a stop sign dented and misdirected, and two injured traffic signals, one of which was lying on its side in the middle of Main Street. The Jeep's front grill looked like it had been through a war.

She nearly convinced herself that someone recognized Lorna sitting alone in the Jeep and brought her back home.

Mercifully, her mind blanked out the shooting. What remained was a deep feeling of unease that she had done something terribly wrong. Dimly remembered of the evening, was Amanda falling asleep, and her taking Lorna to go look for John. But she couldn't remember why she wanted to follow her husband, or why Amanda fell asleep so suddenly. It didn't seem very important now. She just wanted to make sure the baby was okay.

I did a bad thing. I made a horrible mistake, her mind piped up.

Then Kurt Dale's voice echoed in her head, *You shot Richie Welch, that's what you did!*

Gasping, she strong-armed the voices out of her head as neatly and cleanly as her husband had done, when his own interior voice tried to warn him that Ellen was not alright — not alright at all.

Her eyes were blurred with tears and she was seeing the night streets through a shimmering liquid haze. She peeled around the corner onto Lombard Street, brakes squealing.

When she was just a few feet from the Dale's house, Ellen screamed in horror as the headlights washed over the figure standing on the sidewalk with Lorna in his arms. She craned the wheel toward the curb to pull over.

A big dog ran out from nowhere, and she yanked the steering wheel hard to the left to avoid hitting it.

The Cherokee bounced up over the curb with a tooth-rattling jolt and she lost control of the wheel, her plaster clad arm slamming hard against the steering column.

Francis Barclay jumped sideways to avoid being hit by the suddenly approaching vehicle. He landed with a bone-fracturing crash onto his side, his arms still tightly wrapped around the child's waist. His body cushioned her fall and Lorna stayed squarely against his chest when they hit the pavement.

Thinking this was some new variation of the game Airplane that her daddy played with her, Lorna screamed with delight.

"Do it again," she shrieked.

The boy was trying to hoist himself up on his elbows. Just as he began to rise, he felt sharp teeth sink into his leg. He howled in pain, but all that came out was a breathy squeak. The fall knocked the air out of his lungs, and he could do little more than draw in harsh tiny breaths that hurt his chest.

Lorna cried, "Sammie, don't do that!! Bad doggie!" and she reached over him and tried to push the dog away.

Francis Barclay forgot both the baby and the dog mauling him, as he stared in horror at the twin headlights drilling through the small hedges separating the Coombs front yard from the Dale's driveway. They were bearing down on him and the little girl.

His paralysis broke, and he rolled sideways, just as the car jumped the curb and came within two feet of hitting them. Dirt and uprooted shrubbery flew in a dervish around his face.

A slurred male voice yelled something unintelligible and the vehicle canted drunkenly to the left, mowing down a small tree that snapped like a twig.

The Jeep left deep ruts in Kurt's prized lawn. A piercing shriek of terror was torn from Ellen's throat, as she closed her eyes and put her good arm up in a defensive gesture and crashed through Amanda's picture window.

The young cop stood wide-eyed and anxious in the huddle with the rest of the officers listening to Kurt explain the events of that night.

The unspoken pact that they would never tell about this rookie being asleep on the job, as long as he never told that they had numbered four when they arrived, had been born without agreement. Kurt's version of the evening's events was that they sent the officer on a coffee run at some point, and a few minutes after he left on the errand Kurt and John heard shots.

They ran across the street to find out what happened. Once inside the abandoned trailer where they presumed the shots originated, they heard a woman scream, but saw no one until they reached the back bedroom and found Richie Welch dead, shot five times.

They never saw the woman they heard screaming, so could offer no description. The two detectives were quick to advise that they would be canvassing the neighbors and asking questions, so patrol could get back out on the streets to look for a suspect, or out to the woods to look for the murder weapon.

As for Richie, they had no idea what he was doing there in the first place.

"Perhaps," offered Kurt, "He found out where the murderer was holing up, and went after him to avenge Charity's death."

It all made perfect sense, and Kurt felt it somehow added an air of nobility to Richie's tragic death. It was a small thing, but at least it was a kinder tale than John's idea of saying it was probably a drug deal gone bad.

There were few questions asked, and to the officers present, it was no great surprise that notorious town bad boy, Richie Welch, had finally managed to get himself killed.

Not many among their number would shed a single tear. At least half of those present had taken him into custody at one point or another over the years. The fact that he had cleaned up his life was lost on them. Once a criminal — always a criminal was the general consensus about the Richie Welchs' of this world.

At the story's conclusion the young patrol officer nodded once to Kurt, gratitude and something like fear showing in his eyes.

Kurt offered a small, nearly imperceptible nod in return.

Not surprisingly, the canvas performed by the two detectives revealed nothing in the way of a description of the female heard screaming.

Jerry Harper, with his wife at his side, said nothing about the distraught blond woman looking under John's car, and then taking off in a green Jeep like a bat out of hell. Doing so would have only invited another string of accusations from his jealous wife, and possibly landed him in an interrogation room again.

No one else saw her, and even if they had, none would have ever believed Saint Ellen Wyatt capable of murder.

Kurt considered all debts to John Wyatt paid in full.

CHAPTER 31

Amanda was slowly regaining consciousness when the Jeep slammed into her picture window, littering her head and body with bits of broken glass, and hurling the couch she was lying on violently across the room. She tumbled to the floor, miraculously unhurt, and looked around in a daze.

Ellen, who not surprisingly hadn't bothered to fasten her seatbelt, was thrown through the windshield and landed in a broken heap against the fireplace. A single shard of glass jutted grotesquely from between her eyes. Her face was a frightening landscape of bleeding cuts and lacerations.

Amanda brushed bits of glass from her hair and clothes while looking around, and blinking stupidly at the room. Her eyes landed first on her totaled Jeep perched in the middle of her living room, and second on Ellen's ruined face.

"El," she tried to say, but her tongue was stuck to the roof of her mouth. All she could muster was a dry and dusty "Eh." She swallowed hard and crawled toward the fireplace where her friend lay.

Ellen stared straight ahead, her blank and unseeing eyes, the color of faded denim.

When Amanda touched her friend's shoulder, her head lolled sideways at an unnatural angle and blood ran from the corner of her mouth. Amanda gaped in horror and started to shriek, but her throat was still too dry to make much sound.

As she started to back away from Ellen, she knew she must call for help, but she was still so disoriented from the Valium laced wine, not to mention the sudden and unexpected shock from the destruction of her living room, that she didn't know where the phone was.

Her brain registered the Cherokee in the living room. She understood it had smashed through the front of the house, but she thought Ellen was inside when it happened, and had been struck by the out of control driver.

Amanda was unaware that Ellen ever left the house, let alone that she took her child, or that she was the driver of the vehicle when it crashed into the picture window.

Amanda crawled around the dark living room searching for the phone. She heard the baby's voice coming from outside and froze.

"Lorna?" she tried to yell. Amanda pounded her hand in frustration at her dry, useless vocal cords.

She was aware that her finger was bleeding again and was grateful for the pain. It was bringing her back to reality. She grabbed the corner of the overturned couch and hoisted herself up. Her knees let go and the room started spinning. She closed her eyes against a wave of nausea and dizziness, then wretched violently onto the floor. Wiping her mouth with the back of her hand, she started crawling in the direction of the front door.

Everything happened too fast for Russell's alcohol soaked brain to process. He barely noted the Cherokee's sudden approach until it was nearly on top of his dog. He leapt to pull her out of the way. He missed, because at the same moment that he lunged for her, Samantha lunged at the dirty kid holding Lorna.

Russell fell to the sidewalk, scraping the skin on his chin raw, and cried out for the driver to stop when he saw the Jeep barreling down on the disheveled stranger holding Lorna, and maybe his dog as well.

The driver must have heard him because a split second later the Cherokee lurched hard to the left. Russell heard the woman behind the wheel scream, and saw her raise one hand over her face.

Then it sounded like Armageddon. The shattering, explosive sound of breaking glass, followed by the tortured shriek of crumpling metal, as the Jeep plowed into the picture window of his next door neighbor's house.

Russell scrambled to his feet and stumbled over to where the kid with the freaky eyes and Lorna lay. He snatched the baby from the stranger's hands and ran for the Dale's front door.

He called over his shoulder, "You keep him there 'til the cops arrive, Sammie baby."

Sammie baby did as she was told.

Francis Barclay tried to push the dog away, but his strength was nearly gone and she wouldn't budge. Her teeth were buried in the seat of his jeans. She was growling and whipping her head back and forth like he was a rope toy. Each move sending her teeth deeper into his skin.

The irony of him being the bitten, was not lost on Francis Barclay.

He couldn't turn over enough to bite the dog back. He tried to edge away from her and managed to slide a few inches, but Samantha's sharp teeth remained firmly attached.

Reaching out with one flailing hand, he felt his fingers touch something solid. It was a branch of the tree which had been torn out of the ground by the out of control Jeep. He closed his fingers around it and pulled it loose. He twisted backwards as far as he could and tried to whip ineffectually at the dog behind him, but the angle was wrong and he could not reach her. In frustration, he flung the stick sideways.

To his amazement the pressure on his leg and buttocks let up as Samantha, always up for a good game of fetch, went bounding after the tree limb, suddenly more interested in a play date than her career in law enforcement.

She clamped the branch in her jaws and went trotting up the Dale's front lawn after Russell and the crying Lorna. Her muzzle looked like it had been dipped in an oil can.

Francis climbed to his feet on shaking legs, and started for the field behind the house. His only thought was to get away from here.

He was limping badly and bleeding profusely from the army of wounds he incurred during this revenge driven hellish experience.

He no longer cared about his revenge, though a tiny voice in his head reminded him that his hate-filled mission wasn't over. The debt had not been fully paid, the sins not atoned for. However, at this moment he knew he was dying, and he just wanted to die in peace.

Kurt and John drove in silence from the mobile home park after the brief and very perfunctory questioning of the neighbors. They stopped first at John's house to see if Ellen was there, and while John combed the empty house looking for her, Kurt tried to call Amanda repeatedly from his cell phone.

The stuttering *duh-duh-duh* of a busy signal, sent that cold finger of panic sliding up his spine again. He could feel alarm bells sounding in his head, and muttered under his breath, "Where the hell are they?"

John was equally as concerned about Ellen's welfare.

However, Kurt was more worried about what the crazy bitch had done to his family before showing up at the trailer park, than he was about her well-being. He didn't think mentioning this to John would do any good. He still wasn't sure John realized his wife had gone totally and utterly insane.

"Do you suppose she went back to your house?" John asked, as they drove away from his empty home. "She has to be terribly upset that she killed the wrong guy. You realize she had no idea whatsoever that it was Richie? She thought it was Barclay. You know that, right, Kurt?"

Kurt continued to stare straight ahead, his jaw set.

"Um… Thanks for covering things. I uh… I guess I owe you," John said awkwardly.

"You don't owe me a goddamn thing. All debts are paid," Kurt snapped.

"Hey, look, Ellen… she thought she was protecting…" his voice trailed off and he started again, "I mean, Christ, Kurt, I am sure she will explain what she was doing there when we find her. She wouldn't hurt a fly, man. You know that. I mean this is Ellen we are talking about. She just… she was just confused."

His voice had taken on a whiny, pleading quality that Kurt recognized well. It was just usually coming from his throat and not John's. That voice made him even angrier.

"Maybe you can have her explain it to Rachel Clovis," Kurt retorted.

John recoiled. He looked at Kurt with wounded eyes, but said nothing more.

When they turned onto Lombard Street, they were greeted with total chaos. Neither man could believe what they were seeing. The neighborhood had taken on a peculiar resemblance to Happy Wheels. People stood on their front steps in night clothes and messed up hair. Their faces were pale shocked O's. The first flashing blue and red lights were just pulling to a stop in front of Kurt's ruined house. His first reaction was that there was something wrong with the front of his house, but he couldn't quite figure out what. He gasped in disbelief when he realized it was the rear end of his Jeep protruding from what had been his picture window just a few short hours ago.

"Oh Christ!" he cried, as he opened the passenger door of John's car, and climbed out before it even came to a complete stop. He sprinted the rest of the way up the street, and charged through his open front door calling his wife's name. He skidded and nearly fell on the broken glass that littered the entryway. He barely had time to register the sound of his wife and daughter's sobs coming from the kitchen, before Russell Coombs was on him, grabbing his arms.

In a rush of warm, beer-smelling breath, he screamed, "That way! He went that way!" He was pointing toward the back of the house.

"What, Russell? Who went that way?" Kurt asked, totally bewildered.

"The kidnapper that had Lorna. But I took her back. The kid with the creepy eyes. He got away from Sammie, and he's back in the field," Russell rambled.

"Is Lorna okay? Where's Mandy?" Kurt asked.

"They're fine, but you gotta arrest the kidnapper before he gets away." Russell was jumping up and down in his frenzy to make Kurt understand.

Kurt didn't need to ask anything more. Somehow Francis Barclay had gotten his filthy hands on Lorna, and his drunk neighbor had managed to take her away from him.

He shoved past Russell into the kitchen. He looked at Mandy, noting her swollen eyes and bleeding hand. Bits of glass still glittered in her hair and on her clothes. There was a nasty scratch up one cheek.

Other than the fact that she was bellowing at the top of her lungs, Lorna appeared unharmed.

Amanda started to rise from the kitchen chair when she saw him, but was too weak to get up with the weight of the baby on her lap. She swayed and grabbed the table.

"Are you alright?" Kurt asked.

"I don't know," she said truthfully, "Kurt, I think Ellen is dead," she sobbed, as fresh tears coursed down her cheeks.

"Oh Jesus," he sighed, shaking his head. "Where is she?"

"In the living room. The jeep must have hit her when it crashed."

Kurt didn't have the time to explain. "Is the baby hurt?" he asked, while rummaging in a drawer for a flashlight.

"I don't think so, but I was drugged or something. I passed out," she sniffed.

Kurt looked back at Russell, who was now standing behind him. "Tell the cops to get an ambulance down here right away," and he ran out the back door toward the field behind the house.

John felt like he was moving in slow motion as he opened the car door. He approached the front of Kurt's house on watery legs. The sensation was like trudging through knee-deep sand. A loud roaring sound like crashing waves began in his head when he saw the smashed green Cherokee, one blinker winking on and off, like an obscene golden eye. That mental clamor drowned out the howl of approaching sirens and the yelling voices. The chaos was now just background noise. He felt like the sand he was trying to march through was up to his waist as he approached the front door of the Dale's house. He was dimly aware of broken glass crunching under his feet through the roaring in his skull. He saw his wife's splayed feet sticking out and worked his way through the rubble to her side. He felt like he was in a wind tunnel.

Officers were spilling out of vehicles and rushing into the house behind him. Captain Fitzgerald appeared at his side and grabbed his arm. He was speaking to him, and though John saw his lips moving, he couldn't understand what he was saying. The tsunami in his head was just too loud.

John turned from their faces and their unintelligible voices. He sank to his knees beside his wife. He cradled her limp body and gently laid her bloody head in his lap, and with delicate fingers tried to pull the shard of glass from between her glazed, staring eyes. It slid free with a sickening plop and oozed blood onto his fingers. He spit onto the corner of his shirt and dabbed at the roadmap of cuts on her ruined face.

An unknown amount of time later, firm hands gripped his arms and he was gently lifted up and led away. As he looked back, men in white shirts and blue pants, which he knew were paramedics, leaned over his wife's lifeless body, obscuring it from his view. He was pretty sure he told them to be careful with her, but that might have just been in his mind.

Kurt cut across the field, and called out, "Francis! Hey, Francis Barclay! Are you out there?"

The boy stopped running and collapsed some twenty-five feet from where Kurt stood. His feet simply wouldn't carry him any further. He heard the man yelling his name, but didn't answer. Once again he felt bitter irony — *How many people die twice in the same field?*

A small orb of pale yellow light was dancing across the weeds in front of him. With strength he didn't know he still possessed, Francis Barclay pulled himself to his feet. He turned from the sound of the man's voice, and the shadow of his moving flashlight, and limped toward the far edge of the field, looking for the gully where he was murdered by this pursuing stranger's distant relative, so many years before. He stopped when he heard the gun cock only inches behind him.

"Turn around," Kurt growled.

He turned slowly, and at last stood face to face with the man he had returned from the grave to kill.

"Who are you?" Kurt asked.

"You just called me by name," Francis croaked in that disturbing rusted voice.

"We didn't hurt you. I never even heard of you," Kurt cried passionately. "What happened to your people…it…it was so long ago! Centuries! Why did you do this to us? Why now? How… How did you even come back?" Kurt asked, his voice faltering, as the reality of who stood before him truly hit home for the first time.

"So many questions," Francis chuckled. "I'm afraid I don't have the strength to answer right now. Maybe next time we meet I will." He pointed at Kurt's gun, and croaked, "Let's get it over with."

"Did you touch my daughter?" Kurt snarled.

At the mention of Lorna, Francis Barclay's eyes flashed their most brilliant light one final time, and a single tear spilled down his cheek. His eyes glowed fiercer than ever for a moment, stinging Kurt's eyes with their brilliance. Then they winked out like stars.

Francis Barclay turned his back on Kurt and began shuffling toward the edge of the field again.

Kurt watched him go. He slowly lowered his weapon and took a few steps after him.

"Why didn't you hurt her when you had the chance?" He called to the retreating figure. "Wasn't this all about revenge? Why did you spare my little girl?"

Barclay didn't answer. He couldn't. He sunk to his knees and collapsed on his side a few feet away.

Kurt walked over to him and stood looking down for several moments. When the prone figure didn't move, Kurt reached down and seized his wrist. He meant to check for a pulse, but when he picked up the lifeless hand, its loathsome dough-like consistency sickened him, as his fingers sank nearly all the way through the skin. He dropped the ghoul's wrist with a grimace of revulsion, seeing the indentations his fingers left in the waxy flesh. He trained his flashlight on Francis Barclay's face. All that remained was a mottled skull wreathed in long, stringy white hair that grinned malevolently back at him. Kurt took off his jacket and draped it over the hideous thing's face.

He turned and walked slowly back toward his family.

CHAPTER 32

Two weeks after Francis Barclay's second death, Kurt and John sat in their favorite coffee shop for the last time together. Autumn leaves were falling and the temperature had dropped. The sky was gloomy and gray overhead.

"So, what will you do?" Kurt asked tentatively.

John's eyes were red rimmed and swollen. Dark crescents beneath each one, betrayed the fact that he hadn't been getting much sleep. His face was gaunt and he had lost weight.

He looked out the window at the people on the sidewalk and didn't answer right away.

Kurt was content to sip his coffee and wait.

Finally, John said, "I have family in Florida."

Kurt nodded. The only family in Florida John had ever mentioned was an ailing uncle whom he hadn't spoken to in five years. Kurt decided not to remind him of that or press him for any further details.

"Will you try to get a transfer to a local department?"

John shook his head. "No. I will get some money when the house sells, and there is… there's some insurance. It was… a … it was an accident, so they will pay on it."

Kurt reached across the table and patted his partner's arm.

They sat in silence for awhile.

Still gazing out the window, John asked, "Do you think he'll come back?"

Kurt didn't answer right away. He had spent many sleepless nights pondering that same question.

"I watched him go through the incinerator. They cremated what was left of him. There isn't anything to come back," he said with more confidence than he felt.

"Where is he now? I mean where are the ashes?" John asked, still staring out the window at the blowing leaves.

"He was interred in a vault at the cemetery in Oberhart, 300 miles west of here. I didn't want him buried in Alder Lake again. I didn't think anyone would."

John nodded. "Have you spoken to Leroy?"

"No. You?"

"A couple days ago. He saw the For Sale sign on my house when he was making his rounds, so he stopped by."

Kurt waited for him to go on without pressuring him. He knew there was more to say.

John cleared his throat. "He told Rachel he never went with us that night. Said he changed his mind. Everyone seems to believe that Richie went after the killer himself, and died for his efforts."

"Are he and Rachel doing alright?"

John shrugged. "I don't know. There's so many secrets — so many lies. Don't you think someone is going to spill it eventually?"

Kurt had lost plenty of sleep wondering about that too.

"Not for awhile. The wild card in the deck was the officer posted at Norma's. But I don't think we have to worry about him."

John gave him a questioning look. "Oh?"

"Yeah. He put in for a transfer to Parkland. He will be gone by the end of the month."

"You don't think Leroy's guilt will get the best of him?"

Kurt shook his head. "He can't bring Richie back. If he tells the truth now he does nothing but hurt Rachel even worse."

After another long drawn out silence, in a soft voice, John said, "He told me he sees Richie in his dreams…and he's not the only one, Kurt. I see him too — but mostly I see Ellen. I see her how she used to be. Leroy said he's back to three of those AA meetings a day."

"And Rachel?" Kurt asked.

"Rachel isn't going to any meetings." John looked at Kurt with haunted eyes. "She's drinking again," he replied, and looked down at his lap.

Again the silence stretched out between them. Kurt sensed there was more John wanted to say and he sipped his coffee and waited.

Finally, John sighed, "Kurt?"

"Yes?"

"Where is the gun?"

"I threw it in the river."

John nodded and stretched. He slid from the booth.

Kurt made no move to follow him.

John took his wallet out and threw a couple of crumpled dollar bills on the table.

As he turned to leave, he said, "Tell Amanda thanks for packing up Ellen's things, and for all of her help with the funeral," he hesitated a moment, then went on in a faltering voice, "I couldn't have made it through this without her."

Kurt nodded. "Will you stay in touch? Let us know where you are?"

"Yeah. When I get settled I will. Take care, Kurt."

John put his hand out and they shook.

Kurt watched his old friend and partner disappear down the street, looking like a strong wind could have taken him down, and felt tears sting his eyes. He wondered if Florida would be far enough for John to outrun his guilt. Somehow he didn't think so.

Epilogue

SPRING FOUR YEARS LATER

Cord Billings had been a truck driver for twenty-seven years. At sixty-one he was six months away from retirement and the gold watch. Then he and Hannah would board the Winnebago for points unknown. They would travel the country unhurriedly, and send postcards and souvenirs to the kids and grandkids from all the tourist attractions that he and his wife always wanted to see, but never got around to.

He made the same run every week between Curtisville and Oberhart, hauling dairy products to grocery stores in a huge eighteen wheeler with a smiling pink cow painted on the side. And on every run he stopped at the Oberhart Inn, a fancy name for a greasy spoon, truck-stop and gas station, to fortify himself and his rig for the return drive home.

The Inn's Sloppy Joe's gave him a gut full of indigestion, but he ate one every week and then stopped at the Mini-Mart for a six-pack of 7-Up and a roll of Tums. The routine never changed, not once in twenty-seven years.

He had given rides to probably a hundred or more hitchhikers traveling up and down Highway 17 over those years. He heard all kinds of stories, and encountered all kinds of people.

It was just coming dusk, and the evening was mild enough to leave the windows down. Hank Williams blaring from the radio, Cord babied his rig back onto the road from the Oberhart Inn's fuel pumps, and started down the highway headed east. He stopped at the mini-mart for his 7-UP and Tums.

After traveling about twenty miles he saw a skinny boy walking by the side of the road thumbing a ride. He began slowing down. He was pulling his rig off to the shoulder a few feet from the kid, who was now lowering his thumb and looking expectantly up at Cord with brilliant blue eyes.

A light breeze began to blow and Cord gaped curiously at what he was seeing. When the wind kicked up, a flurry of gray chalky powder rose from the kid's shoulders and hair. It blew around his head like a halo before settling back down with the breeze. Several stray particles of the dust, which Cord initially took for the worst case of dandruff he had ever seen, blew into the window of his rig. It gave off a charred odor that Cord later described to his wife as the smell of burnt toast. He ran a finger over the seat where the particles settled, then eyed them closely and sniffed his finger. It took him only a moment to realize the fine cloud of dust he'd seen drift off the boy was ashes. *Kid must really be a heavy smoker,* Cord thought.

Then suddenly, without warning, a chill ran up his spine and he got what his wife always called the tenth sense. He had no idea what seven, eight or nine were, and he had never asked. But Hannah said the tenth sense was that feeling you got way down in your gut that told you that something you were about to do was a bad idea. A *real* bad one.

He jammed his foot down on the accelerator, shifted gears hard enough to make the rig offer a grinding protest, and left the kid standing on the soft shoulder with a puzzled expression on his face.

It wasn't until Cord traveled another fifty miles that his heart returned to its normal pace, and that cold sliver of fear melted away. He loosened his tight grip on the steering wheel. Another hundred miles or so and he called himself a fool for acting that way and broke open a can of 7-Up.

John Wyatt woke with a start. His eyes flew open and he bit his tongue against the scream welling in his throat. His new bride stirred beside him, and looked at the glowing numbers on the digital clock. It was just after 3:00 A.M.

"Was it the dream again?" she asked him, still half asleep.

John reached out for her in the dark, trembling. "Yeah. Same one."

His wife sighed. "Maybe someday you'll tell me about what happened before you moved here," and she closed her eyes to go back to sleep. Her new husband's predawn nightmares were something she had already grown accustomed to.

John used the money he received from the sale of his house and from Ellen's insurance to open a small private detective office in Boca Raton. There were enough cheating spouses in Palm Beach County to keep him busy for years to come.

He met his current wife, Jan, when she came to his office in regard to her brother Chris. She asked John to put him under surveillance because she was worried about him. Their parents both perished in a plane crash the year before, and she was the boy's only guardian. At sixteen Chris went from being a nearly straight A student, to failing most of his classes in his junior year.

There was little money and she worked long hours. She would often come home from her job as an emergency room nurse to find the small apartment they shared empty. Her brother wouldn't show up until the wee hours of the morning, stumbling through the door, disheveled and red-eyed, and she suspected, stoned. Working the swing shift, she couldn't be home to give him the supervision that he obviously needed.

Only in her early twenties, she didn't feel qualified for the huge responsibility that their parent's death foisted on her slender shoulders. She took her meager savings and paid John Wyatt to trail Chris and find out what was going on.

He did so, and then helped her with a painful intervention. He refunded the fee so Jan could use it to pay for the boy's stint in rehab.

They were married six months later in a quiet ceremony at the courthouse.

Her brother, successfully rehabilitated, and hanging out with a better crowd, lived and thrived with them in a comfortable suburban house with a pool. He and John got along well.

Life was good for John Wyatt. All except for the nightmares.

Hearing his wife pull into the driveway, Kurt quickly said goodbye to Carolyn, promised to come see her later, and hastily hung up the phone.

He had transferred out of Violent Crimes and into the Narcotics division three and a half years before. He did it just after the final repairs on their house were finished, and they moved back in from the cramped one bedroom condo they rented from a fellow officer until the house was once again habitable.

Two years later he met Carolyn Devonshire, (just like the cream she liked to say,) a new deputy district attorney for the county. She tried and won a big narcotics smuggling case Kurt had busted. They were thrown together often during the course of their jobs, and he fought his attraction for her as long as he could. He had only given in to his feelings in the last two weeks, and after four years of fidelity the guilt he expected had yet to make an appearance.

Amanda hoisted herself out of the white Nissan Pathfinder, the vehicle that replaced their totaled Jeep. She opened the back door and unfastened Nathan's car seat.

Their second child, a boy, was born three months before. She cradled him in her arms, and called for Kurt and Lorna to come out and unload the groceries. Once inside, she handed the baby to Kurt without a word, and began unpacking the bags.

Kurt sat down at the table and handed her an open letter, postmarked from Florida. She took it from his outstretched hand and read the brief note inside. She studied the two photographs which accompanied the note. She sighed, and put the envelope back on the table.

Turning back to the groceries, she asked, "So, do you think he was upset that we didn't come to the wedding?" she asked.

"No. He knew you were over six months pregnant at that point. You couldn't have traveled. Besides, from what I understand, it was a pretty small affair."

Amanda was quiet and lost in thought. Finishing the unpacking, she sat down across from Kurt. She picked up the letter again and pulled the pictures out.

"She looks a lot like Ellen."

"Yeah. I thought so too," Kurt nodded.

Neither commented on the girl's obvious youth.

Amanda rose and took the baby from him. "I'm going to nurse him and put him down for a nap."

Amanda descended the stairs fifteen minutes later. She saw her daughter sitting on the window ledge staring outside. She walked into the kitchen with a frown.

"What's Lorna doing?" she asked Kurt, nodding her head in the direction of their living room.

"She's been sitting looking out the window for most of the day," Kurt replied.

"Why? Who is she waiting for?"

Kurt shrugged. "I don't know. She hasn't been herself ever since Darlene had to put Samantha to sleep. She had an odd attachment to that dog."

Amanda replied, "That was a month ago already. I thought kids were supposed to be resilient."

Kurt looked at her with something close to contempt. He knew this was the beginning of her postpartum depression, and he hoped like hell she wouldn't wait a year to get the prescription for the little blue pills. He had no intention of stopping her this time.

When he didn't say anything, Amanda asked, "They ever figure out why Samantha started biting people?"

"No," Kurt said. "Russell is still convinced she was contaminated by Francis Barclay's blood when she bit him during that mess all those years ago. But she was always wonderful with Lorna. At the end she was the only person the dog would go near without growling. I guess that's why Lorna is taking it so hard."

Amanda rolled her eyes. "Hey, what the hell can you expect from the town drunk? Contaminated, huh? If you ask me, Samantha just went rabid or something. Her eyes got weird. They went from that dark brown to almost yellow. Surely there was something wrong with her."

"Well, the vet couldn't find anything. They spent a fortune on tests. And Amanda," Kurt said icily, "Russell's been sober for over a year now, so don't call him the town drunk, okay."

She glared at him, not responding.

Kurt rose from the table and went to check on his daughter.

Lorna had grown into a creature of such startling beauty, that people paused to look at her when they saw her on the street. At six years old, her hair was the same auburn red as her mother's, and it fell in soft ringlets to her shoulders. She had a radiant dimpled smile that could light up a room in an instant. She did well in school, and enjoyed ballet and swimming lessons. She had many friends, and was always a favorite guest for a slumber party because she was so well mannered. She could have been a poster child for the all American golden girl.

And practically everyone that met her was nearly mesmerized by, and couldn't help but remark that she had the most brilliant blue eyes they had ever seen.

About the Author

Krystal Lawrence works as a commercial voice over artist and media actress. She lives in Washington where she is working on her second novel, "Be Careful What You Wish For."

www.ingramcontent.com/pod-product-compliance
Lightning Source LLC
Chambersburg PA
CBHW030421310726
48979CB00009B/1563/J